THE SCHOOL GATE SURVIVAL GUIDE

Maia Etxeleku is a cleaner for ladies who lunch. With mop and bucket in tow, she spends her days dashing from house to house cleaning up after them, as they rush from one exhausting Pilates class to the next. But an unusual inheritance catapults her and her children into the very exclusive world of Stirling Hall School — a place where no child can survive without organic apricots and no woman goes a week without a manicure. As Maia and her children, Bronte and Harley, try to settle into their new life, she is inadvertently drawn to the one man who can help her family fit in. But is his interest in her purely professional? And will it win her any favours at the school gate?

THE SCHOOL GATE SURVIVAL GUIDE

KERRY FISHER

ISIS
LARGE
PRINT

First published in Great Britain 2014
by
Avon
A division of HarperCollins*Publishers*

First Isis Edition
published 2016
by arrangement with
HarperCollins*Publishers*

The moral right of the author has been asserted

A catalogue record for this book is available
from the British Library.

ISBN 978–1–78541–145–8 (hb)
ISBN 978–1–78541–151–9 (pb)

Published by
F. A. Thorpe (Publishing)
Anstey, Leicestershire

Set by Words & Graphics Ltd.
Anstey, Leicestershire
Printed and bound in Great Britain by
T. J. International Ltd., Padstow, Cornwall

This book is printed on acid-free paper

To Steve, Cameron and Michaela

Acknowledgements

I've been very lucky to have had some great cheerleaders to get me from "there" to "here". If I hadn't found the creative writing program at UCLA, I'd still be telling a yawning audience about my ambitions to write a novel, so huge thanks to my teachers: Jessica Barksdale Inclán, Lynn Hightower and Robert Eversz and my fellow students: Carol Starr Schneider, Karen Gekelman, Rochelle Staab and Romalyn Tilghman.

On this side of the ocean, Harry Bingham and his team at The Writers' Workshop both spurred me on and offered wise words when needed, as did author Adrienne Dines.

I've had massive support from my family, especially from my husband, Steve, who managed not to say out loud, "When is all this writing nonsense going to stop?" I think some of them may even be a little bit proud now. Friends, way too many to mention, have played their part in pushing me onwards when it was all looking too damned hard. Special thanks to Caroline Broderick, Bushi Pearson and Sharon Woodrow — and my writing buddy, Jenny Ashcroft, without whom I would be rocking in a corner.

Mary Wheeler gave me generous help on police procedure and Mark Collins pointed me in the right direction on probate matters. All mistakes are mine — they knew their stuff.

Some authors have overnight success, many more slog away for years finding the notion of giving up just slightly less bearable than carrying on. I know which category I am in. Consequently, I am so delighted that when things did start to happen for me, I found two lovely people to work with: my editor, Helen Bolton at Avon (and her team) and my agent, Clare Wallace at Darley Anderson. They have both made the publishing process joyous.

Finally . . . I raise a glass to everyone who bought or recommended this book in its previous incarnation as *The Class Ceiling* and created enough success around it to move it to the next stage. Cheers.

CHAPTER
ONE

Posh women with dirty houses sometimes phone me. Posh men never do.

Until today, when this solicitor bod burst into my morning with the sort of booming confidence it would be impossible to argue against. My ears closed down, rejecting the steamroller voice, pushing away his words.

"I'm sorry to be the bearer of ghastly news."

I'd just got home from what was always my worst job of the week — cleaning the changing rooms at Surrey's grottiest leisure centre. The phone rang shortly after I'd gone upstairs for a bath to scrub every trace of old plasters and plughole cack off my skin. As I clumped down to the kitchen wrapped in a towel that barely covered my backside, I was praying that the call was from Colin, with good news about work. Instead I stood there, holding the phone away from my ear so I didn't drip water into the receiver while Mr William Lah-di-dah bellowed away at a slight distance, a sort of old Etonian-cum-Clanger. Then I heard it.

"I'm afraid Professor Rose Stainton passed away last Friday."

I pressed the phone into my forehead as. I tried to take in the fact that my favourite — and best paying —

customer had died. My oddball ally, with her outrageous old lady comments and bursts of unexpected kindness, had gone. I hadn't even said goodbye. Froths of shampoo seeped out from under my towel turban and mingled with the sting in my eyes.

"Mrs Etxeleku? Are you still there?"

"Yes, I'm still here." I couldn't be bothered to correct him. I'm not a Mrs. I'd given up waiting for Colin to pop the question. And my surname is pronounced Ech-eleku, not Et-zeleku. If only my father had hung around long enough for me to be born, I could have had a nice English name — Windsor, Jones, even Sidebottom — on my birth certificate, rather than the blank that made my mother clamp her mouth shut like a Venus flytrap every time I tried to discuss it. Instead I've spent thirty-six years lumbered with a Basque surname no one can pronounce.

"How did she die?" I heard a wobble in my voice. I leant against the wall, the chilly December draught blowing under the back door, licking around my wet knees.

"A heart attack."

"Was she on her own?"

"Yes, she managed to call an ambulance but she was dead by the time they reached her."

He sounded as though he was discussing an order for a Chinese takeaway. I was obviously just a number on his neatly typed list of people to phone — a nobody, someone he needed to tell they no longer had a job. He paused. I imagined him sitting behind a heavy wooden desk, glancing down the page to see who came after "cleaner". The idea that someone who spent her life wiping globs of toothpaste off sinks could be friends with someone who spent hers debating Kafka wouldn't have crossed his mind. I started clattering about, throwing dirty cereal bowls into the sink and hurling trainers and football boots into a heap by the back door. I had no claim on Rose Stainton. I was just the woman with the mop, the skivvy who washed out the kitchen bin.

"Anyway, part of the reason I'm calling is that her solicitor would like to see you," he said.

"Solicitor? Is something missing?" I said, panicking. Surely they weren't trying to track down the parrot head bookends that the old lady had given me. I didn't even like them. In my experience, solicitors weren't people who wanted to see you. They were people who were instructed to see you. Middle-aged men in too tight shirts, who turned up at police stations to work on the pathetic little stories of drug addicts, drunkards and the bog standard low life that hung around our estate. The sort of men who'd saved Colin's sorry little arse on more than one occasion.

"No, Mrs Etxeleku. No, of course not, nothing like that, I believe there was something in the professor's will that Mr Harrison would like to discuss with you."

It was only after I'd put the phone down that the numbness started to fall away. My teeth were chattering. I pulled on the tracksuit bottoms Colin had left on a chair and grabbed my long cardigan, still damp, from the clothes airer. In films you see people burst into tears, sobbing, "I can't believe she's gone."

3

But I started yelling. "Ghastly. Bad. Atrocious. Horrendous. Horrible. Hateful. Crap." That was one of the professor's little games, getting me to think of different words to mean the same thing. When I got to "crap", I banged on the window at the mad git next door who was flicking his terrier's turds through the broken fence again. He appeared to be aiming for our paddling pool, left out since the summer, which had now become a slimy green home to water boatmen and other wildlife. He waved his shovel at me and smiled like a loon.

The professor had always talked to me like my opinions counted. She knew about Shakespeare, Dickens and foreign writers I'd never heard of before. She really liked Gabriel García Márquez and kept asking me to pronounce Spanish words for her. It embarrassed me because most of the time Mum and I had spoken English together, or at least my mother's peculiar version of it. I wish she'd spoken more Spanish or even Basque to me, but 1970s Sandbury wasn't a place to be foreign. It was an English market town, where a wool shop, a cobbler's and a stamp collector's shop were among the high street's thrilling diversions. Mum saw England as the land of opportunity. She might sound like she'd missed her vocation as Manuel's wife in *Fawlty Towers* but she was going to make damned sure that her daughter didn't sound like a "second-class immigrant".

I gave up trying to sort out my shithole of a kitchen and plonked down into a chair. I shoved aside Colin's dirty plate to find the Open University application form

4

that had arrived that morning. I had been intending to tell the prof this week that I was definitely going to enrol. I'd looked forward to seeing her formal manner give way to that excitable hand waving thing she did, which often ended up with her knocking over her little china teacup on the tray. She used to crack me up when she swore. Sometimes she'd say, "bugger me" or "bloody hell", but she never sounded like Colin when he'd been on the Guinness. More like she was just experimenting, seeing how swear words sounded. I loved the way she spoke, all those words perfectly formed, all the letters where they should be. She never used language to make me feel stupid.

I tore the application form up into tiny little pieces, like a dud lottery ticket. There was no way I could afford it now. I watched the paper float down onto the cork floor, noticing again that no matter how often I washed it, something was always gooing up the cracks between the tiles. I couldn't even clean properly. I must have been getting ideas well above my station to think I could do a degree. I just thought that if the kids saw me bettering myself, they might aim a bit higher themselves. At Morlands Juniors, where teachers legged it after two terms and crowd control took priority over teaching, people to look up to were a bit thin on the ground.

There was no point snivelling about things I couldn't change. I wasn't going to think about how frightened the professor would have been when she realised that frail old heart of hers was finally giving out. Or how alone, in that huge house. I hoped she had died in the library with all her books soothing her to sleep. I started pouring bleach on the coffee-stained Formica worktops, trying to get away from the image of her slumped forwards over the creased brown leather of her winged armchair, grey hair escaping from her hairpins, tea — always Earl Grey — cooling beside her. The bleach stung my chapped skin. I made a silent promise to the prof that I'd never drop a "t" again and said, "little, computer, water, butter" out loud.

The front door banged open. Colin stomped down the hallway and into the kitchen, trailing mud right across the floor. I didn't say anything. In fact, I deliberately looked away. He was always as touchy as hell when he got back from the Job Centre. There were so few plates left, we'd be eating straight off the table soon.

"Jesus, that place is a dump. You've got more chance of catching bleeding TB than you have of getting a job there. All them silly questions. What letters have you written this week? Have you been to any interviews? Like you get a fucking interview to paint someone's hallway."

"Did she say you could still get the money, though?" I said, then held my breath.

"Yeah, they're going to 'review' it in a month. S'pose seventy quid a week is better than nothing — least it gets us through Christmas," he said, ripping open a packet of biscuits.

Even though there'd been a drop in unemployment, Colin carried on tutting away, sucking air through his teeth, convinced that the painting and decorating trades would suffer for much longer. "Getting your bathroom painted ain't a priority, is it? No, you mark my words, there ain't gonna be business for me for a long while yet."

Just to be sure that he wouldn't bump into a job offer, he slumped onto a kitchen chair and dedicated himself to eating custard creams like a hamster stockpiling for famine. Unlike me, he was tall so he could get away with it for a while, but the six-pack of manual labour was slowly disappearing into an avalanche of blancmange.

I wanted to tell him about Rose. Just for a moment I wanted to rely on him. I wanted to put my head on his shoulder, have him stroke my hair and cry great big shuddery old sobs until my eyes were like golf balls. I tried to remember if, in nearly nineteen years, I'd ever relied on him. I had to tell him that we had even less cash now. It wasn't like I was expecting him to make up the shortfall. Even if he could, I wouldn't have been able to spend it on the Open University degree. Colin thought education was a waste of TV watching time. Why reach for the sky when you could just tune into it?

I counted to three. "Rose Stainton died on Friday."

"What, that posh old cow at the manor? Jesus, Maia, what we going to do for money now? Her timing stinks. She's been ill for years and has to pick right now to snuff it. Will they pay you to clean up the old girl's stuff at least? You'd better get yourself out there and start looking for another job."

He scraped his chair back and started rummaging in the cupboard like his life depended on finding a tin of ravioli. I tried hard to remember the reason he'd held such a fascination for me. Why I'd loved him enough to have two children with him. Maybe his rebellious streak seemed romantic to me then, the naughtiness that had me skipping school and tearing off to Brighton for the day to eat fish and chips at the beach, shivering under the bandstand, sharing my scarf for warmth. He'd seemed so glamorous and grown-up to me, a twenty-one-year-old with a motorbike and strawberry blond charm. To my teachers' horror, I dumped my A-levels and any notion of university, then hopped, skipped and stamped on my mother's dreams and set off on a career on the tills at Tesco. A promotion to head of the deli serving up Scotch eggs followed. I then climbed to the dizzying heights of deputy fish fryer at the chippy and had now reached my peak as a cleaner to those who would rather die than say "toilet" instead of "lavatory" but still managed to piss on the floor.

Now, finally, I had grown up. In that moment, I wanted to rant about responsibility, smash his skull open with the wooden chopping board and cackle wildly. Instead, I made him a cup of tea and talked to him in the voice I used for Harley and Bronte when they were little and didn't want to go to bed.

"I'll put a notice in the post office window. Did you phone that bloke from the builder's yard who thought they might be looking for someone to help out painting the school?"

"Bloody marvellous. You lose your job and straightaway you're on at me. Get it into your thick head, Maia, there's still a credit crunch, you know.

People aren't paying out to have their spare rooms decorated."

"I know, but this is a school, I just thought —"

Mercury FM came blaring on, blocking out what I just thought.

CHAPTER
TWO

The prof's death brought out the worrier in me. Unlike loads of people round our way who only seemed to remember they had kids when they turned up on the front doorstep next to a man in blue, I liked to know where mine were and what they were up to. Colin didn't like me "bloody mollycoddling" them by meeting them out of school, but that day I was desperate to shake off the dead by hugging the living. I wanted to suck in their just out of school smell, the clammy scent that clung to their clothes, somewhere between lunchtime chicken nuggets, stuffy classrooms and the pong of other people's kids. They liked the prof and had often played in her huge garden while I worked. I wanted to tell them she'd died without Colin making snidey comments in the background.

I stood in the playground on the faded hopscotch squares, craning my neck. Bronte was often out first, walking through the pushing and shoving with what Colin and I secretly laughed about as her "piece of shit" face, or POS for short. Today was no exception. While girls around her came blundering out with rucksacks half open, socks around their ankles and scarves hanging off, Bronte threaded her way through with the poise of a ballerina, her dark curly hair still clipped off her face, her coat zipped up, not even glancing at the bunfight going on around her. She had more togetherness in her nine-year-old little finger than I had managed in three decades. She smiled when she saw me, but enthusiasm wasn't really part of her make-up.

"Mum! What are you doing here?" she said in a tone that could offend a thin-skinned person.

"I had to go to the post office, so I thought I'd walk home with you. I had some bad news today so I felt like getting some fresh air."

Bronte eyed me warily. I could see her closing down, ready to reject any neediness on my part. "What?"

"You remember Rose Stainton, the professor of English, at the big white house? She died last week."

Bronte looked down at the ground. "I liked her. She was nice." I waited for her to ask me something, anything. I suppose I'd thought she might cry. But she'd folded in on herself, shutting me out.

I broke the silence. "Do you want a hand with your bag?" I ached to pull her into a big hug but resisted. No one did ironing board as well as Bronte.

"Okay," she said, with a small shrug of one shoulder. She swung her bag towards me. "Are we waiting for Harley?"

She'd barely finished the question when he came bowling out of school, parka tucked under his arm, white polo shirt nearly as grey as his trousers. With a ten-year-old's lack of understanding of weight, speed and energy, he charged into me. I staggered backwards into the straggle-haired woman next to me whose "Watch where yer going" did nothing to put him off. He threw himself round me, unselfconscious, grey eyes shining up at me. I allowed my face to fall down onto his head, breathing him in and threading my freezing fingers into that warm space where his hair curled down over his collar. His shoulders went up as he registered the cold but he didn't push me off. Harley never hid his feelings; they walked two-by-two across his face, sat in the angles of his body, burst out in his words.

"What are you doing here? I didn't know you were coming today. Brill. Can we go down the bakery and get cakes?"

I needed to say no. Chocolate éclairs weren't going to help the pile of red bills. I could feel some pound coins, fat and solid, in my pocket. Bronte walked next to me, while Harley squashed his nose against car windows, looking at steering wheels, shouting about hubcaps and guff about engine sizes that I'd stopped pretending to understand. I waited until he'd finished peering through the blacked-out windows of a BMW before telling him the news about the prof.

"She was all right, wasn't she? Are you sad?" Harley stopped and gave me a hug. "What did she die of?"

That question was the start of a whole discussion about what's left of a body after twenty years, if worms eat eyeballs, if teeth disintegrate in a cremation, if people are buried naked and whether I knew anyone who'd been put in a coffin alive. I almost preferred Bronte's indifference. I managed to distract Harley by pointing out a Mercedes SLK, no doubt belonging to a local drug dealer.

I turned my attention back to Bronte. "So, who did you play with today?"

"No one."

"You must have played with someone."

"Well, I didn't," Bronte said.

"So did you sit on your own all playtime?"

"Yes."

I sighed. Colin never had to squeeze conversation out of Bronte. They would lie on the front room floor giggling for hours. She'd manage to persuade him to play Polly Pockets with her, his huge hands squishing tiny pink shoes onto webbed feet and lining up miniature cartons of milk in her grocer's shop. I couldn't even get her to tell me who'd shared her crisps.

We walked past a group of teenagers gathered on the wall outside the bakery, all sloppy T-shirts and arses hanging out of their jeans. They were taking it in turns to swing each other around in a Morrisons trolley. The trolley tipped down the high kerb, throwing a boy with a spider tattooed on his neck and "Shit Happens When You Party Naked" written on his sweatshirt headfirst into the road. I winced at the sound of bones meeting tarmac, but where we lived, a lot depended on your ability to look the other way. Hoots and wolf-whistles filled the air. No one jumped down from the wall. I shooed the kids into the bakery where Harley ran to the chocolate doughnuts covered in multi-coloured sprinkles.

"What do you fancy, Bronte?" I asked, squinting out through the reflections on the window into the road. A blonde girl with a glittery thong several inches above her jeans was squatting over the boy.

"I'm going to get a gingerbread man. Are you getting a vanilla slice for Dad?"

I nodded, though Colin didn't need any more blubber stuck on his backside. I'd always loved his muscular build towering above my tiny little frame. But now he was more darts player than rugby player.

Harley had bright pink and yellow sprinkles dotted round his mouth before we'd got out of the shop. Bronte nibbled the gingerbread man limb by ordered limb. The gang had disappeared but the boy was still there, propped up by the kerb, half-sitting, half-lying among the cake wrappers, Coke cans and fag packets. The girl was trying to look at his head.

"I'll be all right in a minute. S'just a cut, innit?" the boy said.

"Are you okay?" I said.

The girl swung round, black eyeliner and thick mascara out of place on her young face. She pulled her sleeves over her hands. "It's Tarants. He says he's good, but he's bleeding from his head, like. I think he needs some stitches or something. The corner of the trolley slashed him."

"Can I look?" I hoped that I wouldn't get a brick through the window later on. I waved Harley and Bronte over to the bench.

The boy took his hand away from his head. His sweatshirt was sodden. I stopped short of hopping

14

about, waving my arms and shouting, "Oh my God, oh my God, you're bleeding to death," but I felt my stomach suck in like a snail into a shell. For the first time I understood what fainting might feel like. I squeezed my eyes tight and fumbled for my phone.

"Sorry, but you really need to get this looked at. I'm calling an ambulance. All right?"

He was rocking gently and sort of singing one note, all that "hard boy, what you lookin' at?" gone out of him. He nodded at me, then started throwing up between his legs, splattering his trainers. I took a step back. Colin did blood and sick in our house. I did nits and threadworm. I held my breath, patted him on the back, and considered putting my coat round him. The blood would never come out of it, though. I shouted at Harley to go into the bakery and ask for a towel. I'd never called an ambulance before. I wasn't sure how bad people had to be for an ambulance. What if I had to pay for it if he wasn't injured enough? Tarants heaved again. I pushed 999.

Bronte slipped her hand into mine. It only needed someone to half-kill themselves for her to feel affectionate. "Is he going to die, Mum?" she said.

"No, no, of course not. A small cut can bleed quite a lot, so it's probably not as bad as it seems," I said, not even daring to look at the trolley in case half of Tarants' scalp, complete with black hedgehog spikes, was dangling there.

Harley spotted the paramedic before I did. I hadn't been expecting a motorbike. The paramedic pulled off his helmet to reveal a lean capable face and dark hair going grey at the temples. With a brisk "I'm Simon," he got straight to work, snapping on gloves and shining a light in Tarants' eyes and ears. I felt responsibility drop off me. Harley edged closer for a better look.

"Mum, will the doctor take him to hospital? Will he have to stay there? Will he get in trouble for messing about with the trolley?" As usual I was torn between pride at Harley's enthusiasm and embarrassment at his appetite for blood and the fact that he couldn't have a conversation that didn't compete with passing jet planes.

Harley bellowing in Simon's ear probably wasn't helping him concentrate. I tried to pull him back, but Harley looked as though he was on for stitching the wound himself. With a little wink, Simon nodded his head to show where Harley could stand for a ringside view without being in the way.

"What's his name?" Simon said.

"Tarants," said the girl. "Short for Tarantula. His real name is Kyle, but no one ever calls him that."

Simon nodded at her as though he came across a lot of people called Black Widow and Daddy Long Legs in his line of work. He examined the wound, his long fingers smoothing and tapping, like he was reading Braille, talking, talking all the time in a soothing voice. Harley had a definite swagger when Simon asked him to fetch a box of bandages from the back of the bike.

"Has anyone phoned his parents?" Simon asked over his shoulder, as he ripped open a dressing.

His shoulders sagged when he learned that Tarants lived with his sister. I looked away. We all knew that our

16

SD1 postcode — stabbings, domestics, heroin overdoses — was the one that the emergency services tried to pass like a forfeit at a party. SD2, a weird oasis of grand Victorian houses bordering our area of flat-roofed sixties flats and terraced stone-clad boxes, was the black fruit gum that everyone wanted — stranded Persian cats, heart attacks, fingers lopped off by pruning secateurs.

When Simon had finished, he smiled round at me, too young for a man who had all of us staring as though he was about to walk on water. Harley didn't seem to suffer from that best-pants-for-the-doctor deference, though. "Cor. How do you know what to do? Have you seen someone die? Will he die? I want to be a doctor like you."

"I have seen someone die. Sometimes it happens even when we try our very best. But Tarants is going to be okay. There's nothing stopping you becoming a doctor. You just have to work hard at school — and have a stomach for blood, which you obviously have." He said it like he really believed Harley could do it. And that made me want to smother him with big fat grateful kisses.

Just as I was noticing that he did have quite nice lips, I heard, "Hey, Bronte. What you doing here? I thought you was late home from school. I came out to see where you'd got to." I turned to see Colin standing behind us, hands on hips. When he came out to see where his little princess was, he was just being a good dad. I, on the other hand, was "blinking neurotic".

17

"Bleeding hell, Maia, I thought you'd be home by four. I didn't realise you was going to get the kids. You're not going to have time to cook tea before you get off to work."

I didn't want to confirm Simon's SD1 expectations by launching into a slanging match in the street. Colin glanced down at Tarants but apparently the thought of his own hand-to-metal contact with a tin opener was a far greater tragedy than leaving your brains splattered on the road.

I tried to pacify him. "I went out to put a notice up in the post office and as it was home time, I thought I'd meet the kids, and then —"

Simon looked up, right into Colin's paint-spattered sweat-shirt. "Your wife saw this young man had hurt himself, so she very kindly called the emergency services and was good enough to stay here to make sure he was okay. He should be fine but I've got an ambulance coming to take him to the hospital so he can be checked over," he said, as though Colin had been falling over himself to make Tarants' welfare his top concern rather than his ever-rumbling belly.

"Mai, you've done your Good Samaritan bit, so stop bloody standing there and get your arse into gear." Colin ignored Simon as though he was just supermarket music.

Simon was obviously a stranger to SD1 customs. He looked over to me and nodded towards Colin. "Don't you mind him talking to you like that?"

For a paramedic with all those qualifications, he wasn't very bright. I shrugged, knowing that getting my arse into gear had rocketed up from an order to an urgent necessity. I started grabbing the school bags, hustling Harley and Bronte on their way as the first darts of panic shot through me.

Colin stood there, arms folded, jaw bull-dogging like a bouncer from a two-bit nightclub.

"Come on, let's go." I grabbed hold of Colin's sleeve.

"Hang on a minute. You got something to say, mate? Maia here's got work to do. She needs to be at home sorting out her own family, not sticking her beak into other people's business and looking for trouble when we got enough of our own. Why don't you get on with saving the world and leave how I talk to the missus to me?"

I wasn't so much grabbing as hanging on now.

"Sorry," Simon said. "I wasn't having a go. I think your wife did a kind thing for Tarants here and it seems disrespectful to speak to her like that. You should be proud of her. You're a lucky man."

I tried to make out the look on Simon's face. Not confrontational, just matter-of-fact. Politely surprised even that Colin had spoken to me like that rather than licking the ground clean in front of me. I willed him to shut up before he became his own customer.

"Since when have you been the expert on me missus?" But I felt the tension in his forearm sag. Colin always loved having something someone else admired: the red Kawasaki when I first knew him; Bronte as a toddler, with her brown ringlets and eyes like little walnuts; that bloody phone that had nearly landed him in prison for handling stolen goods. Simon didn't respond, just carried on packing up, arranging rolls of gauze in his bag and checking the bandage around Tarants' head. Colin was used to men who either quaked in their boots or charged in, arms and legs flying like a *Tom and Jerry* scuffle. Indifference seemed to floor him.

I called Bronte over. "Start walking with Dad, I won't be a minute."

Bronte put her hand into Colin's. "Fuckwit," Colin said over his shoulder, and walked off, all big man swagger. I breathed out.

Harley hung back with me. I said a quiet goodbye to Tarants but he didn't answer. The girl mumbled, "Cheers", and gave me a wave, which round here was almost a handwritten thank you note. There was no shock, no soft sympathy in her face. I braced myself for the pity on Simon's, but instead he thanked me and turned his attention to the ambulance that had just raced round the corner.

CHAPTER
THREE

"Twenty-four thousand pounds a year, until the children are eighteen?" I said. Twenty-four thousand pounds was so many hours of cleaning that I thought I might start laughing and never stop.

The professor's solicitor, Mr Harrison, nodded and shuffled his papers. "Yes, she left enough money so that both children can stay at Stirling Hall School until they finish their A-levels, should they wish to do so."

"Why would she do that?" I asked. "I was thinking that she might've left me something little, y'know, like her reading lamp or some of her books. I mean, not that I would rather have had that, I'm really grateful, but I was just the cleaner." I fidgeted on his very upright chair. I wasn't used to wearing a skirt and I felt as though I had been rootling through my mum's dressing up box. Trousers hadn't seemed right though, and I didn't want this guy in his pinstriped waistcoat to think I wasn't paying proper respect to the prof.

Mr Harrison put the lid on his pen. He had that look about him. Teachers have it on parents' evening, that blank face that doesn't give anything away. "She's written you a letter. Would you like to go into the waiting room to read it? I've got some phone calls to make, so don't rush."

I went and sat in a bright little room next to piles of *Country Life* magazines. My eyes pricked when I saw Professor Stainton's careful writing. She'd addressed the letter to Amaia Etxeleku, which almost made me smile. No one called me Amaia, but Professor Stainton thought nicknames were laziness, "especially if one has a name to reflect one's heritage". The fact that my mother came from a little village in the Basque country fascinated the professor. I hadn't been there since I was a teenager. Mum and I had always planned to go back together but she'd died before there'd ever been enough cash for jaunts abroad. The Basque thing probably wouldn't have meant anything to me at all except it was obvious I wasn't English. I often got mistaken for an Italian with my long dark hair and big cow eyes, just nowhere near as stylish.

I almost didn't want to open the letter. I knew it could change my life, and all change, even change for the good, made me nervous.

Gatsby,
Stamford Avenue,
Sandbury,
Surrey,
SD2 7DJ

23 November 2013

Dear Amaia,
This may come as a surprise to you as I know you never wanted anything from me. I always felt that you

were a very intelligent young woman whose life would have been vastly different had you been afforded a better education. I do not consider it to be too late for you. I know we spoke of you taking an OU degree and I do believe that you will.

However, at my age, I have to make decisions about the future, which is becoming shorter and shorter for me. Since my son died, I have been forced to consider how to make the best use of the little that remains dear to me and consider the legacy I would like to leave to mark my time on this earth. For me, education is the most valuable thing one can have after health, of course, and successful relationships. Therefore it would give me great pleasure to offer your lovely children a good start in life. The time that I have spent with them leads me to believe that they both show intelligence and enthusiasm for learning and I would certainly consider it a wise use of money. Purely because of your domestic circumstances and my fear that my money might find its way onto the horses at Newmarket, I have left my will so that the money can only be used for education at Stirling Hall School. I know from my time as a governor there that it will provide excellent and rounded instruction for your children and open doors for them, which might otherwise remain closed. I hope you will seize the opportunity to help them and keep in mind George Peabody's wise words: "Education: a debt due from present to future generations".

Finally, Amaia, I wish good things for you and your family. I am so grateful to you for making my last few years as comfortable as possible, with your kindness and attention to detail going beyond the call of duty. I urge you to consider my proposal very seriously.

With my very good wishes,
Rose Stainton

Who the hell was George Peabody? Was he famous? The professor couldn't resist leaving me one last little puzzle to expand my mind. I started raking through my hair, pulling out all the loose strands. It was a wonder I wasn't bald.

I screwed up my eyes, trying to find one thought that didn't pull in a knotty old tangle of other problems with it. Sweat started to gather under my armpits, turning my silk blouse from pale blue to navy and reminding me why I kept it for special occasions. By now, I should have learnt that Etxeleku sweat glands and silk didn't mix. I was just considering a damage limitation exercise with the kitchen roll by the water cooler, when Mr Harrison called me back. He looked relieved, as though he had been expecting to hand over his handkerchief for a huge nose blow. He settled back into his big boss's chair and cracked his knuckles. "I assume you are going to take the opportunity to send the children to Stirling Hall?"

Assume. How wonderful to be in a life where you could assume anything. Assume that your husband would take care of you. Assume that your kids would be at a school where their days were about education and not survival. Assume that twenty-four thousand pounds a year was fantastic news, not some Australia-sized crow bar to wrench the lid off Pandora's box.

I remembered my armpits and folded my hands in my lap. "I need to think about it, I mean, I'm grateful, of course, the professor has been very generous, but I need to discuss it with the children's father, like," I said, immediately hearing the professor's voice in my head. "Amaia, 'like' is for people we are friends with."

"May I be so bold as to enquire what the obstacles are?" said Mr Harrison.

I ignored the "being so bold". He could, of course, just ask, though he was trying to be kind. "God, this is so embarrassing. I'm sorry to be so stupid, but how much are the fees at Stirling Hall? You said she was leaving me twenty-four thousand pounds a year. That can't just be school fees."

"I'm afraid it is. Four thousand pounds a term for each child."

"Bloody hell," I said, then squirmed. "Sorry, I mean, that's a heck of a lot of money. Sorry to sound ungrateful. So all that money would just go on the school fees. Wow. That's the only option?"

"I'm afraid the professor has been quite clear. She's tied the money up so that it can only be spent on Stirling Hall. It will be transferred directly to the school at the start of every term. If you don't take up her offer, she has left instructions for the money to go to the cancer hospice in town."

The hair stood up on my arms. Mum had died there three years earlier. I forced away the memory of her little room with the flowery border and the horrible hours I'd spent there, watching her poor, knackered body rise and fall. I needed to think about the next generation, not the last.

"I don't want to sound graspy, but has she left any money for uniforms and that sort of stuff?" I'd seen the piles of hockey sticks, rugby gear and coats for every occasion in the children's bedrooms where I cleaned. I wouldn't be able to get away with any old anorak and a West Ham football kit.

"No, but I believe most of these private schools have good second-hand sales."

My mind was scrambling to see how I could possibly afford it, even second-hand. Harley wouldn't give a stuff about worn elbows or knees. But Bronte would make a right ling-along-a-dance. Even at Morlands, she could make me late for work fussing about matching hair bands and the tiniest ant-sized hole in her tights. It would be like pushing a lamb up the slope to slaughter if I tried to fob her off with something that wasn't brand new.

Unlike Morlands, where a school trip meant walking down to the local museum with its two Roman coins and a few manky old fossils, Stirling Hall was the kingpin of school trips. I'd seen pictures of Stirling Hall's cricket team on tour in Barbados in the *Surrey Mirror*. The bloody Caribbean as a school trip. Just off to the West Indies to whack a few balls. That wasn't going to be a pound in your pocket, a jam sandwich and a packet of Wotsits kind of deal. I'd never be able to afford that for Harley. Still, he'd never played cricket in his life, so hopefully he wouldn't make the team.

I picked at my raggedy nails. An image of Bronte begging me not to come to any school plays, sports days or carol concerts floated into my mind. She hated people knowing I was a cleaner. She kept trying to get me to apply for the *X Factor* so I could become a pop star instead, even though I sounded like a Hoover that had sucked up a sock.

Maybe I was going to need Mr Harrison's handkerchief after all.

CHAPTER
FOUR

"Well then?" Colin said, through a fistful of crisps. "Did the old girl come good?"

"Depends what you mean," I said. I opened the window to let out the smell of Colin's first, though probably not last, joint of the day. I picked up the pages of the *Racing Post* strewn all round the settee.

"Don't play games," Colin said, licking his finger to dab up the crumbs on his T-shirt. "How much did we get? Don't tell me she left you one of her crappy old tea services."

"No, she left us enough money to send the kids to Stirling Hall School."

"You what? I ain't sending my kids to no nobby school. How much did she leave us?"

"Twenty-four thousand pounds a year until they finish their A-levels, but —"

"Twenty-four grand a year? Way to bloody go!" Colin leapt up off the settee and started limbo dancing. "Whe-hey! Fan-bloody-tastic. Let's go on holiday somewhere. D'you fancy Benidorm? Or Corfu?"

"She didn't leave me the money so we could go off sunning ourselves. She left it so we could send the kids to a decent school, get them a good education."

"It's our money. We can spend it on what we like."

"No, we can't. That's the point. You're not listening — unless we send the kids to Stirling Hall, we can't even get the cash in the first place. It'll all go to the cancer hospice."

A great cloud of a scowl rolled across Colin's face. "Let me get this right. That old biddy has left us twenty-four grand a year and we've got to spend it on some fancy pants school or we get absolutely zilcho?"

I moved in front of my favourite red vase. I didn't say anything, just stood absolutely still. The remote control went zinging past my ear, clattering into the front window, taking a bite out of the frame but missing the glass. The batteries pinged out and rolled under the chair.

"Christ Almighty." Colin kicked at the settee. "Snotty-nosed bitch. I bet you put her up to this. Didn't you? Bloody banging on about education, filling the kids' heads with crap about going to university. Sitting there with your nose in a book, bloody *Withering Heights* and *David Crapperfield*. You and your big ideas. Can you imagine Harley in a little green cap and tie? He'd be a laughing stock round here. Get his head kicked in before he got to the end of the road."

"It wasn't anything to do with me. I didn't even know she'd left me anything. For God's sake, it's better than nothing. I think it would be great for Bronte. She's quite bright. She could really go places with the right education." My throat was tight with the effort of not shouting.

"What places is she going to go? She'll probably be up the duff by the time she's sixteen. She needs to start, I dunno, learning to type or something, not having her head filled with a load of old bollocks she'll never use."

"Bronte won't be stupid enough to get pregnant with some no-hoper sponger from round here," I said, looking at Colin's belly hanging out of his T-shirt. Blue fluff nestled in his belly button. I couldn't let Bronte end up with a bloke who thought showers made you shrink.

Colin snatched the paper from me, then blubbered down onto the settee, rattling the sports pages into a position that meant I couldn't see his face. I knew I'd got to him from the way his foot was twitching.

"Don't you want the kids to live better than us? Is your greatest ambition for Harley that he learns the difference between off-white and magnolia? Do you want Bronte to end up scrubbing skid marks out of the toilets of the women whose dads didn't think spelling tests were a waste of time? Or are you just pinning your hopes on Bronte marrying a striker from flaming West Ham?"

He didn't answer. Usually I knew better than to "keep going on" but people like us didn't get a lot of chances. I sat on the end of the settee and put his foot on my lap. "Can you put the paper down, just for a sec?"

He looked sullenly over the top. His eyes were still beautiful.

I persevered. "I think this is a really big chance for them. I never got any qualifications and neither did you, so we're stuck here. Morlands is such a rubbish school that if they stay there, they'll end up like us. We're never going to have enough money to move into a different catchment area. But with a good education at Stirling Hall, the kids could become engineers, architects, doctors, anything. I don't think it's fair to stand in their way."

"Yeah, but what about when they want to bring their mates home? No one is going to come round here in their Beamer in case it ends up on bricks. You ain't thinking it through. Let's say they do go there. We can pay for the school, but what about all the things that go with it? The parents ain't going to want their toffee-nosed little darlings hanging about with Bronts and Harley, are they? Case they catch something awful off of them. They're all going to be living in great big houses — I don't want some kid called Verity or Jasper coming round here to get a look at how poor people live, how Harley pisses against the back fence when I'm on the khazi or how we have to stand on a chair with a match to get the boiler to light every time we want a bloody shower."

I'd worked in houses where guitar lessons, French club and netball matches were the norm, as run-of-the-mill as living in a home where the children had a playroom and the adults had a study. Of course, there'd been some arrogant little shits along the way like the boy who said, "You can't be a mummy. You're a cleaner." But there'd also been some sweet kids, who'd brought out their old dolls, tea sets and jigsaws so I could give them to Bronte.

The one thing they all had in common was this idea, a confidence that when they spoke, they had a right to be listened to. I was thirty-six and still had to work up the courage to say what I thought when they held meetings at school to improve discipline. I'd think, right, I'm going to put my hand up next. No, next. Then someone would drop in a "statistically speaking" or an "economically viable" and I'd decide that my point was probably a bit obvious anyway and some bloke with a clipboard would thank everyone for their useful input and Colin would be moaning about getting down the pub before closing time and that would be that. If money could buy confidence, I had a chance to do one clever thing in my stupid life.

"Talk about glass half bleeding empty," I said. "Yeah, we might get some kids come here who think we're common as pig shit. On the other hand, Harley and Bronte might even make some nice friends, normal kids who don't think that a good Saturday night out is kicking in the car wing mirrors on the estate."

"You just don't get it, do you? They're going to be the council house kids among a bunch of nobs. They ain't ever going to fit in."

"We've got to give them a chance. They might see that there's more to life than a quick shag against the fence in the back alley or getting pissed in the bus shelter on Special Brew." I started combing through all the possible tactics I could use to get Colin to agree. I'd only got as far as two — begging or a blow job — when Colin shrugged.

"I don't fucking know. I think you're wrong. How we going to pay for all the kit and crap that they're gonna need? You're just sticking your head into a bag of trouble," he said.

Colin was voicing my worries. Somehow that made me angrier. "That's typical you. Just sit there and be defeatist. You were just the same when I wanted to go to appeal to get them into a better primary school. Give up before we start instead of using a bit of brain power to see how we could make it work. I'll have to take on more shifts. Maybe things'll pick up and you'll be able to get some work. It's a real opportunity."

"Don't think you can rely on me getting work anytime soon. It's not looking good out there."

I tried to remember that to win this one I needed him on my side. I bit back my "change the record".

He picked at his ear, examined it and wiped it on his tracksuit. "The kids won't thank you for it. Mind you, I might be able to up me rates and find a cushy job with them parents. Some of them must have a nice mansion that could do with a lick of paint," he said.

Once Colin started down the "What's in it for me?" route, I knew that I just had to sneak up and bolt the door behind him. "Can we try it for a term? Morlands is never full. People are petitioning not to go there, so I'm sure we'll get them back in if we need to."

Colin started scrabbling about on the floor for the batteries to the remote. He flicked on the West Ham vs. Arsenal match he'd recorded the night before. I needed to finish the conversation before he started singing the theme tune, "I'm forever blowing bubbles". God, he was starting to hum. I had about five seconds left.

"Colin, listen to me."

"That ref needs bloody glasses. Oy, four eyes! Christ, he wouldn't see a foul if they kicked him on the nose. Did you see that, Maia?" he said, hurling an empty Coke can at the telly and sending an arc of brown drops shooting up the front room wall. He made no move to get a cloth.

I stood in front of the telly.

"Mai! Out the way!"

"Shall I send them for a term?"

"Do what you want but don't come crying to me when it comes back to bite you on the arse," he said, trying to peer round me.

I went straight to my handbag and dug out the solicitor's silver embossed card.

CHAPTER
FIVE

The freezing January mornings didn't agree with my van. It chose the kids' first day at Stirling Hall to start making a chugging sound from the engine. I was terrified that it would grind to a halt with the effort of climbing over the speed bumps along the horseshoe-shaped drive at Stirling Hall. Christ, the school had its own one-way system, a slow-moving line of super-shiny, top of the range cars coming in one entrance and spilling out the other like a Motor Show parade. I had visions of breaking down right in the middle of it all, forcing everyone to squeeze past me. Harley was oblivious, hanging out of the window with his cap sitting at a jaunty angle on his blond curls, shouting about cars.

"Wicked, Mum, look, look, there's a Bentley. A Bentley Continental. Wow. Do you think it actually belongs to one of the parents? Cor, I saw one of them on *Top Gear*. Do you think they might let me have a ride, Mum? Will you ask them for me? Who do you think it belongs to? Do you think they got it new? Jeremy Clarkson says they cost £130,000. Do you think they paid that for it? Cool!"

"Let's see how it goes, Harley. Maybe the boy will be in your class and he might invite you round," I said. I peered at the woman behind the wheel. She didn't have a hairstyle, she had an official hair "do". A big puffy creation that would surely involve rollers. Definitely not a chop with the kitchen scissors in a shaving mirror and a head-upside-down blast from the hair dryer. I'd rather spend the entire day pulling matted hair out of plugholes than have her pass judgement on Harley over a cheese spread sandwich — or a bloody lobster tail or whatever Stirling Hall kids had for tea.

Bronte was clutching her rucksack on her knee, staring straight ahead, looking just like Colin when his horses fell at the last hurdle. That morning I'd gone in to wake her up all jolly and sing-song but she told me to get lost, she wasn't bloody going and held on to the duvet for grim death. She actually swore at me. Little madam. I lost sight of my skipping through the daisies voice in favour of a "you'll do as I say" bellow. I practically dragged her out of bed by her ankles. She got dressed with a slowness that was right on the edge of defiance. She hated the red and green plaid skirt, said it was frumpy and minging and wanted to wear black trousers like she had at Morlands. I helped her into the blazer I'd spent a week's wages on when I could have bought one for £20 second-hand. I had to walk away when I saw her twisting the buttons, complaining that they didn't do up properly. Harley had been twirling his cap round his finger for fifteen minutes by the time Bronte slouched out the door. Just as I started to tell her she looked wonderful, she stared at me, her dark eyes narrowing and said, "You look horrible. Everyone will know you clean up other people's shit."

I decided not to speak to her. My hand tingled with the desire to give her a good slap but attitude adjustments would have to wait for another day. For now, getting her to school was enough. As I looked for somewhere to park, a Mitsubishi Pajero got so close to my bumper that the woman must have been trying to get into my slipstream. I glared into the rear-view mirror and noticed that my foundation looked a bit orange and I'd missed a couple of black hairs on my upper lip with the tweezers. Great. I couldn't wait to be known as Whiskers.

"Wind the window up, Harley. Stop shouting."

"Mum, there's a Porsche Boxster. Jeremy Clarkson says you only buy one of those if you can't afford a 911," said Harley, twisting around in his seat and pushing Bronte onto the gear stick.

"Ouch. Get off," said Bronte. She shoved Harley back.

"Stop pushing her, Harley. Close the window, now." I tried not to shout in case I couldn't stop.

"This is brill, Mum," said Harley, ignoring me and pointing out an open-topped BMW.

I gave up and turned my attention to Bronte. "Hey, Bronte, look at those lawns. They look like somewhere the queen might have a tea party. I bet they play rounders there in the summer. What do you think? Doesn't it look amazing?" I said, hoping to get a small glimmer of reassurance from her. She shook her head.

I tried again. "Come on, love. Let's try and get off to a good start. Everyone feels a bit shy on their first day, isn't that right, Harley? You'll soon make friends."

Harley tried to help out. "Yeah, come on, Bront, it'll be okay. Anyway, Dad says we can go back to Morlands if we don't like it here."

Bronte turned her mouth down so far at the corners, it almost made me laugh. "Dad said Stirling Hall was for tossers, anyway. Though he thought I looked really pretty in my uniform."

Good old Dad. Colin had wandered about the kitchen in his boxers, eating toast without a plate, sounding like he was sucking up his tea through a straw. He made no attempt to help as I double-checked the football socks with named garter, the "laces, no Velcro" rugby boots, the navy "no logo" PE shorts, and every other bloody bit of sports equipment an Olympian in the making could need. I had refused to let myself mourn the days of any T-shirt and a tracksuit, out loud anyway.

I tried to reverse into the one tiny slither of space I could find that wasn't blocked by a monster 4x4. The Mitsubishi woman, "Jen1", leant on the horn as I had a second go. She was obviously in a hurry to get somewhere. Her plastic surgeon probably, judging by her ugly mush. I wished her a flat tyre as I finally managed to park up.

We got out of the van. I adjusted Bronte's hat and looked away from the hands I could see waving behind the Mitsubishi's shiny windscreen. I was never going to beat a Stirling Hall mother in a spelling bee but I'd fancy my chances in a slanging match. I'd get Jen1 back another day.

"Why was that lady waving at you, Mum?" said Harley.

"I've no idea." I shuffled him forward.

"She was trying to talk to you. Won't she think you're rude? You told us to be polite to everyone we met today."

Just when the toothpick holding my patience together looked about to snap, Bronte threw her new rucksack down and ground to a halt like a fat old Labrador that's decided it's not walking one step further.

"Mum, I'm not going. I want to go back to Morlands. We should've started in September. January's too late. Everyone will have made friends and I won't have anyone to play with."

I dug deep. Ferreted about for a kind word. Beamed myself into my other world as Julie Andrews, dancing about in *The Sound of Music* singing "Do-Re-Mi", like I did at work when people who were too lazy to pick their pants off the floor started having a go at me. The voice in my head was screaming, "You ungrateful cow. Here I am making sure you get a fantastic education and all you can do is whine your arse off."

I managed a reasonably calm, "It's too late for that. Don't worry. It's going to be fine. I spoke to your teacher and she seemed really nice." In fact, all I could remember was how I'd nodded blankly at Bronte's teacher as she talked about "prep" for a good fifteen minutes until I realised she was on about homework.

39

I stood on the edge of the sea of green blazers belonging to the prep school kids. A steady stream of older children, dressed in grey, dodged around the little ones and headed over to the senior school building on the far side of the cricket pitch. It had towers. Towers! I would be so proud if Harley and Bronte ended up there. However, the odds weren't looking too hot if I couldn't even get Bronte through the doors of the prep school today.

Harley stood beside me, relaxed, as though we were queuing for the cinema, happily gawping round at the cars. The other kids were swarming through the stone arch into the playground beyond. In my hurry to get away from Colin and his repetitions of "The rain in Spain falls mainly in the plain" in stupid voices, I'd forgotten to re-read the letter and find out where I needed to take them. I glanced around for a mum I liked the look of. Which was more difficult than it first appeared. Not the woman with a long, grey plait down her back. Bloody lentil-eater, for sure. She looked like she knitted her own knickers. Maybe the one next to her. No, she had a briefcase. And stilettos. Obviously rushing off to some mega job in the City. No time for her to be a traffic warden for me when there was a bonus to be had. God, this was hopeless. I felt homesick for the mothers at Morlands with their flip-flops, dark roots and Marlboros, shoving packets of crisps at chubby children and talking about *EastEnders* as though it was real life.

Bronte looked up at me. "I'm not bloody going," she said, her eyes darting around for an escape route. That got me moving. I walked straight up to the nearest person, a young woman with peroxide blonde hair and skintight jeans, holding a spaniel on a lead.

"Excuse me, do you know where 4H or 5R children need to go?"

"Excuse?" she said, untangling herself from the spaniel's lead. "My English very bad."

"Doesn't matter," I said, waving her away. Of course. No nice Morlands grannies with a fag in their mouths and a toffee in their handbags here. Stirling Hall's nannies came with a paid-for car and a foreign accent. Bronte was beginning to cry. Just as I was thinking up my most horrible threat for her, a blonde woman, no Penelope Pitstop hairdo, no red lipstick, no handbag with big gold clasp, came over to me. She was wearing jodhpurs. And if they were really only boobs under her sweatshirt, she had an exceptionally large pair of knockers.

"Hi, are you okay? I heard you asking about 4H and 5R? Is this your first day? It's always mayhem on the first day of term. I'm Clover, by the way." She sounded so like Joanna Lumley in *Absolutely Fabulous* that I thought she might be taking the piss. She thrust out a hand with nails that looked like they spent time in an allotment. My scabby old mitts looked quite refined by comparison.

She turned to Bronte. "Listen, my twins are in 4H." She called over two identical girls with curly white blonde hair trapped into scruffy ponytails. "This is Saffy and this is Sorrel. Just remember that Sorrel has

41

the mole above her left eye. Even I can't tell the difference sometimes."

Bronte made no attempt to say her name, so I filled in the blank. Clover bent right down to Bronte's level, hauling a bra strap against gravity as she went. "Do you know what, Bronte? Your teacher is really lovely. Do you like art? Mrs Harper does the best pictures of horses. She's taught Sorrel to draw a really amazing pony. Will you let the twins take you to class? Look, hold Sorrel's hand, she'll show you where to go."

Miraculously, Bronte's snivelling puttered to a halt. She glanced down at Sorrel's hand, which looked as though it was fresh from digging about in a guinea pig cage. I thought I might have a rebellion to deal with, but Bronte put out a stiff little paw for Sorrel to hang on to while Clover kept up her running commentary. "Bye bye, darlings, be good, Saffy, remember not to imitate Mme Blanchard's accent. And do try and eat your apple at break. Sorrel, did you put your fountain pen in your bag? And tell Mrs Baines that you're not doing drama next term."

"Fucking hell, Mum," Saffy said. "Shu' up."

Bronte looked the most animated I'd seen her all morning. I had to remind myself to close my mouth.

"Saffy, I've told you before about dropping your t's. Don't let me hear any more glottal stops or you'll be mucking out the horses on your own all week."

That "t" thing was becoming a bigger part of my life than I'd expected. At this rate we'd all be in the van chanting the prof's favourite tongue twister: "Betty Botter had some butter . . ." Although I couldn't help

42

feeling that Clover had over-looked something beginning with "F".

She waved the girls off. I felt my shoulders come down from around my ears as Bronte scuffed away with the twins without looking back. Clover turned to me. "Sorry about that. I can't stand glottal stops, can you? Now, let's get your boy sorted out. What's his name? Harley? Orion can drop him at 5R. Orion, Orion, come here."

Orion raced over, lanky limbs flailing, tie pulled to one side and mud down the front of his blazer. His curly brown hair was cropped too close to his head so it stuck out at right angles which made him look a bit odd, but he had a friendly, open face. "Yes?"

Clover dished out instructions to Orion, who turned to shake Harley's hand. Bloody hell, it was like the Freemasons round here. Harley managed to get his hand out of his pocket before it got embarrassing.

"Cor, are you named after a car? That's wicked. Me dad called me after his favourite motorbike."

Orion looked puzzled. "I'm not named after a car. I'm named after the Hunter, the star constellation. My dad does astronomy. It's his hobby."

It was Harley's turn to look puzzled. "Not a Ford Orion then?" But he sounded indignant, as though Orion had somehow messed up the origin of his name. Not humiliated because, among my many other failings as a mother, I hadn't been teaching him flaming star constellations since he was six months old. Watching all that confidence, all that optimism stuffed into one baby-faced ten-year-old made me ache to hug him.

Luckily, the bell rang and Harley gave me a quick wave, a slightly impatient "I'll be fine, Mum" and walked off with Orion.

I heard Harley ask, "So what car's your dad got then?"

I turned away. I didn't want to hear the question — or answer — in reverse. "Thanks for sorting out Bronte. She was really worried about coming here this morning," I said.

"My pleasure. It's difficult starting halfway through the school year, and January's such an atrocious month, but I'm sure they'll absolutely love it here. It's a marvellous school, they'll settle down in no time. You must come to our class coffee morning next week. Monday. We have one at the beginning of every term so all the mums can catch up. It's at Jennifer's, Hugo's mum, he's in Harley's class. I'll pick you up, if you like."

"No, no, it's okay, thanks anyway."

"You will come, won't you? I'll send home directions in Harley's school bag. You'll get to know all the mums so you can sort out playdates. Anyway must go, horses need exercising. Do you ride? No? Bet you do something far more fucking sensible like Pilates. You're lovely and slim. Big tits always been my downfall."

With that, Clover, the mother of a couple of herby girls and a star constellation strode off in her wellies to a muddy old Land Rover. Fucking Clover had saved the day.

CHAPTER
SIX

I looked down again at the note that Clover had sent home. Though she'd obviously written it with a crayon or an eyeliner, it definitely said Little Sandhurst. Which meant Jennifer's house was behind these wrought iron gates, a reddish blur down an avenue lined with horse chestnut trees. Jesus. Before I'd even pressed the button to get in, the gates whirred back and a security camera swivelled above my head. Thank God I'd had the good sense to leave the van in the pub car park at the end of the road, otherwise I'd have definitely been risking directions to the tradesman's entrance.

At the door, I tugged down my T-shirt to make sure my belly button ring wasn't showing. The long walk up the drive hadn't agreed with my underwear and I was just in the middle of pulling my knickers out of my bottom when I suddenly remembered the security cameras. I looked round, praying I wasn't being beamed around the kitchen or the front room, digging between my buttocks for my Asda sideslappers. Then something else caught my attention. A silver Mitsubishi Pajero. Jen Bloody 1. I'd bust a gut, mopping, spraying and hoovering like a chicken on ecstasy to finish early and get over here for coffee with none other than the flaming horn-honker. Stupid cow. For two pins I wouldn't have come, but Harley and Bronte were having a tricky old time fitting in as it was. If I could help by nodding nicely at other mums and crooking my little finger over a Jammie Dodger, bring it on. Hopefully she wouldn't recognise me without the van.

The door opened and Jen1 stood there, a skinny minny with super-straight long blonde hair almost down to her waist. I think it was her waist, anyway. The wide belt around it made it look like my wrist. "You must be Harley's mummy. I'm Hugo's mummy, Jennifer, how do you do?" She held out a hand that had definitely benefited from the sort of creams I dusted on dressing tables — lotions and potions made from nightingale droppings, Chilean snail slime or snake venom at £100 a blob.

"I'm Maia, pleased to meet you, Jenny." I wondered whether Jen1 phoned the hairdresser's and announced herself as Hugo's mummy.

"I prefer Jennifer, if you don't mind," she said, as she did what I always thought of as the elevator look. She started off looking at the top of my head like an exotic parakeet had settled there, then flicked down, taking in my T-shirt, my cardigan with the button missing, my Primark jeans. She got as far as my shoes, then zoomed all the way up again. As soon as she realised that I was so far down the food chain, there was nothing to compete with, her whole attitude shifted. She dug out a different face, like she was picking one out of the wardrobe. The mask she'd chosen for me was a limited amount of smiling and friendliness so I couldn't go away and slag her off but I wouldn't start thinking that I was going to become her bessie mate either.

"Come in, come in, we're all in the kitchen," she said. I stepped into the hall. Pale cream carpet without a single stain, no splodge of tea, no muddy marks. No place for the Crocs that I'd squelched around the football field in at the weekend. I took them off, wishing I'd worn something other than the Boozy Bird socks that Colin had bought me for my birthday.

I followed Jen1's trail of perfume as she led me into the kitchen. About twelve women were standing in various little groups around a black marble-topped island with a built-in wine fridge. Jen1 obviously didn't have to shuffle everything round and stand her milk outside the back door if she'd bought a chicken for Sunday dinner. I handed her the box of bakewell tarts that I'd bought at the Co-op on the way. With barely a thank you, she dumped it down next to a box of Waitrose's mint truffles and a tin of biscuits from Harrods. She introduced me to a few women who had names like Francesca, Elizabeth and Charlotte, all with their own versions of the elevator look.

I heard Clover swearing before I saw her, a helmet of wayward curls among several shiny bobs. She was wearing a pair of thick round glasses that made her look like Velma off *Scooby-Doo*. A kaftan top created a beaded shelf over her enormous boobs like an usherette's ice cream tray. She made her way round to my side of the island.

"Maia, how are you? How are the children settling in? Orrie said something about a problem with Harley's hair? They're such fucking fascists at that school sometimes. I mean, they're great at telling the kids what they're good at, all those star charts and best bloody handwriting awards, but they've got no bastard idea about individuality. Still, I suppose that's what we're paying for. They can instil discipline so we don't have to bother."

When she took a breath, I told her about the note his teacher had sent me, saying that Harley wouldn't be allowed back until he'd had his hair chopped off. That same evening I'd given him a number five in the kitchen with Colin's clippers and watched his curls gather on the floor like an old wig. When I'd finished, my raggle-taggle golden boy looked like he was about to join the army cadets. Harley had run his hand over it, shrugging. "S'all right. It feels like a tennis ball."

When Colin saw it, he did a Sieg Heil salute and told Harley he looked like a BNP supporter. I picked up a curl from the floor, wrapped it in silver foil and put it in the old biscuit tin under my bed where I kept all my precious things. Right on the top of the pile was his school photo from last year. He looked so much younger, scruffy curls falling over his face, cheekily carefree. I had jammed the lid back on.

Jen1 appeared at my side, all buzzy-bottomed and efficient in her black polo-necked jumper and pencil skirt. She offered us a plate of mini chocolate brownies. Clover took one, then scooped up two more. "These are lovely, did you make them?"

"Hugo and I bake every Sunday afternoon. I think it's essential for children to learn to cook. It's no

48

wonder that there are so many of these fat chavvy children about when their mothers just feed them pre-packaged rubbish," Jen1 said.

I glanced over at my bakewell tarts, still in their box, shining with thick white icing and glacé cherries. I took comfort from the fact that she hadn't even let the Harrods pure butter shortbread poison her kitchen.

"We eat organic as far as possible. I'm even getting the gardener to plant some veggies this year. We should have our own rocket, leeks and red peppers by the summer," she said, turning to me. "Would you like coffee, Maia? I've got linizio, livanto or capriccio if you want an espresso or vivalto or finezzo if you want a longer one. Or I've got Mao Feng green tea and white Ginseng tea. Or Tung Ting Oolong."

I didn't have a clue what she was on about. I must've looked a bit dorky because she indicated the coffee machine on the side. "Coffee would be lovely. I don't mind what sort. Thank you," I said.

Clover readjusted a bra strap, temporarily raising her left boob like a put about to be shot. "If you come round to mine, it's just instant," she said, not quite managing to whisper.

A tall woman came trotting over, horsey teeth, bright orange lipstick and frilly Peter Pan collar. "Clover, how are you? And you must be the new boy's mother. How do you do? I'm Venetia Dylan-Jones. Welcome to Stirling Hall, or SH as we like to call it. How is your son settling in?"

"Fine, thank you. I think he's finding some of the work quite hard but hopefully he'll catch up."

"I think reading's key at this age, isn't it? Theo's a great fan of Beverley Naidoo." Venetia had the sort of face on that meant she expected us to be impressed. I obviously didn't get my eyes open wide enough.

"I don't think I know who she is."

"Of course you do. She's written all those books about racism and prejudice in South Africa. You must know *Journey to Jo'burg, No Turning Back*," Venetia said. "It's terribly important for our children to understand other cultures."

"I don't think I've come across her."

Venetia looked as though she thought I might be having her on. She battled on. "Of course, he likes fantasy stories as well. Anthony Horowitz, David Almond and Harry Potter."

"He's read Harry Potter?" Harley was reading *Diary of a Wimpy Kid* and that was a struggle.

Again, Venetia looked at me as though I was speaking a foreign language. "He'd read most of them by the time he was eight." She had that "hasn't everybody?" tone going on. "Not so keen on the last one, I think he was finding it a bit easy."

That morning I'd got really stressed over Harley's spellings because he still hadn't cottoned on to the fact that some words had silent letters, still writing "nife", "nome" and "restling" while Bronte sat there rolling her eyes. Nothing compared to how bloody stressed I was feeling now. Weren't any of the other boys reading *Top Gear* and *Doctor Who* annuals?

Venetia patted my arm. "Perhaps he's more into science?"

50

I didn't tell her that so far we'd only managed to do one of the science homeworks because we needed to use the internet and the one crappy computer at the library had been out of order. I did a half-shrug and said, "We'll see."

Venetia ploughed on. "I've got the number of a terrific science tutor. Even if he doesn't want to do science at university, it might help him get in if there's a struggle for places. We get Theo tutored twice a week in science and he's just started Mandarin as well. My husband is very keen for him to get into Oxford. Languages seem to be terribly important for the best universities."

"How old is he?" I said.

"Rising eleven, he's in Mr Rickson's class with your son. It's vital to start early. Have you thought about universities yet?"

"No, not yet." Though I did make an effort not to look as though the idea had never occurred to me.

"I haven't given it a second thought," Clover said. "I'm not bothered whether the kids go or not. Some of the thickest, dullest people I know went to university. Never saw the need myself. I don't care if my kids spend their lives breeding tropical fish as long as they're passionate about it." She licked the chocolate off her fingers.

"My husband doesn't see it that way. We both went to Oxford and he'd like to see Theo carry on the family tradition." Venetia looked like a cat whose fur had been stroked the wrong way. I wasn't in the "Mandarin by intravenous drip" camp but I did hope that Stirling

Hall would encourage the kids to do something a bit more highbrow than get a few Black Mollies in the family way. God, I was still hoping that it wasn't too late for me, let alone the kids. Even though I couldn't afford Open University, I was working my way through the classics at the library. I'd got most of the A's and B's covered now so as long as people stuck with Jane Austen or the Brontës I had half a chance of sounding a teeny bit educated.

"Where did you study, Maia?" Venetia said.

"I didn't stay on at school."

Venetia looked as though she was going to need smelling salts at the thought of being in the same air space as someone who didn't even have A-levels, let alone a degree. I didn't find her response of "Oh" very articulate for someone who'd been to Oxford.

Clover took my arm. "Would you excuse us for a second, Venetia? I promised to introduce Maia to our celebrity mum." She pointed to a dark-haired woman in the corner. "Do you recognise her? Her name's Frederica Rinton. She's been in *Holby City* and *Casualty* and I think she was in some American soap thing. Can't remember the name."

I looked over. I'd been watching her in a hospital drama the night before. She was a lot slimmer in real life. I wanted to rush over and tell her that I thought she should have won the outstanding drama performance category at the National Telly Awards. She probably wouldn't want reminding of that. I couldn't wait to tell my neighbour, Sandy, that I'd met and actually nibbled chocolate brownies in the company of Frederica. Sandy devoured *Hello!* and *Heat* magazines, talking about TV presenters as though they were her mates. In the meantime, I tried to look like I hobnobbed with celebs all the time.

Clover headed over, weaving her big bum through the chrome stools. "Long time no see, Freddie. I see more of you on the telly than hanging around school. How is the glitzy world of TV? Should we be honoured that you've found time to come to our humble coffee morning?"

Clover introduced me and filled in the gaps for "Freddie". Harley was in the same class as her son, Marlon. I stood there, nodding along to discussions about after-school rugby, the upcoming play, the shocking standard of school lunches. I was trying to remember not to say school dinners. All the time Frederica was talking, I was waiting for her to do something starry, drop some names, names I had only seen in film and TV credits, bitch about her co-stars — yes, deliver me a big fat nugget of showbiz gossip that I could share with Sandy over a Malibu and Coke. I didn't say much, just inspected her face for signs of Botox to report back and wondered how to get her autograph in a cool way. There was no cool way. I eyed the serviette she'd been holding her chocolate brownie on. Sandy would love that. I'd try and snaffle it later.

"I saw you in that costume drama thingy. You lucky bugger, getting to snog Colin Firth; I get to pick up horse shit all day. Life just ain't fair. Tell me he was a dreadful kisser at least?" Clover said.

"I'm going to have to disappoint you: he was the god of kissing. Found it quite difficult to kiss my husband afterwards. But don't tell him that," Frederica said.

I was trying to remember every detail of the conversation for full dramatic recount effect, when Jen1 came twitching over with a list in her hand. "Frederica, as you know, Stirling Hall Fete Day is just around the corner and I've volunteered to coordinate all the stalls. Have you been approached to open the fete? You do such a great job. I know people love to see you there."

"Yeah, like our own Stirling Hall royalty. Frederica is a fantastic queen's name. We'll try and get a red carpet for you this year," Clover said. Jen1 tutted and frowned at her list. Frederica giggled and told Jen1 she'd be happy to do it.

"Right. We need to allocate stalls. If I could just have everyone's attention," Jen1 said, picking up a spoon and dinging it on a glass.

"First off, homemade cake stall. If everyone is in agreement, I'd like to run that one. Everyone needs to contribute at least one cake. I'll be sending home paper plates in the school bags, so look out for them. Last year lots of people donated shop bought cakes, but let's see if this year we can get you all in the kitchen doing your bit. Come on, how difficult can it be? Get cooking with your children, remember, quality time, quality time. Don't forget absolutely no nuts and please list all the ingredients on the label.

"Who wants to run the welly-wanging stall? Emelia? Great. Now, we're getting really subversive this year and having a tattoo stall, wash-off, obviously. Vile, chavvy as anything I know, but the children love them. The headmaster has agreed as long as they are removed for school on the Monday."

She looked round the kitchen. "Maia, you can be our tattoo expert. I think you'd be perfect for that."

"I'll do that with you," Clover said, but not quite quickly enough to cover the silence in the room.

"Okay, fine, let me know what I have to do." I reminded myself that I was here to look nice enough for other mothers to invite my children to play. Which ruled out flashing the love heart on my left buttock or demanding to know why I, above all the others, would be perfect for the tattoo stall rather than the bloody tombola or serving the Pimms? People brought their gazes back from the furthest point of Jen1's manicured lawn as the conversation turned to who was going to provide the "guess the number of sweets" jar.

"Finally, we need volunteers for tickets and refreshments for *Oliver!* It will come round very quickly, though I don't think the children know which roles they have yet, do they?" Jen1 said.

"They do, they've already been rehearsing," said Frederica. "Marlon is playing Oliver."

"Hugo hasn't said anything."

"Isn't he one of the workhouse children?" said Frederica.

"But that's only a small part, isn't it? Hugo always has a lead part. We get a teacher down every Wednesday from LAMDA to tutor him. Who's playing the other big roles, the Artful Dodger? What about Fagin?"

55

I'd never seen *Oliver!* but something about the Artful Dodger rang a bell. The auditions had been on the second day of term though, so I was pretty sure Harley wouldn't have a lead part. He'd only ever been in one play at Morlands as a toy soldier, so I imagined they'd given him some crappo role, like a passerby or a lamp post just to include him.

Frederica glanced at me. "Isn't Harley playing the Artful Dodger?"

"I think he said he was, though I might have got that wrong." I looked at Jen1 whose lips had disappeared completely, wrinkled up like an old sweet wrapper. She hopped off her stool and started scooting about the kitchen picking up coffee cups and crashing them into the dishwasher. I saw her tip the remains of the chocolate brownies into her Brabantia bin. The hostess with the mostest had run out of welcome.

Time to go, but first I needed the loo. Jen1 pointed through the back of the kitchen, with a flick of her wrist. "Out there." It had one of those funny freestanding glass wash basins, which were a bugger to clean because all the splashes of water drip down the outside and collect in a manky puddle at the bottom. I took my time, studying the photo collage of Jen1 in her bikini, in a motorboat, in a hammock, ribs sticking out like she needed a bloody good steak and chips and a couple of cream cakes. I spent ages rubbing in the Molton Brown hand cream. I might as well get silky smooth hands out of my visit.

As I opened the door, I heard her say, "I didn't realise Stirling Hall provided scholarships for poor children. I suppose they are trying to expose our children to all walks of life. Is that a new thing?"

I walked into the kitchen. I failed to keep the tightness out of my voice as I said, "I pay for my kids, just like you do. Nice to meet you, everyone, I need to get off now. Thanks for the coffee, Jenny."

"It's Jennifer."

She didn't show me out.

CHAPTER
SEVEN

Friday was a low point in my week because I spent the entire day in the house I hated cleaning the most — lots of those white ornaments with drippy shapes of women holding babies and whole shelves of decorative bells and silver spoons embossed with Lisbon, Sicily, Madeira and every other place Cecilia and Arthur had been cruising. Plus Cecilia herself, of course, whose idea of letting things slip was not hoovering the back of the airing cupboard every week.

That Friday, nearly two weeks after the kids had started at Stirling Hall, was particularly grim. I'd been dragging the Hoover up and down three flights of stairs as Cecilia had people "coming from the country" for the weekend so she needed me to have a "quick do" on the third floor, but didn't take away any of my usual chores to allow me extra time.

I'd already been late to pick up Harley and Bronte once that week and the school had been very clear. More than ten minutes late and they charged for after-school club. I just had the kitchen floor to mop when Cecilia called me into the "snug", where the smell of lavender was fighting with something citrussy. Cecilia sat propped up on a pile of cushions with her feet in a bubbling foot spa as though there was nothing more pressing to do, while a woman with a tidy ponytail and white uniform perched on a stool, massaging her hands.

"Maia, I'm in such a state. I'm going to a black tie ball with Arthur tonight and I can't decide which nail varnish goes with my dress. Would you be a dear and get it out of the wardrobe for me? It's the long purple one with the fishtail and gold trimming."

I don't think I managed to look overjoyed but I still ran upstairs two at a time and raced back down, not caring that I was scrunching the silk up as I tried not to trip over it. I burst back in, just remembering to hang the dress on the door rather than throw it on the settee.

"Thanks, Maia. Have a look at the nail varnishes and tell me which one you think goes best with it," Cecilia said.

The grandfather clock was chiming three o'clock. I needed to leave in the next thirty seconds. I plumped for a pink thing on the first row of the rack.

"Here, how about Pinking Sheer?" I said, reading the bottom.

"That's quite nice. Can you find Poolside Passion to compare? It's quite a bright colour. That might be it on the second row."

I started turning up the different bottles with all their stupid names, Punks in Pink, Pinking the Perky, Pinking Obvious, but no Poolside Passion.

The beauty therapist carried on massaging cream into Cecilia's hands, making no attempt to help me out. In the hired help category, she obviously considered that someone who ripped out pubic hair was far superior to someone who just cleaned it out of the shower.

"Cecilia, look, I'm really sorry, I'm going to have to go. I have to fetch the children. I've done everything, given the top floor a good clean for your guests, but I'm afraid I haven't managed to mop the kitchen floor. I have hoovered it though, so it just needs a quick flick over."

I said it as an aside, pulling off my work slippers and turning towards the door. But the idea of sullying herself with a bottle of Flash seemed to wind Cecilia up. It was like those rubbish seventies shipwreck films Mum loved, where a light wind starts to ruffle the trees gently and before you know it, the waves are tossing people over the side and sails are ripping in two when a few minutes earlier there wasn't even a ripple in the water.

She sat up very straight on the settee, her dark bob rigid like a tin helmet. "Maia, I'm sorry, but doing half a job doesn't work for me, not when I'm so terribly busy. So I'd be really grateful if you could finish off properly?"

I tried again. "I'm sorry but if I don't go now, I'll have to pay an extra £16 for the children to go into after-school club which I can't afford at the moment. I have managed a lot of extra things today." I smiled to show that I wasn't offended.

"I'm sorry but if you can't stay on for a few more minutes or organise yourself better to fit in a couple of tiny extras, I probably need to think about employing someone more flexible."

"What do you mean? I am flexible. I come in at short notice, I do one-off special cleans when you have people to stay. I pop in on Sundays to tidy up when you've had a dinner party. And they weren't tiny extras, I've cleaned a whole floor from top to bottom."

"I don't want to lose you, but if your other commitments mean that you aren't able to maintain a satisfactory standard, then I think it's better that you seek alternative employment."

I stood, I think the prof used to call it, nonplussed. The beautician's hands slathered and smoothed cream. The spa bath bubbled gently. I couldn't afford to lose another £60 a week. Harley was already clamouring to do guitar lessons at £160 a term. Unfortunately my mouth opened before I got going with the humble pie.

"I'm sorry you feel like that. By the way, I popped your vibrator back in the bathroom cupboard in case you're looking for it."

I saw the beautician's hands slow, then stop. I tossed a "nice working for you" over my shoulder and took a second to enjoy the satisfaction of seeing Cecilia's arched eyebrows disappear into her hairline before the reality of being even worse off depressed the shit out of me.

I decided not to tell Colin about getting the sack. He'd grumped enough when a corpse had made me redundant. I knew he'd somehow bring this latest trouble back to the fact that the kids were at Stirling Hall.

That evening, as soon as he disappeared off down the Working Men's Club for a game of pool — I never dared point out the irony of his choice of venue — I grabbed my bottle of Malibu and headed to Sandy's. I'd lived next door to her for eleven years since the council gave me a house when I was expecting Harley. Colin had disappeared for a few months as soon as the words "I'm pregnant" left my mouth but he reappeared, broke and full of soppy promises when Harley was about four months old. In the meantime, Sandy helped me through the new baby fog, taking Harley next door to give me a break from the crying, and passing on clothes that her son, Denim, had grown out of.

Sandy and I knew details about each other that adults weren't supposed to share. We'd laughed till bubbles came out our noses about the noises men made during sex. Once, after too much Malibu, I'd told her that Colin shouted, "Goal" when he came, so now she always called him the striker. Sometimes she'd ask him, "Played much football lately?" when she knew I could hear. Guilt took the edge off my laughter.

Sandy, on the other hand, took information oversharing to uncomfortable extremes. Instead of saying, "You remember so-and-so, you know, blonde hair, heart tattoo," she'd say, "You remember Dave, the one who liked to watch in the mirror." "You know, Jim, the one who went at it like a hog in heat?" She showed no mercy when it came to describing men's ability in bed, parading across the kitchen doing a reverse fisherman — "It was this big" — and peering at a tiny space between her thumb and forefinger.

Friday nights had become my only little moment of "me" time as the women I worked for called it. They got their feet massaged; I parked myself in Sandy's kitchen and made the miserable events of the week into something we could laugh about. It was like snuggling under a duvet when it's snowing outside.

When Sandy opened the door that evening, she had a line of bleach on her top lip. The mouldy hay smell indicated that henna was working its red magic under the Morrisons carrier bag covering her hair. Bronte and Harley pushed past her as they always did, grunting a hello. They were far more interested in bagging a cushion next to her sons, Gypsy and Denim Blue, and settling down to *Doctor Who* with a jumbo bag of Quavers.

"Hello, Harley, hello, Bronte," Sandy shouted through to the front room. "I thought they'd be coming in shaking me hand and doing little bows. You wanna ask for your money back."

I shrugged and followed her into the kitchen, where I helped myself to a couple of glasses. My sense of humour about Stirling Hall had packed up its troubles in an old kit bag and disappeared completely.

"So, who's the lucky man?" I said, pouring out the Malibu and watching the Coke bubble up into a coconutty froth.

"Who says there's a new man?" she said, a big grin making her little elfin face even pointier.

"Come off it. You only put that rabbit poo on your hair when there's a new bloke about."

Sandy was a single mum who worked shifts packing dog biscuits at the factory down the road. Unlike me, being poor didn't seem to bother her. She didn't care that she relied on the charity foundation in town for her kids' clothes, or that she spent her life switching between credit cards, which even at 0% interest, she had no hope of paying off.

"He's a new guy at the factory," Sandy said.

"Called?"

"Shane."

"When did he start?"

"A few weeks ago." Sandy lit a Marlboro Light. I wondered if the bleach was flammable but I knew she'd start chanting Sensible Susan at me if I said anything.

"Go on, then. Spill the beans. It's not like you to get all secretive," I said.

"I haven't been secretive. You've been too caught up in blazers and book lists to be interested in my shenanigans," she said, in a tone that didn't sound like a simple observation.

"Sorry." I sighed. "I've been really busy." I waited for her to grin, then jump in with marks out of ten, size of willy, number of ex-wives and kids like she normally would. Instead, she sat there blowing smoke rings until I felt I had to explain.

"I haven't had a lot of time for anything. It's a full-time job remembering to buy plain biscuits so that you don't get called in because you've sent in a bloody chocolate HobNob. I spend half my life making sure

Bronte's hair is tied back with green ribbons, not pink elastic bands, and working out how the hell I am going to afford ballet, guitar and flute lessons while losing every decent paying job I've ever had. So I probably have had my head up my arse." I took a big glug of Malibu to disguise the wobble in my lip.

"What? You've lost another job? Jesus, you're gonna beat my record soon." Sandy sounded reasonably sympathetic considering her own working life was one long verbal warning. While I launched into my account of Cecilia, she pulled off her jogging bottoms with a mutter of "You don't mind, do you?" and fetched a little pot of wax off the hob. She splayed her legs and started on her bikini line, her voice fading out like a badly tuned radio when the wax didn't come off in a clean rip.

Harley came bursting in. He stared at Sandy whose red lace thong appeared to be quite fascinating to a ten-year-old. She made no attempt to shut her legs. "You know what they say, Harley, you can't beat an older woman. You come back in a few years' time and I'll show you what I mean."

Harley shrugged but I could tell from the way he backed towards me that he wasn't quite sure if she was joking.

"Mum, Denim says he's got the latest iPhone. But his is only an iPhone 4, isn't it? That's not the latest one, is it? Marlon's got an iPhone 5. He got it early, cos his birthday's next week and his mum bought it when she was filming in America. But Denim keeps hitting me when I say that. Can you tell him that his is an old one? He keeps calling me a liar."

Even though people skills had been the focus of Harley's Personal, Social and Health Education "prep", he could still fit what he'd learnt into an eggcup. I'd taken such a battering that week that my alcohol-dulled reactions were a bit pterodactyl. Sandy, on the other hand, was quick off the mark.

"You spoilt little shit. Do you know how many bloody night shifts it took me to get the money together for that? He's only had it a few months and now he's going to be at me for the new one. Denim and Gypsy not good enough for you now you've got all them poncey little Lord Fauntleroys to play with? Sorry if their stuff isn't quite up to your majesty's high standards."

The colour had risen in Harley's cheeks. His grey eyes were wide, wide open. He glanced sideways at me. I could feel the puzzlement in him. And in me. Sandy had always been such a soft touch, always telling me to "leave off of them, they're just kids".

I pulled Harley to me. Sandy had called my son a shit. I never swore at kids. Especially not other people's. Sandy was bristling away on the other side of the table. We usually ganged up against the woman a few doors down whose kids nicked bikes on the estate, Sandy's bully-boy boss who smelt of Brut, the bastards in the council's housing repairs department. Not each other. I looked straight into Harley's eyes, willing him to go with me on this one.

"Why don't you go and say sorry to Denim and say that you think you made a mistake?"

"I didn't make a mistake. Marlon has got an iPhone 5."

I rolled my eyes and resisted the urge to shake him. "Harley. How would you like it if Denim told you that something you'd got new was a load of old rubbish? You wouldn't. Go. And. Say. You. Are. Sorry. Then I think it's time to go. Tell Bronte."

I screwed the cap back on the Malibu. "Sorry about that."

Sandy carried on attacking some stubborn hairs with her tweezers, head bent over her crotch.

"I s'pose it's to be expected if you fill their heads with fancy ideas. But you're not going to be able to afford all that stuff, neither."

I hated the satisfaction I could hear in her voice.

CHAPTER
EIGHT

End of day dismissal was a formal affair at Stirling Hall. A teacher stood by the door and shook the children's hands before delivering them directly to the collecting parent, unlike Morlands where they spilled out into the playground and were allowed to wander off with anyone who wasn't carrying a shotgun.

Bronte came out, hat on straight, duffle coat buttoned up to the top. Her voice sounded really clear when she said, "Good afternoon, Mr Peters." Not quite top end of town posh but not council estate rough either. My proud mother moment was snuffed out as I realised that Mr Peters, the Head of Upper School, was beckoning to me. As I squeezed forward through the gaggle of parents, Jen1 was coming the other way. I caught her eye and smiled but she looked straight through me. Maybe she could only recognise people dressed in Jasper rather than George.

"Would you have a moment to pop into my office, Ms Etxeleku? Take a seat in reception, I'll be right with you," Mr Peters said.

I nodded, running through the checklist in my head of all my crimes for that week — only ironing cuffs and collars on the school shirts, not ironing Harley's rugby shirt at all, chocolate digestives for snack two days running, forgetting to check Bronte's English homework for capital letters and full stops. I was about to disappear through the door, when Clover pulled on my arm.

"Hi. If you're going to be a few minutes at the school, why don't I relieve you of Bronte? She can play with the twins. You can pick her up when you've finished. We live right at the end of the lane that runs adjacent to the Royal Oak pub. You can't miss us, it's the only house down there."

Bronte was tugging at my T-shirt and hopping from foot to foot. "Can I go with Clover, Mum? I want to see their guinea pigs and rabbits. Please?"

"That would be great. I just need to find Harley and tell him to wait here for me," I said.

Clover fiddled with the toggle on her anorak. "I think Harley is waiting for you in Mr Peters' office. Why don't you bring him over too and stay for supper when you've finished?"

Usually Clover talked loud enough for the whole class to share her thoughts. Her low voice and the way she kept shaking her head at Orion were making me twitchy.

I mumbled a thank you and dived into the entrance corridor lined with posters about five fruit and veg a day, anti-bullying slogans and the benefits of cycling. The squeak of my Crocs on the grey tiles was getting faster and faster. At a corridor crossroads, I saw signs for the physics lab, dance studio, music room but no bloody reception in the business of receiving mothers

69

who were only used to classrooms numbered one to six. Mr Peters caught up with me in a waft of spicy aftershave. "Ms Etxeleku, thank you so much for coming in. I won't keep you a moment, I just wanted a word about Harley."

"Is he okay?" I said, almost having to trot to keep up with his long strides.

"He's fine, absolutely fine." He steered me left into a room with three chairs arranged in a semi-circle in front of a huge mahogany desk. Harley was in the middle one, with his head bent forwards, slumped on the padded velour armrest. He didn't bother to look round.

"Take a seat, Ms Etxeleku."

"Hello, love," I said, reaching for Harley's hand. He squeezed my fingers tightly, needily, staring straight ahead without blinking. His breath was whistling in and out of his nose.

Mr Peters sat on the edge of his desk, his broad shoulders silhouetted against the window. His black shoes were smooth and shiny, teacher-like, but I could see an inch of purple and lime spotty socks peeping out under his trousers. He ran his hand over his short hair. "This is a bit of a delicate matter, Ms Etxeleku, but there's been a little problem today between Harley and one of his classmates. From what I understand, there was a bit of teasing that got out of hand, and then the matter seemed to take rather a violent turn."

"What do you mean, violent turn?"

"Harley punched the boy in question in the face."

70

I didn't speak. I pinched the bridge of my nose and stared down at the hole in the knee of my tracksuit bottoms. All the bad decisions I'd not so much made as allowed to happen — letting Harley mix with the older boys on the estate, shrugging off the odd punch-up in the back alley, not being there when he came home from school — crushed in on me. I'd done my best, which was crap and the crap was about to hit the fan.

Harley tugged at my hand. "Mum. Mum. I'm sorry. He was calling me a pikey. He said that you dressed from jumble sales and Oxfam, that Dad stole car wheels for a living and that we lived in a caravan under the bridge by the station. Dad said if anyone laughed at me, I should punch them hard enough to make their brains rattle."

The desk creaked as Mr Peters stood up. He loosened his tie slightly. "Ms Etxeleku. This wasn't all Harley's fault. Hugo was being very unkind. At Stirling Hall we have a zero-tolerance bullying policy and we do take it very seriously."

Oh God. Hugo. No, please God. "Jennifer's son?"

"Yes, I have already seen Mrs Seaford this afternoon. Hugo did sustain a cut eye and some bruising to his cheek, so as a precaution, she is going to take him to A&E to get him checked out."

I could feel sweat running down my back. "Will the police be involved?"

"As I am sure you will appreciate, Ms Etxeleku, we cannot allow boys to take matters into their own hands, whatever the provocation. Mrs Seaford wanted to involve the police but I think I have managed to dissuade her from that course of action on the grounds that her son's appalling behaviour would also come under scrutiny." His dark eyes were serious but kind.

I kept swallowing but I couldn't seem to get any moisture in my mouth. I looked at Harley. He wasn't making any noise but huge gloopy tears were pouring down his face and making dark circles on his white shirt. I patted his hand gently and he got up and poured himself into my arms, burrowing into my shoulder until I could feel the damp heat of his face.

"May I talk frankly?" Mr Peters said.

I nodded, though I knew that "frankly" meant Harley would be emptying his desk.

"Your son has great potential. I think Stirling Hall could help mould him into a fine young man. He is struggling with the academic work, but we have set up some one-to-one tutoring so we could potentially bridge the gap. He has real sporting talent and Harley's drama teacher tells me he can see star quality there." A cufflink clinked against the desk as he leaned back.

I was getting hot under the weight of Harley leaning into me. I tried to relax my shoulders while I waited for the "but".

"Stirling Hall does have many boys from, let's say, very comfortable backgrounds. However, the philosophy of the school is to ensure that every boy who comes here accesses the same opportunities. That does, of course, mean that all parents need to support our Platinum rules that include 'We solve our disagreements by talking to each other'. I understand your circumstances are quite unique, so a period of adjustment is to be expected while Harley learns what is required of him." He unbuttoned his jacket. To my ironing lady's eye, his blue striped shirt looked hand-tailored.

My heart lifted a little, a bit like it did when I thought I'd missed the bus but a big queue was still standing there when I came racing round the corner.

"But —" he said.

There it was. I looked to see how far it was to the door. I wondered if I could make a dash to the van before I started blubbing.

"But we cannot have boys brawling. I know that some head teachers turn a blind eye to these sorts of disputes, but this is not the way of Stirling Hall."

A shooting pain through my back tooth reminded me to unclench my jaw.

"So. What I propose is that I suspend Harley," Mr Peters said.

"Suspend? What? How long for?"

"I think it would be fair to suspend Harley for two days and Hugo for one, which means Harley would be back in school by Thursday. I do have to say, Ms Etxeleku, if there is another occasion of this severity, Harley is likely to face expulsion. You may wish to convey that to your husband."

Many years of practising good manners obviously helped him to leave out "your arsehole of a husband".

"Of course. Thank you, thank you so much. Harley won't let you down again, will you, Harley?" Something relaxed in my body as though someone had been standing on my shoulders and had finally hoicked

73

themselves over the wall. Mr Peters smiled down at me. He looked quite boyish when he smiled, almost cheeky, probably not much older than me.

Now that a second chance was on the table, I wanted to stop patting Harley's shoulders and drag him outside by the ear. Bellow at him for being so bloody stupid. Shake him till his teeth rattled. Ban him from ever talking to anybody on our estate over the age of five again. Ground him until he was twenty-five. Or maybe I just wanted to cry.

Harley peeled himself off my shoulder. His mouth was twitching with the effort of holding back his tears. He shuffled from one foot to another, staring at the floor, then finally seemed to gather the energy to speak. "I won't let you down. Thank you very much, sir. And sir? I'm really sorry."

"You're a good lad. Now get out of here and learn to keep your fists to yourself. You come to me first if there's a problem."

I wondered if Mr Peters had a wife.

Harley and I drove towards Clover's. We took the turning by the pub where the smart townhouses gave way to fields and farmhouses and the road became an unsurfaced lane. Filthy splurges of water shot up the side of the van every time I clunked down a pothole. At the very end, hidden by mature sycamore and chestnut trees, stood a huge ivy-covered building with a dark slate roof. The windows looked as though random bits of putty were keeping them in their peeling wooden frames. Wellies, riding crops and scooters lay tangled in the front porch. Harley and I weaved our way to the door, dodging mini mountains of horse manure. I lifted the lion's head door knocker. Judging by his green teeth, Brasso wasn't on Clover's shopping list.

Clover opened the door in a black swimming costume patterned with huge poppies. She looked like the potato men Bronte used to make — a big round body stuck on thin little cocktail sticks. Unlike Sandy, she was a stranger to the Brazilian, the Hollywood, and apparently, the Bic. I felt as though I'd blundered in on her in the shower, but she waved us in with all the confidence of a size zero model.

"Come in, come in, hello Harley. Sorry, the girls really wanted to go for a little dip so Bronte borrowed a costume, hope you don't mind. Orion's in the pool as well, so do you want to go in, Harley? I've been in with them but you can all keep an eye on each other now, can't you? Don't worry about taking your shoes off, the whole place is so fucking filthy, keep meaning to get on top of it, but with the horses we're always dragging in more muck so it seems a bit of a waste of time."

We trailed behind Clover. The couldn't-care-less-ness of someone who could greet near strangers in a swimsuit despite having gargoyles of cellulite hanging from her buttocks thrilled and shocked me. She led us into a huge kitchen with an Aga at one end where Y-fronts, stripy tights and hiking socks were drying, filling the room with the smell of damp sheep. A ginger cat as big as a pillow stretched out on the long pine table.

Harley grabbed my arm. "Is that a real bird?" he said, pointing to a blue parrot on the dresser.

75

I was doing a double take when Clover said, "That's Einstein. We found him in the garden about four years ago."

"Wicked! Does he talk?"

"Yes, he says a few things. Orion is really good at getting him to speak, he'll show you later."

I wondered if it pooed everywhere. Clover led us out of a back entrance and into a massive garden full of apple and pear trees. "The pool's out here. Careful where you walk. Orion is supposed to be on bleeding doggy-doo duty but he's not very diligent."

She grabbed Harley's arm and steered him through the mud to the pool house, where shouts and squeals rang out. Through the steamed-up glass, I saw Bronte giggling away as she tried to balance on a blow-up dolphin and keep up with the twins. Orion was sitting on the end of the diving board, swinging his legs. As soon as we stepped through the door, he leapt in and swam over to us.

"Hey, Mike Tyson. Are you coming in?" Orion was on his own in finding Harley's fisticuffs funny, but I felt relieved that at least one child was still speaking to him.

"We'd better go and let you get on," I said to Clover.

"I've got nothing to get on with. I'm going to dig out a pair of swimmies for Harley, then I'll get you a drink."

She found a towelling robe for herself and a pair of Speedos that would have been tight on Action Man for Harley. He stiffened beside me, backing towards the pool door like a dog on its last journey to the vet.

"Have you got boxers on, Harley? You have? Why don't you swim in those?" I said.

76

For once Harley did as I suggested, stripping off his clothes, leaving them in a pile on the floor and dive-bombing the girls. I envied and resented his ability to bounce back when the skin on my face was so tight and pinched that it felt like someone had tied my ponytail too tight.

"Come on, I bet you need a drink," Clover said. I hoped Clover-speak was the same as Sandy-speak and that I wasn't going to get a mug of stewed nettles and cat hair. Back in the kitchen she threw open the fridge and hooked out a bottle. "Drop of shampoo?"

Champagne on a Monday night where I lived was because someone had got out on appeal. "Just a drop, thanks, cos I've got to drive back," I said.

"We'll call you a cab. You can leave the car here."

Clover must have seen the cash register tinging in my eyes. "Anyway, we can worry about that later. You can still have a glass."

I wiped the rim of the tumbler she gave me with the bottom of my sweatshirt while she had her back turned.

"Bottoms up," Clover said. Just as we clinked glasses, the kitchen door opened and a tall, slim man with dark, curly hair came in. It had to be Lawrence, Clover's husband. He was an older, more groomed version of Orion. In his suit, he looked as though he'd stumbled into Glastonbury by mistake. Clover introduced us and he said hello without really registering me, just raised an eyebrow at the champagne bottle. He poked about among the roasting tins, colanders and saucepans piled high in the butler's sink, pulling out a rainbow-coloured welly before he found a mug.

Although nothing suggested he was the least bit interested in who I was or what I was doing there, Clover filled him in. "Poor old Maia's had a terrible day. Hugo was beastly to Maia's son, and they got into a bit of a punch-up and Hugo came off worse. He's an arrogant little sod, he had it coming to him."

"Like mother, like son. Jennifer's pretty arrogant herself," Lawrence said. I was surprised to hear a Mancunian accent.

"She's not that bad. At least she does all the class admin like the fete and tickets for the school play that no one else wants to do." Clover topped up her champagne. I shook my head as she pushed the bottle towards me.

"Don't be so naive. She loves lording it over people. If Jennifer hadn't managed to trap Leo, she would still be touting cheese and pickle rolls around Canary Wharf," Lawrence said.

"That's not fair. Lawrence works in the same department as Jennifer's husband, Leo," she said, turning to me.

"It is fair. You'd think someone who tracks Japanese investments for a living would have enough brains to remember the condoms when he's shagging the sandwich trolley dolly." Lawrence tried to squash an empty jar of coffee into an overflowing bin.

It was so rare for anything to surprise me in a mouth open, bloody hell sort of way, but Jen1 being from the wrong side of the tracks shot onto the list. I sieved through my dealings with her for the tiniest clue that her diamond studs had once been hypoallergenic lumps

78

of glass from Topshop. Nothing. The woman had studied the middle-class stage and learnt her lines well. That accent. Christ, Jen1 could topple Queen Lizzie II off her throne if she got any posher. Still, the mean part of me would always want to start singing, "Prawns and mayonnaise? Bacon butty? Egg and cress?" whenever I saw her now. On the other hand, if I ever managed to get posh myself, she'd be able to sing, "Pan scourer, bog brush, bin bag" at me, so for now, I'd just sing it in my head.

I tried to look as though I wasn't even following the conversation. I didn't want to give Lawrence a reason to ask me about my background. Usually when I said I was a cleaner, a fidgety silence followed while people searched for something good to say about that "career choice". Except Clover who said, "Oh my God, don't tell Lawrence, he'll want to marry you."

Just as I was about to go out to call the children in, they came trooping back, trailing great puddles of water and demanding food. I started rounding mine up to leave when Einstein came flashing through the air to shrieks of delight from Harley and Bronte. Lawrence ducked as Einstein whistled past his head, which made him knock over his coffee.

"Fucking parrot. I'm going to wring its neck one of these days."

The parrot sat perched on the top of the kitchen door. I swear it was smiling.

"Poor old Einstein. He doesn't have very good spatial awareness any more. It's his age." Clover started mopping up the spill with a tracksuit top.

Harley was over by the door, trying to get the parrot to speak. "Pretty Polly, hello, Einstein?" Einstein replied by squirting out a white and brown jet of parrot poo down the door, which had the girls squealing with laughter.

Orion came over. "Listen to this. What's your name?"

"Einstein," came the parrot's raspy voice.

"Where do you live?" Orion waved some kind of seedy snack at him.

"In a fucking mad house," Einstein said, before snatching the snack and cracking it open.

"I spent ages teaching him that."

Out of the corner of my eye, I saw Lawrence shaking his head.

CHAPTER
NINE

Stirling Hall seemed to have a fundraiser almost every week. What they were raising funds for was a mystery, given that there were only so many grand pianos, Mercedes minibuses and Olympic-sized trampolines a school could need. A couple of Saturdays before February half-term it was Fete Day — yet another occasion when Bronte sulked off in front of me and I trailed behind questioning whether I'd made the right decision to send her here.

She stomped into the school hall, without even glancing at the stalls around the edges, as though welly-wanging or marking the treasure on the papier mâché island were beneath her. She was carrying the shoebox she'd covered in old wallpaper and filled with baked beans, bread rolls and teabags destined for the local old people's home. The night before, she'd moaned that all the other mothers went out shopping specially for the Fete Day charity donation rather than bunging in anything that wasn't out of date in the kitchen cupboard. Since the prof had died and Cecilia had given me the boot, I was fast becoming a charity case myself. I hoped that Edna, Gertie or whoever was unlucky enough to get our box would forgive me for the budget biscuits that Colin said tasted like bus tickets.

Just as Bronte was hiding her box in the corner, Jen1 pushed past me in a way that made it difficult to know whether she had underestimated the size of her arse by a few centimetres or was looking for a punch-up. She hadn't glanced in my direction since the Harley–Hugo fiasco. I should have gone over and had a straight conversation with her, but a quiet word was never an option given that the pipe cleaner people she hung out with always surrounded her. Now, at school pick-up, I had to steel myself to get out of the van. I wanted to be oblivious to her but instead I felt the drain of energy it takes to ignore someone.

One thing it was impossible to ignore, however, was her "charitable contribution". All that was missing from her wicker basket was a man with a trumpet. Snuggling in the red tissue paper were pineapples, goji berries, organic lentils, wheat-free muesli, miso soup and a coconut. I imagined some poor sod with arthritic fingers trying to hack into the coconut or getting goji berries stuck in his false teeth when all he wanted was a cup of PG Tips and a ham sandwich. Maybe my baked beans weren't so bad after all.

"Bowl of adzuki beans, anyone?"

I swung round. Clover was a sight to behold in turquoise flares that only a six-foot model should attempt, not a stout woman on the wrong side of short. She pressed a couple of pounds into the twins' hands and told them to "bugger off and have a go on a few stalls, but don't buy any crap".

"Otherwise you find that all the junk you got rid of for the white elephant stall is replaced with someone else's shite," Clover said, taking my arm. "Now, let's get this tattoo stall up and running."

Through the doors leading out into the playground I could see Lawrence setting up the football nets for Five for a Prize. Even though it was drizzling slightly, I wished we were outside. Instead, we fought our way through children clutching coins and grandmas with pushchairs going nowhere fast. Our table was at the side of the hall between the Knock Down the Can and the Wild West shooting stall, where dads were making seven-year-olds cry by hogging the plastic revolvers to prove that they weren't hotshots only at the office.

It was sweatier than the Tube in a July rush hour. I stuck my hands in the bowl of water we were going to use for the tattoos. A few mothers hurried their children past. "No, no, tattoos are so common. No, I don't care if they wash off, they look awful."

Most parents seemed amused, as though they were somehow walking on the wild side themselves by letting their kids have a seahorse on their wrist. They wouldn't be thinking it was such a jolly jape if their darling Henrietta, Rory or Oscar came home with a big declaration of love for Chardonnay or Gav tattooed across their backs in ten years' time. Or a great big spider like Tarants.

A queue formed and Clover and I pressed on butterflies, hearts and flowers, throwing sticky little fifty pences into a Tupperware container. I'd hardly had time to look up when I heard someone call my name.

"Ms Etxeleku. How do you like your first Stirling Hall fete?"

Mr Peters still managed to look formal in jeans and a white linen shirt. I felt as though he'd come to tell me off and my mind immediately started running through apologies, excuses and big fat lies. I should have stuck to a non-nutty "lovely, thank you". Instead I said, "Would you like a tattoo?" and then wanted to kill myself. Heads of Upper School probably didn't go in for a lot of body art.

He surprised me. He laughed. "Very rebel without a cause. What do you suggest?"

I pulled out a new sheet, managing to knock my wet sponge into my crotch as I did so. "What about a devil?"

"I leave being naughty to the kids these days, during the week at least. No, I fancy something a bit exotic," he said.

Clover leaned over. "Mr Peters, that's favouritism, choosing the new girl on the block. What about all us mums who've been slaving away every year since our kids were in nursery? I've got a lovely big dragon here I could stick somewhere secret."

I envied Clover. Being so at ease with it all. But I also wanted her to snout out so I could have Mr Peters to myself, like a child with a protective arm round a bowl of crisps.

"Thanks for the offer, Mrs Wright, but I don't want to get too subversive now, do I? Maybe next year." He turned back to me. "What about that Chinese character?"

84

"Okay, where do you want it?"

There was the slightest pause. A tiny curve upwards at the side of his mouth gave me a glimpse of the man he might have been before he dedicated his life to setting a good example.

"Left or right arm?" I said. Without looking, I knew that a slow flush would be turning my neck and chest blotchy. I pretended to pick something up off the floor so I could dab at the sweat on my upper lip. Mr Peters sat down and rolled up his sleeve. A forearm made for arm-wrestling. Smooth olivey skin, quite hairy. Big hands but slim fingers and clean fingernails. Everything about him was tended, clipped and cared for. I bet his skin smelt of something lemony. And I bet he didn't leave whiskers round the sink.

"Harley seems to be settling down nicely now. In the last couple of weeks since 'the incident', I've seen a big change in him," Mr Peters said, almost drowned out by the noise and excitement of the Knock Down the Can stall next door.

"Yes, I think he's doing much better. Thanks for being so kind to him."

I wasn't about to tell Mr Peters that since Harley had given Hugo what for, he'd become a bit of a hero among the boys. His new nickname was "Mike" and the lunchtime footballing gang seemed to have adopted him as a mascot.

"I wasn't being kind. I was being fair. Between you and me, I think that little event has given him a certain kudos amongst his classmates," he said, leaning in so I could hear him.

Of course. He knew everything. He'd probably worked out that I'd spent ages getting ready that morning, even painting my nails, which was something I rarely did these days. I was glad I had. Didn't want him thinking that I only did holey tracksuits, Crocs and punch-ups.

"How are *you* settling in, Ms Etxeleku?" he asked, clear greeny-grey eyes trapping me in their gaze.

I mumbled, "Fine," and became very focused on sponging his tattoo, which, praise the Lord, went on in one piece.

"Perfect," Mr Peters said. "I could imagine you in a tattoo parlour inking enormous eagles onto bikers' backs."

I think we realised at the same time that might not be as unlikely for me as for most of the mothers at Stirling Hall who were either –ologists of some sort, solicitors, investment bankers or married to one. Mr Peters blushed. "No offence, you know what I mean. It was a compliment to your marvellous artistic skills."

Big red patches like stunted starfish settled on his face. I was fascinated to see a guy with so much going for him, so smart, so in control, blush like that. If I ever got to a place in my life where I could join in a clever conversation and speak with confidence, even on brainy things — politics, literature, the environment — because I had the knowledge to back me up, I swore to God I was never going to waste a minute blushing again.

For the moment, however, I blushed along with him, even though he hadn't offended me at all. My mother

86

used to call it *vergüenza ajena*, a sort of second-hand embarrassment at other people's fuck-ups. I think we were both grateful when the next woman in the queue called Mr Peters' attention. It was the mother of Kuan-Yin, the little Chinese girl who, along with the few other Asian children — sons and daughters of consultants and lawyers — featured heavily in photos around the school as though Stirling Hall was a multicultural hotbed.

"Mr Peters. I see you have the tattoo for love," she said, pointing at his arm with her small elegant fingers.

"Love?"

"Yes, this is the Chinese symbol for love. Does this mean there's someone special in your life?" She smiled so widely that both rows of her neat little teeth were on display.

"I couldn't possibly comment, Mrs Shen," he said, leaning over to put his 50p in my box. He did smell of lemon. "Nice tattoo, thanks," he said, vacating his chair for Kuan-Yin.

As soon as he'd gone, Clover tapped me on the shoulder. "All the mums are dying to get off with him, he's so gorgeous. Must be something to do with all that calm authority that makes him so sexy. Every time he gets seen out on the town with a woman, the Stirling Hall jungle drums go into overdrive. Always seems to go for brunettes, so you're in there."

"I can't resist the beer-bellied, unemployed and in deep debt, myself. I wouldn't know what to do with someone who had a proper job."

Clover laughed and went back to her swords and flowers. I started sticking on a rainbow for Kuan-Yin, quietly looking round the room to see where Mr Peters had gone. He was over by the Bash-a-Rat stand, chatting to bloody Jen1. He looked up and caught my eye. Probably checking that I wasn't making off with the fifty pences.

Frederica came bounding over, looking lovely in a white floaty dress as though she was just off to a shoot for *Hello!* magazine. "Hi. I've been meaning to ring you. Marlon's been on at me to invite Harley over, says he's a footballing wizard."

"Are you sure?"

"Course I'm sure. Can I pick him up from school on Wednesday?"

Maia Etxeleku. Friend of the stars. My son. Going to play at a celebrity's house. I'd have to try and have a little nose about when I went to pick him up. Sandy would want to know all the details. I'd invited her to the fete as a peace offering but she'd told me that not everyone was a woman of means and she was working weekends to cover her credit card bill. Actually I was glad she wasn't there with her shouty old laugh and tendency to take the piss out of people when they were standing next to her. Being glad made me like myself a bit less. However, self-hate wasn't really necessary in the Etxeleku/Caudwell household, as Bronte usually took care of that. She came rushing over with the twins who, for some reason, liked her snotty manner.

"Mum, did you know there's a school disco next Friday? It finishes at ten. Can I go?" Bronte asked.

"I've no problem with you going, but how much are the tickets?" I said.

"Twenty-two pounds. Everyone else is going and you get a proper hot meal. And a cocktail. Not alcoholic."

"Twenty-two pounds? My God. Let me have a think about it."

"That means you're going to say no, cos you always do."

"Let's talk about it when we get home," I said, seeing the whole tattoo queue grow perky with interest.

"Forget it. You'll only say money doesn't grow on trees. You never let me do anything." Bronte stomped off with Sorrel and Saffy. I leaned back in my chair and sighed.

A couple of hours later, when most of the other stalls had ground to a halt, Clover and I were still like a pair of blinking Pied Pipers. Every time I finished sticking on another skull or bow and arrow, I'd have a surreptitious little look to see where Mr Peters was. Out of the corner of my eye, I saw Jen1 take his arm, all swishing hair and breathy smiles. She led him over to the raffle ticket basket. I'd bought one ticket so I didn't look mean or really poor, but other people were splashing out twenty quid a pop. They could have bought five cuddly rabbits or a whole box of old lady's bubble bath for that.

I was just encouraging a little boy to stop flicking my sponge water everywhere when Clover said, "Maia, it's you," and started nodding towards the other side of the hall.

"What?"

"They're doing the raffle. They've called your name. You've won a prize." Clover was pointing over to Mr Peters and Jen1.

I could see Mr Peters smiling like he'd done something really good. Jen1 looked like she'd just sat on a drawing pin. I wanted to crawl under my tattoo table but Clover was hissing at me. Then shouting, "She's here, over here."

I had no choice and scraped my chair back to cries of annoyance from the restless queue of kids. It seemed a long way across the hall. I'd forgotten how I normally walked. I shook Mr Peters' hand, feeling eyes drilling into my back. His hand held safety and protection in its grasp.

"You've won two tickets to the Stirling Hall ball at the end of term."

"Lovely, thank you. Where is it?" I said, even though I had no intention of going.

Jen1 pulled a face as though I'd gobbed in her breakfast. "In my garden."

CHAPTER
TEN

I really wanted to give in to Bronte over the school disco, just to stop her making unhappy shapes and looming up resentfully under her fringe, sucking any tiny drop of happiness out of my bones every time I walked into the room. On the morning of the disco, she stood outside the shower, shouting through the curtain while I let the water run over my head trying to drown her out.

"Have you changed your mind yet? Why can't I go? Everyone's going. Saffy and Sorrel are going and Clover's buying them new leggings and a sequinned top from Next and you won't even buy me a ticket. You're always saying we can't afford things, but you're just tight." On and on it went, followed by a variation on how much she hated me, how I was put on this earth to make her as unhappy as possible and how I should never have had children if we were so poor.

I couldn't give in. I had £3.35 in my purse and the milk was off. We were behind on our rent by several weeks. I'd started leaving the van a few streets away at night in case the council tax people decided to send the bailiffs. Our gas supplier kept making debt repayment plan phone calls. I dreaded picking up the phone but I was paranoid about missing a call from the school in case Harley got into a fight again. I pretended to be a mad Spanish aunt every time a voice I didn't know came on the line but there was only so much "No speak English. Amaia *no está* here. Bysee bye," I could get away with.

Bronte tried to wheedle round Colin. He stroked her hair and promised he'd see what he could do. Unfortunately, seeing what he could do never seemed to involve him getting off his great lard to earn some money. Instead he had a go at me. "You wanted her to go to that bleeding school. You wouldn't listen. So now what are you going to do?"

I sat at the kitchen table, staring at the chip in my mug. I knew, of course, that I'd caused the problem — I always did — and it would be up to me to solve it. I tried to work out when I'd become so alone. I had loved Colin so much once. Maybe the relationship had worn out, like the hall carpet. Did I love him six years ago? Five? Two? There must have been a time when I'd had sex with him, when I still just about loved him. Then there must have been a next time, when a border had been crossed, where some tiny extra bit of dislike had crept in, a blob more affection had seeped away and suddenly I was sleeping with someone I didn't love any more. I couldn't work out where love went.

All the way to school, Harley kept telling Bronte it was just a stupid disco, it would be rubbish and all the girls would be running away from the boys and swapping hair bobbles in the toilets, so big deal. Then he said, "Anyway, Mum's trying as hard as she can, it's not her fault we haven't got any money."

I squeezed his hand. A couple of days before, I'd found a bunch of letters about ski holidays, French exchanges and trips to the theatre in London screwed up in the bottom of his school bag. I think his resignation hurt more than Bronte's angry whining.

As we snaked into the school's one-way system, Bronte demanded to get out so she could walk the rest of the way. I just wanted to escape from her mardy little face before I flipped completely and drove back to Morlands shouting, "It's all been a horrible mistake." She slammed out without saying goodbye and I watched her in the rear-view mirror, scuffing up the drive.

When I got home, Colin was out which went some way to improving my day. At least I used to be paid to hate Fridays when I worked for Cecilia. Now I hated being stuck at home with Colin who was either moaning about his bloody ingrown toenail and picking at his feet or digging about in an empty fridge. He seemed to have got bored with the third option, which was trying to get me into bed. Both a blessing and an insult. Since it was hard to see how I could feel any grumpier, I decided now would be as good a time as any to find out exactly how much money we owed without Colin shouting out instructions from his perch in the front room. After that, if I hadn't eaten the rat poison we'd put down to welcome our friends in the attic, I might call Cecilia and see if I could backtrack, aka beg on bended knee, since all my other efforts to get extra work had come to nothing. Though outing her friendship with Jessica Rabbit wasn't going to help my cause.

As I was sorting out the paperwork, dealing it into piles — rent, electricity, council tax, gas — like a round of poker, the phone rang. Ten o'clock. The council's favourite time for chasing money. I summoned up my imaginary Great Aunt Inmaculada again. "J-ello," I said, in my one foot in the nursing home voice.

There was a pause on the other end of the line. "I'm looking for Ms Etxeleku," said a man with a fairly posh accent, although not quite plummy enough to make it into my hate category. "Have I got the right number?"

I launched into my Amaia Etxeleku gone to live on the moon routine, but I knew I recognised the voice. Maybe I'd just spoken to the guy from the council so often, he sounded like someone I knew. But the council bloke wasn't posh.

As soon as he said, "Is Bronte Caudwell there?" I knew. I knew because the giddiness in my stomach told me a couple of seconds before my brain. I cleared my throat to dislodge Inmaculada.

"Is that Mr Peters? Sorry about that. There's someone I don't want to speak to. You must think I'm completely mad. Bronte's not here. She's at school. Why?"

"She wasn't at morning registration, and as you probably know, we require parents to phone before 9.30 if their child is ill."

"But I dropped her off about 8.15," I said. "She got out at the bottom of the drive because she wanted to

94

walk the rest of the way." I heard my voice rise at the end. Giddiness was gone. Fear, not yet galloping wildly, had replaced it.

"Her form teacher hasn't seen her this morning." Mr Peters went straight into professional mode, calm, kind but thorough. My head was starting to pound. I couldn't take in what he was saying. I stood, jangling the van keys, desperate to go flying up to the school but he told me to stay put in case Bronte turned up.

"Start ringing round her friends and make a list of places she might have gone," he said. "I'll organise a search of the school. She might have decided to go off to the library or hide out in the changing rooms instead of going to lessons. I'll phone you back."

I tried Colin's mobile, getting his cocky voice on the answering service asking me to leave a message "if you think I may want to speak to you".

I couldn't sit down. I put the kettle on, then didn't make tea when it boiled. I tried to work out how long it would take from Stirling Hall to home if she'd got some crazy idea about walking back here. Christ, she could kill herself crossing the dual carriageway. Even dawdling, she could be back in forty minutes, now even, working up the courage to come in. I was sure she was just punishing me. But the bit of me that connected to Bronte in a you-came-out-of-my-body sort of way was aching to see that tiny pause before she let herself smile, to have a chance to brush her hair without being impatient with her knotty curls, just to tell her I loved her and I was sorry I'd made such a mess of everything with all my grand plans.

I ran into the back yard and out into the lane behind our row of terraces. I couldn't bear to look at the burnt-out Fiesta, which had been rusting away out there for years. I'd always hated that car, sitting there all ghostly among the weeds, a trouble magnet. I was terrified that I'd glance over and she'd be propped up against it, blood oozing out of her mouth and tights round her neck.

I'd obviously been watching too many *Trial and Retribution* repeats. There was nothing, not even the mangy cats that roamed the estate. Just the rain plopping down on beer cans, condoms, vodka bottles. Christ, half an hour of worry had sent me loop-de-loop. How did people cope when their kids were missing for days, years even? I tried Colin's mobile again. Never, ever there when I needed him.

I went back inside, peering out of the front window for a forlorn shape lurking. I wished Mum was still alive. She was so capable, she'd have known what to do. I shook my head, trying to connect two thoughts together. Bronte really liked Clover. She might have gone there. I dialled her number and left a madwoman message on her answerphone. I paced about sifting through my little conversations with Bronte, where I'd been scratching away for information among her sulky grunts. Had I missed something? Was this really over a disco evening? Why had I let her get out of the van to walk this morning? Images of perverts pretending to be respectable-looking men in shiny cars outside the school filled my mind. Maybe she hadn't run away at all, maybe someone had taken her. No. This was about the disco. It had to be. Little monkey was probably sitting under a tree somewhere enjoying how worried we'd all be. Anything else was too horrible.

I kept looking at the clock. Nearly three-quarters of an hour since Mr Peters had called. How long did it take to whizz round a school? Finally, the phone rang. I snatched it up.

"Ms Etxeleku, I'm sorry. We've searched everywhere. The next step is to call the police and I think we should do that now," Mr Peters said.

The word "police" moved me from worried to imagination overdrive. I couldn't seem to make my mouth form any words.

"Ms Etxeleku? Are you there? Try to stay calm. The police react to Stirling Hall calls very swiftly." I knew he was right. Authority dealing with authority would get a search party moving more quickly than me not knowing who to speak to and getting fobbed off with some pen-clicking clerk who "couldn't do anything until she's been missing for twenty-four hours". I was sure that the police were much quicker off the mark for burglaries in SD2's neighbourhood than missing children in SD1.

I put the phone down and ran next door to Sandy. All the curtains were still shut. I thumped on the door. I saw her bedroom curtains move, but she didn't come down. The drizzle was gathering force, stingy, sharp darts pinging off my arms. I shouted through the letterbox. "Sandy, I need to speak to you. Bronte's missing."

There was a pause, then the upstairs window scraped open and Sandy's head poked out, her bright red hair sticking up in all directions. She hauled up the strap of something satiny. "Blimey O'Riley, can't a girl get a lie-in round here? What was you yelling at me?"

The sympathy on her face as I shouted up to her broke the last little stitch holding me together. Denim and Gypsy often bunked off school so I'd been expecting her to tell me she'd turn up, to shut up with my mithering and that I was lucky Bronts had never done it before. Instead she ran her fingers through her tufty hair and looked worried. I was trying to force my tears back, shoving against that gathering speed feeling, which started off as quiet, miserable leaking and ended with me howling as though my heart would heave itself out of my chest.

"Did you see Colin leave this morning? I can't get hold of him," I said.

"No, I ain't seen him. I've been on night shift. Hang on, I'll come down."

Sandy opened the door, all floor length leopard skin, lace and baggy boobs. Fluffy tiger slippers peeped out underneath. We ran through the sort of places Bronte might have gone: the rec, the shopping centre, KFC, McDonald's, the sports hall. Sandy kept getting side-tracked by stories of Denim and Gypsy's truancy. She pulled me into a big hug but I was too stressed to let myself be looked after, too many people to phone, too many places to search.

I wriggled free and turned to head home, just as a black Audi drew up. The door opened and Mr Peters got out.

"Mr Peters! Have you found her?"

"I'm sorry, no, Ms Etxeleku. The police thought it would be quicker to have a chat with us both together before I take them up to the school to speak to her form teacher. I said I'd meet them here. I couldn't get through on your mobile."

"Sorry, I was trying to contact my partner."

The rain started to come down in earnest. Mr Peters held his umbrella over me as I turned up my own path.

"Keep an eye open for me, won't you, Sandy?" I shouted over the fence.

"Of course, love. I'll get meself dressed and have a scout round the estate. Take care. Try not to worry."

Mr Peters took my arm. "Come on, you need to get dry. Let me make you some tea before the police get here. They shouldn't be too long."

Mr Peters filled the kettle while I emptied the biros, pencils and money-off coupons out of the teapot. He didn't look like a teabag in the mug sort of guy. I couldn't believe I was even having that thought when some madman might be slitting Bronte's throat at that very moment. I went upstairs to get changed. As I peeled off my wet clothes, I heard the squeak of the back door opening and the thud as the handle crashed into the kitchen wall, followed by "Who are you?" then "Mai! Mai!"

I pulled on a dry T-shirt and still in soaking wet jeans, belted down the stairs two-by-two, thumping my shoulder on the door jamb as I came to a halt.

"Mr Caudwell, Ms Etxeleku will explain everything." Mr Peters had his hand up like a stop sign as Colin hurled his coat onto the table with a clank of keys.

"Maia, what the hell is going on? I just bumped into Sandy and she said Bronts is missing. How can she be missing? Didn't you take her to school this morning? What's he doing here?"

"Mr Peters is Head of Upper School. He's been helping me look for Bronte. She didn't go into school after I dropped her off this morning. The police are on their way."

Mr Peters handed me some tea, much sweeter than I normally drank.

"Police. The police are coming here? What? You don't think something serious has happened, do you? She's just having a strop over that fucking disco, isn't she?" Colin was pacing about, scratching at his stubble.

"I don't know. I think so. I hope so. God, I don't know. Mr Peters has had the whole school searched. I've looked in the back lane. Sandy hasn't seen her," I said.

Colin turned to look out of the window. "Do you think the police will want to search the house?"

I saw the dots join in Colin's brain to form the shape of a marijuana leaf. I looked to Mr Peters who shrugged and said, "They might want to look in her bedroom, or perhaps examine your computer."

"That's easy, we ain't got no computer," Colin said. "I can't just sit here. I'll drive the route to school. And you, you make sure you frigging well phone me this time if anything happens."

He jabbed his finger in my direction. I didn't need to win at that moment. He grabbed the van keys and left without bothering to put on a coat. What freaked me out most was that he didn't even bother to fetch the stash of dope that he kept hidden in the battery compartment of the CD player. I took a deep breath and steeled myself for Mr Peters.

"Sorry about that, I do really appreciate your help," I said.

"It's fine. People react to fear in different ways. Some people get aggressive, some people swear, some people lash out. I see all sorts of behaviour in my job." He sounded so gentle and so capable that I started to cry again.

"And some people just bawl their eyes out." My feeble attempt at humour backfired and a sob stiffened my whole body. I pressed my fingers against my eyes but the tears forced their way through. "I hope she's okay. I should never have moved her to Stirling Hall."

Mr Peters put his hands on my shoulders and looked right into my eyes. Firm, reassuring, certain. "She's your daughter. You wouldn't be normal if you weren't worried. The police are very skilled at this sort of thing. I'm sure they'll find her."

If Mr Peters was in charge, it was almost possible to believe everything might turn out okay. The doorbell rang and I dashed to answer it, a tiny beat of hope in my heart.

Instead of a bedraggled Bronte, a tall brunette with a pointy face, a deep voice, and her hair scraped back into a bun stood at the door.

"PC Blake, but please call me Serena. This is PC Richard Tadman," she said, indicating a stocky man with a jolly smile.

I showed them into the kitchen, managing not to cry. I opened my mouth to introduce Mr Peters but Serena stepped forward and held out her hand to him. "Hello Zachary, long time, no see. You remember Richard?" She sounded very brisk, almost angry. Then she turned to me and said in a much more gentle tone, "Is there somewhere we could sit?"

I took them through into the front room. I tried to stop bustling about like the women I worked for when they had visitors. I found myself doing that "Tea? Coffee?" high-pitched voice thing as though they'd popped in for a bit of Victoria sponge on a Sunday afternoon.

"I'll make some more tea, Ms Etxeleku, you have a seat," Mr Peters said.

"Could I take a quick look at Bronte's bedroom?" PC Tadman asked.

"Of course, it's the first one at the top of the stairs, says 'Top Secret' on the door."

I perched on the settee while Serena pulled out her notebook. Autopilot got me through the basics, name, age, height, last time I saw her, the hoo-ha over the disco that morning, friends and places she might go. I flinched when she asked me if Bronte had a boyfriend.

"Of course not. She's nine years old!"

Serena nodded. "I know, but girls do mature at different rates."

Bronte still went to bed with her toy gorilla. Whatever had happened to her, I was sure she hadn't disappeared with a boyfriend.

Mr Peters came back in with some tea.

"Is she active on social media?" Serena asked.

I shook my head. "We haven't got a computer at home. I'm not sure about school?" I looked at Mr Peters.

"No. The school system is set up so the children can't access those sites," he said.

I was fighting to stay calm. I just wanted Serena to stop asking questions and get out there, on the streets, searching for her.

When she asked for a recent photo, all the fear I'd forced down burst out in some kind of wild animal wail. The sound startled me and then I laughed. It wasn't a noise I'd heard out of myself before, nothing like my giggling at *Only Fools and Horses* or *Mrs Brown's Boys*. It came from deep inside me, boiling up through my chest and splurging out in a wet burst of sound from the back of my throat. I had that out of control feeling as though I would never stop laughing again, even though I knew that it was wrong, really wrong.

I felt the settee sag as Mr Peters sat down next to me, his hand gently patting my back. I leaned into him and he put his arm round me, making a quiet shushing sound. He pressed a handkerchief into my palm. Then the laughing moved into great spitty sucks of air followed by gaspy sobs and I became aware of feeling ridiculous. Serena didn't speak, just sat there, watchful. Almost as though she was waiting for me to stand up and say, "Now, for my next trick."

I was about to pull myself away from Mr Peters, when I heard the front door open and Colin burst in.

"She back?" he said, shaking the water from his hair. I must have moved away a bit jumpily because Colin looked at me, then at Mr Peters. "What the hell's going on here? You two having some kind of cuddle-fest while my daughter is God knows where?"

I saw Mr Peters take a deep breath but Serena stepped in before he could speak. "Mr Caudwell! Your wife, partner, is very upset and Mr Peters was trying to comfort her. Now, please, go and put some dry clothes on and come back down. There are a few questions I'd like to ask you."

"S'pose you think I've buried her body under the patio, do you? You need to get a move on and start looking for her. It'll be dark in a few hours." He had his hands on his hips.

"I understand that, Mr Caudwell, but you may be able to tell us something that speeds the whole process up, so if you'd be so kind."

I had to hand it to Serena. The woman had authority. Colin stomped up the stairs.

I stood up. "I'll just get that photo."

I ran upstairs. PC Tadman was coming out of Bronte's room. "Did you find anything useful?"

He shook his head. "Seeing the child's room just gives us a feel for what they're like, sometimes points us in the right direction." He disappeared off downstairs.

I chased away the thought that I'd never be able to go into Bronte's room again if she didn't come back. I went into our bedroom where Colin was sitting on the bed with his head in his hands. His shoulders were shaking slightly. I lifted his face up towards me.

"Hey. It's going to be okay. The police will find her." I said it as much for me.

Colin threw his arms round my waist. "I don't know what I'll do if anything happens to her, I can't stand it. Where is she? Why would she do this?"

Even in these circumstances, Colin's desperation shocked and frightened me. I couldn't think of any other time when he had cried rather than shouted.

I had no answers. "Come on, the sooner you speak to the police, the sooner they can do their job." I helped him out of his sodden jeans, then I pulled out the box from under the bed. I found my favourite photo of Bronte, taken after Christmas when it had snowed. She was sticking a carrot on her snowman's face, her smile showing the gap where one of her teeth had come out on Christmas Eve, her hair corkscrewed into damp, snow-flecked curls. She looked relaxed, carefree, beyond her normal buttoned-up self. My eyes were sore. I had no more tears.

Colin came over to look at the photo. "She looks just like you there. Beautiful." His voice sounded tight. He pulled me close. His cheek was freezing against mine and we stood there for a moment, united in misery. Colin was so much easier to like when the fight had gone out of him. I squeezed his hand and went back downstairs. PC Tadman was looking at the noticeboard in the kitchen. When I walked into the front room, Mr Peters and Serena started talking loudly as though I'd caught them whispering about us. I didn't have any room left to feel worse.

I handed the photo to Serena. Her face didn't flicker as she looked at it. I don't know what I expected. Probably that she would say she was the most gorgeous child she'd ever seen. To her, Bronte was just another face she'd have to scan onto the missing list.

CHAPTER
ELEVEN

Clover surprised me. When she finally picked up my message, she turned into a one-woman powerhouse. She organised a search of the woods and lanes surrounding her house, phoned every mother in Bronte's class and brought Harley back from school for me. Once word had got out at Stirling Hall, Mr Peters thought it was better for him to come home. I hovered awkwardly on the front step, trying to find the words to thank her. Clover waved me away, her posh voice booming down the street. "Anything I can do, anything at all, just call." I felt as though she meant it.

Harley clung to me, his eyes huge in his face. I found it hard to hug him when my other baby was out there, somewhere, needing me more. Colin fetched Sandy to sit with Harley.

"Maia, love, you poor thing. I'll wait here in case she comes back. You get out looking or you'll both go nutty-balloo, just sitting here." She sounded like the old Sandy I knew.

Colin was clicking the end of a pen. "I'm gonna drive round up by that new park where I took Bronte to ride her bike. That's not far from the school. And that riverbank where we went swimming last summer."

"Good idea. You take the torch in case you're not back before dark. It's under the sink." I went to give him a kiss but he pushed me away.

"Come on, let's get moving, it's one o'clock already."

I watched the van screech away. I stood by the front gate for a moment, trying to focus on logic, not panic. I raked through the people she knew locally. Bronte was reserved like me. She'd never really mixed with the kids on the estate. She preferred to play on her own, pretending to be a teacher to her dolls or writing stories about horses. Some of the kids round here were old before they'd had a chance to be young, mini-louts in the making with their pierced eyebrows, swearing and tribal haircuts. I'd never pushed her to mix with them either.

Where could, where would a kid go on a gloomy rainy day? I was wasting time standing there. I set off, heading towards the recreation ground, a good half an hour's walk away, on the other side of the estate. I hoped she'd have more sense than to go there. All those play tunnels were just asking for evil to hide inside. I shuddered.

The rec was deserted. In all the film I'd seen, no good had ever come from swings dangling in an empty playground. I ran to the big tunnels and forced myself to peer in, almost screaming anyway, even though there were only a few crisp packets and lager cans inside. I climbed the steps of the slide in case she was hiding curled up in the little canopy at the top. From my vantage point, I scanned the playground and beyond, shouting her name, but my voice blew back to me.

It was so cold and damp. I made my way over to the flats on the edge of the estate in case she'd taken refuge in the stairwells there. By the time I'd done ten flights of stairs in six blocks, my legs were shaking with exertion. I sat down on the wall to gather my thoughts and get my breath back, indifferent to the stink of the bins.

It was nearly four o'clock. I hauled myself to my feet, trying to work out a methodical way to search the streets. I was convinced that I'd miss her by a hair, that I'd turn into one road just as she was going round the corner into another. I marched along, the rumbling in my belly reminding me that I hadn't eaten since breakfast. A silver Mercedes with blacked out windows crawled past me. It slowed about three hundred yards further up. I started to run, positive that they were going to throw Bronte out onto the pavement, tied up. Before I'd even got close, a boy, maybe a man, stepped out of the shadows and approached the car. I saw his hand reach through the passenger window and quickly out again. He slipped something into his pocket. I promised myself that one day I'd live in an area where Friday night's entertainment came from a DVD rather than a jacked-up vein. I slowed my pace, hoping they'd been too busy swapping money and crack to notice me flying towards them.

Each street looked the same. Row after row of ugly sixties houses with overgrown front gardens sporting old mattresses, broken chairs and rusty bits of cars. Occasionally there would be a neat lawn with pots and bushes. I called her name over and over again until my throat was sore. Every time I looked at my watch another quarter of an hour had passed. By half past six, my feet were aching and my hands sore from the wind and rain. I forced myself on. I must have been on my fifteenth street when I came up to the community centre, a pre-fab building with pebble-dashed walls sporting the message "If you ain't cool, you can't rule" sprayed in red and blue. The lights were on and the harsh tones of rap music blared out. By the door, a skinhead was snogging a girl up against the wall. Her black puffa jacket was wide open and the boy had his hands up her shirt, kneading her breasts like bread dough, oblivious to the rain.

I hadn't been to the community centre since Bronte was tiny when some well-meaning health visitor did a session about caring for your toddler. When she started teaching us baby yoga, the women practically chased her out of the room, demanding extra benefit payments so they could keep their kids warm. At least back then I'd been able to keep Bronte safe.

I squared my shoulders and marched into the hall, past the gaggle of girls gathered inside the door. Their main purpose in life seemed to be to show lots of flabby flesh, untouched by exercise or fresh fruit. Some of the boys stared in my direction, like dogs who'd spotted a cat and were growling quietly, waiting to see if it dared to come into the garden or not. There was no point in looking for a friendly face. Kids on our estate didn't do friendly so I took a gamble and walked straight over to a tough nut, who was stabbing away at an iPod. He had so many tattoos up his arms that they were like sleeves.

With his black goatee beard and shaven head, he seemed a few years older than the rest, maybe eighteen, perhaps twenty.

"Hi. Don't want to disturb you but could I ask a quick question?"

"Depends what it is." He glared at me, fiddling with the bar through his lower lip. Some of the other boys slouched closer. I hated myself for feeling scared.

"My daughter's missing. She's nine years old. I wondered if anyone here had seen her."

"Christ, we never get any peace here. Something every week. Some kid goes missing and straightaway you're in here pointing the finger at us."

"I'm not pointing the finger at anyone. I just wondered if anyone had noticed her hanging about. I'm asking everyone, I'm so worried," I said.

The boy couldn't have looked less interested. "Why don't you go and get the cops earning their money? They've got plenty of spare time on their hands, they're always down here bothering us. Last week they were on about some bloody pirate DVDs, week before, some dodgy Es. We're just trying to have a good time here, keep off the streets a bit."

Frustration was bubbling up inside me like a saucepan of milk. I wanted to pull him into me by the ring in his eyebrow and shout in his face until he could feel my spit on his skin. I wanted to scream at him: "This is my daughter we are talking about, who could be frightened, shouting out for me, yes, even dying right now and you are telling me to get the cops? Do you think I haven't already done that?"

111

He turned to the guy next to him with white blond spiky hair. "Don't think we can help, can we? No girls hanging around here, 'cept for them old slags out there and nine's too young even for us."

"Please, can you just ask your mates? She's got dark hair like mine. Wearing a red skirt and green blazer. She's got quite dark skin, sort of Spanish looking."

The goatee man looked at me, hooded eyes unfriendly, considering. Then the boy with the blond spiky hair leaned in close to me.

"I know you."

On our estate, those three words usually signalled a punch in the mouth. I pushed down the flutter of panic. I kept myself to myself so it was hard to see how I'd rubbed someone up the wrong way. The boy laughed, showing a chipped front tooth.

"You're the woman who called the ambulance that day I split me head open. I think me brains would've emptied out on the pavement if you hadn't come along."

It was then I noticed the spiderweb half-hidden by the collar of his shirt. "Tarants?"

"Cor, you even remember me name. Is it your little girl who's gone AWOL?"

"Yes. She was there the day you hurt yourself, do you remember her?" He didn't answer for a moment. I wanted to shake him. Think! Think!

"No, but I think I seen her around. She got an older brother, blond, yeah?"

I nodded, feeling like I had all day, that I was wasting my time and that some other place, somewhere I hadn't thought of yet, would be better.

112

"What about today? She's been missing since this morning." I tried to keep the impatience out of my voice.

"No, don't think so. There ain't too many kids round this way in that uniform. It's that posh school, innit? But you're from here, right? What's your kid doing there then?" Now his brain had made a few connections, he'd revved up a gear, lost that dopey look.

"It's a long story. Will you double-check with your mates, though? Please?" I dug my hands deep into my jacket pockets to stop me grabbing his shirt and pleading with him.

"You leave it with me, love. I got friends all over town. Is it that school with all them cricket fields, up near the Royal Oak pub? Me cousin runs in a gang over that way. I'll see if he's seen her." He ran his hand over his spikes as though to check they were still standing to attention.

The goatee boy was twirling the stud in his nose. I sensed my welcome was on a countdown but I wanted to tell Tarants where I lived, scribble my mobile number down and ask him to call me. I was caught between knowing how our estate worked and how I wanted it to work.

"C'mon, you going to put the music on or what?" said the goatee boy, nudging Tarants.

He shoved him back. "Have a bit of fucking respect." He turned back to me. "I'll do what I can, darling."

"I live at 95 Walldon, second to last house on the left."

"Yeah, yeah, I'll find you. You'd better get going, you know how impatient people are round here."

I left, repeating 95 Walldon to him as I walked away and received an irritable nod in return. By the time I'd walked two blocks I was shivering. The rain had stepped up and was bouncing off the pavement in front of me. Cold needles of water pricked my scalp. My hands were so cold they hurt. I shoved them under my armpits. I couldn't go home while my baby was out there. My jeans were dragging down, so heavy with water it was an effort to lift my feet. I pulled my phone out of my pocket, wincing as the thick wet cotton scraped at my freezing skin. I glanced at the screen for messages but it was black. I stabbed at the buttons, desperate to produce a sign of life. Nothing. I'd been walking for nearly six hours. By now, Bronte would normally be snuggled up with Colin on the settee, laughing over some DVD. I would have to go home to find out whether there was any news. I trudged a different route back, not bothering to move out of the way as cars sent sloshes of dirty water across the pavement. My pace quickened as I got close to the house. It was 7.30. Maybe, just maybe, she'd be wrapped in a blanket in the front room with her thumb in her mouth, which she still sucked when she was upset.

One look at Sandy's face told me that was not the case. She rushed off to get me a towel and to put the kettle on. Colin wasn't back yet. I didn't want to phone him. Didn't want to hear the defeat in his voice. Didn't want to have to be strong.

114

"Where's Harley?"

"He was wiped out with crying. He took himself off to bed about twenty minutes ago."

I ran upstairs to see him. He was asleep, grey shadows under his eyes, hands behind his head as though he was sunbathing. I loved the trusting face he had in his sleep, wide open to the world. I stroked his hair and kissed his cheek. Next to him lay Bronte's toy gorilla, Gordon. I eased it out and buried my face in its matted black fur, breathing in hard. I could only smell the plastic of its hands and feet. I tucked it back in next to Harley, wondering whether I'd ever been more miserable.

I was wriggling out of my wet clothes when the phone rang. I flew down the stairs in my bra and jeans and snatched it up.

It was Mr Peters. He told me that the police would call but he had heard "unofficially" that there'd been a sighting of Bronte in the shopping centre, a twenty-five-minute walk from school at about one o'clock in the afternoon. Which meant that seven hours ago she'd been alive. One of the officers had been going through CCTV footage and had captured a picture of her Stirling Hall backpack.

"Was it definitely her? Was she alone?"

"They're pretty certain it was her because her hair is in a plait down the back. It's difficult to tell whether she was on her own because she's going into a shop. They're still searching for other images to see if they can work out which way she went when she came out."

"Which shop was she going into?"

"A fashion shop, H&M, I think. The police are trying to contact the manager of the store at the moment."

I sighed. I was so bone tired. I wanted to feel positive that she'd been seen after she'd left school but anything could have happened in the last few hours.

"Ms Etxeleku? Are you still there?"

"Yes, I'm here."

"Don't give up. I understand how exhausting this is. This is a concrete step forward. I'm sure they will find her. I'd appreciate it if you kept it to yourself that you already knew this piece of information when the police call. I wanted to put you in the picture as soon as possible. You will contact me if there is anything I can do, won't you?"

I wanted him to come over and hold me and tell me that it was all going to be okay. I'd run out of coping. I needed someone else to take the strain. Better still, I wanted him to turn up at the door with Bronte and a plan for how to live the rest of my life after this without turning into a raving loony every time Bronte was out of my sight for five seconds. But it seemed like a big ask even for Mr Peters so I just thanked him and sank into the settee. My teeth were chattering. Sandy stood over me, her face a question mark. I repeated the conversation and saw her features relax, the deep wrinkles of night shifts, twenty a day and Co-op vodka reaching up for air.

"See. I told you she'd be all right. She's a survivor, that Bronte. Like her mother. You better get yourself into some dry togs before you catch your death. S'pose you better ring Colin and let him know, he was looking proper stressed before he went off." She was right. But I didn't want to deal with him. I knew I should go back out into the rain and keep searching. Though I also wanted to hear firsthand from the police what they knew. It might be worse if I shot off like a headless chicken, especially with a dead mobile. I stuck it on charge.

"Sandy, be a love and give Colin a ring for us. I'm going to get dry. His number is, hang on, let me write it down for you."

"It's okay, I've got it."

Upstairs I pulled on the thickest jumper and socks I could find. I was psyching myself up to get back out on my lonely search when there was a knock at the door. It was Serena. My first thought was that she'd have phoned to update me unless Bronte was dead. My belly lurched as though I'd drunk neat lemon juice. She must have read my face because she put her hand on my arm as she stepped inside and said, "I think we're making progress, Ms Etxeleku."

The way her hair was scraped back so tightly was at odds with her kindness. I led her through to the front room where she filled me in on what they'd discovered so far.

I almost wished Mr Peters hadn't phoned me. Keeping my face ready to look surprised was stopping me concentrating. Sandy was acting as though she had a bit part in some cheesy police drama, coming in and out with tea and nodding knowledgeably, muttering stuff like, "They always say it's the quiet ones you've got to watch," until Serena asked her to give us a bit of privacy.

"Has Bronte any history of shoplifting?"

"No, not at all. She's never taken anything." I knew I sounded defensive.

"It's just that when we spoke to the store manager tonight, she remembered Bronte very well because she had tried to steal a sequinned top. Put it on under her school uniform."

A surge of fury shot through me. I almost forgot Bronte was missing. I hadn't brought up my daughter to be a common little thief. Serena probably thought I'd been too lazy to teach her right from wrong.

"Why didn't they call the police straightaway? Then she would never have gone missing," I said.

"They were about to call the police. The security guard saw the sequins hanging down under her blazer. She'd taken the top off and given it back to him when someone else triggered the alarm and in the confusion, she made a run for it. He did chase after her but didn't manage to catch her and because they had the top back, I think they opted for an easy life."

Bronte had always been a quick runner. She was lean and fast. I wasn't surprised she'd outsprinted the security guard. I had to squash down a glimmer of pride. I'd always been a hotshot in the hundred metres on school sports days but I didn't realise the top talent my daughter would inherit from me would be the ability to give a dozy security guard the slip.

"Which other shops does she like apart from Next?" said Serena.

118

"Next? I thought she was in H&M?" I felt my eyes close with the split-second despair that comes from dropping someone you like in the shit.

Serena looked at me. Hard. Brown eyes suddenly matched the harsh hairdo. "How did you know which shop she was in?"

"I had a phone call just before you got here." I was hoping she'd think it was someone from the police station.

"From whom? Why didn't you tell me?"

Jesus. She was going to start taking up the concrete in the back yard if I didn't get my act together.

"Mr Peters rang." I practically heard the splash as the sewage closed over him.

Serena pursed her lips. "I told him that in strictest confidence." Her eyes flicked over me. "Is there anything else you haven't told me?"

"Like what? Why would I keep anything from you when my daughter is missing?"

"Let's start with Mr Peters. You seem very close. Are you seeing him?"

I stared at Serena. "Seeing him?"

"Yes, Ms Etxeleku. Seeing him. Having an affair?"

"No, of course not. He's one of Bronte's teachers, that's all." I could feel myself blushing. "He was trying to help, he knew how worried I was."

"So it would be wide of the mark to suggest that you having an affair with Zachary was one of the reasons Bronte ran away?"

I could see how criminals would crumble under her stare. "Are you joking? I hardly know the man. He's been helping me get the kids settled in at school. He told me something which, unless I've got the wrong end of the stick, you were going to tell me anyway, so big whoopee-doo." Shock had made me slow but I could feel the armies rallying. "I'm not interested in shagging Mr Peters. I'm interested in getting my daughter back."

Serena winced at my language. Bad language except when it came out of my mouth always jolted me too. If I'd wanted to sound like a thicko, I'd done a good job. However, it seemed to do the trick. She stopped banging on about "Zachary", and started outlining what would happen from now on.

"We'll keep reviewing CCTV in the area. If we don't find her tonight, we'll go to the press tomorrow, pull out all the stops to bring your little girl to everyone's attention."

"Why haven't you already done that?" I knew by the way her eyes shot open that I'd sounded rude.

"Statistics show that children usually turn up within forty-eight hours. If we went to the media as soon as a child went missing, ninety-nine times out of a hundred the child would be safely back home before the newspapers hit the stands. The evidence so far leads me to believe that Bronte has run away, not that she has been abducted. I know it's hard but you have to trust me. I've done this before."

I refused to feel like I'd been told off. Forty-eight hours! That was two days. I'd have died of worry before then. I sat picking at the loose threads on the arm of the settee while she ran through how to deal with journalists if any contacted me. Right at the end as she got up to leave, she shook my hand. Her eyes were watchful, suspicious. The big easy smile had made for the hills but I was too tired to work out whether she was mad at me or furious with Mr Peters.

As soon as Serena left, Sandy shot out of the kitchen. "Well? Have those useless boys in blue managed to come up with anything?"

I felt so knackered that I could have easily dropped off mid-sentence as I gave her a rundown of Serena's visit. In different circumstances we'd have hooted our heads off that Serena had thought I was having it away with Mr Peters. Instead Sandy looked all serious. "Are you?"

"Don't you bloody start. I've got enough on my hands with one bloke, let alone trying to find time for a bit on the side. Anyway, Mr Peters wouldn't go for a rough bird like me. He could have anyone."

"Yeah, he looked a bit of all right," said Sandy, handing me the phone. "You'd better give Colin a ring, let him know what's going on. It went straight to voicemail when I tried before."

I could hear a mixture of hope and dread in his voice when he answered. Like me, hearing that Bronte had been seen in the shopping centre didn't reassure him much.

"She ain't there now. I just walked round that way. I've been right up onto the hill in case she decided to go up there. I even drove halfway to Guildford — thought she might walk along the cycle path we went on in the summer. I done the leisure centre, the riverbanks, the shops on the parade, the train and bus station. I'm freezing," he said.

"Come home. We can't do anything now. Serena said to trust the police to find her."

When Colin arrived back about half an hour later, drenched and irritable, he was still cottering on about the bloody police, piss-ups in a brewery and the like. Usually I couldn't stand him going on because Colin couldn't find anything himself if it wasn't dancing a jig and ringing a bell, but on a day when so much had changed, it was comforting to have him rumbling on. I suppose it was like living next to a railway line where the noise of the trains becomes a soothing murmur.

While Colin collapsed onto the settee next to me, Sandy was in and out with coffee and toast. It took all the energy I could muster to rub some warmth back into his numb hands. "I've run you a hot bath, Col," Sandy said, helping him to his feet.

I loved her for babying Colin. I didn't want to, couldn't do it myself. I was filled up with worry about Bronte, with no room left for taking care of anyone else. Although he was quiet now, if he ran true to form, he'd find a way to make his agony over Bronte all about him, his suffering much worse than mine. Eventually it would go full circle and be my fault.

I flicked on the TV. The crappy sitcoms, which usually filled the evenings in our house, seemed pathetic. I pushed back the front room curtains and peered into the darkness. I heard the water slopping over the sides of the bath upstairs. Even with Bronte

122

missing I still felt irritated about having to mop up after Colin. Sandy appeared in the doorway.

"I'll be off now, love. Let us know if you hear anything." She leaned in and hugged me. I pulled her to me gratefully.

I lay down on the settee after she'd gone, wondering whether I'd ever be able to sleep again. How anyone, ever, got on with their lives if their child never came back. I looked at my watch. Nine o'clock. My body ached to sleep, but it seemed wrong. I closed my eyes, terrified that my imagination would parade awful images of Bronte across my eyelids. Nothing. Just black. I was drifting, my mind still turning, walking the estate, the shopping centre, winding down into slow motion when I heard the beep of a text message. I leapt up.

Just wanted you to know that I am thinking of you. Sorry for causing trouble and telling you things I shouldn't have. Done with best intentions. Let me know at once if any news. Take care. Zachary.

Bloody Serena. She'd obviously left here and trotted back to tell him off. I should have warned him. It was alien to have someone apologise to me when I was the one who'd screwed up. I lay back down and concentrated on thinking about Mr Peters to stop replaying my last conversation with Bronte that morning. His hair always looked as though he'd just washed it, maybe in some of that Jo Malone lime, basil and mandarin stuff I often saw spring up in the houses where I worked after Father's Day or birthdays. I was pretty sure he'd never smell of kebabs, or hash, or

Guinness. I loved his manners, all that pulling back of chairs, opening doors. I hoped Harley was learning from him. Mr Peters wouldn't laugh if I told him I wanted to do an Open University degree. He'd sit there looking all public school handsome and show me how to fill in the application form. I wondered what it would be like to kiss him. That was the last thought I had before my limbs sank into the lumpy old foam of the settee and sleep weighed me down like pockets full of stones.

The sound of hammering reached down the dark tunnel to drag me out. Colin was shouting at me to wake up, shaking my shoulder on his way to the door. I blinked for a second before reality rushed in on me again and I sprang to my feet. I glanced at the clock. With a flash of guilt, I realised I'd been asleep for an hour.

By the time I made it the few feet to the door, Colin was on his knees, sobbing, wrapped around Bronte on the front doorstep. All I could hear was "fucking hell, fucking hell," repeated over and over again like a mantra. Bronte looked up at me, brown eyes wide and uncertain, her curly hair so wet it was almost straight, her blazer splattered with mud, a squashed hat under her arm. I flung myself on her, smelling her, touching her face, kissing her head.

"Where have you been? We were so worried about you." My voice sounded harsher, higher than normal.

Her face crumpled and she started to cry. I couldn't make out what she was saying.

124

"Leave it, Mai, let's get her warm. We can have it all out later, don't matter now."

It was only then I remembered the vague shape I'd seen standing in the shadows as I'd run to the door. I looked out.

"Tarants?"

He stepped forward into the dim porch light. "Was it you that found her? Thank you, thank you." I threw my arms round him, registering the stiffness of someone who was used to receiving aggression, not affection. He clamped his arms to his side until the first surge of gratitude had subsided and I remembered the rules of our estate.

He dug his hands in his pockets and shuffled. With a scarf covering his tattoo and his white spiky hair flattened by the rain, he looked quite normal. "S'nothing. I owed you. See you around."

"Wait. Where did you find her?"

He waved. "She'll tell you." Then he was gone, my thank yous and questions washed away with the rain.

CHAPTER
TWELVE

For at least the first hour, I couldn't stop touching Bronte. Kept holding her hand, asking her if she was okay until she got irritated with me. The day had come when Bronte shrugging and telling me to get off filled my heart with joy. I bathed her and wrapped her in a snuggly dressing gown, while Colin phoned the police — "Better tell the fuzz that we've done their job for them." Over endless peanut butter sandwiches, she stumbled out the sorry story of wanting to be like Sorrel and Saffy with a new sequinned top. The escape from the security guard. Hiding at the cemetery where we'd buried Mum three years ago.

"Why did you go there? It's such a horrid place to be, so grey and depressing," I said.

"I dunno. Just wanted to be near to *Amatxi*."

Amatxi was Bronte's name for Mum, grandmother in Basque. They were so alike in some ways. Mum couldn't stand in a queue at the supermarket without discussing the price of plums with the person next to her, but she also had a way of hugging secrets to her, just like Bronte, filtering out information as and when she thought you needed to know. If ever. Bronte was only six when Mum had died, but the long afternoons at the park, the noisy jam tart making sessions in my kitchen, the hours reading and re-reading *Room on the Broom* had helped my mother connect with Bronte in a way I could only dream about.

"How did you get there?" I said. "Surely you didn't walk?"

Bronte nodded. "Yes, I did. I followed the tow path along the river."

"That's about four miles." I bit my lip. I hated her walking anywhere lonely on her own.

She carried on. "It took me ages. It was getting dark when I got there but I thought I'd just go in quickly and see if her grave was tidy."

For God's sake. This was the girl who wouldn't sleep without the landing light on. It was all my fault — she'd been asking to go and visit Mum's grave for ages but I'd kept making excuses. I never went there. I preferred to remember Mum sitting in my kitchen, stirring brandy into her coffee and giving me grief about not going to university nearly twenty years later. "You could 'ave been the Premier Minister. But you meet that not good for anything boy. Colin. Pah."

Bronte's intensity, her desire to do what she set out to do even though she was scared reminded me so much of Mum.

"I got a bit carried away because the grave was quite overgrown so I started tidying up, pulling the weeds off it. I didn't realise how dark it had got because of that streetlight next to *Amatxi*'s grave. Then when I looked around me, I was really frightened. I was about to leave when these two boys came past and started laughing at me, going on about me being a mentalist cos I was talking to myself. I think I must have been whispering to *Amatxi* about the disco and all that."

I waited. That graveyard had a reputation for gangs of teenagers hanging about, doing drugs.

Bronte stirred her hot chocolate. "I told them to get lost, then a whole gang of them appeared and started throwing stones at *Amatxi*'s grave and teasing me about my school uniform. My hat's ruined. I'm really sorry. They snatched it and played Frisbee with it until it fell in a puddle. They said they were going to rip off all my clothes and make me go to school in my knickers. They wouldn't listen to me when I told them I lived on the Walldon Estate. They kept saying, 'Okay yah' and asking if I went to gymkhanas and where Daddy's yacht was. Then they surrounded me. They were holding hands and I couldn't get out of the circle."

Even though we'd put the heating on high, I felt cold. I'd spent nine years protecting her but when she'd needed me, I hadn't been there. If I'd left her at Morlands, none of this would have happened. Colin was silent, chewing the skin round his nails and looking like he might burst into tears at any minute.

"Why did they let you go?" I said.

"It was that girl, Mum. You know, the one who used to go out with Tarants. She was with him that day when he hurt his head. She's called Stace. She doesn't live here any more cos her mum's moved in with her boyfriend on that estate near the underpass. Eastward or something. She's going out with a bloke called Colt now."

I tried to conjure up the girl's face. I could only remember thick black eyeliner. Bronte seemed impatient to get her story out. "Anyway, she turned up with Colt and her dog, Zip, a long-haired Alsatian thing. I was crouched down in the middle of the circle, covering my head with my hands while they were all shouting and throwing cans at me." She stopped, looking worried. "I don't know whether you'll be able to clean my blazer. It's got all beer and Coke down it."

Colin rolled another joint. I stroked Bronte's hair. "I don't care about the blazer, love. We can sort it out." I did wonder how I would ever say no to anything again.

"I tried to run out of the circle but the dog started barking at me. Stace came over to get the dog and then she recognised me from the day that Tarants got hurt. She shouted at them to leave me alone. She told me I shouldn't be hanging about in the graveyard when it was dark and asked me where you were. So I explained what had happened, you know, about the top in Next and stuff. She said you'd be worried and told me to go home. The others didn't believe that she knew me, they thought she was just being wet and kept telling her she'd get chucked out of the gang."

I was ashamed that a part of me wanted to swing round and say, "See? See?" to Colin and remind him what an arsehole he'd been when Tarants had hurt himself. I wished my life was like Clover's where thank yous could be sent by Interflora to people who lived at the same address for more than three months. I'd be lucky to bump into Stace again.

Like Colin, I listened in silence as Bronte told me how Stace had had a big screaming match with Colt because she'd dared to mention Tarants — ex-boyfriend and rival gang member — when she was explaining about Bronte. Colt had smacked her in the mouth, but Stace hadn't gone without a fight either.

"Was she okay?" I said.

"Not really. The others stood round laughing. Colt's the head of the gang so I think he was really angry that she'd dissed him. Her tooth cut her lip so her mouth was bleeding. Then Colt made it worse cos he wears a studded bracelet and it slashed her face. She went nuts at him. He tried to hold her back but she just kept kicking and kicking." Bronte's face was all fidgety and tense.

"What did you do, lovey?" I twisted my hair round and round my finger until it hurt.

"That's just it, Mum. I didn't do anything. There were about seven of them, all clapping and cheering, watching Stace get really hurt. I was so frightened. Colt pushed her over and she hit her head on one of the gravestones. The dog went for Colt, so Stace grabbed me and we ran for ages. She was worried about them coming after us so we went a really long way round all the back streets until we got to that pub by the roundabout. She made me hide by the bins while she got herself cleaned up in the toilets. Then she phoned Tarants. He didn't want to come at first cos he was at some club. But when she told him she was with me, he said he'd come and fetch me. It took him ages to get

130

there, though. Stace bought us some KFC and we waited in a bus shelter because it was so cold."

In the end Bronte looked like she could stay up all night, whereas Colin looked on the verge of collapse. His unspent fury seemed to have turned in on itself. Great surges of shock carried me from one horror to another — drug addict graveyards, bullying teenagers, aggressive dogs — mixed with a sing out loud high that Bronte had made it home safely.

Colin took her upstairs. Bronte had begged to sleep in our bed and neither of us wanted to let her out of our sight. When I went up ten minutes later, they were both flat out. Colin hadn't even bothered to get undressed. He lay with his arm around Bronte who was curled up into his warmth, her face pale, but smooth and unworried. Bronte, one day older. Me, ten years.

I couldn't contemplate getting into bed and going to sleep. My head was buzzing. I wanted to phone everyone, wake up Sandy and get drunk to a point where I wouldn't be asking myself any questions. Life had offered me a second chance. Mr Peters had said to call him if there was any news. I really wanted to talk to someone though, someone who could offer me more than the different types of torture they would inflict on the Eastward gang at a later date. I decided to let the phone ring five times. He picked up on the second ring. "Maia?"

I was thrown by the use of my Christian name. We'd been fannying about Mr and Mrs-ing for weeks. Shyness made me stumble.

"Sorry to be disturbing you so late."

"It's fine, no problem. Is everything okay? Hang on a minute, I'll just turn the music down."

Michael Bublé was singing in the background, then cut off in his prime. Mr Peters came back on the line. "Is there some news?"

I gave him a quick rundown of events. I heard his smile. "That's brilliant. Thank God she's not hurt. We need to get together and work out how to manage Bronte's return to school. Could you come to my office before school starts on Monday, say, eight o'clock?"

"Yes, of course," I said, preparing to hang up.

"Don't rush off. Please." I heard the sound of a door opening and closing and the thud of feet on a wooden floor. "Where's Bronte now? Was she very distressed when she got home?"

I couldn't stop thinking that it was almost midnight and that I should deliver my message and get lost, so I started off "Yes/no/fine". Every answer seemed to lead to another question and eventually I stopped trying to hurry off the phone. Somewhere along the way a bit of banter crept in but it wasn't like chatting to Sandy or even Clover. Every now and again I'd feel self-conscious, squirming because I'd been too familiar. Or used terrible grammar.

"How is your husband, er, partner — Colin, isn't it? — coping in all of this?" The elephant in the corner swinging its trunk and squirting water down its back had finally made an appearance.

"Colin's okay. He's asleep now. Bronte is his princess, so he's found it really hard. Anyway, I'd better let you go now. Thanks for listening to me ramble on."

"You make sure you look after yourself. Get some rest. We'll talk on Monday. One more thing, when we're not at school, you can call me Zachary. Or Zac. Mr Peters makes me feel ninety-five."

I was saying goodnight for the second time when I heard a woman's voice in the background, I didn't catch it all, but I did hear "little chat" and "like a stuffed lemon". I rang off quickly.

Shit. Why didn't he say he had company? What if I'd called him as he was about to get down to business? I remembered Michael Bublé in the background and cringed. Then with no rights, no reason, no warning, the shock of an emotion that I didn't know I was still capable of feeling. Jealousy.

CHAPTER
THIRTEEN

When we got to Stirling Hall on Monday, it felt like five years since I'd last been there. I'd already been up for three hours, done my cleaning shift and rushed home to change. Bronte seemed to have brushed off the whole thing, nattering about seeing Sorrel and Saffy again and somehow turning her role of failed shoplifter and blubbering wreck into some kind of brave, dog-handling heroine. Harley was getting a bit fed up with her being the centre of attention and was saying, "Big deal" to everything. I kept rubbing my lips together. Lipstick always made me feel self-conscious. My early morning eyes were threatening to stream against the unfamiliar mascara.

I parked next to Mr Peters' Audi round the back as he had told me, expecting one of the crusty old secretaries to come flying out at any minute to tell me deliveries were round the other side. As soon as I got out of the van, he was at the door.

"Good morning. Come on in. I've made some coffee. Morning, Harley. You can go straight up to your classroom. Hello, Bronte, how are you?"

Shyness made her whisper.

"No need to be embarrassed. We all make mistakes. It's part of growing up. Remind me to tell you about my eagle tattoo one day."

Bronte looked at me, grinning at this unexpected gem of information that would no doubt fly round 4H. I wasn't sure whether he was joking or not. He looked over at me and winked. Apparently it didn't take much to make me blush these days. Harley raised his eyebrows and gave me a little wave as he disappeared off down the corridor.

In Mr Peters' office I sat in awe as he talked Bronte through what had happened at the school when she was missing, what the other children knew, how to handle their questions. He was serious but kind, and by the time he had finished Bronte was sitting up straight and answering in a strong voice. That alone was choking me up. Bronte was picking up where she left off. I, on the other hand, felt as though I was held together with a paperclip. I didn't want to leave her.

"I'm going to get one of the Year Sixes to take you down to your classroom now while I have a word with your mum," he said, picking up the phone. Bronte hopped up without a care in the world as though Fucked-up Friday was just a summer fly to be flicked away. I was holding on to myself with the tiniest thread of control, everything sucked in as though I was doing the longest pelvic floor exercise in the world. Luckily, a well-spoken boy arrived and started asking Bronte about a picture she'd painted for the display in the corridor.

"Bye, Mum, see you later." No kiss. No "Don't worry about me, I won't do anything stupid". Then just as she got to the door, she ran back and threw her arms around me. She whispered, "Love you." I managed my own strangled reply and clung on to the tears that were gathering along my lower eyelids until Bronte had left the room.

I headed for the door. "I'm sorry, I'm going to have to talk to you another day."

Mr Peters walked in front of me and closed the office door. I heard the lock click. He pulled me round to face him. "Maia. It's really normal to feel like this. You've been through such a lot. Here." He passed me some tissues. I wanted to blow my nose but instead opted for some ineffectual dabbing. I was trying to laugh it off, shrugging and making cracked-voiced jokes about winning the award for the wettest mother in the world.

He took me by the shoulders. Up close, he could have persuaded me to do anything with those eyes. "Look at me. You're doing a great job. It hasn't all come together in the way you wished yet, but you are your children's best chance of a good future. Trust me. You're doing the right thing."

Obviously being nice to me was a mistake. No amount of lip biting could get the blubbing genie back into its box after that. I looked away. Stared down at those shiny shoes in between great swipes of Kleenex. I saw him step closer and felt the light touch of his arms go round my shoulders. Tentative, polite.

"I'm so sorry. I didn't mean to upset you."

Something in me gave up trying to get a grip. I leant into him and sobbed, while he stroked my hair. At some point I realised that his fingers were massaging my scalp. It was so soothing, I wanted to close my eyes and stand there all day but as my snivelling subsided, I became aware of the sounds of the school, the banging of doors, voices, footsteps. This bloke had a job to do beyond offering the feel-good factor to screwball parents.

I looked up. I had to tilt my head right back. He must have been a good eight inches taller than me.

"Sorry. Sorry about that. I'd better go. You've got work to do," I said.

His fingers left my hair and he loosened his grip on me but didn't let go. Cold air settled between us in the warm space where his chest had been. He stared down. "You've got nothing to apologise for."

The 8.30 bell ringing outside his office made us both jump. I pulled away, smoothing down my T-shirt and pushing my hair off my face.

He cleared his throat. "No need to rush off. Take your time." I searched his face for clues that scalp massage didn't come as part of the package with Stirling Hall's fat fees. That given two bottles of wine, Marvin Gaye and a darkened room, we would have had skin against skin. He rubbed his hands over his face. His eyes found mine. Again, that tiny glint of amusement. He looked away before I did. When he looked back again, he'd decided to say something. It was all there in the set of his jaw, and those eyes, no longer laughing.

Before he said a word, there was a knock at the door. I wanted to dive underneath his desk. Mr Peters pointed to a chair and mouthed, "Sit down" at me. He straightened his tie and threw the door open.

His secretary busied in with a bundle of papers, which she put on his desk and then launched into questions about coaches for rugby matches. Mr Peters brushed her off with "I'm just finishing my meeting with Ms Etxeleku, then I'll be right through."

The secretary looked round at me. "There. I could have saved myself the trouble. I've just printed out a reminder for you. Your lunch fees are overdue. I know what it's like, everything's so busy, the little things get overlooked. If you could let me have them as soon as possible." With a jolly smile, she trotted out. I could have taken her bustling little arse and kicked her into next week.

Mr Peters turned back to me, rolling his eyes. "Anyway, where were we?" His voice was clipped, any trace of teasing gone. "Right. I will keep a close eye on Bronte and let you know how she gets on. In the meantime, take care of yourself. You've had an appalling shock and it wouldn't surprise me if there was a delayed reaction. Try and get some rest if you can."

Rest. There was no time for me to rest. I couldn't fit my life in as it was, and I certainly didn't have time for nice little siestas in between buckets of bleach. That silk tie I'd managed to bawl all over probably cost more than a term's lunches. I got up. "Thanks for everything, I mean, the stuff with Bronte, but with Harley as well. You've been very kind to us, Mr Peters."

He sighed. "You can call me Zac."

CHAPTER
FOURTEEN

As I was driving out of school, Clover was in front of me. Her hazard lights came on and she pulled up onto the verge, scoring deep grooves into the turf despite the stern "No Parking on the Grass" signs. She ran towards me in mud-encrusted jodhpurs, a backless mohair jumper and silver wellies. She scooped me into a bear hug, all pillowy bosoms and patchouli oil perfume, with a tinge of greasy hair and booze.

Squeezing my hands tightly, she pulled back from me and launched into her usual scattergun approach. "Maia, thank God. Are you okay? Christ, you look knackered. Then, fucking hell, what do I expect? Is Bronte all right? My two were inconsolable on Friday night. They wouldn't even go to the disco. Said they couldn't dance while they were worrying about Bronte. Is Colin all right? And Harley? Bless him, he must have had a terrible fright."

I thanked her for searching for Bronte and filled her in, cutting corners in the telling as the minute details didn't seem so important any more. In particular, I skated over the community centre and my reunion with Tarants. Clover had welcomed my kids as though they snorkelled in the Bahamas on a regular basis and

139

clip-clopped about with the pony set at the weekends. She didn't need the gory details of our real lives. I didn't want to scare her into locking up the family jewels every time the Caudwell/Etxeleku children visited.

I kept stumbling over what I was saying anyway because Clover's appearance was putting me off. She always looked a bit eccentric but today she'd taken the term "bedhead" to extreme. She resembled one of Bronte's trolls, which was not a kind thought to have about my one posh friend. Her face looked ruddier than normal as though she'd been walking on craggy peaks in wind and rain. As I spoke, she seemed to be struggling to concentrate. When I got to the bit about Bronte turning up late in the evening, soaked to the skin, she started to cry, her face crumpling up like an old piece of tinfoil.

"Clover, it's okay. She's back safely. Really. You don't need to be upset. It's been a horrible time, but it's going to be all right now." Clover's sobs grew louder until her shoulders were heaving and I was asking myself at what point you should smack someone to stop them getting hysterical. Belting someone when they'd already lost the plot had always seemed like such an odd thing to do but I was definitely considering it. Out of the corner of my eye, I saw Jen1 driving past, craning her little chicken neck to see what was going on. Bloody ambulance chaser.

I put my arm round Clover. "Come on, we can't stand here. The whole of the school will be pointing us out as the freak show."

"Have you got time to come back to mine for a coffee?" Actually, it was more of a "glub, glub, sniff, coffee, sob," but I got the gist. Clover looked so done in, I resigned myself to staying up till midnight to do the pile of ironing I'd taken in for one of my customers. I was puzzled that Clover was still in such a state over Bronte. I didn't have her down as a drama queen.

"Are you sure that's all right? Will Lawrence be there?" I asked.

The mention of Lawrence seemed to turn Clover into a sprinkler, waving about and squirting water in all directions. It was a slow process but a light was beginning to go on in my brain.

"Come on, I'll follow you." I poked Clover towards the car and opened the door for her. "Go really slowly."

We came into Clover's drive. Instead of parking right up by the house, she stopped inside the gate. It didn't take me long to see why. Two panels of the drawing room bay window had shattered across the drive and part of the wooden frame was buckled in the middle.

"Christ. Have you been burgled?"

Clover shook her head and heaved open the front door. I followed her into the kitchen.

The state of the house today made the last time I came look like a trip to a hi-tech isolation ward. Parrot shit covered the slate floor tiles. At least three days' worth of plates, mugs and bowls sat among piles of crumbs and toast crusts on the pine table. Two bin bags overflowed, balanced against the kitchen units. Jesus. There had to be a rat in there somewhere. I guided Clover to a chair.

"Let me make you a drink," I said. There was no bloody way I was using a mug I hadn't washed personally. Clover sat down, rubbing her face on her jumper. I plunged my hand into the murky pool in the sink and pulled out a couple of slimy mugs. I sucked some water into an empty bottle of washing up liquid and prayed that the hot tap would deliver on its promise. Thank heavens for the Aga. I made the coffee and watched in dismay as globs of milk curdled on the top. I didn't want to embarrass Clover but I couldn't let her drink cottage cheese.

"The milk seems to be slightly off. Is there any more anywhere?"

"Fucking hell." She didn't answer, just leaned onto the table with her head on her arms and started crying again. "I can't do anything right."

"It's okay. I'll drink mine black."

"I'll have water."

I felt exhausted just managing to produce two drinks that weren't going to give us diarrhoea.

I waited. It was a technique I'd learnt from Mr Peters, who could probably winkle out the true extent of my debts and the colour of my underwear by sitting there silently. It worked. Clover lifted her head. "Lawrence has left me."

"God, Clover. You poor thing. Why?"

"He won't speak to me at the moment but he stormed out on Friday night after I'd got back from looking for Bronte. Said some quite horrible things that I didn't realise he felt."

"Do the children know?"

142

"No, they think he's away on business. He's been such a grump lately, I think they're glad he's not around."

I was still trying to get the hang of acceptable middle-class conversation. Talking money, especially the exact numbers Sandy and I liked to discuss — earnings, the cost of a new telly, size of mortgage or in our case, rent — was as ill-mannered as picking your nose at the dinner table. I was less sure about the boundaries when it came to husband shortcomings, though I was pretty sure Clover wouldn't do a Sandy and start telling me the noises Lawrence made when he was having sex. I sat patiently waiting for Clover to open up, pulling a face at my milkless coffee.

She got to her feet. "You'd better come and look." We walked through an oak panelled hall, where the early February sunlight streamed through a stained glass roof dome. Dust swirled around us as we walked. Clover showed me into the "drawing room". It looked as though a bunch of ravers had recently packed up. The remains of a grandfather clock lay split open, poking through the broken bay window, brass guts everywhere, like something from the Dalí paintings the prof loved so much. A cold breeze was blowing in through the gaps. No one had thought to take down Clover's lovely silk curtains, which were watermarked from the rain.

"The kids were so worried about Bronte that they couldn't settle, so I suggested making a camp in the drawing room to distract them. Just a bit of fun with blankets and cushions and stuff. Orion wanted to convert it into a racetrack for their mountain bikes. I wasn't that keen but it's a hard floor so I didn't want to be the fun monitor either. We moved all the furniture to the side of the room, but when I went out to make some popcorn, Orion had the bright idea of leaping the coffee table. He managed to clip his back wheel and crashed into the grandfather clock at a bit of a pelt. Which, as you can see, smashed through the window." She kicked at some glass fragments on the floor.

"Was he hurt?"

"He bruised his shoulder but he was okay. More pissed off that he'd lost the bet with the twins, I think."

"I'm guessing that when Lawrence came back, he was pretty hacked off?" I was gobsmacked at Clover's easy-come, easy-go attitude to the damage. The clock on its own must have been worth several thousands.

"Lawrence was livid. Told me I was an unfit parent who needed to grow up and stop letting the kids run wild. He said he was sick of living in a shit pit with an idle fat arse fed by a trust fund, while he was out there working his nuts off in an industry full of wankers, just so my family didn't think I'd married a loser."

She ran her hand through her hair, which made it stand up even more. She really did look like she could live under a bridge. She gazed round the room. "I know the house is a bit of a state but he'd always told me he'd hate to be married to someone who fussed about with a duster. I didn't even know the mess bothered him. He'd never said anything before."

I could see why Lawrence might have a problem with coming home to a lounge crunchy underfoot with glass after a long day at work. Mountain biking in the drawing room? Hel-looo? Nothing as freaking normal as a bit of PlayStation or a few Hama beads. Then I remembered that Clover was my friend, which automatically put Lawrence in the wrong. My newly discovered keeping silent skills soon hit the buffers. "You've got a trust fund?" I was finding it hard to match the bag lady in front of me with the Cambridge graduates, pearls and flowing frocks of my imagination. I remembered too late that discussing money was common.

"My grandfather made a fortune dredging clay out of rivers to use in building. Lawrence has always hated the fact that I have my own money, especially without working, because he knows that however much he earns, I'll always have more. He's a flaming northern dinosaur, thinks it's a chap's responsibility to bring home the bacon. He's typically working class with a great big chip on his shoulder, thinks that anyone who inherits money is a spoilt nincompoop."

I tried not to be offended by Clover's view of the working classes.

Her problems should have made me feel great about Colin's willingness to sit on the settee while I brought in every penny. They didn't. Having a problem with your wife's trust fund seemed like a wonderful worry to have.

"I try not to use the money, or at least, not let him know I'm using it, but the truth is, the arse has dropped out of the bonuses in the City and if it weren't for me

145

topping up our cash from the trust fund, we'd have had to move."

"Why does he have a problem with it now? What's changed?" I asked.

"I don't know really. I've always thought that he was happy for the kids to have what he never did. Recently he's started holding forth about them being brats and taking everything for granted. I don't know what I'll do if he never comes back."

"There's something I could help you with."

Clover raised a tiny eyebrow of hope. "What?"

"I can clean. Perhaps if you got the house sorted out, he might feel like talking to you?"

"I can't have you cleaning my house, Maia. I really can't. That's just too much to ask. I've never had cleaners. Lawrence thinks it's despicable to get other people to clean up your crap," Clover said.

"Clover, it's what I do for a living. You should see some of the places I clean."

As in, they never get anywhere near as filthy as this.

"If it hadn't been for you and your kids, we'd never have made any friends at Stirling Hall. You were the only one who didn't look down on us, probably still are. Lawrence doesn't have to know."

"I'll pay you." Clover's voice had taken on a pleading tone.

"I don't want paying," I said.

"Maia, don't be so stupid. I need a job doing and if you're going to give up your time to do it, then I'm going to pay you."

146

We argued backwards and forwards without agreeing, until I marched through to the kitchen and armed myself with a dustpan and brush, black sacks, polish and dusters still in their packets.

Seeing me in motion seemed to jolt Clover out of her misery-filled fog and quite soon we had a good rhythm going — me sweeping all the bits of broken glass out of the corners of the room and Clover hoovering them up. I asked her what she wanted to do with the grandfather clock. "Goodness knows. I didn't even like it. Let's stuff it in a sack. I'll stick it in the garage," she said, poking a brass dial with her toe.

Make do and mend seemed alien to Clover. While we worked, bits of information about her life slipped out, almost as though she was trying to grasp how she'd got from there to here. Lawrence was dirt poor when he was growing up. She'd bumped into him in Hyde Park when she was bunking off finishing school. I didn't even realise "finishing schools" still existed.

"Never did like flower arranging. Stilettos are the death of me, though I can get out of the car without flashing my knickers." Lawrence was a trainee accountant but her family had still been horrified. "He was so prickly. He used to come to dinner wearing PETA T-shirts and sit with his elbows on the table, lecturing my mother about her fur coat."

"I didn't have Lawrence down as an accountant." The backs of my thighs complained as I shoved the big leather settee back into place.

"He'd just done it to get out of Manchester, some scheme for clever kids from poor homes, sponsored by one of the big accounting firms. He didn't want to sponge off me, so I suppose he got sucked into it. He hates not being able to pay his way. Like most young men, he wanted to be a rock star. He's a great singer."

Yep. I could see Lawrence in drainpipes and Sex Pistols T-shirts.

Clover stood back with her hands on her hips. "Fucking hell, Maia. This looks great. I'm going to have to lock the kids in the cellar so they don't mess it up."

"There's still loads to do. No slacking."

"No slacking? This is the most cleaning I've done in years. My mother couldn't relax if a curtain wasn't hanging straight or there was a fingerprint on the window. I obviously don't take after her."

I handed her a bottle of ancient copper cleaner I'd found at the back of the cupboard. "I'll do the wood round the fireplace. You get going on the surround."

Clover hopped to it, her jodhpurs giving her a fetching builder's bum as she got to work on all fours. "I never thought I'd see the day when cleaning made me feel better. Now I do. Thanks, darling. I hope Lawrence comes back to see it."

"I'm sure he will." I wondered if Clover could see the flashing thought bubble above my head that read, "Has he gone off with someone else?" She'd perked up so much, I decided we could pick over possible colleague shagging another day. I pulled out the little occasional tables to polish and discovered water rings like a Spirograph drawing and several attempts by Sorrel at carving her name. I took better care of my Formica

148

kitchen table. Coasters were obviously for the working classes.

I hoovered up the dead earwigs from behind the curtains, sucked out a range of food crumbs from down the back of the settee and cleaned the windows that had escaped the collision with the mountain bike and grandfather clock. Clover had brightened up, singing "We Are the Champions" into the polish can as the drawing room became less of a tip and more of a place for butlers and trays of champagne. We hatched a plan. I would come in for two hours a day for the next month, straight after the new early morning shift I'd started at a gym.

And, yes, I would let Clover pay me. I couldn't afford not to.

CHAPTER
FIFTEEN

By the time the school musical, *Oliver!* rolled around on the day before half-term, I was practically singing "Consider Yourself" in my sleep. Clover had lent us the CD and no breakfast time was complete without the children warbling "Food, Glorious Food". I often walked into the front room to find Harley practising some nifty footwork for "You've Got to Pick-a-Pocket or Two". He'd taken to preening himself in the mirror and making speeches to the audience.

Colin kept poking him and saying, "I hope you ain't going to turn into one of them bleeding ballet dancing poofters, like that bloke, who was it? Billy Elliot. You wanna get yerself a proper job." Stones, glasshouses and all that. Whenever I mentioned Colin coming to watch, his stock response was "I've heard it here five million times. Why do I need to come to the school?"

In the end, I knew he wouldn't let Harley down. I was more nervous about how Colin would perform than Harley.

When the evening arrived, people were crowding up the red carpet that led into the school. I looked round for Mr Peters. As Head of Upper School, I was pretty sure he would be there, but I could only see the headmaster who was greeting parents by name and wafting them inside. The men were moving along in tailor-made suits and silk ties, the women a swirl of floaty dresses and Jimmy Choos. Colin had refused to change out of his West Ham United shirt, clinging to it like a toddler to a teddy. He brightened up when he spotted the sixth formers going up and down the queue with trays of wine. "Great, free booze. Do you think they've got any Newkie Brown?"

I was staring ahead, perfecting my art of not hearing any whispers in the crowd around us. Colin belched. Out of the corner of my eye, I saw him stick an empty glass on the tray and snatch up another one. I couldn't wait to get inside where I would be able to hiss at him. I nudged him with my foot.

"What?" he said.

"You're only supposed to have one."

"Where does it say that?"

I sighed and looked away. I wished I'd come on my own. As we stepped through the door, I found myself standing in front of Mr Peters. I hadn't been that close to him since the morning Bronte went back to school. Just occasionally I'd caught his eye across the playground, which had been enough to make my belly do a little backflip. Standing right next to him shot a burst of heat through my body. I was desperate to stand on tiptoes and sniff his neck. Colin squirting Lynx under his arms and down his crotch didn't have the same pull.

"Ms Etxeleku. Mr Caudwell. Good evening. I saw the dress rehearsal earlier on and I think you will be very impressed with Harley. Please do go through and take a seat," Mr Peters said, waving us through into the hall. With its wood panelling, ornate ceiling and raised seating, I felt as though I was stepping into a West End theatre. At Morlands, I'd been grateful to squeeze half a buttock onto a folding chair.

A tiny corner of my mind was slightly disappointed that Mr Peters hadn't reserved a special little comment for me. Thirty-six going on thirteen. "Let's sit at the front," Colin said, barging through a group of people dithering about the best place to sit "from an acoustic point of view".

Colin stopped in the middle of the front row, picking up the programme on his seat. He'd barely had time to plonk down, when Jen1 came scuttling up. "Excuse me, these seats are reserved."

"What do you mean, reserved?" Colin said.

"There's a whole group of us sitting together, which is why we got here early and put our programmes on the seats."

"I can't see no sign that says reserved. How am I gonna look at a programme and think, oh yeah, that's the seat belonging to the blonde over there? I'm not, am I? I'm gonna think, great, someone's done a good job, they've put a programme out for me."

Jen1's eyes narrowed to little slits. "Mr Etxeleku, I understand you've had rather a problematic time of late with Bronte going missing, so I will excuse your attitude, but I would be grateful if you would move elsewhere as we have already reserved these seats."

152

"Look, love. First things first. I ain't Mr Etxeleku, I'm Mr Caudwell. And secondly, darling, I ain't moving and me attitude has got nothing to do with Bronts. This is me, right, I'm like this. If you wanted to sit here, you should've got your little arsicle on the seat. Maia, sit down."

I was in no man's land, knees bent, halfway between sitting down and running away. "Come on, Colin, look, there are still loads of seats left." I pulled at his arm and pointed towards the back.

"You move if you like, but I'm staying here. Miss Thimble Tits can bugger off and sit somewhere else."

I don't know who gasped first — me or Jen1. Colin did have a point, though. Under that halter-neck top, her chest did look like a couple of hazelnuts nailed onto a stick. Just when I thought the Caudwell/Etxeleku family might add being led away by Stirling Hall security to its list of honours, Jen1 poked Colin in the chest, told him he was a nasty, vulgar little man, then spun round on her stiletto spikes and stomped off. Colin sat down, laughing and congratulating himself on showing that nobby woman a thing or two, banging on about her needing a good shag until the lights went down and the curtains swished back.

I'd been expecting a few children prancing about with tambourines, triangles and a couple of drums against a papier mâché backdrop. Instead, to the side of the stage, a full orchestra belted out "Food, Glorious Food" while Frederica's son, Marlon, stepped into the spotlight and made Oliver all his own. Even Colin was nodding and whispering, "Bloody hell, he's good."

153

I forgot about Jen1, about Colin, as the energy poured off the stage, each carefully timed foot stamp, each pair of outstretched arms sucking me into the story. I was waiting for the moment when Harley would appear as the Artful Dodger. I barely recognised him when he burst onto the stage, his front teeth blacked out and his hair spiked up. He turned to Oliver, and with a wave of his hand, launched into "Consider Yourself". This wasn't the pale boy who sat blubbing in Mr Peters' office a month ago. This was my son, in charge and confident. Colin slipped his hand into mine and squeezed. I squeezed back. My eyes prickled. When Harley pulled a pocket watch from Fagin's waistcoat, the crowd clapped, everyone laughed and cheered. I felt as though I was on stage myself. I glanced at Colin. He didn't normally do "poncey musicals". Without a sneer on his face, he looked almost handsome.

When the curtain came down for the interval, an announcement that drinks were being served in the refectory got Colin scooting to his feet. Pupils from the senior school were moving through the parents with trays of wine and orange juice. I sent up a prayer that I'd be able to keep the show on the road long enough for Bronte and Harley to stay on for the sixth form. These kids were probably only sixteen or seventeen but they seemed so confident. They looked like models to me. There was something so wholesome about them. All that shiny hair and straight teeth. And straight backs, as though they were sure of their place in the world. They didn't have that ready-to-pounce tension, that wary look that the teenagers round our way had.

154

They were so charming. When Colin started talking in a posh voice, asking dumb questions about the vintage of the red wine he was about to chuck down his throat, the young girl smiled like someone in a toothpaste ad and said, "I don't know which year it's from, but I'll get the bottle for you."

Colin winked at me. "Result!"

I looked round to see who I knew. Jen1 was on the other side of the room with her usual bunch of witches, looking angular and tense. I had no doubt that Colin would be a hot topic. I saw Frederica come in, chin up, red carpet poise as though she was about to get papped. She made a beeline for us.

"Isn't Harley amazing? Has he had training? No? He's a natural. You should encourage that. I see very, very few children who have that sort of stage presence, even the ones who've been at Italia Conti since they could walk."

I introduced her to Colin, leading him into the conversation by pointing out that Frederica's son, Marlon, was playing Oliver. Thankfully, even Colin's gnat-sized social skills ran to congratulating her on how good Marlon was. "Haven't I seen you on telly? Weren't you in *Lewis*? That lecturer who got suspended for copping off with a student?" he said.

"I can never get away from my shady past." Frederica flicked her hair back over her shoulder.

"You look much slimmer in real life. And younger."

Frederica grabbed Colin's arm and snuggled up to him. "They did make me up to look older but all compliments welcome." She turned to me. "Such a

155

charmer. Maia, you didn't tell me you had such a gorgeous husband at home. Where have you been hiding him?"

To be honest, I wished he'd stayed hidden but I could've hugged Frederica for making the effort. Colin was all flirtatious, asking Frederica for backstage gossip. I wanted to hear it too, but hadn't asked because I didn't want to look like some desperate groupie. I kept waiting for Frederica to make a "must get another drink" excuse but she stood there for ages, happily dishing the dirt on her co-stars. "Gordon? Looks like someone's jolly uncle on screen, but he's got a nasty temper. The one that plays the blonde sidekick? Not as sexy as she looks. I would say that, wouldn't I? Just jealous, you know. Once she gets that make-up off, skin's terrible. Good boobs though, if you're a boob man."

Frederica was flannelling away about Harley getting his good looks from Colin when Clover joined us. I tapped Colin on the arm and he quickly nodded an "All right?" in Clover's direction without bothering to shake her hand before drooling back to Frederica. Actresses in clingy red dresses were higher up Colin's pecking order than housewives in linen sacks. I consoled myself that Lawrence wasn't Mr Manners either.

"How are you doing?" I said.

"I never come to school functions without Lawrence. I feel as though everyone's looking at me."

"I'm sure they're not. They're probably too busy looking at who's got the latest handbag. If only we knew what the latest handbag was, we could join in."

156

Clover managed a little smile. "It's not fair on the kids, though. He told Orion that he was going to be in New York so he couldn't come but I bet he's in some hotel in Hackney licking chocolate sauce off a twenty-year-old's nipples."

"Ssshhh." I looked round but no one seemed to be listening.

"Well, it's true, isn't it? I mean, not necessarily a twenty-year-old and maybe not chocolate sauce. Maybe he's having dinner with someone my age who only eats tofu and alfalfa sprouts and drinks camomile tea and has an arse half the size of mine. Or someone who licks the bloody skirting boards clean every day and irons underpants and always has things like cocktail nuts and petits fours in the cupboard and a spare pair of tights in her handbag." She looked like she was about to burst into tears.

I would have loved to have joined in with a hundred other ideas of the sort of scuzzy old — or young — women Lawrence might have taken up with in the hope of making Clover laugh, but I couldn't risk it in case I didn't hit the spot and made her cry. Instead I grabbed a glass of wine from a passing sixth former and thrust it in her direction.

"Come on, we'll get him back for you. We'll make your house into such a palace that he won't want to live in some scummy bedsit. All men have a mid-life crisis." I glanced over my shoulder. "I think Frederica is Colin's."

"Do you mind?" Clover asked.

"Couldn't give a shit." The truth of that depressed me. I was glad when the bell rang for us all to go back in. I tapped Colin who said, "You go, I'll be along in a minute, just finish my drink." I looked back to see him necking his wine and having a quick minesweep of a couple of glasses nearby. Clover and I left him to it.

Jen1 reached the door at the same time as me. "Harley makes a fantastic Artful Dodger. You should be really proud of him."

"Thank you." I felt embarrassed. I wasn't sure how to handle praise.

"Then again, I suppose the accent comes easier to him than to the others."

She was gone before my brain caught up with what she meant. I would get her back. One of these days I would wipe that smile off her mean little Botoxed mouth.

Clover squeezed my arm as she left me to squash into her row at the back. "Bloody bitch. Don't take any notice."

Colin squeaked into the seat next to me a couple of seconds before the curtain went up causing great huffing and puffing from the other parents in our row. Colin jigged away in his seat to the music, making loud, though mostly complimentary, comments. I just wanted the show to be over so I could scoop up Harley and shut the door on this weird world, where nothing I did was right. I tried to focus on the story, but the fake Cockney accents didn't seem so funny to me any more. The huge cheer that Harley got at the end, the sheer joy shining out of his face took the edge off my grump, but

I was still the first one out of my seat when the curtain went down for the last time.

"Hang on, hang on, where's the fire?" Colin said, struggling to pull out his jacket from under the chair. He always took his shoes off wherever he sat down, so he still had to put his trainers back on.

"I'm really hot. I'll wait for you outside." I marched out of the hall and headed towards the exit. Mr Peters was standing there with a couple of teaching assistants I recognised from Bronte's year. I said goodbye without making eye contact and burst out into the cold spring air, scurrying across the lawn to wait on a low wall for Colin and Harley, tucked away in the shadows. By the time I looked up, Mr Peters was walking towards me.

"Are you okay?" he said, when he got within talking distance.

"Fine, thanks. Just a bit hot."

"I told you Harley was brilliant. You should be really proud of him."

"I am proud of him. Just as he is." Mr Peters must have caught the curtness in my voice. A puzzled look crossed his face. He raised his eyebrows as though he was expecting me to say something else. I stared up, wanting to pick a fight. He didn't look away and I felt myself unknotting under his gaze, all my wrinkles and crinkles straightening out. I could even feel the beginnings of a tiny smile. He sat down next to me.

"Are you always this self-contained?" he said. I was aware, in a distant way, of two people of different sexes sitting a smidge too close. If I leaned a bit to the left I would have been touching him.

I turned to look at him. "I'm not self-contained with people who know me, but it's hard to be myself when everyone's judging me the whole time."

"I hope you don't put me in that category?"

"Well, aren't you?"

Mr Peters shook his head slowly. "No, I'm not, Maia."

The noisy chatter of parents pouring out of the school floated across the lawn. I blocked it out. Our eyes were doing that dance, mirroring each other, flicking about but never releasing each other. It felt as intimate as tracing his lips with my fingers. Mr Peters broke free first. "Okay. If you're all right, I'd better go and do my bit of PR for the evening. Don't forget you can always give me a ring if there's anything you want to discuss."

I had to hand it to him. He did professional well. And personal, very well indeed.

I stared after him, watching him stride across the lawn. Harley and Colin appeared at the exit as Mr Peters took up his position by the door. They shook hands and Mr Peters pointed Colin in my direction. "All right, love?" Colin said, as he ambled over, shoelaces undone and something a bit unsteady about his walk. We walked back to the van, Harley nattering on, asking whether I noticed he sang the wrong line, if I thought he'd been as good as Marlon, if any of the teachers had said anything about him. For once, Colin's compliments were genuine, with no advice about how to improve things.

160

Colin took my hand as we got to the van. "That school ain't as bad as I thought. Few toffee-nosed parents but Harley's doing good there. I liked that Peters bloke. I told him that I thought the place would be full of wankers but that it had been a nice surprise, like." He leant into my ear and I could smell the wine on him. "Let's get Harley into bed quick when we get home. I feel like giving you a bit of a seeing-to."

Mr Peters was going to have to come to the rescue again, in mind, if not in body.

CHAPTER
SIXTEEN

Policemen have a different knock from friends. Or postmen. Or meter readers. And bailiffs have a different knock from them all. It was the first day back after half-term and I was in that last stressy five minutes before leaving for school. Bronte was complaining that I hadn't done her plaits properly, there was the usual faff to find a pen for me to sign the homework book, plus the discovery that nothing in our cupboard could pass for a "plain" biscuit. A thump on the front door told me I was about to see a meaty fist poking through some splintered wood. I hoped it was one of Colin's grebbo friends come for the repayment of a gambling debt. Harley rushed to open the door, but I shoved in front of him.

I put the chain on and shouted at Bronte to go and get Colin out of bed. One bloody hurdle after another. I opened the door and smiled through the gap. "Hello. Can I help you?"

For a bailiff, he wasn't as brick shithousey as some. I didn't think I'd beat him at an arm wrestle, though. I glanced down at his hands to see if he had any pliers in them, but he just had an ID card which he held close to the door with a gruff "Bailiffs. Need to auction some stuff to pay your council tax debts. You get the letter saying we was coming?"

"I haven't seen a letter." I didn't tell him I'd stopped opening anything that looked like a bill and Colin wasn't much of a secretary.

"By our reckonings, you owe £375 of council tax and we've been ordered to take some stuff. Could you open up for me, love? There isn't any point resisting cos we'll just come back again." He moved a step closer to the door. I backed away. Colin came thumping past me, bare-chested and doing up his jeans. He bellowed something at me as he rushed into the kitchen, but I didn't catch it.

I adopted my most reasonable voice. "You can't come in just like that. We haven't got anything worth anything anyway."

"All right, love. No need to panic. Why don't you let me in so I can be sure that's the case, then I can report back to them and maybe they'll leave you alone?"

I hesitated. He looked like the sort of bloke who would steal a handbag off the back of a baby's pram.

"Come on, love, open up. The sooner you let me in, the sooner we can both get going."

Colin came flying out of the kitchen. He pushed me out of the way and stuck his face in the gap. "Oy, fuck off, do you hear? You ain't coming in here stealing my stuff. Now bugger off." I could see the spit flying out of his mouth and landing on the door. The guy outside started to argue that we needed to sign something so he could leave but Colin didn't give him a chance. He slammed the door shut, then turned on me.

"You stupid cow. You were about to let him in, weren't you? Don't you know fucking anything? The bloody back door was open. He could've just walked in. You've got to keep everything locked, otherwise they'll just come in, climb in through the bloody windows. I promise you, once he's in here, he'll be taking everything — TV, DVD, CD, microwave. They're always telling you to sign stuff but it's to say they can come back and take it. Bloody hell, Mai, you can be one stupid woman."

Shock gave me courage. "Well, let me tell you something. You aren't so clever yourself. If you got off your lazy arse and got a bloody job instead of pissing all my money up a wall, because let's face it, you don't bloody well earn any, we wouldn't be in a position where we had some great lummox turning up to take our stuff. So before you start having a go at me, maybe you should take a look at yourself."

There was more I wanted to say but a shooting pain across my left cheek stopped me dead. That and the force of Colin's fist knocking me into the banister, plus a follow-up slap that made my ear ring.

"You fucking bitch." He marched off into the kitchen where I heard him rattle the jar I kept pound coins in for milk and bread. Then the back door slammed.

I put my hand up. My cheek was wet where his eternity ring had caught me under the eye. I bought him that ring when I was twenty, when he just had to say "Mai?" and I'd run to him like a dog promised a Bonio. Colin had never hit me properly before. A few pushes. The odd unfriendly shove. Loads of threats about me getting a bit of "backhand". But he'd never ever hit me. I sat down on the stairs, too shocked to cry, feeling my face to check the swelling. I didn't want to look in the mirror.

I'd always despised women who let men get away with thumping them, thought they were pathetic for putting up with it. But where was I going to go? Absolutely nowhere. Just this week, the local paper had said our council would take fourteen years to clear its waiting list. I'd be bloody fifty. What was I going to do? Take the kids to Stirling Hall from a caravan on the pikey site down by the railway tracks? Could I make him leave? Bronte would want to go with him. She'd turn against me for sure. I had no choice but to keep buggering on, telling myself that I wouldn't always live like this.

I heard footsteps behind me. Harley handed me a damp tea towel. "Are you okay, Mum?" He was trying not to cry. I hugged him, told him that Dad had made a mistake, he didn't mean to hit me and asked him to fetch my sunglasses from the drawer upstairs.

We were seriously late for school but I daren't step foot outside the house without checking that the bailiff wasn't lurking, ready to spring through the door the second I took the chain off. I checked the back garden and sent Harley round to the front. He banged on the door to say all was clear and Bronte and I scuttled out like a couple of battery hens making a bid for freedom. I was shouting at the kids to hurry up when I suddenly realised there was no van to hurry to. A dry spot further up the road outlined where the van had stood until probably half an hour ago when we'd been so busy making sure all the downstairs windows were shut, it had completely escaped our notice that they'd towed the van away. I cursed myself for not parking it in the next street. My cheek throbbed and the tears I'd been hanging on to refused to cooperate and poured down my face, stinging the cut under my eye.

Harley held my hand. "I know, Mum, let's ask Sandy to take us. She won't mind. We'll still get there in time for first break. We could say that the van broke down, couldn't we? They don't have to know we're so poor they took it away, do they?" I nodded, unable to think of a better plan.

Bronte threw down her bag. "I am not going to school in a Reliant Robin. It's bad enough that we have to go in a van. I'll get the bus." She hesitated. "I'm sorry, Mum. I'm not trying to be difficult, but I can't go in that, everyone in my class will see me."

I grabbed her by the arm and dragged her towards Sandy's house. "You will do what you are told. I am having a shit morning, an absolutely shit day, and you are not going to make it worse. Do you hear me? Get moving, now."

I expected her to fight against me, but I think even she was shocked that Colin had thumped me, so she grumped along beside me. I banged on Sandy's door.

She opened up, a fag in one hand and a can of Coke in the other. She'd gone blonde again since I'd last seen her. "Jesus, Maia, what happened to your face?" I shrugged and darted a look towards the kids. She shook her head. Sandy was no stranger to fat lips and black eyes.

"Can you take us to the school? The bailiffs have taken the van," I said.

"Bastards. Ain't they got nothing better to do? What was it for? The leccy? They took my TV once for that. Council tax? Double bastards. They want to start picking up a bit of litter and sorting out them needles and condoms in that back alley before they start worrying about whether we've bloody paid or not. Come on, I'll get me keys."

Bronte clambered into the back, muttering away. Harley, bless him, was busily telling Sandy about how the *Top Gear* team had tried to convert a Reliant Robin into a space shuttle. I slumped in the front seat, wondering how the hell I was ever going to speak to Colin again. How was I going to get my van back without coughing up £375 plus a huge recovery fee? Without the van I couldn't work, which meant things could only get worse. It was the first time I'd really admitted to myself that my private school experiment had been madness. How I'd thought that I was going to keep the kids in rugby boots, lacrosse sticks and duffle coats when we couldn't even pay the rent on a fleapit, I didn't know. A triumph of optimism over realism. That old professor no doubt thought she was doing me a favour. In fact, all I'd really done was show my kids what they could never have.

Sandy's Reliant Robin laboured up Stirling Hall's drive as she sang, "Who ate all the pies?" Thankfully as we were over an hour late, there was no one about. "Do you want me to wait for you, sweetheart?" she said.

"No, I'll get the bus back. I don't know how long I'll be. I need to sign the kids in. Thanks a lot though." I tried to smile but my whole face creaked.

"Just call me James." She waved and skidded off down the drive, bouncing over the speed bumps till I thought the thing would tip over.

I pulled my sunglasses down over the worst cut, took a deep breath and walked into reception. "Good morning, Ms Etxeleku. Children been to the dentist's, have they?" said the secretary, sliding back the glass window.

I should have gone along with that, but my brain was numb. "No, the car broke down." I couldn't bring myself to say "van".

"Poor you, never mind, these things happen, if you'll sign the late book here. Harley, your class is just about to get changed for swimming. Crikey, Ms Etxeleku, are you okay? Your face?"

"I'm fine, thank you." I didn't offer any explanation, despite the fact that the secretary was practically dangling through the window to get a better look. I turned my back on her to say goodbye to the children and walked out. I hurried away down the drive, past the rugby fields and the tennis courts. Colin was right. I was wrong. We were going to end up on the streets if I carried on fooling myself that Stirling Hall was an option for us. I'd write a letter tonight to give notice and see if I could get the kids back into Morlands.

168

I stood at the end of the drive. I looked back at the grey stone building. The last time I felt so hopeless was when I buried Mum. I thought about Clover and what she'd said about Lawrence and the working-class chip on his shoulder. He and I would be good company for each other right now. There were some things that a woman with a trust fund wouldn't understand as well as a woman with a black eye and a bailiff habit.

I sped up as I heard a car rumbling down the drive. I had seventy-five pence, which meant I would have to get off the bus halfway home. I was just working out which jobs I could walk to, assuming that I could carry all my cleaning stuff, when the car stopped beside me. Mr Peters wound down the window and told me to get in. Obviously, that garrulous old bag of a secretary couldn't keep her mouth shut for two seconds. He sounded stern. I did as I was told.

"What on earth happened to you?"

The "It's nothing" of thousands of women before me formed on my lips. I screwed up my eyes and jumped. We were leaving Stirling Hall anyway. "Colin hit me."

Mr Peters didn't reply to that, but the skin tightened around his mouth. "I gather the van has broken down."

He thought I was scum anyway. "The bailiffs took it."

His shoulders sagged. "Is that linked to the black eye?"

"Yep."

Mr Peters drove out past the last of the built-up area of Sandbury, cut down a long country lane and parked up in some woods. "What are you going to do?"

"What do you mean, do? I'm not going to do anything. I'm going to get on with it. What can I do? Go to the police? Help my kids by giving their dad a criminal record? He's never hurt me before. It was just the shock that things had got so bad that the bailiffs were standing outside our door." Even to my ears, I sounded pathetic.

"Don't make excuses for him, Maia. He's twice the size of you." I'd never heard Mr Peters sound cold before.

"It's not about me making fucking excuses, oh fuck, I said fuck, sorry. I'm not making excuses. Well, I am. But people like you, you don't get it. You live in your fancy houses, drive nice cars and if you get a bill, it's not the end of the world, you can pay it. It's just not like that for me. It's about trying to keep a roof over the kids' heads and, I dunno, getting through the days and feeding them and hoping to have some good times now and again and remembering to keep the bloody kitchen door locked so that the bailiffs can't walk in. I shouldn't have sent them to Stirling Hall, cos that's made everything more difficult and now I can't even go to work cos I've lost the van."

Mr Peters reached over and lifted up my glasses. He winced. And I winced at him seeing me in this state. "What a bastard, excuse my language. You poor thing," he said.

"Don't be nice to me. I'll cry," I said.

"I can cope."

I nearly smiled then.

"Have you put anything on it?" he said.

170

"A damp tea towel." Remembering Harley's face trying to contain his emotions made mine spill over. I really had to stop spending time with Mr Peters. I bet he called me Crybaby behind my back.

Mr Peters unclipped his seatbelt, and mine, then pulled me towards him. "God, Maia, come here." He held me with such tenderness, stroking my back and shushing me so sweetly that the rest of my life seemed even lonelier. When I finally pushed away from him, the concern in his eyes shocked me. The only person who had ever looked that worried about me was Mum, which was the wrong thought to have as it sent a fresh gush of tears flooding out. Very gently he took my sunglasses off.

"Hang on a minute."

He got out of the car and went to the boot. He came back a few seconds later with the first aid kit and proceeded to dab antiseptic wipes onto my cut and massage arnica cream into my cheekbone.

"You're wasted as a teacher," I said.

"You're wasted on Colin."

A look, a flash of surprise, ran over his face as though he hadn't meant to say it out loud. Then, once he had, it was as though he'd crossed a boundary and he bent his head and kissed me, a tiny hesitant touch of the lips. He lifted his head up, tracing my lips with his finger, holding my eyes with his, even though I knew I should look away from that dark-green stare drilling into my soul like a tractor beam. He pressed his mouth onto mine again, softly exploring my lips, then my mouth with his tongue until I forgot about my cheek, the cut

171

under my eye and was conscious only of his breathing, my breathing and the sensations streaming through me as though I'd woken up after a long winter of hibernation. After years of Colin going at my body like it was something to be dominated rather than celebrated, I'd forgotten how powerful a kiss could be.

He pulled away and looked at his watch. "I have to go. I'm teaching your son French in precisely twenty-five minutes."

"Lucky Harley."

"Maia?"

"Don't. I don't know what you're going to say, or maybe I do, but I've got the life I've got, you've got the life you've got and there's no room for them to overlap." I retrieved my sunglasses from the dashboard.

"Listen to me."

"No. Come on, you need to go." I put my seatbelt on.

"Will you listen to me if I tell you how I might be able to help you get the van back?"

Oh yes. The van. That was several lifetimes ago. He started the car.

"How?" I asked.

"By rights, bailiffs can't remove anything that is essential for your work. Your van falls into that category. I know someone on the council. I'll make some phone calls when I get back. Let's find out where it's ended up at least, then we can arrange for you to pick it up."

"I can't pay." Shame was swallowing my voice.

"Doesn't matter. Legally they can't take anything you need for work."

It was all about who you knew. I shoved away my ungrateful thoughts long enough to thank Mr Peters.

"My pleasure," he said.

"I s'pose it's common knowledge round the school now that my husband beats me up?"

"No." He sighed.

"I'm assuming your secretary came scuttling in to tell you."

"Felicity did come 'scuttling in' to tell me. I've told her not to breathe a word unless she wants to walk away with a P45 in her hand."

Despite myself, I couldn't help grinning at Felicity giving herself indigestion with the effort of not opening her big trap. "Oh, to have your magic wand."

A cloud settled over his face. "I wish. There are some things I can make happen, but far too many I can't."

I wondered if he meant me. I didn't want to know if he meant me. It didn't matter anyway.

He frowned. "I suggest you drop the children at the bottom of the drive until your face heals. I'll arrange for them to wait by the school gates in the evening so you don't have to come in." A man who thinks of everything. I nodded.

He dropped me at the bus stop. I shuffled about a bit when he stopped the car because I didn't know how to say goodbye. The moment for kissing was long gone, so I went for a hand pat, the sort you'd give to your Great Uncle Arnold in a nursing home, but he caught my fingers.

"Maia, I'm not a violent man. Not at all. But when Felicity came in to tell me today, I wanted to leap into my car and sort a few things out with your husband. I can't remember the last time I felt so angry." He paused. "I just wanted you to know that."

I allowed myself to think about him on the bus. Then again on my walk home. It was like having a little treasure box, a tin of memories to open. Those eyes narrowing with annoyance, the way he rubbed his thumbs together when he was thinking, his manner of staring that meant I couldn't lie. The memory I loved most of all, the one that made my belly hollow out with desire, was of those gentle fingers working circular patterns of cream into my cheek. I thought about that as I walked up to my front door. I focused on that sensation of leaning against someone solid, someone dependable, while I reassured myself that Colin was still out. Then feeling like a traitor to my kids, the prof and Mr Peters, I went to dig out some writing paper and do what I had to do.

CHAPTER
SEVENTEEN

The van came back that afternoon. I didn't even have to go and pick it up. I watched while a couple of beefy council workers rolled it off their tow truck and clunked it back down onto its ageing axles. One of them came to the door and shoved a form at me to sign.

"You must have some clout. Ain't very often we deliver things back, 'specially not the same day. Even if we give them back to people, they have to get them from the depot." He wiped his nose on his fluorescent jacket, waiting for an answer. I signed in silence and shut the door on him. I wasn't about to let him into the secret world of the wonderful Mr Peters. I texted him to let him know that the van was back safe and sound, debated over signing an "x", then left it blank. He'd know who it was.

I got an immediate response. "*My pleasure. We need to talk when you are ready.*" No kisses. We need to talk? I didn't need to make an appointment to be told that snogging Mr Peters was a fat mistake. I could work that one out myself. Presumably he was kicking himself as well as shitting himself. The headmaster would take a "very dim view", I was quite sure. Once I took the children out of school, he'd never have to see me again. I wanted to warn him before I sent the letter, even though I knew he'd try to talk me out of it. I started to look half-heartedly for a stamp, knowing it was the right thing to do but still hoping for a last-minute get-out when Sandy's coo-eee echoed through the letterbox.

It was over two weeks since she'd been round, not since Bronte went missing. "Hi darling, you all right, love? I was really worried about you this morning. How's that face of yours? That's nasty. Colin do that, did he? They're all the same, aren't they? I've never met a bloke who weren't handy with his fists at some stage. Never mind. It'll be gone next week."

I led her through into the kitchen and filled her in on the row about the bailiffs. "I don't know why he went for me then, we'd been getting on a bit better lately. He even came to watch Harley in a play at school and managed not to be too sniffy about it." I put the kettle on.

"Maybe he's coming round to the idea of that posh school. Blimey, we're going to have to watch our Ps and Qs next door with all of you at it."

I wanted to change the subject. We were never going to see eye-to-eye about Stirling Hall. I stirred her coffee, trying to remember the name of her bloke. "How are you getting on with your new man?"

"Who? Sean? I mean, Shane."

"Well, is it Sean or Shane? How many men have you got?"

"You know me, don't like to put all me eggs in one basket. Sean today, Shane tomorrow." Sandy grimaced as she took a sip of her drink. "Here, you got any sugar?"

"Sorry. You haven't been round for so long, I've forgotten how you take it," I said, digging the bag out the cupboard.

"Yeah, I'm normally at work on Friday nights now, down the factory, so I don't get so much time any more to be lazing about. You still got plenty of jobs going?"

"Still a couple of women I clean for, and the dentists and them offices over by the chippy." I just avoided correcting myself to "those offices" in time. "I need more. We're absolutely skint. I've just got a job at that new gym, it's near the school. They pay good money for three hours a day, four shifts a week. I have to get up at the crack of sparrow's fart, mind, but it gives me free gym membership, so I could get fit too if I find the time to go."

"Sounds all right to me. Cor, you a gym babe. Colin won't know what's hit him, all them pelvic floor muscles giving him what for."

"Don't know about that. After today's handiwork, it'll be a long time before he gets me in bed again. He hasn't seemed that interested lately anyway, though the other night he couldn't get enough of me but I think that was cos he was fantasising about Frederica, you know, the one off *Casualty* — she was flirting with him at the school play and I think it turned his head."

Sandy pursed her lips. "He's a vain one, your Colin. Like a TV star would be interested in him."

Sandy was beginning to hack me off. As if all her men were such lookers. Most of them wouldn't be able to touch their toes for their guts in the way.

"He's not that bad. You should see some of the dads at school. Half of them look like their children's grandfathers. Colin hasn't got a six pack but he's a lot better than some of the fatso City boys with their great expense account bellies."

Sandy shrugged. She picked up her fake Gucci handbag. "Look, I gotta go to work. You take care of yourself. You put something on that face?"

"Yeah, some antiseptic. And some arnica."

"Arnie whatsit?"

"Arnica. It's supposed to stop the bruising, it's some sort of herbal remedy thing."

"TCP too common for you now, is it?" Sandy's face had gone all narrow-eyed and hard.

I remembered why I hadn't seen much of her lately. "No. One of the teachers at school gave it to me. He just happened to have some."

"He? Ooooh, got a little friend, have we? Knight in shining armour come to the rescue? Not the bloke in the swanky car?"

"Don't be stupid. He happened to see me in reception when I took the children in." I could feel my face going red. I turned to pick up the mugs off the table. "Anyway, I'm sending the kids back to Morlands. We can't afford to keep them at Stirling Hall." I couldn't believe I'd blurted that out. I hadn't even discussed it with Colin. Pathetic little me, hoping she'd like me a bit more if I was as hopeless and directionless as she was. "Don't say anything to the kids yet though, cos they don't know. In fact, don't mention it to anyone. I haven't sent the letter yet. I only decided today."

"That's a shame. All that cash you've wasted on new uniforms. Never mind. They didn't fit in that good there anyway, did they?" Sandy said. She looked as though her bonus ball had come up.

I was back where I belonged.

CHAPTER
EIGHTEEN

Clover threw the door open with great gusto when I arrived for my two hours of hard labour the following day. Cleaning was still a novelty to her. I would have liked the chance for a trust fund to be a novelty for me. The big grin on her face soon faded.

"Fucking hell, Maia. What happened to you?"

"Colin. Discussion over money. Long story. I'm not going up to school at the moment."

"Jesus Christ. Have you had it looked at? What happened?"

"It's okay, looks worse than it is. Right, where do you want to start today?"

Clover couldn't take her eyes off me, so I ignored her and said, "How about we start in your bedroom?"

I'd never seen Clover approaching silent before but my very brief explanation about Colin's role in turning my face into a plum punnet seemed to shock all the words out of her. She looked as though she had a lot of questions she wanted to ask but I didn't want to think about the answers. Instead, I followed her up the sort of staircase you imagine floating down in a long dress with a train while someone in a bow tie announces your name. She led me into a huge room with open beams

180

and a vaulted ceiling. An enormous four-poster bed stood against the far wall. Even though Lawrence had been gone for over a fortnight, his jeans and T-shirts were still draped over the end of the bed.

My eyes flicked over the mass of clothes littered around the room. Coats and jackets were hanging on chairs. Lone shoes dotted the carpet. Carrier bags sprouted in every corner. But it was a life-size nude portrait in charcoal that caught my attention. It was Clover, but thin. Clover with high cheekbones and eyes that dominated her face. I did a double take.

"It's me. Lawrence commissioned it with his first bonus when he was twenty-one. I'm nineteen there. I keep it up there to torture myself into losing weight but it's not working."

"Actually, you do look as though you've lost weight." Her face was definitely thinner. It was difficult to judge her body, which she'd chosen to cover in a CND T-shirt and crimson Ali Baba harem pants.

"Maybe a bit. It's the husband-buggered-off-and-is-probably-shagging-a-twenty-year-old diet."

We got to work. It took some time, but we did manage to find an emerald green chaise longue — the sort you'd see in the fancy mansions of celebrities in *Hello!* magazine — under pairs of tights, old jeans, jumpers and even a long sequinned evening gown.

"Oh my giddy aunt, I'd forgotten about that dress. I wore it to Lawrence's Christmas work do. Not last year though. The year before," she said.

I pulled open her wardrobe to hang it up and found a great whirl of sleeves, legs and belts hanging down from the shelves. No wonder she always looked like she'd put on something she'd screwed up and left at the bottom of the ironing pile for six months. I sighed. "Come on, let's pull it all out."

We piled it into the middle of the floor, an exotic bonfire of designer labels in sizes Clover would be lucky to get one leg into now. I was trying to work out a way to suggest dumping some of the stuff without actually saying, "Now you're so fat" when she laughed, one of those bristly, not funny laughs.

"There's no point in putting any of this away. It'll never fit me again. Poor old Lawrence. I was a size eight when we met and now look at me. He'll be divorcing me under the Trade Descriptions Act."

"Come on, he didn't marry you because you were thin."

"It's part of the package though, isn't it? A dolly bird wife you can roll out at corporate events. God knows, he can't stand going as it is. I guess it's much worse to have everyone pointing at him and saying, 'I don't fancy yours much' behind his back." Clover held up a tie-dye T-shirt, stretched it across her boobs and chucked it on the charity pile.

"Don't be ridiculous. Think of the stick women we know, like Jen1. You're not telling me he'd be happier married to her."

"Maybe not Jennifer but not a female sumo wrestler either." She blew out her cheeks.

"Why don't you come to the gym with me? I get free membership now I've started cleaning at Browns. We could get fit together."

Clover looked about to dismiss the idea, then she shrugged. "Why not? It's worth a try. The children will find it highly amusing, the idea of me getting my fat backside into a tracksuit. How much could I lose in a month? I'd love to unveil the new me at the ball and shock them all."

We filled bin bags full of clothes, lots still with labels on, folding and sorting until my back was screaming for mercy. Her wardrobe looked like one of those posh clothes shops where you have to ring a bell to get in. There were just a couple of things folded neatly in the middle of the shelves. Clover pulled out a long red fishtail dress. "You'd look amazing in this. Try it on. You could wear it to the ball."

"I'm not going to the ball."

"You have to. You won tickets at the fete, remember?"

"I know, but I'm not going."

"Please go, Maia. Lawrence is playing in the band. It might be my only chance to see him. He's not answering my calls and if I pick up the phone on the rare occasions he rings to speak to the children, he just says he can't talk to me at the moment. I can't face going on my own with everyone gossiping about me. You know what the jungle drums are like, I bet everyone knows by now. They'll all be whispering about 'Poor old Clover, did you know her husband's dumped her? Well, she had rather let herself go . . .' It'll send the gym memberships soaring round Sandbury. I should charge a commission. Roll up, roll up, get your lard arses through the door or you'll be left high and dry

183

like Fatty here." She stopped shaking out the red dress and flumped down onto the floor.

"Please come with me," she said.

I was trying to harden my heart but she'd been such a good friend to me. I held out my hand for the dress. It seemed prudish to go into the en-suite to change. I turned my back on Clover, feeling self-conscious about the polka dot underwear I got in the Primark sale for 95p. It probably looked tarty to her. I consoled myself that I'd seen her fling a load of grey bras and baggy knickers into her charity sack.

I was gobsmacked when I saw myself in the mirror. I'd never owned anything of such good quality. Looking gorgeous owed a lot to time and money, though good genes helped.

"You look fantastic. You'll have every man at the ball drooling over you. Colin better shape up or you'll be whisked away from under his nose." Clover added, "Bastard," under her breath but I pretended I didn't hear. Clover couldn't possibly understand my circumstances when she was looking at life through a trust fund telescope. But it seemed a bit sour grapey to point that out.

So I made out I was examining my rear view in the mirror. Even though I wasn't vain, I didn't want to take the dress off. I'd spent so many years fading into the furniture in other people's homes that I'd stopped seeing myself at all. It wasn't the sort of dress that you put on to cover your underwear. If I was going to wear it, I needed to develop some attitude. I wondered if I

184

had the nerve to carry it off. I wasn't used to putting my cleavage on display.

"It would be criminal not to come to the ball. You look absolutely amazing."

"Colin won't let me go without him." It was one of those sentences that clunked into a silence.

Clover stopped pairing the mountain of rainbow-coloured socks that sat in front of her. "Can I ask a question?"

"You're going to ask why I don't leave, right?" I said.

"Because you've got nowhere to go. I don't need to ask that question. I see how hard you're working, how much strain the whole Stirling Hall thing is putting on you. If you could be doing it differently, I'm sure you would be."

Something about Clover's unexpected understanding reminded me of the professor. Rose Stainton used to cotter on about how Waitrose no longer made those little chocolate wafers she really liked or how her Glenfiddich whisky wasn't as good as it used to be while I was worrying about how I was going to pay that week's rent. Just when I'd be thinking she hadn't got a bloody clue what a real worry was, she'd insist I brought the children with me when I was working in the school holidays. They'd loved racing around her enormous garden and eating her expensive cookies. She used to read Shakespeare with them, make Harley read the part of Bottom in *A Midsummer Night's Dream*, get Bronte swirling about as Titania. I couldn't think about the prof. She'd have been so disappointed that I was about to give up on Stirling Hall.

"No, my question is, if you had somewhere to go, would you?" Clover asked.

I shrugged. "It's difficult to answer that because I don't."

"I don't want you to go back to Colin. Jesus, Maia, he was lucky not to smash your cheekbone. You can't stay with someone who thinks it's okay to beat you."

I started to argue that it was just a one-off but I knew I'd never feel totally safe again. Clover knew it too. The second I'd heard his key in the lock the night before, my belly had tensed and I'd felt a drag of fear as I jumped to my feet to grab something I could fight back with. He'd come in, stinking of beer, barely capable of standing up, let alone planting a right hook. He'd slurred apologies and love for me, but he'd moved into a different place in my mind. Colin was now an enemy to defend myself against rather than an unreliable partner. I'd concentrated on looking calm, picked up my copy of *A Tale of Two Cities* — at last I was on to Dickens — and told him to go to bed. There was nothing more to say.

Clover passed me a pair of gold Louboutins to go with the dress. "What I'm trying to say is, why don't you come and stay here with the kiddies for a bit? It would give you a chance to think about the future. At the very least, it will give him a fright, even if you do decide to go back. I can take the children to school and pick them up while your face heals. In return, you can stop me hitting the gin every night. Go on, the kids will love it."

I meant to argue. But Colin going for me had changed everything. I was so tired. Tired of struggling, tired of worrying, tired of going round in circles. I still hadn't posted the letter to the school because I couldn't work out what to tell Harley and Bronte. So I nodded and said, "We'll come for a few days. Thank you. Thank you so much." Then I did a little twirl in the unfamiliar high heels.

"One condition though," Clover said, with a wink. "You come to the ball with me."

CHAPTER
NINETEEN

I hadn't really spoken to Colin since he hit me. When I got back from Clover's that day, he breezed in, all chatty and full of some scam he thought he could pull to get more benefits from the dole office. I nodded and shrugged a bit.

"Are you listening to me?"

"Yes, I am." I carried on pulling jacket potatoes out of the microwave.

"What do you think?"

Mainly I thought it was sad that I daren't have my back to him in case he decided to have another crack.

"I think you're incredibly clever to have thought of that and deserve a round of applause," I said. Knowing I had somewhere to go was making me brave — or foolish. I pulled a saucepan out of the cupboard. If he went for me again, I was going to make sure I got a hit in that made his brain sing.

For a moment, he looked as though he'd been asked to do some complicated quadratic equation of the sort Harley still hoped I could help him with. Then he smiled and said, "Are you sulking?" in his wheedling-round-me voice. The man thought he was going to make it up to me in bed.

188

"No, I'm not sulking." I stuck the potatoes on plates, chucked some beans on top and had the satisfying thought that I wouldn't be cooking for Colin again for a few days. I hadn't quite worked out how to tell him that me and the kids, as from tomorrow, would be taking a little holiday in a country mansion. I called Harley and Bronte through. Bronte immediately started complaining that there was no butter on her potato.

"No money either, love, that's why."

"It's a nice potato, though, Mum, and it's healthier without butter, isn't it? We were doing about good and bad fat in science today. We're going to make foam fountains with hydrogen peroxide next week," Harley said. I'd noticed that he was becoming more and more enthusiastic about school as the weeks went by. That sicky feeling washed over me again as I eyed the letter, the traitor letter, propped by the telephone. I would post that tomorrow.

I watched Colin, elbow on the table, shovelling in beans like some mechanical digger programmed to repeat the same action over and over again. He hadn't shaved for a couple of days and it made him look grubby, though he thought it made him look manly and rugged. He finished shovelling and pushed his chair back from the table. A couple of beans sat on his T-shirt. He let out a huge belch, which made Harley and Bronte giggle and try to compete with him.

I left them burping and farting and spluttering with laughter and sloped off upstairs to start putting a few clothes into a bag. I tried to think of it as a mini-break, like my customers, who simply couldn't manage another day without a crystal wand massage or a frangipani flotation at the spa. Staying with Clover wasn't a solution. I wasn't leaving Colin. But I damned well didn't want him to think he'd got away with it, that he could punch my lights out and I'd just say, "Never mind, dear, your hand slipped".

Clover was right. I'd nearly fallen into the trap of thinking that there was nothing I could do, apart from accept my lot and not moan. It wouldn't do Colin any harm at all to spend a week on his own with no purse to help himself to, no underpants fairy, no ironing slave, no bloody punch bag. Clover and I had agreed that she would pick the kids up from school the next day and tell them that we were staying over for a few nights so I could help her clean the house. I didn't want the whole thing ballooning into a "mummy's leaving daddy" discussion because Clover was just a stopgap and I was going to have to come back. I was looking forward to teaching Colin a lesson though.

Once the children were in bed, we sat in silence. I stuck my nose in my book while Colin goggled away at yet another Jackie Chan movie. I went up to check that Bronte and Harley were asleep, unlocked the front door on my way down and picked up the phone from the kitchen. I didn't think I'd call the police if it turned nasty but threatening it might give me breathing space. Now it came to it, my mouth was dry and I had a bit of a goldfish thing going on before I spoke. It took a few "Colins" to tear his attention away from Jackie Chan pirouetting into villains' faces, but eventually he

190

managed to turn a bored face towards me, mouth still hanging open with concentration. "What?"

I got up and stood in front of the telly. I squeezed my knees together to stop my legs trembling. "The kids and I are moving out for a bit."

"Moving out? Where? Where are you getting the money from to go anywhere?"

"I'm going to stay with Clover. I can't stand being here, not knowing if you're going to lose your temper again. It's freaking me out and that's not good for the kids."

His mouth dropped open a little bit further. "What, so you're leaving me to move in with that barrel-shaped bird? No wonder her husband buggered off. She batting for the other side now, is she?"

The gormless git. I felt as though I might start lashing out myself. What came out of my mouth bore no resemblance to the original calm script I had rehearsed in my head. "I know you'll find this hard to believe, but she's my friend and she's worried about me because you split my face open during a tantrum and now I'm frightened of you. I'm hoping I'll feel better when my face heals. In the meantime, Clover can take the children to school for me, so everybody doesn't have to know that Harley and Bronte's dad is a bit handy with his fists. And she's going to pay me to clean her house."

I felt as though I'd run up to a big snarling dog and snatched its bone away. Colin didn't make any move to get up.

"Mai. Mai. Why are you doing this to me? You know I love you. I didn't mean to hit you." He had his arms outstretched, protesting his innocence as though he'd brushed an eyelash off my cheek rather than opened up the front of my face.

"You did mean to hit me. You just thought I wouldn't make a big hoo-ha about it. I don't want Harley growing up thinking that it's okay to smack his girlfriend one if she gets a bit troublesome. Let me ask you this. If it was Bronte, would you be happy if her man blacked her eye now and again, as long as he 'didn't mean to'?"

Colin's lips pursed together. He squared his shoulders. He'd never liked me talking back to him and over time, I suppose I'd saved it for important things, usually to do with the kids, that I couldn't let go. It was ages since I'd had options. My nerves were steadying. I was on the edge of elation. I almost wanted to taunt him, dance around the room going, "Come on, big boy, give us a thump if you think you're hard enough." Just when I was getting ready for him, tensed for a tussle, he relaxed back into his chair and splayed his hands on his knees.

"Mai. I'm sorry. Don't go. I don't know what got into me. It won't happen again." He did look sorry, but that might have been the realisation that he'd have to get himself off the settee a bit more often if he wanted to eat. "Don't leave. I love you. I really do."

He stood up. It was as though Colin hurting me had messed up my ability to read him. Even though he was telling me he loved me, I was backing away, ready to

192

grab his metal darts trophy off the top of the TV. He came towards me slowly and tried to pull me into a hug. I shook my head and pushed him away. I didn't want him near me. I should have been crying, churned up, but I didn't feel anything except a sense of failure. Perhaps he did love me. Maybe I'd nagged too much, maybe the stress of not having a job had finished him off, maybe the bailiffs had sent him over the edge. Maybe he hadn't really meant to hit me. I could hear Mr Peters in the back of my mind. "Don't make excuses for him."

If I hadn't seen him glance past me to Jackie Chan, making me walking out on him a bit less worrying than grasping the full technique of karate-chopping a villain in the neck, I might have weakened. I marched past him.

"You're really going, aren't you?" he said.

"I certainly am. When you've sorted yourself out, I might come back. I will leave forever if you lay a single finger on me again. For the moment, I'm going to tell the children that we're moving in with Clover to give her house a spring clean. If you don't want to make this harder than it already is, you will go along with that too."

Colin picked up his sweatshirt off the floor and stomped to the door. He'd never done sorry well. "You always thought you were so damned special. Don't wait too long to come back. You ain't the only woman in the world, you know."

The front door slammed and the Working Men's Club prepared to welcome its latest misfit.

CHAPTER
TWENTY

I lay awake half the night listening for the sound of Colin's key scratching around the lock. I'd never thought of myself as a coward before but lying there with my face throbbing was making me dread the mood he might be in after a few beers. I fidgeted about trying to get comfortable, but every position put pressure on my bruises. Any noise — shouting outside, cans being kicked about, car doors slamming — made me lift my head off the pillow. Somewhere around midnight I heard Sandy's bed springs getting some action with Sean — or was it Shane? — and tried not to listen to the post-shag murmuring and giggling on the other side of the wall.

I must have dropped off in the early hours of Wednesday morning. The beep of a text jolted me into an aching consciousness at seven o'clock. My right eye was refusing to open properly and when I looked down I could see my cheek. I reached for the phone and read, *"Could you give me a call, please?"* The display read Mary. Mr Peters to everyone, but Mary to me — and Colin — if he picked up my phone. There was something gorgeous about someone gorgeous thinking about you first thing in the morning. I looked at Colin's side of the bed. He definitely hadn't been home. Which meant he could turn up at any time. I didn't wish him dead, just temporarily paralysed in a booze-induced stupor on someone's settee. I nipped downstairs to double-check that he wasn't snoring away in the front room, then put the kettle on. I rang Mr Peters. He answered straightaway. He sounded as though he'd been up for hours. I imagined him jogging in the park at dawn, showering with some posh products and eating a breakfast of oats, apricots and natural yoghurt. He always looked as though he'd just towel-dried his hair and filed his nails.

"Maia! Can you talk? Good. How's your face? Are you okay? I've been worried about you. You should go to the police about Colin. He shouldn't get away with that."

"I can't. How can I explain to the children that I've deliberately got their dad in trouble with the police? It won't solve anything. Just make things worse." I sniffed the milk before pouring it into my tea.

"Was he okay with you last night?"

I went through to the front room and looked out of the window, scanning the street for Colin. "Yeah. I'm sorry, I'm going to have to go. Colin's not here at the moment and I want to get out before he comes back. I'm moving in with Orion Wright's mum for a few days."

"You're leaving Colin?" He sounded relieved.

"Not really. I'm going to come back, but Clover can do the school run while my face gets better." There was silence on the other end of the line.

"Can I see you?" he said, finally.

"See me? What? In a school way?"

"Partly in a school way. But also in a Maia–Zac way. I need to talk to you."

He sounded so nervous, so tentative, I nearly burst out laughing. The wonderful Mr Peters, heartthrob of all the mothers, tiptoeing around me. "I'm hardly fit for public viewing at the moment."

"Why don't you meet me at my house? I've got a free lesson before lunch. Could you manage 12.30-ish? I'll even make you a sandwich," he said.

If I'd been able to lift my eyelid, I'm quite sure it would have flown wide open. I'd bet my bottom dollar on granary bread. "I'll have to come straight from work. That means crappy old clothes and stinking of bleach."

"Maia. I don't care. Just come." He gave me the address. A flat near the school.

I heard movement upstairs. "I've got to go."

Bronte appeared at the top of the stairs. "Who were you talking to?"

"I was arranging for us to go to Clover's for a while. She needs help with some cleaning and she thought it might work best if we stayed with her for a few days so we could really get on top of it." I couldn't begin to imagine how many lies got told when people had affairs.

Bronte's face lit up. "Can I go riding?"

"I should think so. I'm sure Clover won't mind." Bronte started to bounce up and down. I laughed. "I packed last night, so you just need to bring Gordon the Gorilla."

Bronte turned towards her room, then stopped. "Is Dad coming?"

"No, sweetheart. He's going to look after the house until we get back."

"Where is he?"

"I'm not quite sure at the moment. We'll give him a ring later. Come on, we don't want to be late." She moved towards her room. For the time being, going riding outweighed saying goodbye to Colin. Harley did his usual go-with-the-flow shrug when I told him, handing me a few *Top Gear* annuals and helping me carry the bags to the van.

I dropped the kids at school and raced through my work that morning. I spent a long time polishing the mirrors, studying my face as I rubbed, wondering whether it was worth covering up my black eye with foundation. I tried not to think about Mr Peters, but every now and then, I'd be wiping round the loo or tying the handles of a pongy old kitchen bin and I'd catch myself grinning. Or I'd do a little shimmy as I shook the towels out, a dance with the Hoover, a super-vigorous shake of the cushions. Excitement and nerves were making me sweat. I swilled my mouth out with a blob of toothpaste and pinched a quick squirt of the woman's deodorant before I left. By the time I drew up outside the converted Edwardian building that housed Mr Peters' flat, I was jittery, as though I'd eaten candy floss for breakfast.

By the looks of the names on the intercom, the building was a one-stop health and beauty shop. I bet it had a gym and swimming pool in the basement. There was a homeopath, beautician and reflexologist on the ground floor. Of course, the residents couldn't possibly survive without a homeopath to press a little pill into their hands every time they got an ache in their big toe. Half the people I worked for swore that a tiny tablet of some stupid herb diluted a million times cured everything from arthritis to psoriasis. Shame it didn't cure their stupidity at wasting money on crackpot ideas. I'd have to find out if Mr Peters was a gnat's piss convert. I checked my teeth in my little compact mirror and rang the bell. He buzzed the front door open straightaway and was leaning over the banister beckoning me up as soon as I got into the lobby.

I tried not to pant up the stairs. Without his jacket and tie, he looked much more approachable. He ushered me into his flat, straight into a light open plan room, all wooden floors and cream walls except for one bright orange one. The furniture was what all those housey magazines I sorted into neat piles would describe as "statement" — enormous stripy olive green, orange and brown settees and armchairs. No cushions, vases, ornaments or plants. Good.

"Thanks for coming," he said, shaking his head as he looked at my face. I didn't blame him. There was something of the elephant woman about me. He pulled out a tall stool for me at a granite breakfast bar. "Coffee?"

198

I nodded, looking down at my clothes. "Sorry for looking such a state. I didn't have time to go home." I shrugged. "Wherever home is."

"Stop fishing. Most of the mothers at Stirling Hall would give their right arms to look as good as you." He wasn't going to pretend nothing had happened, then. He didn't say anything for a moment, just ferreted around in the freezer. "Why don't you lie down on the sofa with this ice pack on your face, while I make coffee?"

"No, no, it's fine, honestly. I'm okay."

"You are not okay. You can't even open your eye. Come on, you'll feel so much better."

"I thought you wanted to talk to me, not nurse me."

"I do want to talk to you. But I also want to look after you." One raise of an eyebrow and I obediently shuffled off to the settee. Or sofa, as he called it.

I was terrified that some blob of bleach or horrible chemical from my clothes would take the dye out of his upholstery so I made him find a sheet for me to lie on. Not, of course, a raggedy old grey thing he would have got in my house, but some super-cotton, super-ironed, super-white number that made me want to snuggle down and go to sleep. He held me gently by the shoulders and eased me into position, slipping a pillow under my head. He came close enough for me to smell his aftershave. And see a hole in his earlobe. Mr Peters with an earring? Maybe he gelled his hair into a baby Mohican at weekends and put in a dangly cannabis leaf earring. I couldn't conjure up the picture. He put the mask over my bad eye and cheek. "Stay still for ten minutes. That should ease the swelling."

In the meantime I heard the fridge open and close, cutlery and glasses clink down onto the granite top, the bread knife sawing away. With my good eye, I tried to snoop as much as possible. I could see one photo on the windowsill but couldn't make out who was in it. I'd have to have a nosey at that when I got up. Check out the competition past. Or maybe even present. A rack of magazines stood by the fireplace. *Private Eye*. I hoped he didn't expect me to get all those political jokes. The *BBC Good Food* magazine? Either he was dicing and slicing himself, or there was a woman around the place.

After a few minutes, he peeled back the ice pack, patted me dry with a towel and rubbed in some cream, tutting away as he did. My good intentions had grown wings. I was in no hurry to get up. He knelt on the floor beside me. "That looks a bit better." He leaned closer. If I lifted my head a fraction, I could kiss his chin. He looked at me with a question in his eyes and I must have held the right — or wrong — answer in mine. He lowered his mouth onto mine with such gentleness, that I felt every "mustn't do this" thought fade away. He smoothed my hair back from my face, kissing me over and over until my head was spinning. I moved over to let him come onto the settee. He lay down beside me, slipped his arm under my head and whispered, "Am I hurting you?" before carrying on where he left off. My body had turned hussy and was crying out for the man to clamber on top of me. But in the same way he opened doors for me, Mr Peters was nothing if not well-mannered. Damn him. Eventually, he pulled himself up onto one elbow to look at me.

"What?" I said. I always sounded aggressive when I was embarrassed.

"I really didn't want to do that." He blushed, which made him look like a teenager. "I did want to do that, I mean, of course I did, but I wanted to talk to you first. I don't mean, first, before, well, you know. God, it doesn't matter." He pressed his fingertips to his eyes and got to his feet, adjusting his cuffs and tucking his shirt in again. "I've made you some lunch. Hope you like crayfish and rocket salad." Right then, I would have fallen at his feet for a fish paste sandwich.

He hauled me up. I glanced over to the photo while pretending to be checking the weather. Older lady with a big woolly scarf. Didn't look like someone he would sleep with.

He pulled out a stool for me at the breakfast bar, then sat down beside me. "I didn't get you round here to kiss you. Even though you're absolutely lovely. I wanted to talk to you about your family."

I rolled my eyes. My family wasn't much of a family right now.

"Hear me out. Then you can tell me to get lost if you want to," he said.

I nodded.

"It's kind of difficult for me to have this conversation now, because I've destroyed any official credibility that I might have had. But I need to say this, and then even if you never speak to me again, I can live with myself." Mr Peters passed me the olive oil and balsamic vinegar.

He took a sip of his coffee. "I grew up on a rough estate in Bolton."

"Bolton? You sound like you were born in Guildford."

"Appearances can be deceptive," he said, in a perfect Lancashire accent. He unbuttoned the top of his shirt and pulled it to one side to reveal the tattoo of an eagle just above his left nipple.

"Oh my God. You weren't joking when you told Bronte you had a tattoo. I thought you were having her on." I was struggling to match up the Mr Peters of the suit and how-do-you-do manner with the one who had once been a customer of some hairy biker boy tatt shop.

He carried on in pure Boltonian. "I was expelled from school for brawling just before I took my CSEs. No one at my school did O-levels. Dad left when I was five and Mum didn't really get education. Thought I should stop mithering about stuffin' me bonce with facts and gerr'out and earn some money."

"Can you go back to your normal voice now?" I said. He was freaking me out. I felt as though I was having lunch with Peter Kay and any minute now he'd ask if I wanted some *gaaarlic* bread.

"That is my normal voice. Well, one of them." Phew. Mr Posh Peters was back. "Sorry to do a Zachary Peters *This is Your Life* on you but there is a point to this. I ended up on a building site, no qualifications, no prospects. My old history teacher happened to walk past one day and saw me there, shovelling gravel. He wouldn't go away. He sat on the pavement reading his

202

newspaper until I finished my shift, then he took me home."

I sat very quietly. I'd never seen Mr Peters so earnest. He sounded a bit choked. "That teacher always wore shirts with cufflinks and a suit. I remember feeling so ashamed because Mum was wearing her coat and a woolly hat like a tea cosy because we didn't have any heating in the house. He told Mum that I had so much potential, that it would be criminal for me not to continue my education. He persuaded her to let me apply for a bursary for a private sixth form that his cousin ran in Surrey."

"So that's how you ended up here?" I tried to imagine Mr Peters as a scruffy lout catapulted into posh surroundings.

"Yes. I boarded for two years, got good A-levels and made it to university. I'm not trying to make out that it was a dream come true. It wasn't. I got into an awful lot of fights, mainly with other boys teasing me about my accent and my strange 'northern' vocabulary. In the end, I started talking like them and now it's become a habit. But I'd probably have got into drugs and petty crime if I'd have stayed where I was."

A bit of Boltonian accent dobbed in and out of his speech as though talking about it took him back there.

"Everything I have now is the result of someone believing in me when I was on the verge of pissing my life up a wall." The swearing sounded funny coming out of his mouth. His cheeks were mottled with pink. He took my hand. My fingers tightened around his. Everything he was telling me was coming from a raw place deep inside, which, of course, made me want to laugh hysterically.

"Are you laughing at me?" he asked with mock severity.

"No, not at all. It's just so weird to hear you swear. I sit in the van saying, 'Piss, bum, bollocks' to get it all out of my system before I have to come in and see you. You make me nervous."

He stood up. "You make me nervous. There's always so much I want to say, then I say it and wish I'd kept me bloody gob shut." He was back in Boltonian mode. He swivelled my stool round and took my face in his hands. "It's a good job I met you now. I have to admit I'm struggling here. I couldn't have been this restrained in my youth."

"What do you mean, 'restrained'?" I thought I'd enjoy my moment of power for a bit longer.

He smiled, a naughty, if-you're-not-careful-I'll-show-you smile. "Fighting wasn't my only vice." He blew out his cheeks. "I'd better sit down. I have serious things to say and I can't think straight when I'm touching you."

My whole body missed him the second he moved away, though he didn't let me go with his eyes. He went back to sounding all strung out and angry. "What I am trying to say is that I don't want you or your children to miss out. You've got an opportunity to turn your life around, just like I had. If you're not careful, Colin is going to ruin it for you. He is making it impossible for your kids to be the best they can be. He's scrounging off you, he's beating you up, he's a terrible role model, especially for Harley."

204

I shifted on the stool. "I know all that but right now there's not a lot I can do about it." I felt criticised for cocking up the choice of father for my children. I hated the way he'd skipped from soft and sexy to some kind of busybody preacher. I had to work hard not to look sulky.

Mr Peters was one step ahead. "Don't get me wrong. I admire you. You get on with life, you don't mope about feeling sorry for yourself but you are capable of so much more. You're bright. You're funny." He took my hand and turned it over, tracing circles on my palm, which made me long to have a sticky beak at that eagle tattoo.

"Funny doesn't pay the rent though." I knew he was telling me all this for the right reasons, but that didn't make me want to listen. Colin thumping me, leaving home to stay with Clover, snogging my son's teacher . . . my memory card was full, no room to store anything else. I couldn't get my head round leaving Colin permanently. And when Mr Peters was so busy admiring me for "getting on with life" — ha bloody ha — how could I possibly shout out that my kids were coming out of Stirling Hall? I couldn't look at him. I felt as though I had FRAUD stamped on my forehead. I chased a piece of crayfish round my plate.

"You could get training, get a better job than cleaning. God knows, Maia, you're capable of it. I think you'd make a brilliant teacher. I've seen how you handle Harley and Bronte, how you encourage them. That's half the battle. Making them want to do well."

"Me a teacher? That's a laugh." That was probably the biggest compliment I'd ever had.

"Why not? You're brighter than lots of teachers I know. You could study in the evening. I'm sure the Open University does a whole range of courses for people like you who missed out on a formal education first time around. In the meantime, why not look for a job as a housekeeper, somewhere you could live with the children? Lots of families round here have annexes or cottages in the garden. Promise me you'll think about it. Colin will still be able to see the children, but you'll have a much more stable life. And you won't have to worry about whether he's going to hit you again."

"Do you really think I could teach?"

"I'm sure you could. You've got natural empathy with children and you're not a pushover."

"I am for you." The words came wanging out of my mouth before I could get them back in.

"Are you? That's good to know. I can't imagine you being a pushover for anyone." Good job we weren't lying on his bed, really. He leant over and caught a long strand of my hair. "Maia, you are really special. I'm sorry because I've complicated the whole thing by getting too close to you. I'm trying to tell you this as a neutral observer, not as a man who has very inappropriate thoughts whenever you walk into the room."

Joy that Mr Peters found me attractive mingled with irritation that now he'd voiced his concerns, he'd be waiting for me to do something about them. Could I find a way to keep the kids at Stirling Hall without ending up homeless? We were so far in arrears with the rent, the council wouldn't wait much longer. The ache in my face was making it difficult to think. I looked at my watch. "I've got to go. I've got a shift at the leisure centre in half an hour."

"Will you think about what I've said?" He came round to help me off the stool, his hand firm under my elbow.

"Yeah. I will. I just feel that my whole life is two steps forward, one step back."

"Hang on in there. I know you can get through this. If you let me, I could really help you."

"You've helped me enough." I was dying to come clean, tell him that I was going to let him down, fuck it all up, send my kids back to Morlands to a dead-end future. There was no time for that. I couldn't have that conversation in two minutes.

"Thanks for lunch — and the pep talk." I hesitated. He didn't. I braced myself against the granite island to stop my body shaking as he pulled me close.

"I didn't even get round to talking about us," he said into my hair.

"What us?" I felt him sigh against me. He tried to silence me with a kiss. I allowed myself a mini-melt for a moment, but I had to be heard. "You've worked very hard to get where you are. I'm not going to ruin it for you. In a few years, you could be head of Stirling Hall, if you don't mess up by sleeping with white trash."

I pulled a face to show that I was half-joking but he didn't crack a smile. I peeled myself away from him. I reached up for a final sweet peck on the lips and forced myself out of the door.

My mops were waiting.

CHAPTER
TWENTY-ONE

I could hear the shouts of laughter from the end of the lane as I drove back from my shift at the dentist's. We'd been at Clover's nearly a week and the kids were as happy as pigs in shit. When Bronte wasn't walking Weirdo, their Old English sheepdog, in the orchards, she was camped in the outhouse with the guinea pigs and rabbits. Orion made the mistake of saying there was a quad bike in the garage and since then, I'd barely dared look out of the kitchen window as Harley flew past the statues in the gardens and out into the paddocks at the back. Our little terraced house was going to seem like a right shoebox when we finally went back.

Clover seemed to love the company. Even though I had to stop myself telling her children off for swearing and bouncing on the furniture, my kids didn't seem to irritate her at all. She'd started to teach Bronte how to ride and the sight of her straight-backed, heels down, on the little white pony made me want to stop the clock and stay here forever. As the kids played hide and seek, racing round and round the house, dodging each other by scooting up and down the servants' staircases, screeching with laughter, I forced myself not to worry about what would happen when we had to go home. And we would have to go home, though for the moment I was earning my keep in elbow grease. Whenever we finished a room, Clover would dig a bottle of champagne out of the wine cellar and toast us like a couple of explorers back from Antarctica.

As I pulled into the drive, the screams and shouts got louder. I followed the noise to the back of the house. Clover was standing with a stopwatch and the kids were taking it in turns to complete an obstacle course — clambering over garden chairs, flying round the orchard on Orion's bike, bouncing off the trampoline onto an old mattress and swinging themselves onto the monkey bars. I never saw her kids gawking at the telly in the same way mine would sit there, mouth open, deaf to every word until I blocked their view. When I got back from my shifts, there was still so much to do in my own home, I didn't have the imagination or energy for playing. I suppose that's where a trust fund helped out.

Clover saw me and beckoned me over. "Who wants Maia to have a turn?"

All the kids clamoured for me to join in. I was nervous about knocking my face but I didn't want to mention it and remind them. Harley grabbed me by the feet and wheelbarrowed me down the slope to the orchard. "Go Mum, go Mum, go, go, go." I kept falling on my belly on the wet grass but Harley was determined to make me finish the course. It was years since I'd been on monkey bars but I was still strong — all that polishing must have been good for something. I was so smug as I swung to the end, though my hamstrings were killing me as I ran the last few yards, with Clover keeping a running commentary about how I might just beat Saffy if I put my back into it. I insisted that Clover had a turn, then everyone wanted to see if they could beat their first time and we all went round again, faces shining pink in the cold.

It was only when my whole body was shivering and I was gagging for the warmth of Clover's Aga, that I realised that I needed to be at Harley's parents' evening in half an hour. I'd gone for the early slot so Clover could look after the children until I got back, then we could swap over. I ran inside, glorying in the fact that I had my own en-suite shower and didn't have to stand trying to light the boiler for twenty minutes before I could thaw out.

I wrapped myself in a towel and studied my face in the mirror. My skin looked all outdoor healthy. The dark smudges under my eyes had gone. Country mansions obviously agreed with me. I didn't wear a lot of make-up but I imagined that turfing up at school without even a lick of lipstick was a bit like going out in just a bra. I did a quick flick of mascara and eyeliner then spent ages covering the yellowing bruises on my cheek with thick concealer. The swelling had gone down and I'd been telling anyone who asked that I'd cut my face on a Velux window when I was cleaning someone's attic. I threw on my one pair of decent black trousers and a green jumper and ran out of the house, stepping over a pile of children playing Twister in the hallway.

I was expecting the meetings to take place in the classrooms but an assistant waved me towards the hall where the teachers sat behind desks. Confident couples stood around chatting with other confident couples. I hovered inside the door, trying to spot Harley's teacher, the bald-headed Mr Rickson. Venetia of the "OMG, you didn't go to university" horror came in, looking like she was about to audition for *Strictly Come Dancing*. "It's Amayra, isn't it?" I nodded. She was never going to be my friend. "If you're looking for Mr Rickson, he's not here. His wife's gone into labour. Mr Peters has stepped in to do his meetings."

A minute ago I'd been shy. Now I was shaking. I had two minutes to collect myself. "Thanks. Are you seeing him now?"

"No, we're after you on the list. You'd better go first. We might be a while because I've got some issues with Theo's maths achievements. I need to find out if I can get a Kumon maths tutor to come into the school at lunchtime because he has tutors for other things after school."

Christ. I might not be out by Easter. "I'll go now then. I shouldn't be too long." What the hell was Kumon maths?

I really wanted to nip to the loos and check for spinach, or rather Bourbon biscuit, in my teeth but I didn't feel I could hold up the juggernaut of Venetia's ambition shuddering along behind me. I walked over to Mr Peters' desk, managed a hello, then sat down and blushed until it wasn't possible to go any redder.

212

"Ms Etxeleku, how are you?" His eyes fixed on my bruises.

"Fine, thank you," I said, conscious that Venetia and her husband were waiting a few yards behind us, no doubt equipped with special bugging devices to make sure Theo wasn't lagging behind Harley in anything other than near-expulsions.

"Your face is looking better," he said, in a whisper. Then more loudly, "So, let's take a look at Harley's marks. He's doing extremely well."

I was only a tiny bit tempted to look round and say, "See!" to Venetia.

He opened a big book and started reading down the columns. Little images of those lovely hands stroking my face were distracting me from the results of Harley's spelling tests. Considering the only reason I was at Stirling Hall at all was to get a better education for the kids, it seemed a bit off that I couldn't concentrate on whether or not they had made any progress. I think the basic gist was that Harley had a natural gift for languages — "He's a very good mimic" — and was still struggling in maths but everything else was "going great guns with a tremendous aptitude for drama".

I almost wished he was telling me that the whole experiment had been a royal balls-up because I still needed to broach the subject of Harley and Bronte leaving Stirling Hall. I'd decided that I couldn't possibly send the letter without telling Mr Peters first. When he finished with, "I know Harley has had a few tricky times here, but what he's achieved in such a short space of time is outstanding," I didn't feel I could piss on his parade at that particular moment, especially as I was feeling under pressure to relinquish the hot seat to Venetia. Any minute now she was going to topple off her chair with the effort of trying to overhear. I was about to get up when he scribbled something on a piece of paper and pushed it towards me. I read, "I've thought about you an awful lot." I stared down to make sure it didn't mean something different I was too thick to get. When I looked up, his eyes were teasing me.

"I'm interested to hear that." I hadn't flirted in a million years and my witty one-liners were a little rusty, along with my voice, which suddenly sounded as though I'd been working down the mines for thirty years.

I heard Venetia fidgeting behind me, tap, tap, tap on the arm of her chair. I'd probably had far more than the ten minutes allowed. I was trying to signal to Mr Peters with my eyes that she was listening to every word. Luckily, he was slightly more evolved than Colin who would have been going, "What? Why are you looking at me funny?"

"Okay, I'll just make a note of these marks, so you can read over them at your leisure." He quickly scribbled, "Leave now before I'm tempted to kiss you again." I picked up the piece of paper and pretended to look closely at it.

"That's wonderful. Thank you very much for your time." I had to concentrate on making my legs stand me up. When he shook my hand, every nerve in my body paid attention. There was a dangerous moment when it would have been easy to forget that there were other people in the room. Mr Peters let go.

"Nice to see you, Ms Etxeleku." I think he meant it.

As I walked back past Venetia, she said, "Did you talk to him about Kumon maths?"

"Yeah. He thinks the kids are better off watching *The Simpsons*."

CHAPTER
TWENTY-TWO

As soon as I got back, Clover swanned out the door, complete with the lace elbow-length gloves we'd discovered at the back of her wardrobe during one of our mammoth tidying sessions. She looked as though she was trying out for a part in *Moulin Rouge*. I got going on bedtime for five children, which was hard work in Clover's household. Orion, Saffy and Sorrel didn't really understand bedtime, which was having a knock-on effect for my two, especially Bronte who needed her sleep and was getting lippier by the day. At home I bundled them off to bed well before nine but Clover's three were still paddling about at ten o'clock, roasting marshmallows in the Aga and making chocolate milkshakes, usually with Clover saying, "Well, you've only got RE and Art first thing tomorrow. No one ever died because they couldn't draw a tree."

Trying to force them up the stairs a bit earlier was not without the risk of being told to fuck off back to my own house. There was a lot to be said for one house, one staircase. Keeping an eye on where each child was, plus teeth cleaning and uniforms for the morning, was like trying to gather up a field of rabbits.

So it wasn't until I plonked down into the leather armchair in the drawing room to watch the *BBC News at Ten* that I started to wonder where Clover was. She'd had the latest appointment at parents' evening which was nine o'clock, but given that I regularly saw her shouting, "Tell Mrs Harper that the horses ate your homework" or "Say that Daddy put your maths in the shredder by mistake", I guessed she'd be in and out of there fairly sharpish.

I wasn't used to being in big houses late at night. I didn't miss my life with Colin at all but I missed the noises of it: the rumble of buses, the sound of people going home from the pub, the foxes rootling through the bins in the back alleyway and Denim and Gypsy clumping up and down the stairs next door. As for Colin himself, I hadn't even spoken to him, simply passed the phone straight over to Bronte when I saw his name flash up. Even she pulled a face if he was interrupting her games with the twins.

I closed the curtains against the black and the silence, peering down the drive looking for headlights. Something was scratching against the window at the other end of the drawing room. I got my phone out of my pocket and switched all the lights off. As my eyes began to focus in the darkness, I prepared myself for some wild-eyed madman to have his nose pressed up against the window. I saw something moving about and forced myself closer. Just when I thought Clover might come back to find a SOCO team studying spurts of blood, I realised that my enemy was the wisteria, banging on the window pane in the wind.

I snapped the lights back on, furious with myself. I picked up *The Guardian*, which Clover insisted she needed to keep reading to stop herself becoming too right wing as she got older, turned the telly up and told myself to stop being such a wuss. I was still happy to hear the scratch of wheels on the gravel and the muffled sound of the kitchen door. Clover must have come in round the back. I stopped myself from scurrying out to her on the grounds that no one likes an ambush in their own home. When Mum was alive, I hated it when she used to greet me at the door, giving me every last detail of how she'd made me some special soup before I had time to take my coat off. Of course, now I'd love the chance to get pissed off about her exact method of sweating the garlic and onions.

So I sat there rustling the paper, flicking through the channels and trying to look to the manor born. I heard her go upstairs and smiled. Clover might appear laid back but she obviously couldn't wait to tell Orion what his teachers had said about him. He was very popular despite the "rabbit scoffed my homework" stories. He must still have been awake, as I could hear quite a lot of clodding about. Wooden floor-boards carried the noise, especially at night. My crappy 1970s carpets back home weren't so bad after all. I couldn't hear any talking. Maybe she'd gone straight to bed, but it seemed odd that she hadn't bothered to come and speak to me. I immediately started stressing that she couldn't wait to be shot of us all.

I crept out of the drawing room and listened at the bottom of the stairs. Someone was definitely moving about. I reassured myself that Weirdo would have barked if it wasn't Clover. Then I had the very unreassuring thought that the stupid mutt would do anything for a custard cream. I was debating whether to go outside and check whether Clover's Land Rover was back when I heard the familiar squeak of her bedroom door, then footsteps on the stairs. I pretended to be walking to the kitchen rather than have Clover catch me skulking about like a loony. Out of the corner of my eye, I saw a shape that wasn't Clover, and when I snapped my head round, it was a man with a beard in a black Al Capone hat, black raincoat and a bin bag in his hand. The gangsters had come to town and the only thing I had to protect myself and five children was the wooden carving of a tall giraffe, which stood in the hallway. I'd always expected that I would shit myself and flee for the hills in that sort of situation but I surprised myself. I picked the giraffe up by its neck and jabbed the legs at him. In terms of a weapon, it was looking a little spindly but anger had made a Rottweiler out of me. The loudness of my voice surprised me. "Put the bag down. Put it down now. Get your hands on the banister before I call the police."

"For fuck's sake, I bloody live here. Who the hell are you?"

I gasped. A Mancunian accent. "Lawrence! Oh my God. I am so sorry. You must think I am a complete madwoman. I thought you were a burglar. Shit. I didn't recognise you. The beard's new, isn't it?" I rallied slightly. "You might have come in and told me you were here." I turned away and lowered my giraffe battering ram back onto its hooves. He was more dishevelled than I remembered. His hair was curling out from under that bloody Mafia hat and he looked like he'd been sleeping in his clothes.

"And you are?"

"I'm Maia, we met once before, a while ago now. I'm looking after the children because Clover's at parents' evening." I didn't think this was the moment to tell him that the kids and I had arrived with our suitcases the second his back was turned.

"I know she's at parents' evening. That's why I came now. Get a few things without any drama. Thought she might have got her mother in to babysit as a last resort, so I was trying to creep out without getting spotted. Wanted to sidestep a bit of earache." He shrugged in apology.

"She'll be back soon. I'm expecting her any minute." I tried to think of a way to keep him there but since I'd nearly taken his eye out with a wooden hoof, I wasn't sure he'd want to party with me.

"As I said, I don't want any aggro, so I'll be on my way. Just tell her I popped in. Give my love to the kids. I miss them." He looked quite watery-eyed for a moment. Then he nodded, looking round. "House looks amazing. Have the burglars been and tidied up?" He indicated the bin bag. "Couldn't find my clothes. Didn't think to look in the drawer at first."

With that, he walked off towards the kitchen. I heard him talking to Weirdo before the back door slammed. I slumped down onto the stairs. At least he'd noticed that the house was clean. It was a step in the right direction. I was still replaying the embarrassment of threatening Lawrence in his own home when Clover came bowling through the door.

"What are you doing sitting on the stairs?" she said.

"Lawrence was here. I thought he was a burglar and I went for him with the giraffe."

Clover looked around, puzzled. "Lawrence was here? What for? Had he come to see me?"

"No, he knew you were at a parents' evening. He came to get some clothes."

Clover's face crumpled. I could hear the sound of pedals whizzing backwards as I rethought my Diplomat of the Year approach. "He seemed a bit upset, sort of sad. He did say he missed you all." I was sure he meant to include Clover with the kids. If he didn't miss her, we'd find out soon enough.

"Did he? Did he look okay?"

"No, he had a beard and looked like an East End hoodlum." I filled Clover in on my encounter.

God love her, she had the good grace to laugh. "Fucking Jennifer. If she hadn't cornered me, I'd have been here. She came over to do her 'I'm sorry to hear your bad news, do tell me all the gory details.' Sorry, my arse. I bet she's loving it. I've no doubt she'll be scouring the *Surrey Mirror* every week to see if the house is on the market. And then she'll be trapping me in the playground with 'It's probably for the best. A new start in a more manageable house will do you good.' I couldn't get away from her. She was doing that hand on the arm thing, you know, that 'I feel your pain', patting away like I had some terminal disease rather than a terminal divorce."

"You don't know that he wants a divorce. Until you speak to him, you can't know what he's thinking. He didn't look like a man with a mistress tending to his every need though."

Clover chucked her coat on the end of the banister. "Doesn't mean that he's not shacked up with some bimbo with a nutcracker arse, does it? Maybe he's gone for the great sex rather than the great cooking, cleaning or ironing?"

"He did notice that the house was looking good, so that's something."

"I need a drink," Clover said. "At least if he doesn't come back, I'll have had the satisfaction of emptying his wine cellar."

Halfway through her second bottle of champagne and every Thorntons chocolate in the box except the nut brittle "too hard on my poor old teeth", Clover saw the light. "Right. I am going to compete with any li'l nutcracker arse. I'm gonna get my own pair of perfeck buns. I'm gonna get down that gym of yours." Then she dug into the next layer for a butterscotch fudge, nodding wisely, while I wondered how soon I could creep off to bed to stand any chance of waking up for my 5a.m. shift at the gym.

CHAPTER
TWENTY-THREE

Clover didn't turn up to the gym the day after she'd discovered the answers to life in a bottle of Dom Pérignon. I got home after my early morning shift expecting to find her slumped on the settee in her dressing gown eating fried egg butties but she met me at the door all triumphant. "Sorry, Maia. Thought I might vomit if I went near a running machine. I was so dehydrated I would have turned inside out like a slug sprinkled with salt, but I haven't been totally useless." She pointed into the garden. "See that compost heap?" I nodded, wondering what that had to do with transforming Clover into a lean, mean, fitness machine.

"I've buried the key to the wine cellar in the bottom of it. So now if I want a drink, I'll have to go excavating amongst the rotting bananas and rancid eggshells. Should be an incentive to keep off the pop. It'll be smashing to wake up without a hangover."

I didn't share her enthusiasm for a champagne-free lifestyle. I was going to miss that "pop, glug, fizz" thing that was quickly becoming part of my life.

"I am very impressed," I said, secretly disappointed.

From then on, though, for a woman who said herself that she'd had it easy all her life, Clover showed a will to give Maggie Thatcher a run for her money. I'd expected her to come to the gym once, see all the teeny tiny girls with their sit-up-and-beg breasts and feel the immediate need for a jam doughnut and a siesta. I don't know whether it was because she was desperate to lose weight or because she needed aching limbs to blot out her aching heart, but whenever I had a shift at the gym, she raced in, raring to go, shortly after I finished at 8a.m. Life was so much easier for me now that Clover did the school drop-off in the mornings. When I finally went back to Colin, it would be a shock to my system to have to rally drive across Sandbury again to grab the kids and squeak up to Stirling Hall seconds before the bell went.

When they'd told me I could use the gym as a perk of the job, I'd thought I might have a ten-minute pedal on the bike every now and then, or a quick wave around of those kettle things when no one was looking. What I got, thanks to Clover, were regular hour-long sessions with a personal trainer. "I'll never keep it up if I'm messing about by myself. I need someone to make me suffer but I'd feel ridiculous on my own," she said.

I came to see it as a rent payment, a straight swap — short-term agony for what was looking like long-term lodgings — the week time limit I'd set myself for staying at Clover's had already stretched to ten days but no one seemed to care. Whenever I mentioned leaving, she threw her hands up theatrically and said, "Stay forever!"

In the meantime, she'd dug up a blond monster of a man, who introduced himself as "Tristram, but everyone calls me Ram". Clover laughed out loud but got the joke about "Is that in or out of bed?" out of the way. Ram looked like he should have been shouting, "About turn" on a parade ground except that he spent more time flexing his muscles in the mirror than the army would have allowed.

So that was how we came to have our arses in the air, bunny hopping up and down the gym, when Jen1 came strolling in, wearing black Lycra leggings and a green thong leotard which separated her tiny butt cheeks like a Christmas ribbon. She did the whole "Hey, Ram, just a quick question about my heart rate, would you mind looking at my food diary, is soya better than milk for losing weight . . ." before making a big palaver out of pointing to some invisible bits of chub she reckoned were love handles. Personally, I didn't think someone as bitchy as Jen1 was in danger of getting love handles.

She didn't spot me at first. "Clover! So this is where you've been hiding."

Tristram wasn't going to allow Clover to stop so she panted out a hello between her legs. "Punishment for talking! Star jump squats." I laughed, because as a result of Clover's boot camp regime, we could barely walk up the stairs, let alone do star jumps. No woman who's had a baby should have to do that. I was concentrating very hard on holding my pelvic floor in but Clover yelled, "Oh my God, I've wet myself." Ram backed away and pointed in the direction of the loos. Jen1 pulled a face and trotted onto the treadmill, her spindly little spaghetti legs going like a baby deer on speed.

When Clover returned, Jen1 tried to ignore her, avoiding her eye in the mirror but Clover kept laughing and saying, "A lot to be said for having one child, Jennifer. Those bloody twins have done for me. Maybe I need to get some of those love eggs. They're supposed to be good for your pelvic floor, aren't they? Kill two birds with one egg as it were." Jen1's eyes flew open so wide she looked like a child's drawing. She was obviously a curtains drawn, strictly missionary kind of girl.

We finally got off the subject of incontinence pants before Ram banned us from his gym. Ram came up with yet another method of torture that involved Clover and me pulling on a stretchy band behind our backs. I could feel Jen1 watching us, smirking her face off every time the bands pinged out of our hands while she pedalled away as though she was leading the Tour de France. But Ram believed in teamwork. Every day he made me sprint five hundred metres on the running machine while Clover did the plank, some disgusting Pilates move that made time stand still and your belly muscles rip open. I ran as fast as possible to minimise Clover's misery. I'd only done fifty-five metres when she started screaming for me to hurry up. By two hundred and fifty, she was swearing and by four hundred metres, it was impossible to make out anything other than her favourite F-word.

When she finally caved in, squirming in agony, Jen1 pranced by and patted her on the back. "Good for you. I must tell Lawrence that he won't recognise you next time he sees you."

"That's the fucking plan," Clover said through clenched teeth. I was pretty warm myself but Clover was so purple when we left the gym that I tried to remember what to do when people have heart attacks.

That evening Clover munched her way through a huge pile of alfalfa shoots, lentils and chickpeas. When I came in from my shift at the posh offices where I'd left everything smelling of lavender and furniture wax, I walked into a kitchen smelling of horse manure. I honestly thought that Weirdo had left a turd somewhere in the room, but given that Clover — miraculously — had kept the kitchen spotless, anything out of place was easy to see. I wrinkled my nose. It was hard to believe that one woman could produce such a terrible smell without a dead rat actually decomposing somewhere about her body.

"Sorry. I think it was better when I ate junk food. The kids are threatening to make me sleep in the pool house." Clover didn't look the slightest bit bothered.

"I'm going to light some candles." It still gave me great pleasure to open up her kitchen drawers and find everything from Sellotape to string and matches neatly arranged.

"Why? Are you Catholic? Is it a feast day for gym babes?" Clover flexed her arms like Popeye.

"I am Catholic, lapsed, obviously. But candles get rid of awful smells."

Clover picked unenthusiastically at a bowl of pumpkin seeds.

"God, Maia, you are the font of all knowledge. How will I survive when you leave?"

227

"You'll have Lawrence back by then, so you won't need me."

Clover's eyes filled. "I don't know about that. Even when he does answer my phone calls, he won't talk about us, only the children. I've no idea what he's thinking but I know that if I demand answers or back him into a corner, he'll close down and won't tell me anything. I'm too scared to ask him if he'll ever come back." She fidgeted. "I could murder a glass of Sauvignon Blanc."

"Gooseberries," I said, obediently.

"Brilliant!" said Clover, clapping her hands. I'd made it my mission to teach her about cleaning. She'd made it hers to teach me about wine. She was just looking as though digging deep into the compost heap for the wine cellar key might become a possibility when there was a loud banging on the front door. A bailiff-type thump. I was glad to be in a home where the ownership of the toaster was never in doubt.

Clover looked at her watch. "Who the hell's that at ten o'clock at night?"

"Maybe it's Lawrence." I prepared to disappear.

"Nah. He'd let himself in through the back door. He had a thing about the front door. Said he was more comfortable with the tradesman's entrance."

Clover obviously worried a lot less about headless axemen than I did and opened the door without asking who it was. There in all his glory stood Colin. He stumbled towards us stinking of booze and looking as though he hadn't bothered to light the boiler in the three weeks I'd been gone. What was it with these men?

Did they need a wife or girlfriend to remind them to shower? By the smell of Colin, the answer was yes.

"Colin." Clover was very clipped.

"I'll handle this." I wasn't sure I would but it would be rude not to try.

"What are you doing here?" I said. Pity, fear, embarrassment, distaste. They were all shaking around like some multi-coloured cocktail.

"You gotta come back. You's my wife. You b'long with me."

"I'm not actually your wife. You could never be bothered to marry me. But anyway." It wasn't a time to be splitting hairs.

"You always was a lippy cow. Where's me kids? I wanna see the kids." He tried to get through the door.

Clover stood in his way. "Listen, Colin, I don't want to be inhospitable but it's late and you've obviously had the odd sherbet or two, so why don't you get along home and Maia will talk to you in the morning?"

"Wossit got to do with you? If it weren't for you, she'd be at home with me."

Clover wasn't having any of it. Oddly enough, she reminded me of my mother, who always liked to give people a piece of her mind. Or her "brain" as Mum liked to say. "No, Colin. The reason she is here with me, is that you punched her in the face. So I suggest you leave, sober up and buck up your ideas. Then you might stand half a chance of getting her back."

I could see Colin weighing up the pros and cons of forcing his way in. He had that "I'll pretend I'm listening" look on his face as he swayed from one foot to the other, one eye closed.

In her bare feet Clover only came halfway up Colin's chest. But she wasn't about to back down. She stood, arms folded, square in the doorway — though a lot less square since her gym sessions with Ram-alam-a-ding-dong. Colin didn't look like he was leaving anytime soon. He was trying to talk to me over Clover's head. In an undertone, she said, "Shall I get rid of him?" I nodded. I couldn't see the point of having the serious conversations we should have had over the last ten years when Colin could see two of me.

"I'll be right back. Don't let him in." Clover sped off down the hallway.

I wasn't half as brave without Clover. Colin leered towards me. "C'mon babe. You've had yer fun. Come home with me. It ain't the same without you."

"In what way?"

"I'm not cut out for livin' on me own. House feels really empty without the kids. An' you, of course. Too big for just me. And I ain't eating properly. I've even got meself a job."

"Where?" That was the point where I should have been really interested in what Colin had to say. Instead, he seemed like a throwback from another era, like someone walking around with an Elvis quiff and thinking he was trendy.

"The betting shop. But not betting." He hiccupped out a laugh. "Painting. Doing the front up. All the signs are hanging off so I'm sorting it out. I ain't been paid yet, but it'll see us right. Keep them bastard bailiffs away for a bit."

Which proved to me that Colin had no idea what we owed. I didn't hold out much hope that the most interesting destination for a bunch of twenties pushed into his hand at the end of the week would be rent arrears rather than the 2.20p.m. at Kempton races. I was looking for something enthusiastic to say on the grounds that, like it or not, I'd have to share a house with him again soon. Before I came up with anything approaching positive, Colin gabbled on.

"How are the kids? I've missed them, you know. And you." He stepped towards me to give me a hug. When I backed away, he got all aggressive. "Too good for me now, are you? You better not stop me seeing the kids."

"I'm not stopping you seeing them. You haven't tried to arrange anything."

Colin looked at his feet. Shifting his eyes off something level seemed to unbalance him and he ended up doing a little crab walk. "I thought you'd be home after a few days. S'pose they've forgotten all about me, now they're living in this big old pile."

"Bronte is learning to ride which she's always wanted to do. And Harley loves having a dog. But they miss you. Especially Bronte."

His face softened. I might have felt a tiny bit of pity for him if he hadn't started jabbing his finger in my face. He shouted, "This is all your fault. You with your fancy ideas. You thinking you're better than everyone else, not even telling me you was taking the kids out of

Stirling Hall. I am their father, you know. I've got me rights."

Colin loved a good "right". Shame he hadn't thought that his rights included responsibilities, like putting food on the table and paying the electricity.

I stepped back from him. "I thought you'd be pleased I was moving the kids back to Morlands. You've won. I was wrong. I thought I could manage, but I can't." I stopped. I hadn't sent the letter yet, or mentioned it to anyone, not even Clover. "How did you know anyway?"

"You told Sandy, didn't you? Felt like a right plonker hearing it from her."

Sandy. Bloody cow. She obviously couldn't wait to stick her nose into that one. I could imagine her calling to Colin over the hedge. "'Ere, Col, sorry to hear your kids have to leave Stirling Hall. Still, you was never for it in the first place, was you?" And her dancing a little jig when she realised he didn't even know. She hadn't texted me to find out where I was. Then again, I hadn't told her I was leaving. I was just as bad, though I wanted to believe that I'd be a bit more generous-spirited if things turned up trumps for her.

Colin lunged forward to grab my arm. "Come on, you're coming home with me."

I pushed him off. "I'm not coming back tonight. The kids are in bed."

"I'll wake them up myself in a minute. Go and fetch them."

"No. I don't want them to see you like this, anyway."

"Oooh, their old dad too rough for them now, is he?" He grabbed me again and for someone who would struggle to walk in a straight line, he was hanging on well.

"Get off. Off!" I fought against him as he pulled me out of the house.

"No. You are going to get it into your thick head that I am the man of the house and you will do as I say. All this bloody liberal crap that your friend, Flowerpot or whatever her name is, is filling your head with. You are coming home with me. Get the children. Now."

He was beginning to twist my arm well beyond comfortable, when a shot, a bloody gunshot, echoed round the garden. Colin dived to the ground. I leapt back over the threshold and slammed the door. Another shot rang out. Then I heard Clover's voice shouting down from upstairs.

"Bugger off. Just fuck off. Next time I'll shoot you in the goolies."

I peered through the hall window. From upstairs I could hear Clover yelling every single swear word that finished with "off". Colin was flicking the "V"s, shaking his fist and holding his own on slinging the insults. But those little drunken feet were flying over the gravel, until soon, I couldn't see him at all.

Clover came down the stairs, rifle under her arm, thumbs tucked in her pockets, walking like John Wayne and talking in a Texan drawl. "I'll be darned. That there rifle came in handy after all, dirty rotten scoundrel." And other miscellaneous movie lines which should have wound me up. I wanted to be cross. I really did. But

233

relief that we weren't the target of professional raiders and the memory of Colin's feet skidding off down the drive tapped into my "shouldn't be laughing" gene and off I went, trying to disapprove but snorting and giggling instead. I was just thankful that the solid old walls of Clover's house meant that the kids had slept through the whole commotion. I wasn't in the mood for any "Clover wasn't really trying to blow your Daddy's brains out" conversations tonight.

Clover was as high as a kite. "I've always wanted to do that. Lawrence keeps it in the garage to shoot the squirrels — they keep getting in the roof and chewing through the wires. I was never going to hit him, you know. I aimed at the chestnut tree by the gates."

I praised the Lord for the key in the bottom of the compost heap.

CHAPTER
TWENTY-FOUR

The next day was Bronte's class assembly. All parents were invited so I finished my shift at the gym early and made it back to Clover's in time to join in all the fun of the breakfast bunfight, against a backdrop of Einstein's swearing, Weirdo's barking and the odd rabbit or guinea pig hopping about the room. Since our massive clean-up, Clover had clamped down on outdoor pets coming in the house, but the kids had made a sport out of smuggling them in. I could hear the shower running upstairs, which explained how a huge white rabbit called Blizzard had managed to slip under Clover's radar to scoff up a hearty breakfast directly from the children's bowls.

Clover's fitness fad had led to a Sugar Puffs and Coco Pops ban in favour of organic cereals with happy-clappy names like Tiger Tastic and Monkey Mayhem but which were actually gluten-free, nut-free, taste-free lumps of hippo poo wearing honey as a disguise. The real enemy in the camp though was not the hippo poo, but the amaranth, a cereal which, according to Clover, was bursting with potassium, calcium and goodness knows what, but turned into the texture of a fresh cowpat when milk was added — and tasted worse. Orion was trying to spoon lumps of the stuff into Bronte's bowl without her noticing. He'd point to the parrot and say, "I think Einstein is about to crap." She'd turn to look and Orion would dollop in a spoonful of amaranth. I knew there'd be trouble as Bronte's sense of humour was about as noticeable as Colin's work ethic. Sure enough, after a few "Look at Blizzard, he's eating a spider" comments, Bronte started shoving Orion and shouting at him.

"I hate you. You could make a dot-to-dot on your spots."

"You could park a car in your big mouth. No one asked you to come and live here. Why don't you go back to your own house?" Orion said.

I put my hand on Bronte's shoulder. "Come on, now. Orion was just having a bit of fun. Why don't I chop you up a banana? We need to get going because we don't want to be late for your assembly, do we?"

Bronte shrugged me off. "I'm sick of living here. I want to go home. I want to be with Dad, not stupid Clover and her stupid children." I was glad that Clover wasn't there to catch the full force of Bronte's ungratefulness.

"Bronte. They are not stupid and they have been very generous letting us stay here. Come on, let's finish breakfast."

"I hate them. I really hate them. Where's Dad? I want to see Dad. Doesn't he love us any more? Why doesn't he come to see us?" She shoved her bowl so hard it knocked into Orion's and sent them both crashing onto the floor. I didn't feel that it was the right time to tell her that Colin had turned up and Clover had practically peppered his arse with shotgun pellets.

Orion did what ten-year-old boys do. He started laughing and pulling faces. Harley was trying not to join in but I could see the appeal as Bronte grew more and more purple, finally screaming at Orion. "I don't know what you're laughing at. Your dad has left you. He hardly ever phones you. He doesn't love you any more and I don't blame him."

"You bloody liar. He hasn't left us. He's away working. America and now Scandinavia, I think." Orion's face clouded with uncertainty.

I nodded until my neck hurt. "Yes, your mum said northern Scandinavia, a really remote part, without any telephone masts." I needed to shut up before I started naming Swedish tennis players and pop groups, talking about herring factories, snow sports, any random rubbish to back up my lie.

I grabbed hold of Bronte and prised her away from the table. She resisted me at first, but as soon as we got into the hallway, she started to cry, big chunky sobs, right from the heart. "Where is Dad? I thought you said we were just staying here for a bit while you helped Clover clean. Have you left him?"

"No, I haven't left him."

"But you're going to, aren't you?" Her eyes were demanding the truth from me. Half an hour before her starring role in assembly as a dung beetle wasn't the moment.

"I am not leaving your dad. Of course I'm not. He was very unkind to me when he hit me. Now I hope he's learnt his lesson. As soon as I've finished cleaning the house with Clover, we'll be going home." I almost wished that I was lying, but I couldn't keep behaving like an ostrich and chucking another bucket of sand over my head.

"When?" Bronte's eyebrows were nearly meeting in the middle.

"Soon, very soon. Now, where's that dung beetle costume?"

My heart did its usual dance as we drove up to the school. I was looking forward to a fix of a certain dark-haired man. Since parents' evening over a week ago, he'd rung me every day. Whenever "Mary" flashed up on the screen, I felt as though I was hugging a happy little secret. Every time I answered a call I promised myself it would be the last one. The truth was, he made me feel special. Way too special. We'd spoken long past midnight the night before as I told him about Colin's unexpected appearance and Clover's special method of helping him leave. We'd both killed ourselves laughing. I loved being able to make him laugh like that, even if it was at Colin's expense. Especially if it was at Colin's expense.

"Do you think you'll go back to him?" he asked.

"I don't want to but the kids are getting fidgety. They really miss him and he is trying to be a bit better. He's got a job now." I could picture Mr Peters shaking his head.

"Promise me you won't go back without telling me." There was a silence. "I'd really like to see you, Maia. I keep thinking about you."

238

I did what I always did. Made a joke. "You'll see me tomorrow at the dung beetle parade." I closed the conversation down. I knew that I couldn't let Mr Peters get any more involved with me. He'd bust a gut to get from fast-fisted hooligan to well-respected teacher. I could only bring trouble to the party so it was better not to accept the invitation. I just needed to find the strength to refuse.

As we walked into school I was grateful for Bronte's fussing about whether her dung beetle horns were on properly. I'd spotted Mr Peters by the hall and the last-minute costume faff meant I didn't have to make eye contact until I got to the door. He was wearing a khaki suit with a pink shirt. I'd never liked pink on men — too long living with Colin and his "pink is for poofters" prejudices, I suppose — but he looked like he'd stepped out from an advert for a top-of-the-range watch. The headmaster was standing next to him, all pointy-faced and frumpy silver-rimmed glasses. I saw the headmaster look at me, then say something out of the corner of his mouth to Mr Peters. Mr Peters shrugged. The headmaster greeted me with a breezy "Good morning" but I didn't care about him. Mr Peters said a quiet hello and smiled the sort of smile that didn't even move the corners of his mouth.

I picked a seat on the end, a few rows back from the stage. The teachers gradually trooped in to take their positions along the side of the hall. Mr Peters sat a couple of yards in front of me, to my left. I waited for him to look up and catch my eye but he was staring at the floor. Maybe that grouchy old headmaster had got wind of the fact that the Head of Upper School was providing a little too much "support" for me, but I couldn't believe anyone had real proof. Mr Peters would piss me off if he gave up on me, even though I'd been encouraging him to do just that.

I turned back to the stage as Bronte pushed a huge brown ball along in her dung beetle role, lecturing the audience on CO_2 gases produced by not composting your vegetable peelings. I was in the mood to be irritated. Setting up wormeries to eat your leftover mangetout and using banana skins to fertilise your roses was such middle-class bollocks. The prof would have tutted and told me that intelligent people are not governed by class. It was still bollocks. I was too busy trying to earn enough to buy food to worry about whether my carrot tops were making November a bit warmer. I clapped as though it was the most entertaining thing I'd ever heard, maybe a bit too loudly, in case Mr Peters hadn't actually clocked I was there. The dung beetles gave way to a group of boys failing to keep a straight face as they read out little gems about recycling human waste — "Don't waste your wee. It's rich in nitrogen. Mix it with sawdust and use it as bedding for lettuces."

I wondered if I was the only one who preferred pee-free iceberg. I glanced at Mr Peters. Judging by the big scowl on his face, he didn't find the idea too appetising either. When it was prayer time, I squinted at him through half-closed eyes, while listening to the cheery words of "Greedy lifestyles, piles of waste, boundless avarice and irrational hate, excess packaging, contaminated air, mountains of rubbish, is anyone there?"

I was feeling as though I'd sucked up a few evil chemicals myself. God was moving in very mysterious ways. I wanted a sign that Mr Peters wasn't like all the rest. I didn't need him to feed the five thousand, a little flicker of those eyes in my direction would do. Instead he sat there, serious-faced, clutching his hymnbook like he was scared "Abide with Me" might escape.

I brought my attention back to "The world gets hotter, forests disappear, animals are dying out, can anyone hear?" What was wrong with the Lord's Prayer? The mumbling continued. I don't think the kids even knew what they were saying, just trotting out the words like the five times table. I wasn't feeling eco-friendly. Or anything friendly. I couldn't find it in me to be bothered about non-organic pesticides and how they might make my eyelashes fall out when Mr Peters was doing the deep freeze. He'd obviously decided to put the mistake I was behind him. The last conversation we'd had, we'd joked about going to the Basque country together. Now it looked like we wouldn't even be going for a coffee.

I glanced past him down the row to the other teachers. The headmaster was looking at me. Or probably looking down on me. I wished I had the guts to flash my tits at him. How could he know anything about me and Mr Peters? Maybe that nebby old bag of a secretary had opened her big mouth and dropped Mr Peters in it. Copping off with pupils' parents, especially poor parents with no money to chuck at a new library/climbing wall/driving range would not be a good career move.

Finally, after the one hymn I recognised — "All Things Bright and Beautiful" — we all shuffled out. I waved goodbye to Bronte. She was giggly and glowing which made me slightly less pissed off that the hour wasted at school would mean making up lost ironing time that evening. Mr Peters, on the other hand, stood by the door, the opposite of glowing. In non-professor speak, he had a right gob on him. His natural PR skills had taken a day off. He rewarded all those mothers trying to dazzle him with their sunniest smiles with a curt, "Goodbye, thank you for coming." I dawdled about, pretending to fiddle with my jacket zip until most people had gone. As soon as I spotted a decent — sized gap in the line, I nipped in and said, "Goodbye" loudly, adding, "Are you okay?" in a whisper.

He glared back at me, eyes dark with anger. "No, I am not okay. Why didn't you tell me?"

"Tell you what?" He shook his head, as though I was super-thick. My mind was jumping about, trying to find the right direction to run in, when I saw the headmaster approaching out of the corner of my eye and had no choice but to leave, forcing out a "Thank you for a lovely service, very original", as I went.

I stood by the van for ages. I thought he might come out but twenty minutes later, I realised that the Etxeleku Effect was over.

CHAPTER
TWENTY-FIVE

I'd texted Mr Peters after the assembly to ask what he was on about but he hadn't bothered to reply. In between tidying up other people's papers and bleaching sinks, I kept fishing the phone out of my pocket to double-check that I hadn't somehow missed a message. I preferred life before mobile phones when two little bleeps didn't make or break my day.

However, I did discover a voice message from Colin, left earlier that morning while I was suffering toxic overload. "Darl, s'me. Sorry about last night. Sorry. It just didn't come out right. I need you home, darl. I'm trying really hard, working and everything. Give me a chance. At least come and see what I done to the house. I've tried to make it nice for you."

There was a time in my life when Colin promising to try harder would have guaranteed instant forgiveness. Instead, he just reminded me of a toddler whining to stay a bit longer at the park.

Mr Peters wasn't going to save me. Clover wasn't going to save me. No one was. I had to stop pretending I had choices and get back to my old life. I needed to do it before the children could no longer rough themselves back down. If I was to survive there again, I was going to have a conversation with Colin to lay a few ground rules without the children as an audience. No hitting would be a great starting point, followed by a regular job. I'd go back all right but Mouse Maia was gone forever.

Now was as good a time as any. I steered towards home. I turned left where the fancy Victorian houses began to look a bit more run down, rusty gates, garden sheds in need of a coat of Cuprinol, weedy, stringy lawns. Then right into the Victorian terraces, where the front gardens had long been tarmacked over and vans and L-reg Fiestas took the place of roses. And finally, round the bend to our sixties rabbit hutches with stone cladding and small windows in a sea of concrete.

My heart didn't lift. I didn't belong. Not at all. It was amazing how quickly I'd adapted to Clover's big rambly house. But bed, lie in it and all that. Everything in me was sinking as I walked up the path. The hedge between mine and Sandy's house had a few more crisp packets in it. The paint on the front door had peeled a bit more. Only one of the curtains in the front room was open.

I didn't knock, but I felt as though I should. The house had that empty, still feel. I called out "Hello?" but no answer. Colin must have been telling the truth when he said he had a job. The mat was littered with flyers for junk food, Lidl's and a dodgy place that cashed cheques, no questions asked. Colin had kicked the free newspapers out of the way rather than risk burning a calorie to pick them up. Made it nice for me, my arse. I could smell paint somewhere. Jesus, the great lard had actually moved off the settee in my absence. I opened the living room door. The dirty eggshell blue walls were now a bright pale cream. I pushed back the curtains. The spring sunlight drifted into the room. It looked much larger now. I wanted to be grateful. I'd been nagging him for long enough. But now he'd finally done it, I realised I didn't want to be here, magnolia walls or not. My furniture looked shabbier and more old-fashioned than I remembered. I wondered if the children would notice and whine to get back to Clover's.

I went out to the kitchen. Colin had either worn himself out lifting the paintbrush or hadn't expected me back so soon. The table was covered in empty KFC boxes, McDonald's wrappers, blobs of curry and empty cans of Lidl lager. He hated Malibu but he'd even swigged that down. I could smell the bin.

There was a pile of brown envelopes on the side, all unopened, The next forty years were looking horribly long. I picked them up, flicking through a series of unpaid life. In the middle of all the cheap brown utility envelopes was a good quality white envelope. I turned it over. On the back flap was the crest of Stirling Hall. I ripped it open. As soon as I read ". . . acknowledge receipt of your letter informing us of the withdrawal of Harley and Bronte Caudwell from Stirling Hall . . .", the blurry bits of my life started to move into focus, sharpened by my anger that Colin, that lazy lump who would struggle to reach for a bucket of water if his arse was on fire, had somehow managed to post my letter. Which I hadn't firmly, decisively, categorically, positively, definitively, decided to post. It probably wasn't the moment to think about how much faith the prof had shown in me. Or Mr Peters. No wonder he had the hump with me. His words, "Keep talking to me, Maia, keep talking to me," kept coming back to me. Finding out from someone else — probably that Felicity secretary woman with the motor mouth — that the kids were leaving must have felt like a sharp jab of the two fingers.

I stomped upstairs. I'd fucked up. Not just the letter, but everything. Getting together with Colin in the first place. Allowing myself to get dragged down to his level, instead of yanking him up to mine. I glanced into Bronte's bedroom. Colin had painted it a pale lilac. She'd love that. He did love the kids. But would that be enough? I felt like a rat trapped in a kitchen, scuttling about, banging into things, trying to find a hole to shoot out of.

I walked into our bedroom. It smelt of greasy hair, sheets gone too long without washing, morning breath trapped in a too small space. I'd have to have sex with Colin again. I couldn't imagine his chubby fingers on me after Mr Peters' gentle touch. I opened the window, feeling the weak sunshine on my face. I bet Mr Peters' bedroom smelt of aftershave and shower gel. I'd nosed in when I'd been to the loo. It wasn't perfect — a pair of trousers hanging over the back of a chair, an overnight bag still to unpack — but the bed was made, a big white duvet perfect for snuggling under.

Footsteps on the stairs next door broke into my daydream. I heard the muffled sound of a loud drawn out fart. The loo flushed. I'd forgotten how much of Sandy's life I could share without her even knowing. Then the thumping started. I didn't take much notice at first, still drifting in and out of the shock of discovering that a lot of people knew Harley and Bronte were leaving Stirling Hall before me. I needed to tell the kids and Clover before the Chinese whispers started up. Happy days.

The thumping got more rhythmical, faster. Sandy must have friction burns on her fanny. When she wasn't at work, she was at it. I started flicking through my wardrobe, looking at my stuff as though it belonged to another life, trying to block out images of Sandy in her leopard skin stilettos. The girl wasn't going to let me off that easily. I could hear her shouting encouragement, sounding as though she was doing singing scales before exploding in a "Yes, yes, yes! Go for it, right between the posts!" I got up to go back downstairs. Other people's orgasms were ridiculous. Then I heard it. The deep, unmistakable roar of "Gooo-aaaal!"

How long? How bloody long? How long had my "best" mate been shagging my not-quite-husband? She was always taking the piss out of him. Always going on about what a thicko he was. What a lazy git. How fat he'd got. How he was such a loser. I tried to shove away an image of them lying in bed, giggling about their little secret while I lay on the other side of the wall nursing my black eye. Clouds of realisation started to drift in. She knew his mobile number when Bronte was missing. The reason I'd never once spotted Sean, Shane or any other shithead beginning with "Sh", was because the shithead began with "C". She didn't care about Stirling Hall. She just wanted a reason to fall out with me, so she could see Colin on Friday nights instead of me when he was supposed to be at the Working Men's Club. Her brilliant smokescreen of slagging him off at every opportunity. The empty Malibu. And Mr Peters said I was bright.

The thought that they'd been sniggering about me behind my back made me want to put my fist through the wall. Punch a hole in it — it wouldn't take much — and stick my head through it. "Helloooo-eee." I couldn't face the picture of Sandy's little chicken legs wrapped around Colin's blubber imprinted on my mind forever. I stood in the doorway debating what to do. Bastards. I felt like forcing my way into her house and seeing the panic as they snatched up their clothes, Colin stuttering and flapping about. I itched to bang on the wall and shout through to Sandy to watch out for Colin wiping his willy on her dressing gown. I'd get revenge.

Relief joined my rage. Hoo-rah. Sandy's responsibility now. She wanted to open her legs for him, so over to her. She wasn't going to hand him back to me. She could support him, listen to him drivelling on about bloody West Ham, wipe his wee off the bathroom floor, deal with the endless stream of low life coming to demand money for his gambling debts. I wanted to go round and snap her raddled little neck for pulling a fast one on me. But real sadness that she'd had the honour of Colin humping away, grunting with pleasure like a pig in potatoes? No. It was Sandy's turn to be poked

248

awake to pretend to be a streaker at a football stadium now.

Excitement calmed my fury. Colin wanted to get me back here for a reason. I didn't know what that reason was, but it had nothing to do with love. That suited me, because he'd chipped away at that huge love I'd once had for him until the remaining grains had blown away, leaving nothing but a few good memories and a shedload of bad ones. We could stop pretending. Perhaps not yet, not before I'd had time to think of a plan. Harley and Bronte would have enough to deal with changing back to their old school again. I couldn't drop this on them as well. Somewhere, in the back of my mind, a tiny thought was stretching itself out. I was free. So was Mr Peters. I had to talk to him.

I pulled my memory box out from under the bed and tiptoed downstairs. I wasn't about to start sewing prawns into the lining of the curtains because I'd definitely have to come back with the kids even if I managed to get rid of Colin. Instead I buried the TV remote under the cleaning cloths in the kitchen.

Then I was gone.

CHAPTER
TWENTY-SIX

The need to speak to Mr Peters consumed me. I stomped about in Clover's house, trying his mobile over and over again like someone who puts things with long ears and white fluffy tails into big saucepans on a regular basis. I needed to get on with ironing the shirts I'd picked up from one of my customers but I couldn't settle. Egyptian cotton was a bastard to get right on a good day, but today, I was making more creases than I was taking out. After my fifth go at pressing the darts in the back of one shirt, I gave up.

I could either go steaming up to the school, burst into his office and tell him he'd got it all wrong, which would be like taking out a full page ad in the *Surrey Mirror* — Etxeleku has got the hots for Peters — or I could phone the secretary and ask to speak to him. I kept rehearsing what I wanted to say, trying to get it into my head that I was a paying parent, at least until the end of next term, and I had every right to be put through to the Head of Upper School. My voice kept coming out like a relative of the queen. I brought myself back down to earth by imitating Sandy. Slapper. Eventually I dialled the number. Felicity answered, sounding as though she'd recently come back from a pheasant shoot. "I'm dreadfully sorry, Mrs Etxeleku, Mr Peters isn't on the premises at the moment. Is there something I could help you with?"

I trotted out my speech. "As I'm sure you are aware, the kids, I mean, my children, are leaving at the end of next term and I wanted a word with Mr Peters about some information I need for their new school."

"If it's for the end of next term, the summer term, I'm not sure he's the best person to ask because he's leaving us at Easter. Let me see if I can put you through to Mrs Saltrey, she's going to be his replacement."

"No, no, hang on a minute. Mr Peters is leaving? When?" My voice had become a shriek. When the hell did Mr Peters, who up until two days ago was on the blower to me every day, decide he was jumping ship? With no warning?

"There'll be a formal announcement going out soon, but he's being seconded for a year to a state school on special measures." She was typing away while she spoke to me, Little Miss Efficiency. "Stirling Hall management and governors are fully in favour of it because they think he'll bring new ideas when he returns. Move with the times and all that. Anyway, I'll just transfer you."

I got a surprised-sounding Mrs Saltrey on the phone. My garbled request obviously puzzled her, given that I was having to invent some guff on the spot about the school needing to know which reading levels they were on. Having established that the kids were off to Morlands, she said, "I think you can rest assured that both Harley and Bronte will be far in advance of their

251

peers in the same age group," in a tone of voice that suggested they would be reciting Latin prose from memory while everyone else was on *The Beano*. I thanked her and slammed the phone down.

I couldn't stand it. When exactly was he going to tell me that he was off? That he would no longer be able to support me or help Harley and Bronte to find their niche at school? He must have made the decision to leave before he knew I was taking the children out. The difference was his leaving was about choice; mine was about necessity. All that bollocks about "keep talking to me", when he was about to pull the biggest bloody Houdini stunt of all. Pretending he'd always be there for me. Making out he was keeping an eye on the kids when in fact, he was just marching on the spot, waiting to find some interesting little thing to add to his CV. Moves like that didn't get made overnight. There was me thinking that we were friends. At the very least, friends.

Hurt spread from my head, through my heart and squeezed at my belly. I'd nearly begun to believe in him. Nearly begun to think that however complicated, however hard, that man, with all that kindness, might have been meant for me.

I looked at my watch. 12.30. I knew he sometimes went home on Wednesdays because he had a free lesson before lunchtime. I might just find him there. I didn't know what I was going to say, but I had nothing to lose. It wasn't long till the end of term and then he'd be gone and I'd never see him again. I drove — with a trigger-happy use of the horn — to his flat. I cursed the fancy underground car park that meant I couldn't see whether his car was there or not. I looked up at the windows to work out which balcony belonged to him. First floor I seemed to remember. Yes, there it was, with the stripy olive and orange curtains. I couldn't see any movement.

I walked up to the front door, remembering the last time I'd been there, after Colin had given me a black eye. I'd never trust anyone again if that turned out to be some great big piss-take. I stood there summoning up my courage to press the doorbell, scared that he'd answer and refuse to see me. Scared that he wouldn't answer and I would have to simmer away, not understanding what the hell had happened forever more. A big bust-up was better than nothing. My finger was hovering over the button when the front door opened. A tall woman with long brown hair came out. She looked a bit familiar.

She smiled uncertainly. "It's Maia, isn't it?"

I nodded, taking a moment to place her. Then the light went on. Serena, the policewoman who'd helped me find Bronte. Last time I'd seen her she'd been in uniform with her hair in a tight bun. Now she was all flowing locks and Timberland casual but I'd recognise that deep voice anywhere.

"What brings you to this part of town?" she said. Something was odd about her. I looked more closely. She was red all round her mouth and chin. She looked like someone had been kissing her face off. God, I was slow. The familiarity yet strange tension at my house

253

between Serena and Mr Peters. The snippy "Long time, no see". By the looks of things, she'd remedied that.

The hot spike of jealousy that sliced through me made me feel sick. I glanced at the names on the doorbells. "I'm on my way to see the homeopath." Even though all my religious belief had disappeared years ago, the Catholic in me still struggled to lie.

I saw her shoulders relax. She didn't seem very keen on meeting my eye. "I've heard good things about homeopathy. I'll be interested to know if it works for you. Bronte all right now?" She sounded in a rush to get away, as though she was asking out of duty rather than interest.

I wanted to say, "Too busy having sex to ask Mr Peters?" Pride saved me. "She's doing well, thank you, no more hiccups so far."

"Good. Pleased to hear it. Good luck with everything." She held the door for me and I walked through, but I had no intention of going to see Mr Peters. I couldn't bear watching him dart guiltily round that kitchen, tidying away the two post-rumpy coffee cups. I didn't want to look down the corridor and see the ruffled bed. And I definitely didn't want to see his dark hair all mussed up. I'd be able to smell her Armani on him. I couldn't compete with Serena. Educated, successful, tall, pretty. God knows what made me think I'd ever been in with a chance.

I lurked around the bottom of the staircase, waiting until I could be sure that Serena had gone. I didn't know what I'd do if he stepped out of the lift. He'd never been serious about me. He'd probably been laughing about my pathetic attempts to educate myself and my kids. Why behave like he was interested? Maybe I was some social study, some weird modern day *My Fair Lady*. Or perhaps he did like me, but when push came to shove, he was terrified I'd sink him back to where he came from, away from his crayfish salad, oak-aged Modena balsamic vinegar and cold-pressed olive oil to a world of Pot Noodle, battered sausages and KFC Bargain Buckets. I heard the lift crank into action and ran out of the building, bolting back to the van.

Clover turned up from horse riding to find me in a big cupboard cleaning frenzy, sorting out her millions of sandwich boxes so that we didn't get buried in an avalanche of plastic every time we needed a packed lunch. We'd come to read each other's moods well. If Clover was standing up, eating cereal out of the box or spooning peanut butter out of the jar, I trod carefully. If I was on the obsessive edge of cleaning — tops of cupboards, bleaching the grout in the kitchen tiles — Clover knew that I was trying to turn my smash-your-face-in energy into something useful. It was so much easier to live with a woman than have to spell out your moods in mile-high glittering letters to a man.

Even so, I couldn't bring myself to serve up the whole Mr Peters humiliation. I'd never mentioned him to Clover. She loved gory details and I wasn't yet ready for one of her interrogations — "Did you get him in bed? What's his house like? Did you see his bathroom?"

— so I fed her the Colin–Sandy scenario. Which was humiliating enough.

"I should have blasted Colin's brains out whilst I had the chance. So much simpler," she said.

"I don't love him any more. I don't. But I'm going to have to put up with him. The kids will have left home by the time the council can rehouse me." I chucked out a pile of mouldy takeaway containers.

"You're not leaving me! I'm not letting you go back there. You might not love him, but surely you're not going to put up with him screwing Sandy whilst you're cooking his tea next door? I mean, it's one thing if he's had a dalliance, seen the error of his ways and come to his senses, but you're not going to let him have his cake and eat it, are you?" Clover said.

"No. Even I'm not stupid enough to let him carry on with Sandy while I skivvy after him. But it's not your problem, Clover. We've loved the fortnight we've spent with you here but this isn't my life. It's your life. When Lawrence comes back, he's not going to want the Etxeleku/Caudwells hanging round. You've been really, really generous, with everything. Enough is enough." I closed my eyes. "The kids are going back to Morlands. I can't afford to keep them at Stirling Hall."

"No! No! You can't do that. You can't, Maia. They're excelling there. You can't remove them now. That's insane. Bronte's in all the top groups now, spelling, maths. Saffy says she's the one everyone wants to beat. And Harley, he's managed to elbow Hugo out of the A-team in football and rugby. I imagine Jennifer is at the school banging on the headmaster's door now. He's doing so well in drama, I could see him on stage." She tried to make me laugh. "Christ, Harley's even made it onto the A-list of birthday guests — he's got an invitation to Hugo's tank and paintballing party. Ten-year-old boys would auction their mothers for one of those."

"I've already given notice. They leave at the end of next term."

Rich people saw things differently. Clover might pretend she was like me. Sure, we both got frustrated with the kids. We both had problems with our men. We both loved each other's company, quite often staying up till one or two in the morning to check there wasn't a detail about each other we hadn't picked over or taken the piss out of. She made me laugh with impressions of her mother whose idea of relaxed was serving home-baked Victoria sponge without a doily underneath. I made her cry talking about how much I missed Mum and my frustration at never finding out who my father was. She was growing more like me — she could now wipe up something sticky before it got covered in cat hair and I was growing more like her — I caught myself saying "clearly, obviously, frankly" quite often. But we were separated by several hundreds of thousands of pounds, which right now wiped out all our similarities. And I was in the mood to take things the wrong way.

"For God's sake, Clover. None of this is about the bloody school. It's about money, as in, I don't have any, as in, the bloody bailiffs are round my house trying to take my crappy telly, as in, I don't have a fucking choice." I banged the cupboard door shut.

Her eyes flew open. "Sorry. I'm really sorry. That was really tactless and stupid of me. There I go with my hobnailed boots again." She scrabbled in her bag and produced a dog-eared chequebook. "You've got the fees covered, so why don't you let me lend you some money to tide you over and you can pay me back when you can? Even in twenty years?"

She was being generous beyond the call of duty, and I needed to be grateful. In that moment I hated everyone who had an easier life than me. I managed to soften my face. "I can't let you do that. But thank you." She tried to stop me getting up and I just managed to disguise my desire to push her away as a gentle pat on the arm. There was only one place for me when I felt like this.

I drove straight to the gym. Ram took one look at me and got the boxing gloves out. I slugged away, fury seeping out of every pore. Uppercut. Hook. Straight arm. I pounded into his hands, punch after punch until my shoulders ached and sweat was flying off my hair. Every now and then I'd catch a glimpse of myself in the mirror, wet strands of hair plastered to my forehead, my T-shirt clinging as though someone had chucked a bucket of water over me, plus mad-woman-escaped-from-the-attic sort of eyes. Ram stopped to let me get my breath. I buried my face in my towel, glugged down a whole bottle of water and carried on. Left, right, hook, foot forward, swinging at the waist, belting imaginary blows into Colin, into Sandy, into the wall between the bedrooms. I wanted to slug one in for Mr Peters as well but every time I thought of him, the

258

anger that had been boiling away in me all day dropped away, and a sadness, the sort that would need hot water bottles and fleecy blankets over many months, rushed into its place. Anger, for now, was easier.

"Okay?" Ram said, as I slowly ground to a halt, each blow becoming weaker as my wrists complained. I nodded. He looked as though he was going to stray off his professional autopilot of "Make hunger your friend", "Don't eat for an hour after exercise", "Winners make goals, losers make excuses" mantra and put the personal into trainer. I gathered up my towel and walked away. I didn't want anyone else's advice today. And I needed to have someone left to fall out with another day.

CHAPTER
TWENTY-SEVEN

The next morning everything hurt. Even pulling back the duvet sent a jag of pain squealing through my shoulders and down through my back. My body was nothing compared with my head. I vaguely remembered Clover deciding that there'd been such a lot of upset that we couldn't get through it without alcohol. "We need the Tatty, darling." She'd powered up her wind-up torch and trundled down the garden in her riding boots in the dark, to return a good twenty minutes later with a slimy key to the wine cellar. "Fucking hell, that's the last time I chuck anything on the compost heap. The bloody rats have made a nest in there. I thought it was a stringy old parsnip until it started wriggling and shot off across my feet. If I didn't need a drink before, I do now."

And drink we did. Champagne. Mostly pink Taittinger. Then she got the Kir out. I groaned at the memory. She'd been determined to convince me to stay and also to keep the kids at Stirling Hall. "I'll make you Kir Royales every night of your life."

I couldn't allow myself to borrow money. I'd never be able to repay it. If Lawrence didn't come back, she'd need her trust fund. Maybe I was of "parochial mind" as the prof used to say about anyone who couldn't recite at least ten poems off by heart, but surely even Clover couldn't lend me £15,000 without noticing the difference. And £15,000 would probably only pay off the debts I had now and see the kids through another few years before I'd be out with the begging bowl again. She seemed almost insulted I wouldn't accept her offer.

"Darling, I wouldn't suggest it if I couldn't afford it," was as close as she got to saying, "It's nothing to me." I loved her for not ramming that point home.

I frowned. My eyes stung as though some elf had been sandpapering them smooth during the night. A blurry recollection of eventually giving in to Clover and agreeing to stay until after the ball next Friday was fighting its way through the morning fog. Clover had said she needed someone to drown her sorrows with if Lawrence left permanently, then burst into tears. I'd surrendered, somewhere between finishing off the champagne and hoovering up the stale Wotsits that had escaped Clover's health blitz. Just over a week to plan my dead-end future.

I fumbled for my mobile and switched it on. One serious-sounding message from Mr Peters left at midnight: "Your withdrawal letter for the children appeared on my desk about five minutes before assembly. It made me think I'd got you all wrong but we should at least talk." And a text sent at 6 a.m. "*Maia, please call me.*"

Got me wrong? What about leaving Stirling Hall without breathing a word? And forgetting to mention that he'd been up close and personal with Serena's underwear? I already had Colin lying his arse off to me, I didn't need to find his twin. Mr Peters was intelligent. He'd be much better at it. If I spoke to him, he'd out-clever me and talk me round. I struggled into a semi-sitting position and texted back, "*No point. Nothing to say.*" The phone rang immediately. "Mary" flashed up. I watched it ring. My fingers twitched to pick it up, to hear his voice, to let him say what I wanted to believe. He didn't leave a message. Not that bothered then.

I swung my legs over the side of the bed, wondering if I should have a quick cry in the shower and get it over with. The mobile rang again. My heart lifted and crashed back down. Colin.

"Mai, Mai, it's me, Colin. You all right? Did you come back home yesterday? Yeah? What time did you come by? Ten-thirty? I must've missed you. Prob'ly down the betting shop. Painting, that is, not betting. I've given up that lark. Not completely, of course, never know when you might get the big one, but sensible, like."

Colin always talked too much when he was guilty of something. I was restricting my comments to "Mmm". Men were such lying shits.

"Are you coming back, darl?" I'd give him "darl". "Did you like me painting? Looks good, don't it? I tried to surprise you. Thing is, I really need you, darl. I don't want you living over there and me here on me own. I want us to be a family again."

I sat up. There was something in his voice. It wasn't love, desire or even loneliness. I'd had lots of practice at spotting Colin up to no good. I'd play along, even though a picture of his balls and a pair of pinking shears was flashing through my mind. I couldn't bear the thought that he'd be sitting there, rolling a spliff, perhaps even winking at Sandy, thinking he'd got away with it.

I flicked the "V's" at the phone but contented myself with "I'll be back a week on Monday. Can you get Harley's room painted as well? I don't want him to feel left out. And tidy up the kitchen." Now wasn't the time to confront him about Sandy. If I was going to stand any chance of booting Colin out and getting the house back for myself, I'd need an element of surprise on my side.

Relief made Colin generous. "See what I can do. I think there's some blue down at the betting shop. I'll try and get me hands on some of that. And the kitchen. Sorry about that."

I rang off. He'd got what he wanted. Now it was my turn.

CHAPTER
TWENTY-EIGHT

Stirling Hall was on holiday for nineteen weeks a year but the teachers still couldn't find the time to have a spot of training without a flaming inset day. Jen1, who probably had her diary mapped out for the next five years, had spotted a gap between Hugo's drama and clarinet lessons and filled it with a tank party for his birthday. Harley and Orion spent the whole journey there pretending to be SAS commandos in Afghanistan. Noise never bothered Clover but by the time the Land Rover bounced up the muddy farm track, my nerves were shot. As we rounded the corner to the barn, a silver limousine decorated with "Happy Eleventh Birthday, Hugo" balloons greeted us. A silver limousine stuck in the mud, wheels spinning, sending great splatters of gungy slime over the four men trying to push it out of its soggy pit. Jen1 was running up and down, shouting orders to the driver and the pushers.

Harley leapt out of the Land Rover. "Wicked! Come on, Orion, let's go and help."

Before I managed to yell at them to stay away from the car, a huge spray of brown sludge shot over them both. They started slinging globs of mud at each other, slamming each other over and killing themselves laughing. Hugo and Marlon rushed to join in. Venetia's son, Theo, shouted at them to stop, standing with his arms folded, looking just like his fussy father when a big splat landed square on his chest. Suddenly all the violin lessons, all the Mandarin tuition, all the Kumon maths rolled off him as he hurled himself at Harley, joining in with more spirit than I'd ever seen in him.

One of the men suddenly stopped pushing the car and came running over to them. I steeled myself for them getting banned from the tank driving. Instead, the man pulled Orion into his arms.

Clover's hand flew to her mouth. "That's Lawrence. Fucking hell. I haven't seen him in six weeks and here I am in his old jumper. Not even lipstick."

"Go and say hello."

"I can't. I feel sick."

We watched as he hugged Orion and Orion hugged him back, not giving a monkey that all his friends were there. Lawrence waved at Clover.

"I'll just go and pop the presents in the barn," I said.

Clover's hand shot out. "No, stay, don't leave me."

Lawrence looked like a clay figure plastered from head to toe in gunge as he squelched up to us.

"Hello love."

Clover had emotions bubbling up to her eyeballs. She gasped a hello. I couldn't bear it. There were some things a wife had to do without a friend in tow. Sex and tricky conversations about relationships were in that category. Especially as last time I'd met Lawrence, I'd threatened to poke his brains out with a wooden giraffe. I waved a hello and raced off. The other men had taken a break from trying to budge the limousine, so I went over to Jen1. She was wearing a sweatshirt with a baby photo of Hugo and eleventh birthday nonsense all over it.

I didn't want to sound like I was crowing so I didn't mention the car. "You're very brave hosting a party the day before the ball. You must be so organised. Harley was really excited about it."

"We booked it as soon as we knew about the teachers' training day. I wasn't about to tell Hugo he couldn't have a party because mummy was too busy with the school ball. He's only going to be eleven once — my little baby is eleven! He can't help that it's his birthday today. I've been baking all week and freezing the food, so I only had to pull it all out this morning."

"Jeepers. When my kids were little, I used to move their birthday to a day more convenient to me," I said.

"What? If Harley's birthday was on a Tuesday, you'd move it to a Thursday if that suited you better?"

"Yes."

"But you gave them presents on their real birthday, right?" Jen1 stared at me as though I'd told her that I'd put whisky in their bottles when they were babies so they'd sleep while I went down the pub.

"Wrong. I just moved the whole thing to two or three days later. They didn't even know." I smiled and handed her the presents. I'd have liked to see her face when Hugo opened them. She'd asked me for some vouchers for the Royal Opera House — "He's dying to go and see *Cosi Fan Tutte*" — which didn't really fit into my £5 a present allocation. She'd suggested a bird table to Clover — "Hugo loves watching the birds in the garden. We spotted a green woodpecker this morning."

Clover had snorted and said, "Poor little bugger, I bet he hates birds and dreads being dragged along to some vile opera when he'd rather go and watch some computer-generated rubbish at the cinema. I'm going to buy him a huge bucket of sweets and a catapult to frighten the birds." I totally ignored Jen1 and trotted off to Oxfam, thrilled to find *Mockingjay*, the third book in Suzanne Collins' trilogy for 75p. I knew from Harley that Hugo was reading the second one so I decided that I would look thoughtful, if not generous. Anyway, ignoring what she'd asked for didn't seem any ruder to me than dictating what people should buy in the first place.

I looked over at Clover and Lawrence. Orion was still standing with his arms round his dad. He'd forgotten any ten-year-old cool.

"What's Lawrence doing here?" I said to Jen1.

"He and Leo are terrifically good friends and Lawrence has always wanted to drive a tank apparently, so Leo told him to come along. I meant to warn Clover, but I got waylaid making Hugo's cake. It's a chameleon. I had to use about six different colours of icing. It's not as hard as it looks. A bit fiddly cutting out every little scale separately but it's turned out fabulously well."

"I'm sure Clover will be delighted that Hugo has got a wonderful cake."

Jen1 stared at me as though she was trying to work out whether I was serious or not. I wondered whether Leo had ever had a good laugh with her in his life.

Lawrence stepped away from Orion as Leo shouted to everyone to push the car again. Clover came over to me looking as though she needed to get out of there quickly before she made a show of herself. I raised my eyebrows. She shrugged. "We couldn't talk because Orrie was there. Lawrence said he'd done a lot of thinking. And that he'd missed the children terribly. I couldn't tell whether he'd missed me though. I made him agree to come round next week, so we can make some decisions. I managed to whisper that I loved him."

"Did he say anything?"

"No. He just gave me a tiny wink. I do really, really love him." Tears were leaking down her face.

I took her arm. "Come on, let's go. I'm not helping Jen1 get her stupid limousine out of the mud. Silly cow." And to prove that good things come to those who hang about long enough, Jen1 chose that moment to fall flat on her face in a mud bath, her blonde mane hanging round her shoulders like a muddy octopus. I waved a very cheery goodbye to Harley and leapt in the Land Rover, shoulders shaking.

CHAPTER
TWENTY-NINE

Clover made me jump on the morning of the ball. It was 6.30a.m. and nothing usually disturbed my porridge eating, apart from Weirdo who would roll onto his back for a tummy tickle. She came clattering in, rustling about in the cupboards for something less healthy than a bran muffin. It was probably a bit rich for me to feel grumpy that she'd come into her own kitchen but I'd never been a morning person.

We'd already discussed five hundred — or possibly five thousand — Lawrence scenarios the night before, ranging from him suddenly fancying men to sleeping with prostitutes to falling in love with a school friend he'd found on Facebook. Clover kept wanting reassurances from me that she was, above anyone else we could think of, the perfect match for Lawrence. The problem was I didn't know enough about him to have a clue. If what you wanted from marriage was a huge-hearted, generous and funny human being then Clover was your girl, but if you were in the market for shiny skirting boards, polished shoes and an ability never to run out of kitchen roll, then she probably wasn't.

At the crack of dawn I didn't want to discuss Lawrence any more. I don't think there was ever a moment in Clover's life when her jaw wasn't in constant jabbering motion. It normally didn't bother me because she made me laugh, but I was having my own Mr Peters trauma. I'd ignored so many texts and phone calls from him now, there was no going back. I needed a bit of quiet time to work out what face to put on if he did show up at the ball. I didn't really think he would — busman's holiday and all that, at eighty-five quid a ticket to boot — but I needed to be ready on the off chance. I couldn't do that while Clover needed an answer every two minutes. I did an "Oh my God, is that the time?" and made a break for the van before she started debating whether the woman who changed the bin liners where Lawrence worked might have stolen his heart.

My cleaning shifts passed in a blur. My customers would have nothing to complain about. Wherever I could, I took rugs outside and beat the shit out of them. I plumped pillows until feathers threatened to fly everywhere. I polished tables until my angry little face glowed back. It was nearly twenty years since I'd first been stupid enough to fall in love with Colin, but I couldn't remember him ever getting such a reaction from me. Even though I was furious with Mr Peters, my belly kept doing that flapping fish thing every time I thought about him. I was going to have to take up boxing as a second career to stop myself going mad.

When I got home, Clover was standing on her head against the wall. She'd covered her face in black mud.

"I read somewhere that standing on your head boosts the circulation to your face. Thought it might help my wrinkles. This mud stuff is from the Dead Sea. Not sure that's a selling point but it's supposed to rejuvenate. Do I look eighteen yet?" She was scissoring her legs while she balanced.

I didn't want to offend her by laughing, but I didn't think Lawrence would be making similar preparations. "You haven't got any wrinkles." I wasn't being kind. Despite Clover's beauty regime of a splash of water and a dab of patchouli oil, she had great skin. And her high cheekbones were beginning to stand out again.

"I still look a bit chipmunky though. Still, can't do anything about it now. I daren't eat any more of that rabbit food. Popping lethal farts in his face isn't going to win him back." Amen to that.

I carried a huge bundle of ironing into the kitchen, leaving Clover to head off upstairs to ladle on the Immac. I needed to get the shirts out of the way so I could spend a bit of time getting ready. I wasn't going to make a silk purse out of a sow's ear but with the dress Clover was lending me, if Peters did turn up, there was half a chance that he wouldn't be shouting "Hallelujah!" on his lucky escape.

Seventeen shirts and many mad conversations in my mind with both Colin and Mr Peters later, I headed upstairs. I'd expected Clover to be twirling around dancing to Hot Chocolate like she normally did when she was getting ready to go out. But no "You Sexy Thing", no "It Started with a Kiss". "Clover? Clover?" I knocked on her door.

She appeared in a fluffy dressing gown, hair wrapped in a towel, her cheerful face all upside-down clown. I didn't even have to ask what was wrong.

"What if he doesn't want me?"

I hustled her into the bedroom. "There is absolutely no way he is not going to want you. Look at you, you're gorgeous. Come on, let me blow dry your hair."

Time was ticking away. Six o'clock and we had to leave in an hour. I'd just have to look like shit. It wouldn't change the outcome of my life. I tamed Clover's blonde mane until it hung smooth and relatively frizz-free. She kept telling me to leave her and get ready but by now, the rebel in me had gained the upper hand and I felt like showing up in my tracksuit to prove to everyone they could chant "Chavarama" at me and I wouldn't care.

I handed Clover a little brown bottle of Rescue Remedy, rolling my eyes as I did so. Rescue Remedy was in the same category as homeopaths, chakras and auras. Before I put it back in the bathroom, I had a quick swig. Tonight was a night for bet hedging. I zipped Clover up into her brand new lime green dress. She stepped into her silver stilettos. Any resemblance to a farmer's wife had disappeared. She looked every inch the grand lady. The square frame of a few weeks earlier was now a curvy, busty silhouette. I turned her round to face the mirror. I could see belief and relief in her eyes.

I left her trying on different earrings. I threw myself in the shower and dried my hair upside down on full blast until I looked like I'd been swept in off the moors.

The taxi was hooting. I ran downstairs, zipping up the red dress, still in my Crocs, sandals in hand. I shouted goodbye to the kids who were playing a rowdy game of table football with the babysitter refereeing. Bronte came to the door and waved. "You look lovely. Not like a cleaner. Like a princess." I still felt like a cleaner.

We bundled into the taxi where I put my hair up with the black plastic crocodile clip I used for work, did my make-up in a compact mirror and painted the two toenails that would be visible in the gorgeous gold Louboutins Clover had lent me.

When the cab pulled through the gates at Jen1's, I realised that a twenty-minute turnaround wasn't the way to go. I'd never been to a ball before. I knew it wouldn't be jeans and fleeces in the village hall, but I hadn't expected it to be like a bloody film festival in the South of France. The entire driveway was decked with pink fairy lights, strung from tree to tree. Oil lamps burnt on the ground. At the side of the house a red carpet led to the marquee. Black dominated. Long, short, lacy, frilly, sequinned, with a bit of gold or red thrown in. Clover and I shuffled out. A flash went off in my face. I vaguely recognised one of the dads behind the camera. No doubt I was pulling a face like the village idiot after too much cider. I looked down. I had the bloody gold sandals in my hand and my sludge green Crocs peeping out under my dress. You couldn't take the SD1 out of the girl.

I wanted to hunch over and rush inside. Preferably to the ladies and not come out again. I knew Clover was nervous. That's where confidence, paid for at finishing school, stepped in. As soon as she put an ankle out of the car, it was showtime. She was waving, joking, posing in a ta-da way for the camera, kissing other people's husbands, never doing that awkward nose crash tangle. I followed her, smiling gawkily, trying not to show my teeth in case I had lipstick on them. As soon as we made it into the shadows of the marquee, I headed to the toilet, leaving Clover holding two glasses of Buck's Fizz.

I should have known that the school ball would have doubled the turnover of hairdressers, beauticians and shoe shops for March. I stood messing about in front of the mirror for ages. Hair clipped up like a cleaner? Or down like Morticia from *The Addams Family?* I quietly opened the cabinet under the sink to see if there was a brush or some perfume I could borrow but bleach and Glade were my only friends. I dragged my fingers through my hair and left it down. I made do with a big squidge of hand cream that I rubbed into my arms, calves and chest. Someone was knocking on the door. I shoved my Crocs under the sink, stuck the sandals on my feet and with a "Here goes nothing", I stepped out. Straight into Serena.

"Hello, hello again," I said, as though she was the person I'd most looked forward to seeing. My belly clenched so tight I wished Ram was there to see it. What the F was she doing there? She'd had her hair curled which made her look so much less sturdy-shoes-and-notebook and far more sex-plaything-draped-on-an-animal-skin. Everything about her was glossy. Bright red lips. Bright red nails. Beautifully plucked eyebrows.

274

The sort of long glittery halter-neck dress that people over five foot nine could carry off in a way I never would. She'd better not have come with Mr Peters.

She smiled. "We must stop bumping into each other like this. Nice to see you again — you look gorgeous. I'll catch up with you later — you must tell me what you thought of the homeopath."

I nodded vacantly. "Mmm. Yes. The homeopath was interesting. See you later," I said, as she disappeared into the toilet. Homeopath. Shit. I'd have to make up some old guff.

I found my way back to the marquee and stood against the back wall. The draught grouched across the top of my sandals. The heaters were on but cold gusted down my back. I wished I was at home. Even shitty Colin home. I couldn't see Clover. But I wasn't looking for her really. I was looking for Mr Peters, praying to my mother's favourite saint, St Jude, the patron saint of hopeless cases, that he wouldn't be there. I could hear Mum's guttural voice in my mind, "Amaia, San Judas Tadeo, his help come at last minute. You believe, you pray, he always respond."

St Jude must have been on a coffee break or maybe I was too hopeless even for him. Mr Peters was there all right, with his back to me, talking to the headmaster. I knew he would look gorgeous in black tie. I reminded myself that he'd done a runner on me without a word, long before he knew that I was taking the kids out of school. He turned round. I deliberately looked towards the stage so I didn't catch his eye. I had no idea what

I'd find there. Pity, hate, anger? Or maybe he just wouldn't give a shit. Better not to know.

Clover appeared at my side. "I've seen Lawrence."

"And?"

"I lost my nerve. I dived into the kitchen."

"He must know you're here, though. Why don't you wait until he's played the first set and then go and talk to him? He must be feeling nervous about performing in front of people he knows."

"You're probably right. Here, let's get some more champagne." Clover took a couple of glasses off a passing waitress.

"Might be a good idea to take it easy on the booze, so you're not stumbling into the plant pots when you do finally speak to him."

"Stop being so hideously sensible. I might be devastated tomorrow, so let's have a bit of a hoot now." Instead of passing me the second glass, she glugged it down herself and scooped up two more. I took one from her. Thankfully someone banged a spoon on a glass and called us to our tables. Clover already had that slightly lairy look about her.

Clover and I arrived at the table first. A huge orchid sat in the middle, surrounded by fake rose petals and gold sequins. Little gilt-edged place cards dictated where we sat. Clover started snatching them up. "Good, Frederica's with us. Bad, so's Venetia 'my son's violin playing brings a tear to my eye' Dylan-Jones. Oooh, lucky you, you're next to Mr Peters. Who's Serena Blake? She's on his other side."

"Serena's the policewoman who helped find Bronte." I thought I might cry. "I can't sit next to Mr Peters. Will you swap with me?" I was hissing in a sort of desperate way.

"Whatever for? I'm next to Venetia's husband, Randolph. His idea of scintillating conversation is how to build a telescope from scratch. You stay where you are."

"No, no, it's fine. Let's swap." I snatched up my place card.

"Maia, that's beyond the call of duty. I can't subject you to an evening of 'my child is a genius, I'm not sure the school can contain him' when you could be having a tête-à-tête with Mr Peters."

"I don't mind at all. Come on, please. Mr Peters really likes you. He definitely won't want to sit next to me. Do you think we can stick Frederica next to him?"

"Maia, you've got to grow out of your fear of authority. Mr Peters is just a teacher."

I started to protest but shut up quickly when we heard, "Good evening, Mrs Wright, Ms Etxeleku," behind us. Clover laughed and gave Mr Peters a cheeky wave.

Mr Peters rested one hand on the back of the chair next to me, His other hand was on Serena's waist, guiding her to her place. Watching him touch her made my belly twist in on itself. I hated her in a way that made me look at her through slitty eyes. Mr Peters looked as though he'd been born to wear a dinner suit. No one would, ever know he'd been a one-time lout. I had a sudden picture of him at home at the end of the evening, bow tie undone, hanging loosely, shirt open. Something inside me lurched.

"Mrs Wright, this is PC Blake." Mr Peters went round the table introducing Frederica and her husband, Lloyd, Venetia and Randolph, and a man called Howard whose reedy, recently beaten dog appearance probably explained the fact that he didn't have a wife with him.

"Ms Etxeleku, you've met PC Blake before," Mr Peters said.

"Do call me Serena."

I wanted to answer, "Maia, aka Mr Peters' fling. Know about that, do you?" Instead I nodded like a fluffy dog hanging off a rear-view mirror.

"Could we drop the Stirling Hall formality for this evening and use Christian names? Otherwise it feels like parents' evening. Please feel free to call me Zac," Mr Peters said. Everyone said their first names. I mumbled mine in the direction of Venetia who wiggled her fingers at me and boomed, "Evening, Amayra."

We sat down. I could feel Mr Peters right next to me. He was such a people magnet, bouncing the conversation along, managing to include everyone. I didn't want to be part of his audience, even though he was smiling away, filling up my water glass and passing me the butter. He could pretend that I was just another mother but I would never be able to pretend that he was just another teacher. I tried to move my chair away so that his jacket didn't keep brushing my arm. I couldn't let any part of me touch any part of him because I could go either way. I might slap him. Or I

278

might sob. Nine of us were on a table for eight — they'd obviously lumped all the singletons together — so I managed to scrape about two centimetres closer to Howard on my right. His breath encouraged me to scrape four centimetres back again.

Howard was one of those blokes whose chat-up lines didn't take into account his malnourished mongrel looks. "So, Megan, how come I haven't seen you before? I'd have remembered a gorgeous woman like you." I tried to time my breathing so my in-breath of oxygen didn't coincide with his out-breath of horseshit.

"Better not drink too much, Megan, you might let me have my wicked way with you," he said, topping up my glass with white wine. "I'm not much of a Chablis man myself. I prefer Chardonnay."

"Chablis *is* made from Chardonnay." Clover had taught me well. I hadn't meant to correct him, I was just excited to know something that I thought posh people usually knew. But Howard wasn't so keen on someone common knowing something posh. He tried to enlist the help of Frederica to prove me wrong. She looked at him as though he'd just dived in front of her on the red carpet and said, "How the bloody hell should I know? I drink the stuff, not pick it off the vine."

Thankfully, the starters arrived. Prawns on a bed of mango and coriander. Frederica immediately complained that the prawns were in their shells. "I don't do bones, shells or anything that reminds me it once had a life. Bring back the bloody prawn cocktail."

I was concentrating on not shooting prawn juice over my dress when Howard leaned towards me. "The little bowls with lemon are for washing your fingers."

I felt a movement beside me. Mr Peters was obviously a closet woman and could listen to two conversations at once. "Mr Sutton, or rather, Howard, did you know that Maia's mother was a chef? I'm sure Maia would be delighted to share some of her Basque recipes and cookery tips with you."

I didn't think it was the right moment to point out my mother was a cook, a housekeeper, rather than a Jamie Oliver wannabe.

Howard blustered. "I didn't mean any offence, it was just a joke."

Mr Peters didn't smile. "I'm always saying this to the children. It's only a joke if everyone's laughing." He carried on peeling his prawns as though nothing had happened. Howard shrunk down in his seat. I nearly felt sorry for him. I glanced sideways at Mr Peters. He was shaking his head, jaw set.

Serena was talking to Clover in that deep Lauren Bacall voice of hers. No one was asking her if she could handle the starter. Even in a posh frock I must have looked like a right pikey. It must be so obvious to everyone else that I didn't fit in, that Mr Peters couldn't quite shake off his habit of sticking up for me.

My appetite had disappeared, but I didn't want to draw even more attention to myself by not eating. I stuck a prawn in my mouth and immediately regretted it. Along with the lime and coriander was chilli, which didn't agree with me. A bolt of heat shot through me.

Sweat broke out on my forehead. I dabbed at my upper lip with my serviette. Or was it napkin? I could never remember which one marked you out as rough. I knew my cheeks were turning bright red. I took a slug of water, then another. I knew that for the next twenty minutes I'd be leaking from every pore. I excused myself and went outside to stand in the cold to see if I could short-circuit my boiling blood.

I sat on a bench under a big sycamore tree watching the stars, feeling the sweat drying on my face and arms and the scorch of chilli heat slowing to a simmer. The cold air carried shouts and laughter. The quiet murmur of voices in the shadows on the other side of the marquee reached me through the dark. I heard a woman say, "I don't know what I'd do without you," but didn't catch the answering baritone.

I hugged my knees to me. Earflapping on someone else's love story just underlined my own failure. I got to my feet and went round the side to avoid walking past them. As I walked through Jen1's kitchen, I glanced at the CCTV monitor. It was flicking between views of the garage, front gates and both sides of the marquee. The grainy image shifted slightly. A man with dark tousled hair was cuddling a woman with a blonde chignon. Lawrence. But that wasn't Clover. I stared. Jen fucking 1.

CHAPTER
THIRTY

"Where have you been?" Clover said, or rather slurred, as I got back to the table. My heart was still jumping. Shit. Lawrence and Jen1. How was I going to tell Clover? Would I be better off waiting for a sober moment? Or was a body blow better with booze? If she decided to shoot the messenger, she could blast my bloody head off. I didn't mention my chilli allergy — every child at Stirling Hall was allergic to some damn thing, peanuts, eggs, milk, wheat — I didn't want to look like I was jumping on the bandwagon. I drivelled something about needing some fresh air.

Serena and Clover seemed to be having a great time, hooting over cop shows on TV and debating whether they represented real life or not. Venetia was on the sidelines with a fixed grin like she wanted to join in but had only ever watched *Panorama*, *Newsnight* and *University Challenge*. I wanted to tap Serena on the shoulder and tell her to get lost, that she already had my man, so she could keep her hands off my friend. Mr Peters was in my seat and was having some hoo-ha about the length of teachers' holidays with Howard and Lloyd.

He stood up as I got close to the table. "Maia, here, have your seat back."

"No, it's fine, I wanted to have a word with Frederica, anyway."

He was trying to lock me in, chiselling into my secrets with that steely stare. I wasn't falling for that old bollocks again. "So you are speaking to me then." He was talking very quietly with his back to the others.

"There's no point in speaking if there's nothing to say." I took a gulp of my wine, trying for a woman of the world flounce and hoping he didn't see me dribble it down my chin.

"Have you been okay?" he asked.

I glanced at Serena, shrugged slightly and said, "Spiffing. Marvellous. Fine and dandy."

He looked as though he was about to say something, but I could see the excuses, the lies gathering like pigeons on a phone wire. I left him standing there and walked round to Frederica. Out of the corner of my eye, I saw him shake his head and just managed to stop myself shouting, "What? What? What's your bloody problem?"

Frederica beckoned to me, bellowing in her stage voice as though she was trying to reach the cheap seats. "So, Maia, where's that gorgeous husband of yours tonight? Now, there's a man who'd look good in a tux. I do think there's something a bit Daniel Craig-ish about Colin."

My jaw thudding open must have registered on the earthquake scale. "This isn't really his kind of thing.

He's more a pie and a pint sort of man. I came along to keep Clover company."

"You look fantastic." Frederica paused. "Did Harley tell Marlon that you were living at Clover's at the moment? Or did I make that up? I never know what to believe."

"I've been helping her out a bit while, you know, Lawrence and all that. Anyway, we're going home on Monday." I tried to make light of it and move the conversation on. I didn't want Mr Peters to overhear and think I was crawling back to Colin with my tail between my legs. Frederica was still projecting her voice to the other end of the marquee, when Clover, not short of a foghorn or two herself, joined in.

"She's had enough of the Wright family. I keep trying to get her to stay, but no, seems Colin is more of a pull than me." That did piss me off. Colin didn't come into it and she knew it.

"Gorgeous man like that, Clover? Are you surprised, darling? You've got many qualities but I expect there are some areas that Colin trumps you in. Isn't that right, Maia?" And off Frederica went, cackling at her own joke. I was relieved when the lamb shanks arrived and I could sit down again. Serena leapt up and started spooning out the asparagus, mangetout and dauphinoise potatoes, patting the men on the shoulder and salsaing round the table like she'd known everyone for years.

When she was right over the other side, Mr Peters bent his head towards me. "So you're going back to Colin?"

"You have a problem with that?"

"Yes. Same one that I always had. He's an arsehole."

"Takes one to know one." I sounded about twelve but it couldn't be helped. There was a tiny moment when I thought I'd gone too far and my shoulders came up round my ears in that "oh shit" position. I wasn't quite ready to be the talk of Stirling Hall.

Mr Peters was far too classy to make a scene. He made a sound as though someone had punched him in the stomach. "Has something happened I don't know about? I didn't get the impression you thought I was an arsehole before."

I could feel myself backing away from confrontation with him. I reminded myself that I wasn't a pupil having to explain myself to him, he wasn't my teacher, he was a man, nothing special, just been to school a bit more than me. I redoubled my efforts and found a lovely pit of anger. "Since you ask, it really fucked me off to find out that you're leaving Stirling Hall and hadn't bothered to mention it."

"Who told you that?" he asked.

"Is it true?"

"Yes, but —"

"But bloody what?" I saw Serena glance in our direction. Every muscle in my face strained with the effort of smiling at her. Mr Peters leant over and filled up her wine glass. We both sat with fixed grins on our faces until she went back to her conversation with Clover. I whispered. "But what? Why didn't you say anything?"

"God, this is complicated." I could hear the northern inflection in his voice. He was fiddling with his cufflinks. His voice was so low I had to lean towards him to hear. "I could say the same about you. I wasn't too pleased myself to have a letter thump on my desk saying that you'd withdrawn Harley and Bronte without even discussing it with me."

"I didn't send that."

"Colin's taken to forging your signature now, has he?" He was drumming his fingers on his glass.

"No. I mean, I did write the letter but I was going to talk to you about it. I'd left it at the house because I was still thinking about it. He posted it before I could speak to you."

His eyes narrowed and then his face relaxed. He ran his fingers through his hair. "You went all funny on me before I could tell you about changing jobs. There was a good reason for it."

I never got to find out. Serena took Mr Peters' hand and butted in. "Weren't you saying you wanted to go to Florence, Zac? Venetia went at half-term."

And like a preacher sharing the gospel with the great unwashed, Venetia spouted out her views on Florence and Mr Peters had no choice but to listen. "We thought it terribly important for Theo to see the *Birth of Venus* in the flesh as it were. Interestingly, he preferred Giotto to Botticelli. Of course, there are so many amazing churches. We had to set ourselves a limit of two a day. My personal favourite was Santa Croce." Venetia was really giving it some on the Italian pronunciation front, sounding like an advert for pasta sauce with her "Santa Crrrrotchaaay".

Clover started sniggering. "Is that where you pray to God for a big cock to come visiting?"

Venetia looked like she was going to answer that one seriously. Just in time she realised it was a joke and bared her teeth in a thin smile. Frederica was talking about Mauritius and some amazing place on stilts; Howard started banging on about his holiday home in St Lucia. Even bloody Serena had slummed it off to California touring the Napa Valley — "Zinfandel Blush is to die for". I was dying to imitate her.

Mr Peters didn't seem about to enlighten us on whether the sky-high fees at Stirling Hall were funding luxury cruises in the Galapagos. He nodded in the right places but he didn't offer a view. I couldn't see whether he was still holding hands with Serena. I sat there picking at my lamb, desperate for the band to come on and drown them all out.

"What about you, Amayra? Is it Greece you're from? Do you go back there every year?" Venetia said.

My will to live had seeped away. "I just took the kids camping in Suffolk."

Venetia clapped her hands. "Oooh, glamping. It's all the rage. Did you stay in one of those big yurts with a wood burner stove? Did it have a solar-powered shower? Did you have to pedal a bike to generate your own electricity? Most places are getting so eco-friendly these days. It must be such fun."

"This was just a normal campsite." I didn't add that it rained all week and the four of us squashed into a tent that stunk of mould because Colin had put it away wet the year before.

"Oooh," Venetia said again. "British seaside holidays are so trendy now. Makes the Caribbean sound so passe. You are brave though, Amayra, I don't know whether I could face camping."

Not brave. Just poor.

"Whereabouts in Suffolk?" Venetia said.

"Sizewell."

"Isn't that where the nuclear reactor is?" Randolph suddenly rattled into life. "Aren't they planning to build underground caverns to house nuclear waste there?" Off he went into a rant about the "monumental folly" of this, that and the other plan. Even Clover pretending to snooze didn't make me crack a smile.

Just when I thought it couldn't get any worse, Serena turned to me. "So, Maia, how did you get on at the homeopath's? I've been wondering if homeopathy could help with my hormones. As Zac knows, I get quite bad-tempered at certain times of the month." A little knee pat.

"I just thought that was your personality," Mr Peters said, deadpan.

Annoyance flashed across Serena's face. She ploughed on. "I forgot to tell you that I bumped into Maia at yours the other day."

My turn to be annoyed. "I go to see the homeopath there. She helps me with my eczema. I think the cleaning stuff causes it."

Serena's eyebrows knitted together. "She? I thought the homeopath was a man?"

288

Shit. "I think there are two of them. The woman only does a few hours a week, I think." I looked at Mr Peters.

He said, "I've never seen a woman homeopath there. Maybe it was Mandy, the beautician who shares the studio?"

"I go to Mandy," Serena said. She leant over, putting her hand in front of her mouth like a schoolgirl with a secret, and whispered: "She does electrolysis on my face." She started speaking loudly again. "Mandy's never mentioned homeopathy to me. Come on, Maia, admit it to us, you were really there for a Brazilian, weren't you?"

Serena found herself hilarious. I wondered if she was sporting a landing strip that she'd be putting on show for Mr Peters later that night. His face was wary, as though he didn't like the way the conversation was heading.

A great big flush was spreading across my chest. I couldn't think of a single girl's name. I was searching round for inspiration when I saw sherry vinegar on the menu. "I think she's called Sherry. Anyway, I've only been a couple of times, so I don't know whether it works or not."

"What did she give you?" Serena said.

"I can't remember now. Some pill thing."

Thankfully, just as I was digging myself a hole so deep I could shake hands with a kangaroo, the cheese plate arrived. Venetia was out of her seat with excitement. "Ooooh, look, Duchy Originals biscuits. And Cambozola. Scrummy."

"I think that's Dolcelatte, not Cambozola," Serena said.

Venetia frowned. "I did do a Cordon Bleu cookery course. Cheese identification was part of it."

"Sorry, I was just saying."

Venetia harrumphed and carried on pointing at the cheese plate. "That's Cornish Yarg, look, it's got the nettles round it. That's Norbury Blue. They make that on a farm over at Mickleham. I think that's ordinary Brie."

"Jesus, just when I was longing for a bit of Edam," Frederica said, winking in my direction.

Howard passed me the plate. "You go first, Megan." I dreaded to think what he'd smell like after a round of blue cheese. I'd just taken a piece of the identity crisis Cambozola/Dolcelatte and was in the process of cutting some Brie, when Howard shrieked, "Megan!" I looked round for the fire, or the man with a machine gun, or the big fat hornet with a sting the size of a drill.

"What?" I asked.

"You've cut the nose off the Brie," Howard said.

"What?"

"You can't cut the nose off the Brie."

Saying "What?" for the third time was going to make me seem a bit short of imagination. Clover stepped in. "Fuck off, Howard. Get a bloody life. If you're worried about who is cutting the pointy bit off the Brie or whether someone uses the right fucking fork, you are not busy enough." You had to love the girl. She'd actually managed to tell me what Howard was on about, without having to take me to one side and spell

290

it out. I mouthed a thank you at her. Clover did a not very discreet tosser gesture in return.

Howard spluttered but didn't try and argue back. Venetia started off on some boring technical explanation about how it was important to keep the cheese in its original shape so everyone got exactly the same amount of good and bad bits. Howard nodded away, a ridiculous flappy bit of hair bouncing up and down. How could there be a right or wrong way to cut a piece of cheese? I got the point of knife rules if you were operating on someone's brain, carving a piece of wood or carrying out scientific research on rats, but cutting a piece of cheese? Was there someone sitting in an office somewhere making up stupid rules for posh people? Did it only apply to Brie or was it the same for Dairylea Triangles, Philadelphia and Babybel? And if you were posh, how could it be considered good manners to point out the social cock-ups of people who didn't know any better?

Thankfully, the lights dimmed and the growly throb of an electric guitar started up before I used the cheese knife to gouge out Howard's Adam's apple. The joy of a diversion from all these people with their heads up their backsides nearly had me whipping off my dress and streaking across the marquee singing, "Get yer tits out for the lads." Clover had gone still. Venetia was trying to shout about the advantages of a cheese wire over a cheese knife above the music but Clover had turned her back on her to look at the stage. Lawrence came on, looking much younger than his forty-two years, in drainpipe jeans, Andy Warhol T-shirt and a leather jacket. With his curly black hair and blue eyes, he looked as though he'd hopped down from a Romany caravan in Galway. He bowed low and then broke into "I Love Rock "n" Roll".

Howard leaned towards me. Tiramisu-mixed-with-dustbin-left-in-the-sun breath gusted over me. "Every middle-aged man a rock star."

I wanted to pretend he was invisible but I needed to defend Lawrence. "He's brilliant though, look at him." Lawrence was living and breathing every chord, eyes half-closed, looking as though this was what he was born to do. I couldn't imagine him squinting over sheets of figures and sitting in meetings with dandruffy old bankers. Then I remembered he was having an affair with Jen1 and hoped that he would be forced to bean count from here to eternity and that tonsillitis would plague him into old age.

Clover's eyes were dancing with delight. Frederica was raising her glass and hooting. When the music changed to "Twist and Shout", Lloyd pulled Frederica to her feet, which broke the ice and everyone crowded onto the dance floor, twisting up and down. Even Venetia was grooving. Her great arse was wobbling as though someone had strapped a beanbag to it. In a white flouncy dress with frilly tiers, she looked like a wedding cake on the move, while Randolph was doing this pointing at the ceiling thing, a bit like a Pinocchio puppet Bronte used to have.

Howard tapped me on the arm. "Come on, Megan, let's show them how it's done." I beckoned to Clover who giggled and waved me onto the dance floor. I tried glaring and pulling desperate faces but the old baggage refused to come to my rescue. She sat there grinning over the top of her wine glass. Howard was all I'd expected but with BO thrown in. He'd taken his jacket off, presumably to free himself up for the Freddie Mercury crossed with Russian Cossack dancer moves for "Good Vibrations". When I looked over to Clover, she had her head on her arms, but I could see her shoulders heaving up and down with laughter. I'd get her back.

Mr Peters and Serena were turned in towards each other, faces serious. She kept touching his knee when she was talking. I hated her for having that privilege. I hated her for looking at him, head on one side, puppy dog eyes, simpering away. She was playing the "I love Jimmy Choos and fluffy kittens" card when she'd probably do you in with a pair of Doc Martens and a rusty screwdriver if push came to shove. I wanted to kill her for butting in when we had one tiny chance to straighten out a few things. Too late now. Mr Peters loved someone else. Someone smart. Love didn't have much of a place in my world anyway. What a dumbo for thinking it did.

When the music changed to "(I Can't Get No) Satisfaction" I couldn't face the prospect of Howard's arms in the air and told him that Clover loved the song and he should ask her to dance. He scampered across to the table and dragged her to her feet. I waved and watched as a big cloud of BO filtered through to her. The only people left at the table were Mr Peters and Serena. Seeing the back of his neck with the funny little swirl of hairs made me long to touch him. I hovered on the edge of the dance floor. Frederica spotted me and swept me in, bringing me into her circle of foot stampers and air thumpers. Diamond necklaces bounced up and down on cleavages. Fat stomachs bulged over cummerbunds. Rolexes glittered on wrists. And everyone danced as though they were at the Scout Hut jamboree, knocking back the cider rather than the Châteauneuf.

Then the music changed. Lawrence looked out into the audience. His eyes settled on Clover. "This song is for a very special person. She knows who she is, but is probably wondering who the hell I am right now. This is for you."

The chords of "Just the Way You Are" rang out. Then Lawrence's deep voice filled the marquee and couples moved into each other's arms. Out of the corner of my eye, I saw Mr Peters and Serena get to their feet. Clover stood in the middle of the dance floor, eyes brimming, oblivious to everyone else around her. Howard hung around at her side for a few seconds before even he had the sense to slink off. Lawrence sang into the crowd, never taking his eyes off Clover. It was a first-class shafting from a two-timing arsehole. What a brilliant way to cover your tracks — sing a soppy love song to your wife with everyone there to witness it. I couldn't watch.

I marched off to the loo, but not before I'd seen Serena wind her arms around Mr Peters' neck. I stared at myself in the mirror to see if the sick jealousy churning my insides showed on my face. I couldn't believe how normal I looked, apart from my eyebrows, which were sticking up like some has-been politician's. I'd never managed to train them into elegant curves. I didn't want to go back out so I had another little nose at the photos of Jen1, Leo and Hugo. Hugo had that sly, sharp edge about him that Jen1 had. The sort of look teenage girls have when they're smoking in school uniform. Leo had a much more open face. There he was at a posh event with Lawrence, holding up some kind of award. They were both in DJs. Leo was bursting, delighted with himself. Lawrence still managed to look scruffy, hair tumbling about as though he'd blundered into the ceremony during a gale-force wind. He had a half-smile on his face, as though he was about to break into a sarky speech, "And I'd like to thank my agent, my make-up artist and my manicurist."

I wondered if Leo knew Lawrence was banging his wife.

Someone rattled the toilet door handle. The throb of music that had been making my buttocks judder had stopped, which meant more sitting round the table nicey-nicey with Serena simpering over Mr Peters'. I couldn't face trying to look pleased for Clover, when heartbreak was heading her way. I pulled my Crocs from their hiding place under the sink, grabbed the gold sandals and crept down the hallway. I peered into the kitchen. There was Jen1, ordering the coffee girls about like a Victorian mistress of the manor. "Jessica, no, plee-aase don't slop it in the saucer. No, give it to me. Goodness me, don't they teach you anything at catering college?"

How could Lawrence possibly prefer that uptight gold-digger to Clover? I opened the front door and stepped out. Tiny spots of drizzle pattered down onto my arms. I looked up at the CCTV camera, gave it the finger in case Jen1 was watching and set off down the drive.

CHAPTER
THIRTY-ONE

Once I got outside the gates guarding Jen1's palace, I walked towards the pub, feeling the hem of Clover's beautiful dress dragging along the pavement now I'd taken my high heels off. I hitched it up. It was 11.15. If I was lucky, I'd make it to the pub before chucking out time and they'd be able to call me a cab. A few people were straggling out as I clumped into the car park. I walked into the bar. The landlord looked up from washing glasses and offered a surly "We're closed". He didn't bat an eyelid at the fact that I had no coat, my hair was wet and I was in a ball dress.

"I know, I just wanted a number for a cab."

He nodded towards the corridor. "On the wall out there." I punched the number into my phone, and as there was no offer for me to wait inside, I walked back out again. By the time the cab arrived, I was shivering.

"Bloody hell, love, where's your coat? You girls. Catch your death. Good evening, was it? Where we off to then?" the cabby said.

I hadn't planned it. It just came out. Rowley Road, SD1. I saw his eyebrows shoot up in the rear-view mirror. "Bit far from home, aren't we? Gonna cost you. You got the fare? You ain't gonna get much change out of a twenty." I thought about all the things I could do with twenty pounds. But going back to Clover's wasn't an option. I couldn't stand it if she turned up with Lawrence. I didn't have the stomach for watching anyone being lovey-dovey.

The cab driver nattered on. "First time I pick up anyone from round your way in a ball frock. I don't go there normally. Too many druggies. Used to work that patch between the rec and Walldon Estate but got puke in me car too many times. You live there, do you? It's a lot worse since all them Eastern Europeans came over. They've started taking our jobs on the taxis now. Can hardly speak English, let alone find their way around Sandbury. If you need a taxi, love, you make sure you call my cab company and ask for Ronnie. I know where I'm going, I do."

And on it went. I looked out of the window, wondering if Mr Peters had noticed I'd gone. I texted Clover to tell her I'd had to go home, no emergency, I'd be over for the kids in the morning. She rang as I was getting out of the cab. She was talking fast. Excited and happy. I fobbed her off, saying I wanted her to have the house to herself. She didn't put up much of an argument once she knew I was safe.

I stared at the house. There were no lights on. Next door, Sandy's bedroom was lit up and I could hear the faint strains of Bob Marley. Sandy's bonking music. I crept up the path, sandals and shiny little evening bag in hand. I opened the door. The house was still. I stood in the hallway and listened, watching my breath form puffy little clouds in the freezing air. Once I'd turned the thermostat up, I tiptoed upstairs. I hung Clover's dress on a hanger, pulled on an old tracksuit and got to work. I fetched some bin bags from the kitchen and stuffed Colin's clothes in, willy-nilly, pissed off that I'd wasted time ironing his T-shirts. Never mind. Sandy's problem now. In went the lucky West Ham pants, the England shirt, the baseball cap with the "I'm Forever Blowing Bubbles" logo. I tossed in a pile of rusty Bic razors, the dog-eared toothbrush, all the socks he hadn't bothered to pair up since I'd been gone. Next, the little darts shield he'd won in the pub league, old copies of *Racing Post* that he'd been too lazy to chuck out and all the old boots, sweatshirts and holey jeans that had been mouldering away in the bottom of the wardrobe.

In less than an hour, I'd packed Colin into a couple of black bin bags. I hopped over the little fence into Sandy's garden. "No Woman, No Cry" was seeping down into the darkness. One bin bag. Two bin bags. A pile of crappy CDs. Colin's collection of high body count DVDs. Blow-up football armchair. I rang the bell. There was a thud upstairs. The music went off. Sandy's shrill voice. Colin's grumble. Heavy footsteps on the stairs. Colin's voice, grumpy and aggressive. "Who is it?"

I didn't answer, just stood there. I knew curiosity would get the better of him.

The key turned in the lock. Colin, shirtless, in a pair of tracksuit bottoms.

He took a step back. "Maia!"

"I gather you've moved out. You forgot some of your things so I've packed them up for you."

"Mai." Colin's mouth was moving up and down, but he was struggling to get a sound out. "It's not what it looks like."

"What does it look like? You having a neighbourly cup of tea with Sandy? You unblocking the lav? Colin, save it. I heard you the other week with your 'Goaaaal'. Not very original, are you? She can have you, and all the crap that goes with you."

"You can't chuck me out like that."

"Just watch me." I picked up one of his Doc Martens and slung it into the hallway. "You're gone, Colin. History. Sandy can put up with you humping away like a donkey in heat now. You can score as many 'goooooaaaaals' as you like."

"Oy! You always said I was good in bed."

"No, you always said you were good in bed."

Colin's eyebrows knitted together as he tried to figure out whether that was true or not. He started to bluster. "You can't just turn up and turf me out."

"I just have. And if you don't want me to shop you for working while you're on benefits, you'll stay out. Don't forget I know where all the skeletons are, starting with the dodgy DVD players and the mobile phones. It won't be just you I dob in, I'll finger your mates too, so if the cops don't get you, then I suspect Big Harry or Bruno will." I could see Colin's brain cranking into gear as he totted up the damage I could do him.

Sandy appeared behind him in a lacy dressing gown, a post-goal cigarette hanging out her mouth. She should have been shaking in her fluffy mules. But Sandy being Sandy, she stood with one hand on her hip, a "bring it on" set to her jaw.

I should have flown at her, told her she was a homewrecker, slung a few insults about her being a slag and shitty friend. I couldn't summon up the energy. It was like finding a home for a settee you wanted shut of, without the effort of taking it down the dump. The biggest surprise to me was that I didn't feel angry, just resigned. Not much to show for nineteen years' hard labour with one man.

I leaned round Colin. "You've done me a favour, love. He's yours. I'm not having him back."

She put a hand on Colin's shoulder. "I never have understood what you was moaning about."

"Give it time." I turned back to my house, then stopped. "Just answer me one thing, Colin. Why did you want me back?"

"I didn't."

I registered a tiny fork jab of hurt. Pride, probably. "But you practically begged me to come back."

"House is in your name, innit? There's been a bloke from the council poking his nose in cos we're behind on the rent and you ain't around. Told me that unless you turned up this week, we'd lose the house. They're having a crackdown. They ain't gonna let a single bloke stay in a three-bed house."

I nodded. "Thank God for that. I thought you were thinking of someone else apart from yourself. Now that would have been scary."

"You'd better get the rent sorted though, or move back in with that posh Flowerpot friend of yours. I don't want me kids with nowhere to live."

The first thing that came to hand was his West Ham mug, which hit the banister with a satisfying smash.

CHAPTER
THIRTY-TWO

The birds were singing by the time I dropped off. Once the adrenaline of giving Colin his marching orders had worn off, I'd realised that the boiler wasn't working. I'd stood shivering on a stool for ages, pressing the ignition button till my finger hurt. I slouched off upstairs wondering how long it would take the council to sort that out.

I didn't want to get into the bed I'd shared with Colin in case he'd been at it with Sandy there. I climbed into Harley's bed under every duvet and sleeping bag I could find. The bed didn't smell of Harley. It was cold and unloved, like the rest of the house. I tried to practise thinking of happy things, which is what I told the children when they couldn't get to sleep, but my brain was locked into misery, stuck on images of Serena and Mr Peters, which made me hug my knees into my chest and curl up into a tight ball. Eventually my mind strayed off into Lawrence in a clinch, the horrible Howard and his BO, a quick flash of humiliation over the cheese, then back to Colin and the way Sandy didn't give a monkey that she'd stolen my man, before ending up in the black sludge of thoughts about my future.

Was I really going to live here with Bronte and Harley, burying my head under the pillow so I couldn't hear Colin and Sandy next door? What about the kids? Gypsy and Denim had never known their dads. Would Colin step up to the plate? Bronte would hate that. The prof would have wrinkled her nose. "Sordid, Maia, perfectly sordid." She would have trotted out one of her favourite phrases, "You can do better than that, dear, much better. Lovely young woman like you." I missed having her on my side. For some reason she'd believed in me. I cried until water ran into my ears and the pillow felt and smelt like one of Harley's swimming towels, rotting in his school bag from one week to the next.

So when the world was slowly coming alive on Saturday morning, I was in the deep, deep sleep of the emotionally exhausted. It took some time for the thumping on the front door to filter through and even longer for me to go and investigate. If that was Colin, he could toss off. I was amazed he'd taken me seriously and hadn't let himself in. I opened the door a fraction and peered out. A man in blue overalls waved a clipboard at me. "Morning, sorry to disturb you so early. I'm here about the gas."

"Oh." I crossed my arms over my chest. "Excuse the pyjamas, I was expecting someone else. I didn't realise you guys worked at weekends. Anyway, brilliant, come in." I waved him through. "The boiler's in the kitchen, through there. It won't light. Give me a sec, I'll go and get dressed." I raced upstairs, having the first kind thought about Colin I'd had for a while. At least he'd bothered to phone the council. That probably meant moving out had come as a surprise to him. Good.

I threw on a pair of jeans and a sweatshirt and ran back downstairs. I expected the bloke to be tinkering with the boiler but in fact, he was standing in the kitchen, scribbling something down and looking round as though he was sizing up the joint.

"Have you had a look? What do you think?" I stayed in the doorway in case I'd welcomed someone into the house who was going to slit my throat. In fact, now I looked properly, there wasn't much of a toolbox thing going on. He turned round. Something sympathetic flashed across his face. I knew before he said a word.

"I'm not here to fix the boiler. I'm here on behalf of the gas company because your bill hasn't been paid." He looked down at his notes. "Since last November." He patted his identification card as though I'd challenged him.

I'd spent all that time pretending to be my Great Aunt Inmaculada, talking in a ridiculous Spanish accent to avoid phone calls from the people we owed money to. But when it mattered most, I'd opened my door and practically provided a trolley for him to wheel away our stuff. I looked down at my feet. My two bright red toenails stood out against the three I'd left unpainted during my quick fix on the way to the ball the night before. I waited.

The man rotated one shoulder as though he'd slept on it funny. "Do you know how much you owe?"

I wanted to explain. Explain that I hadn't been here. Colin not working. The whole school money drain. He wasn't going to be interested in my non-payment of the gas bill in favour of the new trainers I'd had to buy Harley because they had to be completely white, not the white with black stripes I'd sent in. Or the fifteen pounds I'd spent on a huge French dictionary for Bronte, plus four on Ferrero Rocher chocolates she'd demanded to take in on Italian day and a couple of quid on neon laces for Funky Footwear Friday. "I'm not sure."

He flicked a page over. "It's one hundred and ninety-seven pounds, twenty-three pence." Panic jolted through me. I had ninety-five pounds rolled up in an elastic band at the back of one of the drawers at Clover's. My emergency money.

"I can't pay that. I haven't got the money." I thought of Colin, curled up on the settee eating Jaffa Cakes through the autumn and winter with the heating high enough to grow orchids. "Can I pay a bit off a month?"

"You could have. But the gas company has sent so many letters and called so many times with no response that they've lost patience." He was shrugging his shoulders.

"My kids are coming home today. We can't live without any heating. And my hob's gas too. I've got to be able to cook."

"I'm sorry. If you don't let me install a pre-payment meter which works with a pay-as-you-go card, you'll get disconnected completely."

I had visions of the money running out in the middle of cooking dinner, endless freezing showers, the heating going off in the evening when there was no chance of

306

topping up the payment card. It was just another rung down the ladder, another confirmation that we really were the welfare family. I imagined Harley's posh friends sitting there while I nipped down the corner shop to recharge the gas card so I could heat up baked beans. No doubt the electricity would be next. The guy was tapping his pen in a "let's get this show on the road" sort of way.

I held my hand up. "Just give me a minute, will you? I need to talk to my husband." Husband seemed much easier than explaining about the loser who'd never married me who was now shacked up with the bird next door. I darted outside, slopping down the path in a pair of Colin's work boots I'd missed in my blitz the day before. I hammered on Sandy's door and shouted through the letterbox.

"Colin! Colin! Colin!"

The bedroom window opened and a very mussed-up Colin stuck his head out. "What? Bloody hell, Maia. What you making a racket for this early?"

"Sorry to drag you away from that beauty you're playing housey-housey with but I've got the guy from the gas company next door. He wants to install a pre-payment meter, otherwise we'll get cut off. We owe about two hundred quid."

"Don't look at me. I ain't got no money."

"Colin, don't you care that your kids will be living in a house without any heating, hot water or any way of cooking anything? This is not just my responsibility. You could have paid a bit towards it from your benefit, you could have, God forbid, opened an envelope while I've been away, or let's go wild, got off your fat arse and looked a bit harder for a job. It's not bloody good enough to stand there saying, 'Don't look at me'." I was shouting so loud, my throat was vibrating.

A sulk descended on him. Sandy was calling out something I couldn't quite catch. "Don't change the fact I ain't got no money. Hang on a sec." He disappeared from view. I heard him grumbling and rumbling to Sandy and a swirl of short, high-pitched answers.

His head reappeared. "I can give you forty quid. That's all."

"Whoop bloody whoop. I need it now, like, he's waiting next door, ready with his spanner."

Colin huffed off inside. A few minutes later he stood at the door in his boxers, his belly hanging over them in a freckly blubber. He handed me a pile of dog-eared fivers, a pound coin and a pile of two pences.

"Great. He already thinks we're scum and I'm going to stand there counting out eighteen, twenty, twenty-two."

Colin scratched his belly. The nails he kept long for the guitar he never played rasped across his skin. "What about that posh friend of yours? Can't you tap her for a bit of a loan?"

The fact that Colin even dared to mention Clover made me want to lunge at him with a baseball bat. Sandy deserved my thanks, not my anger. I would do everything I could to make sure that Colin didn't come boomeranging back to me. Ever. He couldn't even be bothered to come next door and make sure that the house where his children would be living, had heating. Colin loved the kids, but not as much as he loved himself.

"A thank you would be nice," he said.

I ignored him and stomped back off to find the gas man standing in the kitchen.

I held out my hand. "I can give you forty quid now."

"I'm sorry. I'm not authorised to take it. Let me install the meter. It stores the debt and takes an agreed amount each week."

I couldn't argue. There didn't seem to be enough air in me to form a strong voice. I considered my options. Clover. Mr Peters. The meter. Queuing up at the corner shop to top up my gas card seemed less shameful than making a begging phone call. "Okay, the meter."

He nodded. "It's for the best, really it is. Some people say they wouldn't be without it, even when they didn't want one to start with. It will help you budget."

I texted Clover to say I was going to be late for the children and received a text full of smiley faces back. I put on my biggest jumper, gathered up all the envelopes stacked on the side and set them out in piles on the front room floor. Gas, electricity, phone, council tax. All red, official and threatening. Every time I opened an envelope I closed my eyes and had a little bet on how bad it could be. If we owed less than £150 in electricity, that would be good. More than £200, terrible. Less than £40 on the phone, okay. More than £85, disaster. Each time it was more than I'd guessed at. By the time I'd finished, I worked out we owed about £825, plus Colin had credit card bills of more than £1500. I didn't even know he had one. His debts could be a nice little moving in present for Sandy.

I wondered how desperate people felt when their businesses collapsed owing millions. I couldn't imagine feeling like this, times a hundred, let alone a million. My mind was racing. Maybe the children would get taken into care because I couldn't afford to look after them. Perhaps we'd get evicted. Maybe we'd all end up living next door at Sandy's, with Colin lording it like some sultan with his harem. Maybe we would have to move to a caravan. I lay on my back on the floor. Me and my big dreams of the kids speaking nicely, learning Latin, for God's sake. Of me getting an Open University degree. It was laughable, beyond ridiculous. The prof would have called it "delusions of grandeur". I let the tears pour down my face. I didn't care what the gas bloke thought, or anyone. I deserved to have people look down on me for my stupid, stupid, stupid choices.

There was one envelope left which didn't look like a bill. Handwritten in blue ink. I looked at the postmark. Sandbury. Briefly I thought Mr Peters might have written to me. He wouldn't write to me where Colin could open it. He wouldn't write to me, full stop.

I braced myself for some other horror I hadn't thought of yet. I pulled out a single sheet of paper with the red letterhead of the prof's solicitors, Harrison & Harrold.

Dear Ms Etxeleku,
    We have received correspondence from Stirling Hall regarding the education of Miss Bronte Caudwell and

310

Master Harley Caudwell. We would welcome the opportunity to discuss this with you and propose a meeting at our offices at 10a.m. on Monday 24 March. We look forward to seeing you then unless you advise us to the contrary.
Yours sincerely,
Peter J. Harrison

Two days until I had to sit in front of Mr Harrison and admit to being an official failure. I rolled over, put my head on my arms and sobbed until my throat was raw.

CHAPTER
THIRTY-THREE

I rang Clover to brief her on the Colin situation. I swear I heard her clapping her hands, though she said all the right things and told me she'd bring the children home for me. When they arrived, Harley rushed back into the house as though he had turned up at some luxury Spanish villa and it was all to explore. Bronte stood grumpily by my side while I talked to Clover on the doorstep. I invited her in.

"No, darling, I'm going to leave you to it, you'll want to have a bit of a catch up *with the kids*," she said, none too discreetly.

Yes. I knew I had the joy of explaining that I'd chucked Colin out to look forward to. "Is everything all right with you?" I said, knowing she'd get that I meant Lawrence.

She gave me such a happy smile that my belly churned at the thought of telling her about Jen1. I'd want someone to tell me though.

"There's been plenty of talking going on. I'm beginning to understand a lot of things." She didn't look like one of the things that had become clear was that her husband was copping off with someone else.

She glanced down at Bronte. "Anyway, we'll catch up soon. You go and sort the children out."

She handed me a couple of bags of the children's clothes. I thanked her and hugged her really hard. At least I already knew my children's dad was a good-for-nothing arsehole. She still had that discovery ahead. I waved her off.

"Where's Dad?" Bronte said.

"He's next door at the moment."

"At Sandy's? Is he putting up shelves in her bedroom again?"

"Shelves?" I said.

"Yeah, Gypsy said Dad's always putting up shelves in Sandy's bedroom."

I'd never known Colin to put up a shelf anywhere. It was better for everyone if we believed that Colin had suddenly developed DIY skills.

"I'll let him know you're back. I know he's dying to see you."

Bronte was frowning, trying to puzzle it out so I ran next door. I could see Colin sitting at Sandy's little kitchen table, dipping biscuits in his tea and laughing with Gypsy and Denim. How much that hurt surprised me. I didn't think anything to do with Colin hurt any more. I rapped on the window. Sandy looked up without smiling but the kids waved at me and Colin immediately appeared at the door.

"I saw them get out of the car. Can I come round?" The aggression was gone, replaced by something softer.

Bronte came flying down the path. He swung her high into the air, kissing her and swirling her round.

"How's my little princess? Still talking to your old dad, then, not gone all hoity-toity on me? What they been feeding you? You've grown six inches."

"You'd better come in. Harley wants to see you too." I tried not to sound too accusing.

He stepped into the hall and started rubbing his hands together. "Cor, it's cold in here, innit?" I felt the right hook I'd got to grips with in my boxing classes with Ram flex in my fingers.

Brawling in the hallway wasn't going to get our family powwow about our new living arrangements off to a good start. I left Colin swinging Bronte by her ankles in the front room and went upstairs to find Harley. He was in his bedroom squeezing between his bed and his wardrobe to find his slippers. I'd got so used to seeing him rattling about in a bedroom big enough to play Scalextric in, it felt as though the whole house had shrunk around us. I stood staring for a moment.

"Mum, stop standing in doorways looking at me, it's freaky." But he was laughing.

"Sorry. I'm trying to get used to being here again. It feels funny seeing you in your tiny bedroom."

"I like being back." Harley shrugged. "I like having all my things again."

"Do you really?"

"Yeah. Just the four of us. The twins got on my nerves a bit, all that silly singing and dancing and doing their hair and trying clothes on. I miss the quad bike. And the dogs. And Orion, a bit, I suppose. But I see him at school."

314

Oh yes. I hadn't had the school discussion yet. Before that little joy, we had the "Mum's not living with Dad any more, it's just the three of us" conversation to get through.

"Dad's downstairs," I said.

"Yeah, I heard him. Thought I'd let Bronte say hello to him first or she'll only start whining that she's left out."

But he moved down the stairs pretty quickly and threw his arms round Colin who ruffled his hair and did some play punches. I bit back a bitchy remark about hoping Sandy was worth giving up family life for and went off to make a cup of tea. The kids deserved a couple of minutes with Colin, a few last happy moments before we stuck our hand-grenades under their lives.

I took a deep breath before I walked back into the front room. I saw immediately that Colin had already ripped away another strip of childhood. Bronte was sitting on his lap, sucking her thumb. Harley was all big eyes, looking as though he expected me to say it wasn't true. Neither of them was crying, which cranked up the pressure on me to sound like this was a jolly day, a great new beginning for all of us.

"Is Dad going to be Gypsy and Denim's dad as well, Mum?" Bronte said.

"He'll always be your dad, yours and Harley's. I mean, he'll live there so he's going to spend a bit of time with Gypsy and Denim because they'll be in the same house, but you'll see him all the time. He's only going to be next door." I hoped I made that sound like a good thing.

"So is Sandy going to be our mum as well, then? Are we going to live with her?" Harley chipped in, with wonderful timing as usual.

"No!" I knew I'd shouted. I got my voice down to a manageable level. "No, she won't be your mum, because I'm here and nothing will ever change that. You'll still live with me, in this house, and I'll look after you and be responsible for you." I crossed my arms to stop them shaking.

Harley smiled. "Good. I don't really like Sandy. She always looks sort of dirty. And her bathroom smells funny."

I did my best "told you so" face at Colin. He looked at the floor.

"Everyone has a different way of living, but let's all try and get on together," I said. Jesus, I'd be going on about respecting diversity like the bloody Stirling Hall brochure soon.

"Will we all spend Christmas together? Will we get two lots of Christmas presents like Suki in my class? Her parents are divorced and she got a Wii and a PlayStation for Christmas," Bronte said.

"Mum and Dad aren't married, stupid, so they won't get divorced. Derrr." Harley pulled a face at Bronte.

I smiled, more a stretching of the skin on my lips, but it seemed to reassure her. "We'll work something out. Don't worry."

I looked at Colin who was scratching at the worn velour on the settee. As usual he'd delivered the killer blow, then left me to pick up the pieces, while he sat there, gob open, as though he'd fallen into the front room by chance.

"Why does Dad want to live with Sandy and her kids instead of us?" Bronte managed to ask the question as though it was somehow my fault.

"Colin? I think you should answer this one." I wanted to stab him in the eye with the screwdriver he wasn't using to put shelves up.

He rubbed his bottom lip. "Your mum and I, I suppose, we haven't really been getting on that well lately. We met a long time ago and people kind of change when they have kids and stuff."

The children sat staring at him. He appeared to think he'd come up with an explanation. "So is it our fault?" I could hear the uncertainty in Harley's voice.

I pulled him to me, straightening out one of his blond curls. "Of course not. Not at all. Don't ever think that. You and Bronte are the best thing that ever happened to Dad and me. No, we are splitting up because we don't love each other any more and Dad loves Sandy now. But we both still really, really love you two and we'll always be so, so happy that we had you both."

Colin nodded along. Bronte snuggled in closer to him. Harley looked at me as though he was expecting some very wise words to make this whole mess go away. No one said anything. My face muscles started to twitch. I held my breath but it was no good. My mouth was contorting and little snorts were escaping. I pursed my lips tighter, clenching my teeth.

"Why are you laughing, Mummy?" Harley asked.

It was a very good question.

CHAPTER
THIRTY-FOUR

Clover was glowing when I saw her at school drop-off. She was waiting for me, lurking by the van, rosy-cheeked under her blue bobble hat. I waved to her, delaying the moment when I'd have to deal with her happiness. Or ruin it. I watched Bronte slouch slowly into school. It was hard to tell if she was upset about Colin leaving because she was such a misery guts in the morning anyway — definitely one of the "monosyllabic youths" the prof used to rant about — but she looked paler than usual. Once I was sure she'd actually gone in, I plastered on a smile and walked over to Clover. The joy on her face filled me with dread. If I got this wrong, our friendship would be on the skids.

"How's it going?" I searched her face for a tiny shadow of doubt, a hint that all was not well in the world. But no shadows, only brilliant sunshine. I leaned back on the van, rain dripping off my hair and listened while she filled me in on Lawrence.

"He'd lost his job. He was going to tell me that evening, but then Orion smashed the window with his bike and he just blew up. Poor man, all that worry on his own. Men are funny like that, aren't they? Defined by their careers. Preposterous really. I mean, you read about men putting on their suits and pretending to go to work, but you never think it will be your husband. Made me feel ghastly that he couldn't talk to me."

All the energy that I noticed about Clover when I first met her was back, her slightly too fast way of talking, lots of swearing, hands waving about all over the place. She drew breath. "Sorry, I want to know about you and Colin, I'm being frightfully self-centred here." I shook my head and off she went again. "Anyway, we've decided that he's going to set up a business teaching music. He'll run it from home at first."

The words "But he's copping off with Jen1" were vibrating on my lips. I managed, "Do you know where he was living yet?"

"That's the hilarious thing. You know Lawrence has never really liked Jennifer? Leo insisted that Lawrence stayed in the cottage in the garden at their house. God knows how he persuaded Jennifer into that. According to Lawrence, she made him very welcome."

Yes, I bet she bloody did. Clover was still rattling on. "Though I must admit I feel a bit foolish that she was talking to me about Lawrence and all the time he was living at the bottom of her garden. Had a bit of an F and Blind over that. Made me look so fucking stupid. But then he got me into bed and well, I forgave him." She gave an embarrassed giggle. "Sorry, too much information. Lawrence had told Jennifer not to tell anyone where he was. Which I suppose means she's quite trustworthy in a funny sort of way."

I was surprised she couldn't hear my saliva sizzling trying to hold back the truth. Out of the corner of my eye I saw Jen1's Mitsubishi snaking out of the school drive, sandwiched between Venetia's X5 and Frederica's vintage MG. She pulled over a little way past us and walked back with a bag in her hand.

"Maia, I'm glad I saw you. I've been meaning to give this back to you. Hugo's already got the book you bought him for his birthday so I was wondering if you could take it back and exchange it for something else if you've still got the receipt? I'm sorry but Hugo did tell Harley he had the whole trilogy. I assume Harley didn't know what 'trilogy' meant. Something by Tolkien would be marvellous, though he's read *The Hobbit*."

My mouth must have been open. I held out my hand for the bag. Even Clover stood in silence as Jen1 smiled, one of those smiles which made her cheeks go higher but didn't go anywhere near her eyes. "Must run," she said, "I'm having my nails done in London and I need to get some petrol."

I watched her walk away. Clover shook her head and said, "She can be so fucking rude. I don't know why she does things like that. I'm sure she's got a good heart but she doesn't think before she speaks."

That nearly sent me thundering after Jen1. I couldn't bear Clover bumbling along, giving her the benefit of the doubt when Jen1 was doing the dirty on her. Wild images of me jumping on the bonnet of the Mitsubishi and clinging to the windscreen wipers darted through my mind. But I couldn't drop the truth on Clover like that. At the very least she deserved to hear the bombshell in private. I looked down at my watch. "Damn, I forgot, I've got to see the solicitor this morning. I'd better go."

I followed Clover out of the drive. She turned right for SD2, I turned left for scumbaggy SD1. As I drove past the BP garage, I saw Jen1 filling up. The indicator on the van kept pace with my thumping heart. I drew up and strolled over.

She put on her St Francis-talking-to-the-animals face. "Maia. Hello."

"How long have you been having an affair with Lawrence?" I stared straight at her, waiting for her to flinch.

"Lawrence?" She didn't look away but she did look puzzled which hacked me off. She'd been acting the part for so long, she wasn't going to be tricked out of it easily.

"Yes, Lawrence, you know, Clover's husband, the one she's desperate to get back with? The one who stood up there on Friday night singing love songs to fuck with her head while he's screwing you."

She shook her head. "What? What? I'm not having an affair with Lawrence."

"You fucking liar. There you are, pretending to be a listening ear. I saw you on your camera thing. All snuggled up in his arms."

"You're mad, Maia. You've no idea what you're on about. Lawrence is just a friend, a really good friend, to me and to Leo." She had her scrawny little arms on her scrawny little hips. With her lips curled back she looked like an angry chihuahua.

"I heard you. 'I don't know what I'd do without you, Lawrence'." I was jabbing my finger in her face. I was turning into Colin but at that moment, I didn't care.

"If you wave that finger at me one more time, I'll twist it off. Now go away and let me finish buying my petrol in peace. No wonder Harley thinks he can solve everything with his fists with a mother like you."

"Leave Harley out of it. Leave him out of it or you really will be sorry." For some reason, I hadn't prepared myself for her fighting back. I'd assumed she'd beg me not to say anything. "You've got nothing, nothing to be snobby about. If you hadn't married Leo, you'd still be hawking ham sandwiches round Canary Wharf so you can piss off pretending that you are any better than me." Shock marbled her face. She hadn't expected me to know that. Everyone knew where I came from, whereas Jen1 had dedicated her life to covering it up.

"Stay away from Lawrence or I will tell Clover and Leo exactly what you have been up to," I said. The rain was starting to come down more heavily now, but I wasn't about to head for cover.

Jen1 seemed to gather herself. "I haven't been up to anything. Lawrence was made redundant because the department he was running closed down. He was so furious when they gave him notice that Leo thought he was going to do something stupid, so he invited him to stay in our cottage."

"So why couldn't Clover know that? Instead of you creeping around, pretending you didn't know anything about it?" I asked.

"I had to promise not to tell. He was in such a bad way. He's been seeing a therapist every day to sort his head out. Clover's family have never thought he was good enough for her. He can't face going back into the financial industry but he couldn't bear them to think he was a sponger."

Jen1 and Lawrence had obviously practised their stories together. They weren't going to fool me like they'd fooled Clover. "That's bollocks. Complete bollocks. I saw you. I heard you together."

Jen1 pulled the petrol pump out and started to fill the car. She was shouting at me over her shoulder, looking like she had just chewed on a bad Brazil nut. "Aren't you the clever one? Sort your facts out, Maia, before you go round accusing people of things they haven't done. Leo was going to lose his job as well, but because Lawrence recommended him to the person merging the departments, Leo's got a promotion. So that was why I was thanking him. We've been having sleepless nights. I thought we'd have to sell the ski lodge and maybe our house here as well."

"Not the ski lodge. How would you survive without a pad in St Moritz?" My anger wasn't about to make a U-turn. It was like a runaway racehorse, still jumping fences though the rider was off. Panic was making me really bitchy. I didn't want to believe her. But although she was the biggest fake I knew with her French manicured nails, hair extensions and organic baking shite, my conviction was faltering. I still couldn't find my back pedal, much less my brake. "You thank all the men by throwing yourself into their arms?"

"You wouldn't understand, Maia. It's a middle-class thing. We like to hug and kiss. Working-class people don't go in for it much."

I thought of Colin, of the blokes down the Working Men's Club, of the young lads round our way. They never greeted anyone with that silly cheek-kissing thing. A nod and an "all right?" maybe, hands in pockets. Any woman who gave them a big hug without a very good reason would be considered "up for it". I wasn't going to let that go. "You're right. How would I know what the middle classes do? But then again, how would you?"

That's when I copped it. A great zinging slap across my face that rearranged my brain cells. I rubbed my face. "See? You're just a working-class brawler at heart. The Duchess from Dagenham. Or should I call you the Posh Pajero after your car? You know 'pajero' means 'wanker' in Spanish, don't you?" I was aware of a few startled faces peering over the tops of cars. I glared at a bloke craning over his BMW. He quickly looked away.

Jen1 was beside herself. She shoved the petrol pump back into its holder and started pushing me backwards. "Working class" seemed to ignite her like a blowtorch. "Fuck off. Just fuck off. Go on, sling it. You little cow. God knows how you ever managed to get your kids into Stirling Hall, you common little tart."

"Same as you, Jenny. They don't care about breeding, only money." That pushing reminded me of Colin, thinking he could treat me any way he wanted. I daren't push her back, because the fury in my body was not just about Jen1, it was about Colin, Sandy, Mr

Peters. I could probably have pushed a juggernaut out of the way. I'd be no good to the kids behind bars for manslaughter. I reached for the bucket of water provided to wash the windscreen and slopped the whole lot over her, delighting in the sloshing noise and the satisfying slap as it splatted to the ground, washing off a bit of make-up and a lot of smugness as it went.

Through the glass front of the garage I could see the cashier squawking her head round, trying to get a better look at the two grown women, one in a very wet Prada coat and soggy Uggs, one in Asda jeans, parka and wellies, screaming at each other across the forecourt. Fear, shock, death wish — I don't know what it was but for the second time in twenty-four hours I started to kill myself laughing.

I had to go. Mr Harrison was waiting. At least I didn't have to go in and pay for petrol.

CHAPTER
THIRTY-FIVE

I paused outside the solicitor's office to look at myself in the rear-view mirror. Anger was still pumping round my body, tinged with panic that I might have got the wrong end of the stick. My left cheek had a clear four-finger outline. My hair was hanging down in wet, wavy strings. I was already ten minutes late so there was no time for a last-ditch effort to make myself more presentable.

The receptionist smiled as though I was dressed in a twinset and pearls, glanced down at her appointment book and pointed towards the stairs. "He's expecting you, just go straight in."

Walking up with dread in my heart took me back to the day Harley had given Hugo a thumping and we'd sat in front of Mr Peters waiting to hear our fate. That seemed so long ago, I felt as though I'd lived a whole extra life since then. I hesitated on the top step, then strode towards Mr Harrison's office. He could look down on me as much as he wanted for messing up the Stirling Hall chance. I bet he wasn't going home worrying about whether the leccy would be cut off or someone would turn up to make off with the microwave. My fighting thoughts became a feeble knock on the door.

"Come in."

Mr Harrison stood up, offered to take my parka and pulled out a chair for me. I bumbled some apology about arriving late and dripping wet. He waved it away politely and lifted a big box file onto the desk.

"So, Ms Etxeleku, how have things been?"

Clover was right. I did have a pathetic respect for people in authority. I choked back the honest answer of "My partner has gone off with the slapper next door. I've shown my kids the good life and am now going to plunge them back into the bad life. We've got no heating and I'm up to my eyes in debt. I've just thrown a bucket of muddy water over someone who is so far up her arse she can't see daylight, and the man I think I love, although I'm not sure I know what love is, is in love with someone else."

Instead I said, "I'm not going to be able to keep the children at Stirling Hall. I can't afford all the extras, the uniform, the books." The defeat in my words rushed out like bleach down a drain.

He steepled his fingers. I hated men who did that. It was always men. He wasn't sneering at me, though. In fact, he looked quite concerned. "I have had some communication from Stirling Hall. I understand the children are to leave at the end of next term, the summer term?"

"I had to give a term's notice, and I knew the fees would have to be paid next term anyway, whether they went or not. I didn't want to waste Professor Stainton's money, I mean, she'd put her trust in me, like." I pulled a face. I gave a mental nod to the prof. Yes, yes, I knew, "like" was for friends. I hardly ever said that any more. "So they'll go for next term, I'll just have to manage. I don't know how, actually. Then they are going back to Morlands, the school they were at before."

"Is it purely a financial consideration? I mean, all things being equal, are you happy with the school?" he asked.

"I love the school. The children have really started to settle in and improve so much." I looked away. "It's been quite exciting to watch." I could hear my voice starting to catch.

Mr Harrison smiled. "The professor's library has not yet been distributed. Do you think there would be anything useful there to help you get through the next few months?"

My heart quickened. The prof had loads of classics, Austen, Dickens, Oscar Wilde, Virginia Woolf. I used to pull them out every couple of months or so to dust the shelves thoroughly. It took me ages because I couldn't resist reading a few pages before I put them back. I'd kill to own them but I couldn't pretend they were for the children. Bronte had loved the prof's collection of Lewis Carroll poems. An image of the prof sitting in her armchair, reading Bronte *Jabberwocky* came to mind. Harley used to beg her to read *The Hunting of the Snark*. Maybe it was her facial expressions, her voices, her hand movements that had given him his love of drama.

328

"You can't just give her books to me. What about, I don't know, her relatives? Don't they want them? Surely she must have left them to someone?" I tried to remember her mentioning anyone apart from her son, Dominic, who died in a car crash in Australia.

"As it happens, Professor Stainton appointed me executor of the will, so I can assure you it doesn't present a problem. Would it be convenient for you to accompany me to her house now? Then perhaps you could choose some books that might be useful to you."

"I loved her books but I don't want to take anything that belongs to someone else, don't want any comeback later, a big fuss because the cleaner made off with her first editions," I said.

"I promise there hasn't been a stampede to claim the professor's library. Shall we go?"

I followed Mr Harrison in the van. The prof's house wasn't on any of my usual routes so I hadn't been past it since she died four months earlier. The gates to her long driveway were already open. The daffodils were out, lovely golden clusters all over the garden. Tulips — the prof loved tulips — nodded away in tubs by the front door. Perhaps the powers that be had kept the gardener on until the house was sold. Mr Harrison pulled his Jag into what I considered to be my spot, a little clearing by the weeping willow, where the prof's pet poodle, Iago, had been buried a few years earlier.

Mr Harrison produced a bunch of keys, fiddling away to find the right ones.

I held my hand out. "Would you like me to do it? I can tell by looking which ones fit the locks."

He handed them over. I had to remind myself that the prof wouldn't be sitting in the drawing room with her *Chambers Crossword Dictionary* beside her. As the front door clicked open, dust danced in the daylight that filtered through the Edwardian bay windows. The house had missed me at least. I'd expected it to feel hollow and damp but in fact, it felt warm and comfortable. The boiler was obviously working better than mine. I waited for Mr Harrison to take me through to the library. He hesitated in the hallway, looking from one door to the other. "This way," I said, nodding to the first oak door.

I stood in the doorway while the memories crowded in. The prof shouting the answers to *University Challenge*. Cursing her knotted arthritic fingers as she taught Bronte how to knit one, purl one. Showing Harley pictures of her father posing in his goggles at the Brooklands racetrack in the 1920s. My heart lurched as I spotted her little silver-rimmed glasses on the side table, sitting on top of *The Times*. I wondered who had cancelled the papers. Mr Harrison coughed behind me. "Feel free to enter and have a look at the books. See if there are any you'd like. I need to get something from the professor's study, so I'll leave you to it."

I walked over to the built-in bookshelves that stretched from floor to ceiling on two sides of the room. I pulled out *Great Expectations*. It felt solid and smooth in my hand. I held it to my face. I loved the old smell, slightly fusty, of all those words put together so cleverly. The prof had always encouraged me to borrow books but I never did. I couldn't bear the thought that

Colin would leave a coffee ring on one. I used the local library instead. I ran my hand along the bookshelf until I found my favourite book of poems with a shiny silver cover. Not for the first time, I read the inscription inside.

"*To Mother, Sorry I can't be with you but I will be thinking of you across the miles. Read the poem on P.31. Missing you! Love, Dominic. 15 August 1977.*"

The year I was born. I wondered how long afterwards he'd been killed in the car crash. I glanced at the photo of him on the mantelpiece, trapped forever in his twenties, suntanned and smiling, posing next to a kangaroo. I shook my head to chase away the thought of Harley or Bronte dying before me and turned my attention back to the book.

It fell open naturally at page 31. I smiled as I read it, hearing the prof's voice in my head as she read out Jenny Joseph's poem, "Warning", about becoming an old woman in purple and blowing her cash on booze and fancy sandals. I could almost hear her giggle, a light bird-like sound. I missed her.

I shut the book quickly as Mr Harrison's footsteps echoed on the parquet floor in the hall. I should have been gathering up the books I wanted. I hadn't even looked to see if there was anything to help the children. Harley had said something about studying First World War poets, bursting in at odd moments with "If I should die, think only this of me". I looked along the bottom shelf for her anthology of Rupert Brooke's poems. And Shakespeare. They would definitely study Shakespeare. I started pulling out the tragedies, then the comedies, feeling a flutter of panic. Too much choice. I didn't want to look greedy. But I couldn't stand the idea of these beautiful books being packed into cardboard boxes and left to rot in some spidery attic.

I turned round as Mr Harrison came in. "Sorry, I haven't quite finished yet. I won't be a sec. Are you in a hurry?"

"No, not at all. The professor left this for you." He held out an A4 envelope.

"For me?" I took it. "Amaia Etxeleku. To be opened at the end of the first term at Stirling Hall" was written on the front in her old lady's writing, neat, flowery letters.

"Where did you find this?" Something in me was backing away. The whole thing of people speaking from the dead freaked me out.

"It was in her safe."

"Here?"

"Yes. She sent a copy to the office a few days before she died. She was quite clear that you were to have the version from the safe." Mr Harrison had that blank gaze back again, very "see no evil, hear no evil, speak no evil". I wondered how many times he had quietly sorted out stuff left to mistresses without the wife ever knowing.

"Do you know what's in it?"

"As the executor of her will, I have been party to all of Professor Stainton's paperwork whilst dealing with probate." He wasn't going to give me any clues.

I tipped the envelope up and felt something heavier than a letter slide to the other end.

My fingers were all clumsy, ripping the envelope as I opened it. A pile of photos, some black and white, some coloured, fell to the floor. I knelt down to gather them up. The prof with Dominic as a baby in one of those huge Silver Cross prams. Dominic and a gorgeous dark-haired girl standing in front of, was that Big Ben? She looked foreign, but there was a London bus in the background. The same couple dancing, Dominic looking very handsome in a DJ. The woman was in a bright red halter-necked maxi dress, a bit like the one Mum had when I was little.

My eyes were drawn to her dangly gold and jade earrings. They were very familiar. That *was* Mum.

"What's going on? That's my mother's photo in there. With the professor's son."

"Why don't you sit down and read the letter? It will explain everything. Would you like me to sit with you? Or would you rather read it on your own? I really don't mind."

"I think I want to be on my own." I couldn't take my eyes off the photo of them dancing. They fitted together, as though they had melted into each other somehow, the chemistry between them shimmering in the stiff little Polaroid picture.

Mr Harrison tucked a pen into his inside pocket and nodded towards the car. "I'll wait outside for you."

I scrabbled at the photos on the floor, all fingers and thumbs. I piled them onto the prof's little side table, gently putting her glasses to one side, then sat down in her armchair. I'd never sat in it before. It felt wrong. But not as wrong as this flipping letter turning up from the prof several months after she'd died. I flicked through the photos until I found one of Mum, dark hair swirled up in a lovely chignon like a 1950s film star. I propped it on the side. I pulled out the letter, surprised to see that it was several sheets long. Basildon Bond. Of course.

Dear Amaia,

This will no doubt come as a shock to you, but when you have had time to process all the information, I do hope that you will have a clearer understanding of the events leading up to this letter. I must endeavour to be as clear as possible as it is not my intention to leave you with unanswered questions, however painful you may find the truth. For this purpose, I must start from the beginning.

My son, Dominic, met your mother, Josune, when she worked as a housekeeper with the Watson family before you were born. He had been at Charterhouse School with their son, Robert, and they were very good friends. To cut a long story short, Dominic fell in love with your mother. I think she was quite cool with him at first — she was three years older than Dominic and such a proud person. She would never let anyone pay for anything, even though she was clearly not well off. Dominic persisted with her. He was twenty-one and in his last year at Cambridge. He started to come home every weekend, staying in with Josune to babysit

Robert's younger brothers instead of going out with his friends. He was besotted by her.

When he graduated in economics and found a job working in a bank up in London, I suppose we thought that Dominic would meet a City girl and forget all about Josune. Instead, I think it was after two years (it is all so long ago now), when he'd been promoted at the bank, he told us he wanted to marry your mother. I have to be truthful. I loved your mother and although she was not what I expected when I had imagined a daughter-in-law, I could see how happy they were. Her heart was a good one. I greatly admired her. She was such a capable woman. She'd made her way to England and forged a life for herself.

I feel ashamed to write this next piece knowing it will hurt you. I am asking an awful lot of you, but you must try to take into account that this all happened nearly four decades ago and times were different then. Herbert, my husband, thought Dominic could do better. He liked Josune but he was always a little xenophobic. He was a good man but his horizons were limited. He'd been a bank manager for years. Everyone he knew, everyone we socialised with, was English, white and middle class. He'd had almost no need to confront any variation on that in the real world. Your mother was so tactile, so enthusiastic and gregarious, I think he was almost scared of her. He used to stand behind the armchair in the drawing room whenever Josune came in until he was absolutely sure she wasn't going to try to kiss him.

Anyway, through his contacts, he arranged a transfer for Dominic to the Commonwealth Bank in Sydney, Australia. Dominic was furious and refused to go — Australia was a world away, a place where people emigrated and only saw their families again once or twice before they died. People didn't have "gap years" then. It was like being sent to the moon. But Herbert argued, threatened and cajoled until he finally persuaded Dominic to take a contract for a year. Herbert agreed that if he still wanted to marry Josune when he came home, then he would do so with our blessing.

I don't need to tell you that Josune was devastated. She was smart. Whatever we said about them being too young or Dominic needing to get some experience or see a bit of the world, she knew that we, or rather Herbert (and I was too weak to stand up to him), disapproved of her and that he hoped that distance would do anything other than make the heart grow fonder. She felt betrayed by Dominic for not resisting us. She refused to go to the airport to see him off, though I know she wrote to him every week once he was there because her letters were returned to us with his belongings. Dominic, for his part, never stopped mentioning Josune in his letters, always asking if we'd seen her. She wouldn't communicate with us at all. We'd humiliated her and she never forgave us.

I rubbed my eyes. Mum had had to fight for everything in her life. Maybe that's why she'd died young — nothing left to fight the biggest battle of all, against cancer. I wished she was there to make sense of all this for me. It sounded like her not to speak to them. I could imagine her: "They think I am not good enough for the son, so they are not good enough for me. So I don't speak with them. It is a simple thing." She was very black and white like that. It was so her, it almost made me smile. I took a deep breath and turned to the next page.

He'd only been there five months when we got a call to say he'd been killed in a car crash, a completely banal accident — someone misjudged their overtaking and Dominic was the casualty. At eleven o'clock at night on 28 August 1977 his boss at the bank called us. I remember that we talked over each other because of the time delay on the telephone. I can't think about it now, more than thirty-six years later, without imagining those words travelling from the other side of the world suspended in time, my life still the same for a split second before they reached me.

The writing was starting to get larger and untidier as though the effort to get it all on paper was sucking the life out of the poor old prof. My thoughts were all over the place. I looked out to Mr Harrison's Jag. He was sitting in the front seat, reading *The Daily Telegraph*, flicking through the pages as all the important bits in my life were fed into a blender. The writing changed from black ink to blue, as though the prof had returned to it after some time.

I went to see your mother the next day. My recollection of our meeting might be unfair, coloured as it was with my own indescribable feelings. All I can remember is her pointing at me. She was wearing bright red nail varnish, which never seemed to chip, however much housework she did. She just kept saying over and over again, "Tiene usted la culpa, tiene usted la culpa. This is your fault. You. You. Your fault." And howling, howling like something in the most terrible pain. It had a feral sound to it. Your mother was very petite, very slender, but when she stood up and put her hands on her hips, I saw that she was pregnant. I knew, of course, I knew the baby was Dominic's but grief made me clumsy and I made the mistake of asking whether it was his, searching as I was for some solace, some tiny glimmer of anything other than total despair on which to throw myself. I was no match for your mother. She forced me out of the door.

You have said you don't know who your father is. Since you came to work for me any doubts I harboured have long since dissipated. Dominic is there in the way you arch your left eyebrow when you are puzzled. The way you curl your hair around your index finger when you are reading. Your acute observations of human nature. Your love of language, the sound of words. I am asking myself as I write this whether it is fair to burden you with this knowledge now, when those who can help you understand it are no longer around — me, your mother; Dominic, even Herbert. How I wish Dominic had known you. I know he would have been

immensely, immeasurably proud of the wonderful
young woman you are and of course, of your children.

I had a dad. I had a dad. That blank on the birth
certificate was Dominic Stainton. I had a dad with an
English surname. Stainton. I rolled it round my tongue
like a cherry stone. Amaia Stainton. Frightfully proper.
I was bowled over by the fact that I was made out of
love, not violence, as Mum's tight-lipped silence had
led me to believe.

I picked up the photo of him in the tux and studied
his face. I felt disloyal to Mum, but I wanted to see
myself there. I stared at every feature. Perhaps the
mouth, those full lips. Mum's lips were thinner, less
bow-shaped. It was difficult to judge. He did look a lot
like Bronte, those wide-spaced eyes with thick lashes.
That was my dad there, in that photo, concrete and
real, not just the rock star/James Bond of my
imagination. I read on, forcing myself not to skip lines
or to turn to the last page.

I am sure you will ask yourself why, why on God's
earth, I didn't say something before I died? Of course I
wanted to. I promised myself that once I knew you a
bit better and I felt that you trusted me, I would. As
with all these things, the perfect moment hasn't yet
presented itself and I think that it never will. I am
dying, my heart is slowly giving out and I don't have
the energy for fighting. So, you can say, I lack courage.
But my fear is that having found you, you might also
reject me once you know the full story.

Her writing, neat and straight at the top of the page, was veering down in sloping lines. I couldn't bear to think what a strain it must have put on her to write this, dredging up all those horrible feelings from long ago.

After your mother threw me out, I tried, I don't know how many times, to contact her. She refused to see me, to accept my calls. Any letters were returned unopened. I wanted to offer her money, the gatehouse in the garden, Lord knows, I wanted to look after her. But she was so vehement in her fury, her hatred. I couldn't get through to her.

The Watsons were very fond of your mother and kept her on after you were born. Mrs Watson had three sons and I think she was quite pleased to have a little girl to spoil after all this time. She never was the sort to care much what other people thought, even though children out of wedlock were still very frowned upon in the seventies. I recognise how selfish this must sound, but it hurt me terribly that Mrs Watson was able to see you every day while I was banished. Josune lived with the Watsons for some years, I no longer recall how many, before she got the council flat over by the Common. Once you started school in Queen's Drive, I used to time my walking the dog with playtime, so I could watch you through the railings. Nowadays I would probably be arrested.

I bumped into your mother in town when you were about eight, a gorgeous little thing, shiny, bright eyes, full of curiosity. Your mother rushed you away from me as though I carried some terrible contagious disease. I think that last incident finally eradicated any fight I had left. I knew she would never forgive me.

I trawled through my memory but couldn't remember that meeting. Mum had never done forgiveness well. I was trying to make the shift from Professor Stainton, the elegant old lady I cleaned for, to Rose, my grandmother. Frustration was rushing around in all directions. My mother for being so bloody stubborn. Herbert for packing Dominic off to Australia. Rose for, I don't know, not spitting out the truth over the Earl Grey.

I glimpsed you a few times in town as you were growing up. I kept distant tabs on you over the years. I knew you had moved to the Walldon Estate because I found you in the phone book. I made a point of coming to your checkout when you worked at Tesco. Herbert was very against it. He thought that it was all "water under the bridge". He was probably right but I couldn't let it go. I think perhaps a mother feels the death of a child more keenly than a father. As long as I saw you, a tiny fragment of Dominic was still available to me.

When I saw your mother's death in the *Surrey Mirror*, I felt it nearly as much as when Dominic died. She was still so young, just sixty. I wanted to be with you afterwards, to comfort you. I was in slightly better health then. I couldn't drive any more but when Herbert went off to play golf, I used to get the bus into town, then out to the Walldon Estate. I spent hours walking up and down, hanging about outside your house, trying to gather the courage to present myself at your door. I never did. Your mother and I had hurt each other enough. It seemed almost foolish to invite any more pain.

I couldn't imagine frail little Rose coping with the bus journey, getting off at the estate, picking her way through the dog shit, ignoring the shouts from the louts. She always wore a string of real pearls. Jesus, she was lucky not to be mugged. Why had I never noticed her?

Then one day, not long after Herbert had died, I was in the post office and I saw the card advertising your services as a cleaner in the window. The name was Etxeleku. It had to be you. Excitement made my hands so uncooperative I had to ask the girl behind the till to write the number down for me.

I remembered Rose calling me. I snatched her hand off because she offered me £15 an hour — "I'm prepared to pay over the odds, because I can't clean in between." It was my cushiest job, six hours on a Tuesday and Thursday. She'd ask me to make a pot of Earl Grey, then invite me to sit down with her. I could never relax properly because I should have been hoovering instead of scoffing her Clotted Cream Thins which arrived every so often in a Fortnum & Mason delivery. She could be quite nosey for an old bird who looked like a strong wind might snap her in two. "So

342

your young man, this Colin, what does he do?" "Do you keep some money of your own, dear?" "Did your mother ever talk about your father?"

I leaned back in her armchair. She could have told me. There were so many openings in our conversations. I thumped the armrest. Dust puffed up. The place needed a good clean. I supposed that the person who bought the house would chuck out all her lovely old furniture. Well, lovely to me. A lot of it was a bit shabby, but cosy and well-weathered, rather than crap quality.

I loved it when you came to work for me. You really helped me through that period of early widowhood. I found it incredibly comforting to have my "other" family close. In particular, I looked forward to the school holidays when Bronte and Harley came with you. I'd pushed away all that maternal love, channelled it instead into my career. Having you and your children around seemed to awaken something in me — I was old but young again. Through Harley and Bronte I felt I was regaining a little of the time I lost when you were growing up. In Harley, I could see so much of Dominic, similar mannerisms, even a way of expressing himself. And of course, Bronte resembles him in appearance.

The writing was becoming harder to read, fainter on the page.

I do not have much time left, though I hope to see this Christmas or at least a few more Tuesdays and

Thursdays. However, if you are reading this, it is because I am dead and the children have completed a term at Stirling Hall. I hope you are seeing the benefits, although I have no doubt that you have had to make some sacrifices to keep them there. I know money was always scarce in your household and I suspect that the hidden extras of private schooling will have represented an ongoing burden. It was not my intention to create extra stress for you. I simply felt that if I left you a sum of money before you had experienced and recognised the value to your children of a Stirling Hall education, there might have been more possibility of Colin appropriating — and potentially gambling away — money designed to give your children the best possible start in life.

It was weird to be pissed off with a dead person. Rose hadn't trusted me enough to keep her money out of Colin's sweaty paws to make sure the kids could stay at Stirling Hall. Resentment flashed through me. From the way my teeth were grinding together, I realised that Rose had told me something I didn't want to hear. The truth. Maybe I would have disappeared off to Corfu for six weeks in the sun or got swept along by Colin and bought a flashy car. That Maia seemed like another person now.

I am quite confident that even one term of Stirling Hall education will have brought about a significant change in all of your lives. I hope, I trust, that seeing your children realise their potential will have inspired you to reflect on your own priorities. For this reason, I bequeath my entire estate to you, which should at least allow you the possibility to pursue further education for yourself. By the time you read this, Mr Harrison should have completed the probate process and you should be able to move into your new life with the minimum of delay.

Amaia. Life is precious. Make the most of it. I have the utmost faith that you will.
With love,
Your grandmother, Rose xxxx

I read the last few lines again. My heart was beating so fast, I couldn't help thinking that I might have a heart attack like my gran while Mr Harrison sat outside puzzling over his Sudoku. My sweaty fingers were making damp furrows in the notepaper. She couldn't mean I owned the house? But an estate, that was the house too, right? Maia Etxeleku, Lady of the Manor. Butler? Tea, please. The books. They were all mine. Seven bedrooms. Mine. Apple orchards. Mine. Cheese knives. I'd always wanted a cheese knife. I'd never cut the nose off the Brie again. Not one, but two staircases. Everything, absolutely everything, mine. Harley and Bronte were going to love this. They'd be able to do everything they wanted, carry on to the senior school at Stirling Hall, go on the rugby tour to South Africa, the politics trip to the USA, even the tropical ecosystem trip to Belize, for God's sake.

I was going to love telling Colin. Mansion, mine. Council house and Sandy, yours.

CHAPTER
THIRTY-SIX

I couldn't take it in. Mr Harrison had informed me, with a note of satisfaction in his voice, that in the months since the professor — my grandmother — had died, he'd completed the legal formalities and the inheritance was mine "as soon as I was ready".

Strangely enough, I didn't feel the need for any further delay. However, for the next five days, until term finished, I carried on turning up to work as normal. Now I didn't have to do it, I didn't mind as much. I didn't breathe a word to anyone, not even the children. I nearly blew my cover by paying £60 for Harley to go on a school day trip to France to see the First World War battlefields. The amazement and delight on his face filled me with the sort of joy that made my feet float. I nearly let the cat out of the bag loads of times but I wanted to have the Easter holidays to get used to being our new non-welfare selves without the whole world whispering about us.

On the last day of term I dropped the children off earlier than usual. The van had developed a cough that blew out a cloud of black smoke every time I changed into third. Knowing I could march off to the garage and buy a Lamborghini if the fancy took me made me wave at Jen1 as she made an exaggerated detour around us. When I went into reception, I rang the bell for attention, rather than skulking about on the other side of the glass hatch hoping that someone would notice me. I could see down the corridor to Mr Peters' office. I willed the door to open. I willed the door to stay shut. My heart leapt every time I heard footsteps, then sank again as the wrong faces came into sight.

Felicity bustled out. "Good morning, Mrs Etxeleku, what can I do for you?"

I wondered if she ever went anywhere without a little clipboard. "I wanted to let you know that circumstances have changed. The children will be staying on at Stirling Hall after next term."

"Let me just check, Mrs Etxeleku. I don't think their places have been allocated yet. Just bear with me a moment." She pulled down a big file and started leafing through the pages, sharp pencil twitching. It had never occurred to me that there might not be room for them, even though I was now in a position to come and dump great bags of swag on her desk. If she said they had to leave anyway, I thought I might burst through the glass partition like a rhino with a dart in its backside, roaring and spearing all who crossed my path.

Felicity was scribbling something in her file. I balanced on tiptoes to see what she was writing.

She looked up. "Wonderful. All done. Luckily because it's been so busy, we haven't had time to reassign places yet. There are six on the waiting list for Bronte's class and three for Harley's."

Felicity obviously thought I should be grateful to be allowed to spend over twenty-four thousand pounds a year at Stirling Hall. I was. Fantastically, ecstatically, massively, wildly, wonderfully grateful that I'd got one thing right in the huge dung heap of everything I'd got wrong.

"I also need to give you my new address. We're moving in today." As soon as I pronounced the words "Gatsby, Stamford Avenue", she scrumpled her face up as though she was trying to understand an immigrant with a particularly heavy accent. I would never get tired of saying SD2. Or of seeing the look of surprise when they realised that Maia Etxeleku, bog cleaner, van driver, tracksuit wearer, lived in — what had Mr Harrison called it? — one of the premier roads in Sandbury. I ignored my natural urge to explain how I ended up there.

I smiled right into her bemused face, then bent down, pretending to do up my trainers. I didn't want to leave without seeing Mr Peters, even if it only gave me the opportunity to ignore him, but I couldn't hang around any more without beaky old Felicity getting all suspicious. Maybe he'd already left for the other school. Maybe he was, at that moment, touching Serena's face as gently as he'd touched mine. Just the night before I'd been reading Tennyson's poem *In Memoriam*, trying to convince myself that it really was better to have loved and lost than never to have loved at all. I needed to grow up and stop wanting the complete fairy tale. The prof had already taken the role as the knight in shining armour. A grand future for the children was fairy tale enough.

I headed back to my old house, trying to get rid of the feeling that Mr Peters had been hiding in his office, waiting for the all clear that I'd left the building.

As I drew up outside, I noticed the ugly square windows with their yellowing PVC frames for the first time. I'd always considered windows a barrier to burglars rather than works of art. I went into the house and started at the top, walking from room to room, scanning for anything I couldn't leave behind. I picked up a little doll in traditional Basque dress off Bronte's chest of drawers. My mum gave her that. I scooped up Gordon the Gorilla. I chucked Harley's *Top Gear* annuals into a carrier bag, then picked up the prof's ugly old parrot head bookends. I paused in the doorway of my bedroom. I didn't want anything that reminded me of Colin. Nothing at all. I took off my eternity ring, the closest he'd ever got to romantic, and left it on the bedside table. He could recycle it to Sandy.

I didn't even go into the front room. I wasn't about to start making off down the path with crappy old armchairs. Enough. I'd buy anything I needed. I loved how arrogant that sounded.

I paused on the threshold and said a loud goodbye into the hall, then banged the door shut. Just one more thing left to do, then it was time for the curtain to fall on Maia Etxeleku, Act One. I knocked on Sandy's door. When she saw it was me, she took a step forwards and jutted her chin out. "What?" She rasped up a phlegmy cough without bothering to put her hand in front of her mouth.

"Is Colin in?"

She shouted back into the house. "Col, it's Maia."

He appeared, unshaven, a big blob of some ketchup-looking thing on his T-shirt. He wasn't about to waste any words either. "Yes?"

Jesus. Where did all that love go? How many people were floating about the world looking at people they used to kiss, tongues and all, and thinking, "You grubby jowly-faced frog, don't touch me because I'll scream"? He had a big spot with a whitehead on the side of his neck. I'd never be able to kiss anyone less fragrant than Mr Peters ever again.

I held out the keys to the house. "Good news. I'm moving out. You can have the house — get in touch with the council and find out what I need to do to sign it over to you. Give me a ring when you want to see the kids."

His mouth fell open slightly. I could see his brain struggling against spliff-induced slowness. If Colin had been a car, the sound of backfiring would have filled the air. "Where you going?"

"Stamford Avenue."

He peered out at me as though he needed glasses. "Stamford Avenue? What? You got a job as a housekeeper?"

"No. I own a house there. The prof that died? She left her house to me. So we're moving in today."

I stood there just long enough to watch the first drops of realisation filter through. If I knew Colin, the old back pedals would start flinging round at any moment, now that a meal ticket for life was on the table.

"When did you find out? Why didn't you tell me?" Indignation was pogoing all over his face.

I couldn't be bothered to explain anything. I'd found leaving jobs I hated more difficult than this. Nineteen years and all I could think about was whether I had time to go to Homebase for some sweet pea seeds before I picked the kids up at lunchtime.

"Bye, Colin. I'll give the kids your love."

I left him grunting and spluttering, next door to the house where I'd lived for over a decade. I sat Gordon the Gorilla on the passenger seat and hopped into the van without the slightest twinge, as though I'd been a plane in a holding pattern, waiting to land at the right destination.

Some goodbyes were turning out to be easier than others.

CHAPTER
THIRTY-SEVEN

I drove up to Stirling Hall with little squeaks of excitement vibrating in my throat. Shuffling from foot to foot, I waited for Harley and Bronte right at the front, scanning the children's faces as they came bowling out, weighed down with papier mâché volcanoes, hockey sticks and their own Kandinsky creations. When Harley and Bronte finally surged out, I couldn't concentrate on their chatter at all. Even when Harley thrust his drama cup into my hands, I had to work hard to find a "well done". Bronte was the first to clock that I wasn't driving straight home.

"Where are we going?" Bronte could never do neutral, only accusatory. Today she couldn't touch me.

"It's a surprise."

"Give us a clue," Harley said.

"You wait and see."

Bronte hunched down in the front of the van, grumbling under her breath about wanting to get home and chill out. I turned into Stamford Avenue and flicked the automatic gate opening gizmo.

Harley was first to react. "Why are we coming to the professor's house? Are you going to clean it up?"

Bronte was sitting up a bit straighter. "How long are you going to be? Can we go and play tennis while you clean?"

"No, not today you can't." I threw the van door open. Bronte and Harley scrambled out, Bronte frowning, ready to moan. I didn't want to spoil the moment so I said, very quickly, "You can't play tennis today because you need to choose a bedroom."

Bronte scowled. "What do you mean? Have we got to help you?"

I pushed away the thought that she reminded me of Colin, always scared of wearing himself out if he did anything that didn't directly benefit him.

"It's our house now," I said. There was a silence, a puzzled shoulder shrug from Bronte, then Harley started to grin, his eyebrows raised in a question. I nodded.

"What do you mean? This is our house? What? Forever? How did that happen?" Harley said, throwing his arms round me. Even Bronte started jumping up and down on the spot, whooping and yeehahing. I told them that Rose Stainton had left it to us and I would tell them all about it later. For the moment, I wanted to focus on the future. The past wasn't going to change if I left it half an hour.

I opened the door, loving the solid clunk as the key turned in the brass lock. I stood back as the children elbowed each other to be first through the door. The grandness of the huge hall with its grandfather clock and massive gilt mirrors seemed to act as a brake and they came to a halt, gazing about, as though they were waiting for the real owner to appear and tell them to take their shoes off.

"Go on, go and explore. It really is ours." Harley and Bronte stampeded up the main staircase, ringing the servants' bells and counting the bedrooms. I walked up slowly, running my hand along the solid oak banister. Bronte came bursting out of a bedroom overlooking the orchards. She beckoned me up.

"Can I have this room, Mum? I really like it, it's got a window seat and everything. I could keep all my Polly Pockets in that cupboard. Those little shelves could be their home. Can I have one of those lava lamps like Saffy's got?" I nodded. My new bank account could run to a lava lamp. Bronte rewarded me with a hug so tight I heard my lungs empty.

Harley chose the smallest room, a funny little semi-hexagonal box room in a turret on the second floor. "I love this room. I feel like Harry Potter. Can't wait until Orion comes over here. Will you buy me a telly? And a PlayStation? And a computer? And can I have a dog now we've got the space? Maybe Bronte could have a horse. Then we won't argue over it. I want one of those Pyrenean mountain dogs. Or a Great Dane."

I didn't make any promises, just laughed and said I'd think about it once we'd settled in. I needed time to work out what was right, not just what was rich. I still couldn't get used to going into Morrisons and picking up anything I wanted. I'd stood struggling with myself for ages before putting blueberries in my trolley at £2.99 a punnet. Even then I only ate a few a day and wanted to have a right go when Harley crammed them into his mouth willy-nilly.

Now the children knew the good news, I was free to tell Clover who sounded more excited than we were, if that was possible. She wasted no time in checking out the good fortune of the Etxeleku/Caudwells and arrived for a thorough inspection the very next day. I threw the door open with a dramatic "Welcome to my humble abode" then did a double take as all five of them — including Lawrence — stood there.

"You expected me to bring Lawrence, didn't you?" Clover said as the kids charged upstairs in a big jumble. "Forgot to ask on the phone. We can put him to work, he's very good with his hands." She gave a saucy little laugh.

I'd been so obsessed with my own goings-on that I hadn't really got my head round the fact that he was back on the scene. So I arranged my face into some kind of welcome.

"Of course I expected Lawrence, come in, come in. I promise not to attack you," I said. I struggled not to sound grumpy that the day I had planned with Clover was now going to become a polite getting-to-know-you session with Lawrence. He didn't even look that thrilled to be there, standing in the entrance hall with his hands in his pockets.

"Nice pad," he said. No doubt turning up to the houses of friends he wasn't the slightest bit interested in was the downside of being back in the bosom of the family.

Clover clapped her hands together. "Can we have the grand tour then? This is a gorgeous house. I suppose the kids are staying at Stirling Hall now? You'll have to be class representative next year so you can invite everyone back for coffee. I'd love to see Jennifer's face. She'd kill to live on the 'right side' of Sandbury. Wouldn't we all?"

At the mention of Jen1, I stared at Lawrence to see if he was squirming. He didn't look embarrassed. Just blank, as though he'd whitewashed all the emotion off his face. Maybe I was so burnt by Colin and Mr Peters that I saw betrayals and lies behind every curtain when really the poor bloke was just a man who'd lost his marbles for a while. I needed to let that whole Lawrence–Jen1 thing go.

I took them upstairs, hearing the thumps and bangs of a rough game of hide and seek as the children clumped up and down the servants' stairs and climbed into cupboards. I hated them marauding about but I knew Clover wouldn't say anything. I couldn't bear it if anything got broken before I'd had time to decide I didn't like it. Harley came barging past us, his shirt hanging out, crashing into the banister as he went. I tried not to shout but I couldn't help it.

"Right. I think it's time you went outside. Go and get the others and have a game of tennis. Or see if you can find some tadpoles in the stream."

"That's boring. We're having really good fun. This house is wicked for hide and seek," Harley said.

One day in the new mansion and the boy was already bored. I'd never invited any kids from Stirling Hall over when we lived on the Walldon Estate because I was ashamed of where we lived. Now I could invite them over, I didn't want them there. I was giving Harley my "NOW!" look when Lawrence came to my rescue. "I'm sure your mother doesn't want everyone stampeding round the house. Why don't you get the others together and I'll come down and you can show me the garden?"

"That would be great, thanks, Lawrence. I'll make some coffee in a moment. There's a lovely little walled garden at the side. It's quite sheltered so we could sit out," I said.

He stroked Clover's arm. "Is that okay, love?"

"Course." They held each other's eyes for a second. I couldn't read whether it was an "I love you" moment or a "Be on your best behaviour" moment.

I wanted to talk to someone with my eyes.

Lawrence slung his arm round Saffy's shoulders as the five children clattered down the stairs, trailing grubby little hands down the walls.

I took Clover round the house, straightening the bedcovers and closing wardrobe doors as we went. "This is marvellous," she said, pressing her nose against the porthole window in Harley's room. "I'm so pleased for you. I always knew that you were destined for better things."

I grinned. "Anyway, enough about me. How are things with you, with Lawrence, I mean?" I watched her carefully.

Clover picked up a model of a James Bond Aston Martin DB5 and the Chitty Chitty Bang Bang car that Harley had discovered in a cupboard. "I had these as a kid." There was a slight pause. She turned to me. "Okay, I think. He gets a bit funny when I ask him about his time at Leo and Jennifer's. He doesn't really like talking about it. I think he feels a bit ashamed. I don't know whether he had an actual breakdown, but whatever, I don't think he thinks it was a very virile way of going on."

There it was again. That edge of a cliff feeling as though I was about to shout out the truth. "Do you think he's got it together now though?"

"I don't know. I hope so. I find it a bit galling that Jennifer knows more about my husband than I do."

"Is Lawrence still friendly with her? Does he ever see her now?" I said. "Or Leo?"

"Lawrence isn't terribly fond of chatting on the phone. He's spoken to Leo a few times. I keep thinking I should invite them over to supper to thank them for what they did but every time I imagine Jennifer pushing food round her plate and holding forth about only eating organic bloody lamb and spinach washed in spring water, it makes me want to disappear to Africa and never come back."

She adjusted Truly Scrumptious in the car and lined it up on the windowsill. "It's a bit weird him going to live there though. And them keeping it a secret. I mean, he wasn't that friendly with Leo. He's always been utterly disparaging about Jennifer but now he keeps defending her. Maybe he just got to know her better. Though frankly, I'm not sure getting to know her better would be a bonus. I think we'd just discover more things about her to dislike."

358

It was my chance. I smoothed Harley's duvet and looked out of the window at the kids splashing about in the stream, shoes kicked off, trousers rolled up but not far enough. Bronte was jumping from one side of the stream to the other. I was still organising my words when Clover broke in. "Maybe he fancies her. She does look good."

"She looks good if pipe cleaners turn you on. You're far more gorgeous than she is." I would have to stick to the facts if I did tell Clover, not make a cuddle on camera sound like a great big affair because I wanted to have my own pop at Jen1.

"Don't think I'll bother asking that question. Don't want to know that my poor husband is lumbered with a gigantic bubble of a pear when he'd rather be having sex with a string bean. Perhaps they did have it off while he was there." She shrugged, laughing as though the thought was ridiculous. "Anyway, I don't want to know. He's back and he seems fairly contented. He's a bit more patient with the children and he's loving the music teaching. He's so restless most of the time, but when I see him teaching, he seems almost serene."

Never mind the bloody guitar lessons and Lawrence's Zen state when he was plinking about on the piano. I tried again. "Would you really not want to know?" My heart was heaving in my rib cage.

"Fuck, no. What's the point? I love him. I don't want him to leave me. It's just sex at the end of the day. If it's over, I don't need to know. I mean, if Mr Peters turned up in my bedroom in his birthday suit, who's to say I wouldn't give in to temptation?"

I couldn't quite pin down the emotion that shot through me at the mention of Mr Peters. Jealousy that Clover should even think of him like that, plus some kind of missing him feeling, sadness that he'd only ever been part of the lows in my life. I tried to re-order my thoughts on the "to blab or not to blab" dilemma.

Clover was flicking her hands about. "Christ, is there anything more hideous than people who think you need to know the truth? Half the time they only tell you the details to make you feel dreadful, not because you need to know. Truth be known, I bet ninety per cent of happily married couples have had a dalliance somewhere along the line. That whole splitting the assets, fighting over the family dog and who keeps Aunt Ethel's teapot seems a high price to pay for a quick roll in the hay that doesn't mean anything."

She looked out of the window and beckoned me over. Lawrence had all the children chasing up and down an obstacle course that ended with a dash through the stream. It was the perfect snapshot of how children should look — carefree, rosy-cheeked, excited. "Anyway, he's the disciplinarian in our house. I'm not much good at any of that, bit of a lousy old mother to tell the truth. God knows how unruly the kids would be if he didn't lick them into shape. Orion's already nearly as tall as me."

I was clear. It didn't actually matter whether or not Lawrence had had an affair with Jen1. Even if I could prove it, Clover didn't want to know. Time for coffee, Waitrose *tarte aux pommes* and shutting my big trap forever. But I'd be watching.

CHAPTER
THIRTY-EIGHT

Although it was only mid-April, the walled kitchen garden was such a little suntrap that I could hang out the washing there. Living next door to the turd flicker meant I'd always had to dry my clothes inside. After years of stiff socks and trousers dried to a crisp on storage heaters, laundry flapping out in the fresh air filled me with a ridiculous amount of joy. I was humming "Wonderful Life" to myself, smoothing out some Egyptian cotton sheets that I'd discovered hidden away in a linen box. During the three weeks we'd been at Rose's house, I'd taken to luxury quite well. I'd never be able to do brushed nylon again. I pulled the sheets into a square, feeling the sun on my face and picturing the geraniums and dahlias I would grow in the summer. Footsteps on the path behind me made me look round. My hand flew to the scarf turban I'd tied my hair in to keep it out of the way while I worked.

Mr Peters.

The blush was instant.

"Hi." He was leaning against the archway.

"Hello." My lungs appeared to have a bit less puff in them. I was feeling good, for the first time in ages. I didn't need him coming along to remind me what I couldn't have. He looked gorgeous in his checked shirt, jacket and jeans. Now it was the Easter holidays, he'd obviously decided to funk up his look to fit in at the state school. His hair was a bit longer, quite wavy now it wasn't so closely cropped. I ignored the begging in my stomach and folded my arms.

He pulled at the collar on his shirt. "Sorry to disturb you while you're working, but could I talk to you for a few minutes?"

"How did you know I was here?"

"I went to the gatehouse. A bloke with a spider's web on his neck gave me the third degree before he told me where you were. Didn't look like the normal inhabitant of Stamford Avenue."

"That's Tarants. He does the garden and the odd jobs. He's taken it upon himself to double up as a security guard. Anyway, I didn't mean how did you know I was hanging out my sheets, I meant how did you know I was living here?"

He smiled. Longing swept through my belly. Or stomach, as Mr Peters would say. "I knew you wouldn't answer the phone if I rang, so I went to your house. I've been there every day for the last couple of weeks but there's never been anyone there. Your neighbour yelled out of the window that you didn't live there any more or 'had buggered off' as she put it. She slammed the window shut before I could ask her any more and she started shouting some very rude words through the door when I knocked. I take it she's not very keen on you?"

362

"You can say that again. Colin's bit on the side. So how did you find me?"

"I rang Felicity to see if you'd left any change of address." He put his hands up. "I know, I know. I expect the whole world now knows that I was looking for you but I couldn't think of what else to do. Anyway, is it convenient to speak for a moment? Or shall I come back later when you've finished?"

I could practically hear my better judgement galloping off down to the stream at the bottom of the garden. "I'm only hanging out the washing. I'll make you a coffee." I nodded towards the French windows into the kitchen.

"Are you sure it's okay for me to come in?" Mr Peters seemed fidgety.

"Of course. The kids are down in the orchard, building dens. They absolutely love it here." I pulled the scarf off my head and shook my hair free.

"I bet. Looks like you could have a mean game of football on that back lawn."

We ducked under the magnolia tree, bursting with great bowls of pink flowers and stepped into the sunny kitchen. I put the kettle on the Aga, then leant against it feeling the warmth of the oven through my jeans. He was rubbing his hands together, biting his lip as though he had something unpleasant to say. He started rolling up his sleeves. I couldn't stand it.

"So what brings you here?" I was preparing my face muscles to form a smile if he announced that he was marrying Serena.

"I heard Harley tell Orion in my French lesson that Colin had moved out. Is that right?"

Harley and his bloody foghorn. "Yeah."

"Are you okay about it?"

"Why wouldn't I be? To use your words, he was an arsehole. He was having an affair with Sandy, the woman who told you I'd gone away."

"Why didn't you tell me?"

I felt my face fall into that "doh" face that Bronte made when I was being particularly uncool. The kettle started whistling behind me and I was glad of an excuse to turn round. I couldn't seem to get my brain working quickly enough. Truth? That I'd turned up at his house and bumped into Serena coming out with a snog rash all over her face. Lie? I couldn't even think up a lie. There must have been one out there I could trot out and save a tiny scrap of pride.

I warmed the teapot. Rose had insisted on it. I preferred my tea made in a mug, soupy and strong, but for the moment, I was trying out all sorts of middle-class nonsense to see if it fitted. Make my grandmother proud.

"Maia? Why didn't you tell me?"

"For God's sake. I came round to tell you but I bumped into Serena when she was leaving your flat and I felt ridiculous because I didn't know you were seeing her as well as sort of, well, not seeing me, but you know what I mean. I'd obviously got totally the wrong end of the stick like a complete dork." My voice was rising. I could feel tears looming in the distance.

"I'm not seeing Serena."

364

I set down Rose's blue and white Wedgwood teacups. I frowned. He was doing my head in. "What? She knows that, does she?"

Mr Peters nodded.

"That must be a recent thing then because I saw her come out of your block of flats and she was all over you like an ivy at the ball, just a few weeks ago." I poured a tiny drop of milk into his tea and hated myself for storing the useless piece of knowledge that he liked his tea almost black.

"I went out with her ages ago, a couple of years ago now. Not for long. She's a lovely girl but she wasn't right for me."

"But you were at the ball holding hands with her." I could see her reaching out for him in my mind and yes, I would still like to belt her one.

Mr Peters stirred his tea even though he didn't take sugar. I pulled out a chair for him but he started pacing around the table.

"Maia. Christ, where to start?" He ran his hands through his hair, leaving it sticking up in gorgeous little tufts that made him look like he'd just got out of bed. Bed thoughts couldn't come into this discussion. He looked at his watch. "Shit, I'm taking up loads of your time. Is this okay?"

"Yeah, spit out whatever you came to say." Colin screwing Sandy hadn't hurt me anywhere near as much as Mr Peters holding hands with Serena.

His face set. "Make it easy for me, why don't you, Maia?"

I shrugged. "Well?"

He didn't look at me. We both jumped as the cuckoo flew out of Rose's clock as it chimed eleven. The noise seemed to jerk him out of whatever trance he was in.

"Maia, this is the truth and I'll have to go and kill myself with embarrassment afterwards but here goes. When Bronte went missing, I knew I was getting too close to you. When I was holding you on the sofa when you were crying, I just didn't want to let you go. I didn't want to leave you there with Colin. You seemed so alone, so vulnerable. I promised myself then that I would stay away from you. I was desperate not to cause trouble for you or the children at Stirling Hall. I could see that you had enough to deal with without everyone gossiping. The problem was, I couldn't stop thinking about you. I had all these moments in staff meetings when I needed to be firm and decisive and I'd be daydreaming about you. I'd look up and there would be an array of puzzled faces waiting to hear how we were going to approach the parents of a bully or what the budget for next year's drama production would be."

He turned his back on me and leaned on the worktop, apparently intent on Robert Frost's poem, "The Road Not Taken", which hung on the wall. Just as well really, otherwise he'd have seen the great Etxeleku gob clanging open.

"You were daydreaming about me?" I started to laugh. When I'd been conjuring up his face in the mirror while I polished, he'd been dripping about at staff meetings. What a pair.

"Don't laugh. I know I sound like a teenager having his first crush. I knew that I couldn't be Head of Upper

School and become involved with the mother of two of my pupils. And to start with, I didn't want to split you and Colin up because of the children, but then you came in with the black eye and I knew that you'd be better off without him. So I started to engineer a transfer to that other school. I didn't tell you because I knew you'd try and stop me. You were always saying that you were afraid you'd mess up my life. I thought you'd refuse to see me if you knew, so I decided to present you with a *fait accompli*."

"You did that so you could carry on seeing me?"

"Yes. I did. Didn't you realise how much I thought of you? It must be my northern working-class ways. Can't do all that middle-class touchy-feely stuff." He was looking away again. "I was absolutely overwhelmed by you. Your timing was brilliant though. I got the phone call about the secondment the same day your letter arrived saying you were taking the children out of Stirling Hall."

"Why didn't you talk to me about it? I could've explained," I said.

"Okay. You're going to laugh at me now. I'd moved heaven and earth to get into another school. I wanted to ask you to come and live with me. I couldn't stand the thought of you staying with Colin, in case he turned on you again. When I got that letter, it made me feel like I couldn't trust you, that I didn't know you at all, that you'd been using me."

I stared. I cursed myself for leaving that bloody letter where Colin could get his hands on it. "Move in with you? But you've never even lived with anyone. And I wouldn't have come without Bronte and Harley anyway."

"I was expecting you to bring them as well, of course."

My eyes widened at the thought of trying to keep Harley contained in that immaculate flat. "So are you taking the secondment or not?" I wasn't sure how to break the news that the kids were staying on at Stirling Hall.

He put his teacup down with a rattle. "Yes. Luckily, I think it will be very interesting."

I hoped like mad that all the teachers at his new school would have crossed eyes, great big lardy arses and sensible lace-ups. "I'm really sorry that I didn't talk to you about taking the kids out. You had such faith in me that I didn't know how to disappoint you. Then once I was at Clover's away from the bailiffs and the debts and everything, I suppose I buried my head in the sand a bit and of course, Colin got involved. There's no way I would have sent that letter without telling you first. Do you at least believe that?"

He put his head on one side. "Yes, I think I do. But you wouldn't speak to me. I couldn't work out what was going on."

"I found out you'd been seeing Serena. You're banging on about how you were mooning about, overwhelmed by me, or whatever your words were but you still had PC Plod on the backburner. Hedging your bets, were you?" I could hear the poison tumbling out of me but I couldn't seem to get the stopper back in the bottle.

Annoyance flickered over his face. He put his hand up. "Hang on a minute. You were the one with the partner, not me. Up until a few weeks ago, you were going back to Colin." He stepped towards me. "Okay. I'm getting the message that Serena is the sticking point here. Let's deal with her first. She liked me more than I liked her. We had a few dates but I let it fizzle out."

I wasn't letting him get away with that. "But she was there when I phoned you, after Bronte was found. I heard her, whining about sitting there like a 'stuffed lemon' while you were talking to me." I made a conscious effort to take my hands off my hips, but then I couldn't think how to stand naturally.

Mr Peters shook his head. "I hadn't seen her for ages before Bronte went missing. I think she felt as though fate had brought us together again. She made an excuse to come over to discuss the school's strategy for dealing with Bronte's disappearance and I was glad of the distraction. It all ended rather badly because she thought she'd be staying the night and I called her a cab just after I spoke to you."

I hated the idea of Serena lounging about in Mr Peters' flat, preparing to make a night of it, all come hither eyes and girlie giggles. I wasn't about to be fobbed off with that. "But I saw her coming out of your building about a month ago. I'm not making that up."

Exasperation was creeping into Mr Peters' voice. "She goes to the beautician to have facials or whatever stuff you women have done. I heard her say that to you at the ball. That's nothing to do with me. I swear I have seen her once since Bronte was found and that was at the ball."

I didn't know what to believe. Maybe that snog-fest look was an electrolysis thing rather than a Mr Peters thing. I stared at him. He wasn't fidgeting or looking away like Colin used to when he was feeding me a line.

"But you must have invited her to the ball?" I said.

"I hold my hand up to that. I don't know what I was thinking. The headmaster had already caught a whisper that I was involved with you, probably from Felicity. Of course, I denied it flat out but he was watching me. Watching us. He's keen on the whole community relations thing and had drawn up a list of the local great and good to invite to the ball from the police, council and various charities — including Serena. All the senior staff had to escort someone. You weren't answering my calls, so I just took the easy option and chose Serena. I suppose I thought it would stop people gossiping. About you and me, anyway."

He glanced at my Open University forms that I'd left on the side. A huge grin spread over his face, then he seemed to realise it wasn't the moment. "Right, this doesn't show me in a very good light. I also agreed to escort Serena because I thought it might make you a bit jealous." He looked down. "Maia, I wanted some sign from you that it wasn't all a game. Then when I got to the ball, I didn't want to make you jealous, I just wanted to be with you."

His voice trailed off. He closed his eyes. "I could have punched that horrible Howard bloke. I could see him hitting on you but also trying to humiliate you and

370

I just hated it. Then you told Frederica you were going back to Colin and I realised I'd missed my chance. I came outside to look for you, to try and talk to you but you'd already gone."

"Yeah. I went home to throw Colin out. And to cry my eyes out over you." I studied his face, trying to read the truth there. A little — what did Rose used to say? — "scintilla" of excitement sparked somewhere deep inside me.

Mr Peters walked over to me. I caught the scent of his aftershave and a memory of him lying on top of me in his flat wafted into my mind. He stood within touching distance and I held my breath.

"I must let you get on." He glanced behind him towards the open kitchen door. "Okay, this isn't very northern lad, a bit gushy for a Boltonian boy, but I really like you." The man was blushing. Really blushing. "I don't know how you got under my skin so easily. Anyway, I'd better go before you get the sack."

"I don't think I'm likely to get the sack," I said. I stared at him to see if he was having me on. For such a bright bloke, it appeared he hadn't completely understood my change in circumstances.

"Who are the owners, anyway?" he said.

"A wonderful woman, a single mum, with two lovely children. She's just missing the gorgeous boyfriend now." I started to laugh and moved in a bit closer. I could see the tip of the eagle's beak poking out of his shirt.

Mr Peters looked confused. "What?" He drew away from me slightly. "I'm thinking that I need to be concentrating on this conversation. It's a bit tricky when you're standing so close."

He shook his head but didn't try to stop me as I undid a couple of buttons on his shirt. I kissed the eagle and put my ear against his chest. His heart was thudding. When I looked up, those dark grey-green eyes were questioning me but he didn't look like he was rushing to get away. I brushed his lips with mine. His hands threaded into my hair.

I murmured into his ear. "I thought you knew. This is the professor's old house, you know, Professor Stainton, the one who left me the money for the school fees? I only found out a few weeks ago that she also left me the house. And rather a lot of money. It's a long story, but she was actually my grandmother."

He drew away from me. "Your grandmother? You've inherited all this? I thought you were, I don't know, living on the top floor with the children or something. That's brilliant. Oh my God. You're not joking about owning it. And there was me, riding to the rescue, thinking you'd want to move into my two-bedroom flat. What a moron."

I pulled him back towards me. My legs were trembling. Every nerve in my body was waiting to be soothed by him. He lowered his face to mine, kissing me softly, tiny little kisses, pausing every now and then to look at me with those headlamp eyes. I could feel him holding back, not wanting to scare me off. I needed more than that. "Zac, it's okay." I felt his lips curve when I said his name. He pressed his mouth hard onto mine, kissing me until there was no room for any thoughts, just giddiness. I could practically hear the blood pumping round my body.

Zac buried his face in my hair. His hands were moving up my T-shirt and I was having to concentrate on keeping my breathing even. "How many bedrooms did you say there were?" he asked.

I didn't get to reply. The kids came barging through the front door, charging into the kitchen and doing a cartoon screech to a halt as they clocked Zac.

"Hello, sir. How are you?" Harley was all smiles and mud. Even Bronte broke into a big grin, her cheeks flushed and eyes bright from the fresh air.

I pretended to look for something in the fridge so I could adjust my T-shirt. Zac's shirt was gaping open but he managed to look cool and trendy rather than undressed. Zac took it all in his stride. "Morning, you two. Just popped in to discuss a few things with your mother. I gather you're quite enjoying living here."

Harley rushed out hundreds of details, how he was going to get a quad bike, how he was playing tennis every day, what fish he'd caught, before flying off upstairs to ring the servants' bell in his bedroom which showed up on a panel in the kitchen. Bronte contented herself with getting out Rose's book of wild birds and showing him a picture of a kingfisher she'd seen at the stream. He was so easy with them, so interested.

Half an hour later, I walked out to the car with him. "Will you tell the children?" he asked, as he opened the door.

"Tell them what?"

"That I'm your new boyfriend?"

"Are you my new boyfriend?"

"I'd like to be. That is, if you don't mind dating the lower classes now you're part of the aristocracy." He had his arms folded, rocking backwards and forwards on his heels.

I reached for his hand. "I like a bit of rough."

He laughed and pulled me into his arms. "Maia, I don't want to let you go again. I've faffed about, got it all wrong and I just want a chance now to behave a bit bloody normally."

He kissed me gently, then not so gently. He glanced over my shoulder, back to the house. "I'm going. You need to talk to the children before they see us together. I love you."

"Love me? You haven't even had dinner with me." I had yet to learn that smart-arse remarks weren't always the answer to embarrassment.

He shook his head. "Go. Go now. Tell the children I'm going to be around for a very long time. I'm serious."

I didn't feel like a cleaner. I felt like a princess. And that was nothing to do with money.

THE ALTOGETHER UNEXPECTED DISAPPEARANCE OF ATTICUS CRAFTSMAN

Mamen Sanchez

Atticus Craftsman never travels without a supply of Earl Grey and a favourite book. So when he is sent to shut down a failing literary magazine in Madrid, he packs both. A short Spanish jaunt later, he'll be back in Kent, cup of tea and smoked salmon sandwich in hand. But the five ladies who run the magazine have other ideas. They'll do anything to keep their cosy office together — even if it involves hoodwinking Atticus with flashing eyes, the ghosts of literature past, and a winding journey into the heart of Andalucía. With not the most efficient of detectives in hot pursuit, it's only a matter of time before Atticus Craftsman either falls in love, disappears completely, or — worst of all — runs out of Earl Grey.

LIFTED BY THE GREAT NOTHING

Karim Dimechkie

Max lives with his father, Rasheed, and doesn't remember his mother, who was murdered by burglars before father and son were forced to emigrate from Beirut to New Jersey. Rasheed is enamoured of his idea of American culture — baseball and barbecues — and has tried to shed his Lebanese heritage completely. He has a single purpose in life: to provide Max with a joyful childhood; though sometimes his efforts do more harm than good. When Max turns seventeen, he discovers that his father has been lying to him — about everything — and their peaceful universe is destroyed. As Max ventures on an uncertain journey to Beirut, he must ask himself, what happens when your truth is a fable? And can some lies be a sacrifice in disguise?